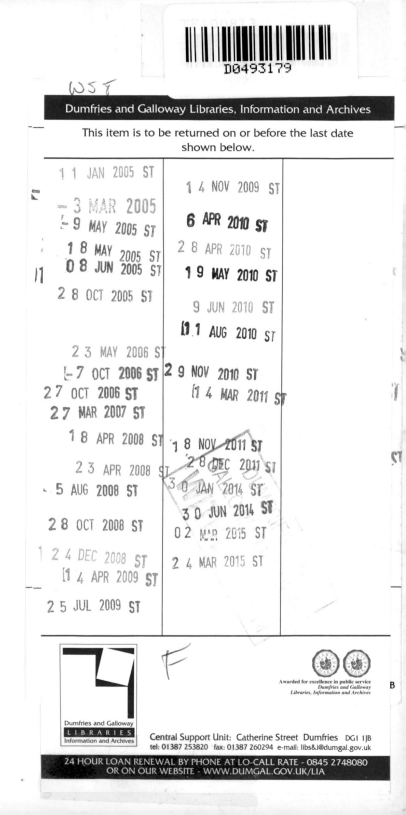

WST

D0493179

Dumfries and Galloway
L I B R A R I E S
Information and Archives

Awarded for excellence in public service
Dumfries and Galloway
Libraries, Information and Archives

Central Support Unit: Catherine Street Dumfries DG1 1JB
tel: 01387 253820 fax: 01387 260294 e-mail: libs&i@dumgal.gov.uk

24 HOUR LOAN RENEWAL BY PHONE AT LO-CALL RATE - 0845 2748080
OR ON OUR WEBSITE - WWW.DUMGAL.GOV.UK/LIA

THE PRIVATEERSMAN

Recent Titles by Richard Woodman from Severn House

THE ACCIDENT
ACT OF TERROR
THE ANTIGONE
CAPTAIN OF THE CARYATID
THE CRUISE OF THE COMMISSIONER

THE NAVAL HISTORICAL SERIES

THE GUINEAMAN
THE PRIVATEERSMAN

THE PRIVATEERSMAN

Richard Woodman

severn
House

This first world edition published in Great Britain 2000 by
SEVERN HOUSE PUBLISHERS LTD of
9–15 High Street, Sutton, Surrey SM1 1DF.
This first world edition published in the USA 2000 by
SEVERN HOUSE PUBLISHERS INC of
595 Madison Avenue, New York, N.Y. 10022.

British Library Cataloguing in Publication Data

Woodman, Richard, 1944-
    The privateersman
    1.   Sea stories
    I.   Title
    823.9'14 [F]

    ISBN 0-7278-5593-X

Typeset by Palimpsest Book Production Ltd.,
Polmont, Stirlingshire, Scotland.
Printed and bound in Great Britain by
MPG Books Ltd., Bodmin, Cornwall.

Part One

Death

The Rice-Water Fever

The wind thrust him forward with palpable force, raising the capes of his heavy coat and pattering them across his shoulders with a strange fluttering insistence, so that he thought of black crows assaulting him, the frenzied beating of their wings just beyond his vision. The power of this image raised his heartbeat and made him fearful of the dark, stormy night. It was, he knew, populated with more than mere visions, for he could hear the whispers of the *obeah* women of the Guinea coast and the moans from the slave decks of a Guineaman sailing as swift as an arrow through the stunning beauty of a tropical night, a night whose perfection was marred by the sickly sweet stench rising from the gratings over her slave-rooms below.

Spiritually oppressed and instinctively wary, he hefted his heavy cane and gripped it like a club, half expecting to be attacked by footpads as he approached the corner, but the night was too foul for even those most opportunist of thieves.

He turned the corner and the thrust of the wind changed to a buffeting irregularity as it coursed up the rising street of tall and elegant houses. As the ground rose the wind came more directly off the River Mersey behind him and he felt its full force. A coach stood outside one house, a bright patch of light spilling from its open door, but the flaring torches of two patiently waiting link boys dissipated the domesticity of the scene, giving it instead a hellish aspect only added to by the figure of the coachman unmoving upon his box. The gale snatched away any noise of voices, giving it a detached, otherworldly appearance that was in accord with his mood. This was a night for death and dark deeds, not frivolous rioting.

He crossed the street rather than pass through that puddle of light and feel an irresistible compulsion to glance into the

3

hallway. The lives of others had no part in his desperate fear and misery. Halfway across the cobbled carriageway the rain began, with a gust of wind that threatened to unseat his tricorne, and he hurriedly put his left hand up to its fore-cock to avoid losing it. The skirts of his heavy coat clung to his legs. He quickened his pace but the first sheeting squall struck him and drove at the nape of his neck with a chill sensation as if all the corvine birds in hell were flying to harry him. His heavy boots tripped on the uneven cobbles as he struggled uphill and he swore as he caught his balance, glancing behind him as if real crows terrorised him.

"You damned fool!" he hissed, forcing himself to stop and turn, to confront his primitive irrational fear with the cool logic of his solitude. Then the coach was coming up the hill behind him, its two lamps glowing like eyes and the black gleam of the straining horses' wet bodies presided over by the untidy black hump of the coachman atop the neat regularity of its swaying body. He watched it go past, blinds up and passengers oblivious to the drenching rain that in a matter of moments had turned the street into a hissing torrent of water. A footman on the box gave him a glance of commiseration and then it was gone.

The rain, almost horizontal in the little light escaping between the shutters, drove him uphill. The occasional sconced lamp only added to the desolation. Was it possible, he thought for one moment, to be *so* alone when surrounded by such habitations? But he already knew the answer: the presence of death isolated even those huddled now round their fires of sea coal in a lamplit atmosphere of familial conviviality. For cholera, like the tall and lonely figure, stalked the sea port of Liverpool.

By the time he turned the final corner, into a street that ran parallel to the distant river and whose houses thus afforded him a timely lee, his stock was sodden and the rain poured from the tricorne as if from three gutters. He clumped up the steps to the door and pulled the bell, turning to stare up and down the street as he waited, unconsciously pounding the step with his cane.

The door opened and he turned as the maid drew aside and bobbed a curtsy.

"Good evening, Captain."

"Evening, Bridget." He nodded at the Irish girl and stood in the hallway, the water pouring off him. "I'm sorry, m'dear . . ."

" 'Tis no matter, sir." She took his hat, cane and gloves and waited as he removed his greatcoat.

"Is there any news?"

"No, sir, nothing new . . ."

"Who is it, Bridget?"

" 'Tis the Captain, Miss Katherine."

As Bridget sank under the weight of his sodden coat he looked up to see Katherine Makepeace halfway down the stairs. The younger woman managed a wan smile. "Uncle William . . ."

"Kate . . . There's no change, I understand."

"No, no change."

"I am sorry."

"May I speak to you – please?" She indicated a door off the hallway, descended the stairs and, as he stood back, led him into the withdrawing room. A single candelabra burnt on a side table and the low light threw the young woman's face into stark relief. Growing fast beyond the age then considered as being marriageable, she was plain and almost severe in her looks, though her face lit up when she smiled, for she had perfect teeth. But she had nothing to smile about on this filthy night which rattled the sashes as the rain fell like a lash upon the windowpanes.

"What is it, m'dear?"

She drew herself up and faced him. "Uncle William, I fear the worst."

He nodded. "Yes, I understand. I know of no one who recovers once the disease has taken such a hold. You are taking those precautions that I advised?"

"Yes, insofar as we can."

"They must be most stringently enforced," he said, "with absolute authority, particularly so below stairs. It is imperative, Kate, or you, your mother and your servants will succumb."

"I have given instructions that all water is to be boiled and that they are to wash their hands when handling anything from the sick-room."

"Let us hope that is sufficient." Seeing the agonised look on the young woman's face, he added, "As I am sure it will prove." He touched her arm and smiled. "Bear up, Katherine, your mother will need all your help in the coming days."

"But –" she looked at him – "how did Father catch this disease?"

"It is everywhere, my dear, even up here," he suppressed any hint of irony, "and your father spent much time down in the docks and the lower part of town."

She was not listening and interrupted him, her eyes wide with concern. "Oh, forgive me, I forgot to ask after little William."

"He died this afternoon."

"Oh." The long expected news seemed to stun her. "Oh dear . . ." She hesitated, not knowing what to say. "I . . . I am so very sorry." The tears ran down her cheeks. "And it was the same?"

He nodded. "Yes, the rice-water sickness."

"And Puella?"

He shook his head and she heard the tremble in his voice. "I do not think she will last a month."

"She has the cholera too?"

He shook his head again. "No, but she has lost the will to live. I have seen her this way before; she withdraws inside herself and – " he sighed – "I am the author of her misfortune, hence my presence here, for I cannot remain at home this evening, though I suppose I must return later."

"You may stay here."

"No, that would be desertion and I cannot have that charge laid against me." He looked her in the eye. "I did have another reason for calling."

"About the ship?"

"Yes, I thought it best that your father did not know."

Katherine shook her head. "It is too late. Mother told him this morning. She was unable to prevent herself . . . I do not think my father took the news to heart, he was already in a high fever and seems unaware of anything happening around him."

"Well, there is nothing to be done. She is only our second loss in all these years, but it comes at a hard time."

"Uncle William, if – I mean when – Father dies, what will become of us?"

He looked at her and smiled. "Your mother will have a small fortune, my dear, a sufficient competence to sustain you and your two brothers. That is something upon which you may rest easy." He paused. "By the by, have your brothers been summoned?"

She nodded. "They are expected tomorrow, or the following day . . ." She seemed preoccupied and Kite asked if there was some other matter that troubled her.

"I have heard Father talking about money, fretting over some private matter, and Mother I know was anxious, so anxious in fact that she confronted him with the loss of the *African Princess* as though it was the summit of our calamities."

"I think not, Kate; that would be a gross exaggeration." He smiled at her again. "When the time comes I shall explain matters to your mother, and to you if you wish."

"Thank you."

But to Kite it seemed that this was no real reassurance. "Where is your mother now?" he asked.

"She is asleep beside Father, that is why I was anxious to know who it was calling at this hour."

"I am sorry, I really had no idea of the time."

"Oh no, I did not mind it being you. I was only anxious that it was not Frith. He will fuss so and pleads all sorts of excuses to disturb Father."

"Frith? You mean Samuel Frith?" He frowned.

"Yes."

"What business has Samuel Frith with your father at this time?" He tried to clear the fog of his own preoccupations away from his mind. Frith had called several times at the counting house to see Makepeace of late and the latter had dismissed his visits as being personal and not of much significance. "D'you know, Kate?"

She shook her head, a look of uncertainty crossing her face so that he was driven to dissemble. "Ah, I recollect," he said hurriedly, "I had forgot, your father offered him an interest in a Guinea voyage; nothing was concluded and I suppose Frith has grown anxious lest your father's illness interposed and stopped him participating."

"I do not much care for him, Uncle William."

"No, my dear, neither do I, and I should advise against either you or your mother entertaining him." This he said with perfect truth, adding, "I do not know why your father wished to solicit his interest."

Katherine looked at the floor. "Mr Frith had made Father a proposition regarding myself, Uncle."

"You?" Was this the personal nature of Frith's business with Makepeace? And was the opportunity to speculate on a voyage part of some proposed marriage settlement? Frith and Katherine were not likely bed-partners, though there were some advantages to be gained from the union commercially, and perhaps Frith might benefit from her embraces. He looked at her unhappy face as she confronted him.

"Yes." She shook her head. "I did not wish to accept, but . . ."

"Your father would not listen to you, I suppose. I did not know of this; but what was your mother's part?"

Katherine dropped her voice to a whisper, as though fearful of the very walls retaining her confidence. "She it was who proposed the union."

"I see." The ever-practical Martha's hand was not hard to discern.

"So," Katherine said, her voice hardening, "the death of Father will do nothing to loosen our bond with Mr Frith, rather it will be enhanced and Mother may feel compelled to unite our families in the interests of Charlie's and Henry's futures."

"For which you will be the guarantor."

"Yes."

"I see."

"Will you . . . ? Can you . . . ?"

"I will do what I can, Katherine," he said, wondering what on earth lay within the bounds of possibility. Katherine was entirely dependent upon her father, and if he died, Kite supposed her mother would have a greater influence upon the fortunes of her children. In the years he had known her, he had never entirely warmed to Martha Makepeace. Kate, however, was a sweet creature and not a marketable commodity. He tried to reassure her. "Thank you for your confidences; pray remember that you may rely upon me."

"Thank you, dear Uncle William." She leaned forward and kissed his cheek.

"I am not truly your Uncle William, Katherine, m'dear, but I hope you may count me a true friend. Now, if you will ring for little Bridget, I had better return to Puella."

"Poor Puella. You will give her my kindest regards." Katherine crossed the room to the bell pull.

"I shall. And please do you keep me informed of your father's condition. It were best, when the end comes, that you let me know first. Send Bridget; she is to be trusted, I think."

8

"I will." Their conversation ended as Bridget entered. "The Captain's leaving, Bridget."

As he left he turned in the doorway, a flurry of rain drove past him into the hall. "It is late," he said, "you should get some sleep."

One

Captain "Topsy-Turvy"

It was almost midnight when Captain William Kite reached his own house, buffeted by the gale against which it had been necessary to struggle. He went immediately to the bedroom, where the candle had almost burnt out. It seemed the only thing that had changed, for Puella sat in the darkness as she had when he had left, hours earlier. He stared at her, but she seemed unaware of his presence, staring straight ahead of her into the gloom, seeing at once the past and the future.

"Puella . . ." He called her name softly, but she did not stir, her handsome black features immobile, as though carved out of the ebony she so much resembled in the candlelight. He had removed his boots below and crept across the rich carpet to fish a new candle from the box she kept them in, for Puella hated the dark winter nights of these unfamiliar, hostile northern latitudes. Lighting it from the first, he replaced the old with the new candle and then lit another. Having reassured himself that Puella was beyond his contact, he left the room.

Holding the other candle he ascended to the upper floor, his heart beating heavily in his breast. He hesitated before entering his son's bedroom, then with a sigh, he turned the door handle and went inside. The candlelight fell on the body of the boy. The curly hair and the broad, flaring nostrils had all the beauty of his mother's, though the shape of his head was inherited from his father, as was the tall build and the line of his chin. "You would have been handsome, my darling buckaroo," he murmured, "like your beautiful mother and the brother that you never knew." He touched the boy's brow and the chill of the flesh still had the power to shock him, though he was no stranger to death. The finality of it had an absolute quality that was so at variance with the petty aspirations of his busy life; it mocked him with a quiet, eternal jeering that was inescapable. Contemptuous of the solicitous intervention of priests, he felt again that solitary acquaintanceship with the ineffable and numinous power that bestrode the universe, familiar to seamen, hermits and the *obeah* women whose blood had so recently flowed in his dead son's veins. The sensation brought him no comfort, but with it came an unresentful acceptance. He, like his wife, bowed to the inevitable but in contrast to Puella he gathered himself again and in going on attracted her contempt and enmity.

Sighing, he rose and bid his son farewell. The dead boy would be buried tomorrow.

Kite softly walked down the stairs to his study where he picked up a blanket kept there for the purpose and made himself as comfortable as he could on the couch. When the spirits took a hold of his black wife, William Kite found it impossible to spend the night in the same room.

But he could not sleep alone either. The rain beat upon his window and the gale howled relentlessly, booming in the cold chimney and lifting the heavy curtains, so that he lay awake, tense and uneasy, as he had once lain in the cabin of the *Spitfire* as a hurricane attempted to dismember the schooner. With a monstrous effort he turned his mind from the cold body lying in the room above him and the immobile figure of his beautiful wife sitting with the past and the future gathered about her in the next room.

Grief over young William's death and a cold despair over his estrangement from Puella slowly ebbed. Instead his active mind reverted to the distraction of the evening, the situation in the household of his business partner, Captain Makepeace. Both had served in the slaver *Enterprize*, Makepeace as commander, and they had become joint shipowners in Liverpool towards the end of the Seven Years' War, men whose family lives were almost as interwoven as their business relationship. But what was he to make of Katherine's revelations about Frith?

Makepeace had never mentioned the matter of a liaison. Could his wife have been behind the match? That was a distinct possibility, Kite thought, sitting up. Martha Makepeace was a competent woman who in the years since her husband retired from the sea had lost some of her autonomy. By way of compensation, she had taken to manipulating other people. Kite himself had been relieved when she had, with every appearance of cordiality, arranged matters between his sister Helen and Lieutenant Henry Hope of the Royal Navy. But even supposing his conjecture was accurate, surely Makepeace would have made some allusion to it? He knew too much of the captain's past, of his flagrant philandering on the Guinea coast, and this shady history linked them so that they might have considered themselves confidants. In the years of association in Liverpool their combined ventures had drawn them closer, so that vexed asides about Martha's occasional extravagances, the exasperations of fatherhood and the intermittent discord endemic in any household led him to the odd revelation. Surely, only a desire to conceal something from his partner could explain Makepeace's silence on the subject of Frith.

Kite considered the matter further. In recent weeks, it was true, Makepeace had been bound up with the purchase of a new vessel, the *Pride of Galway*, but his preoccupation did not necessarily conceal ulterior motives. Or did it? And had Katherine got wind of something when she asked what would happen to her and her brothers when her father died, as die he surely must? He would follow his dead godson William Kite into eternity, for once the dreaded cholera had induced its filthy rice-water flux there was no hope of recovery.

"Christ!" Kite flung aside his blanket and rose to his feet. He felt like death himself as he drew back the curtains. He wondered if he had dozed, for it was light and the rain had stopped, but he could see by the rigid winged flight of the gulls above the chimneys that the gale blew with unabated fury. The wind had shifted though, scouring the sky clear of clouds.

"A north-wester," he muttered.

"Kite."

He spun round, startled. Puella stood in the doorway.

"Puella! You startled me . . ."

"I have seen into the future tonight."

"Yes," he said drily, "I thought you had."

"You will not be happy, Kite."

"That is scarcely surprising."

"Listen, Kite. Do not mock me."

"I do not mock you, Puella."

"You brought me to this terrible place, Kite."

He sighed, closing his eyes. He was too tired to remonstrate; besides, it did no good. Puella was fixed in her views. As his old father had observed long since, "she ploughs her own dark and incomprehensible furrow".

He bowed his head and when he looked up, she had gone. He followed her through into the bedroom. She lay on the bed, staring up at the ceiling.

"Puella," he began, sitting on the edge on the mattress.

She closed her eyes in dismissal and all he could do was touch her hand.

Puella refused to break her fast the following morning, or to leave her bed. She did not accompany him to the church for William's funeral, and the congregation was pitifully small. Katherine was there, as was his chief clerk, Jasper Watkinson, with Mrs Watkinson, and the assistant clerk Nathan Johnstone, whose wife had died in child-bed only two weeks earlier. Helen was in London with her husband, so poor little William had few to see him lowered into the cold earth. The gale only added a haste to the proceedings which Kite found deeply troubling as he fought to keep his balance in the buffeting wind.

Kite stood beside the priest as he intoned the committal. The man's surplice flapped with a furious distraction, like a flag, and his words were torn away in a mumbled incoherence. Kite's own coat remained sodden from the previous night and he felt the weight of it irksome. He was ashamed of this, guilt-ridden that it dulled the keen edge of grief, but the feeling of detachment was as much a consequence of his lack of sleep as was the gritty sensation in his eyes. Patches of sunlight streamed up the hill, over the distant masts and yards of the moored ships and the smoking chimneys, rising, it seemed, from the grey expanse of the Mersey, rather than emanating from the cloudy sky. The brilliant sunny patches were followed by deep, chill shadows, so that the change of temperature was as palpable as the unpredictable visitations of death itself.

Afterwards he stood and mumbled his thanks as Watkinson and his spouse awkwardly expressed their condolences. Johnstone followed, uncontrollably lachrymose, for the funeral too closely followed the burial of his own young wife.

"I'm so sorry, sir, so very, very sorry . . ."

"Thank you, Nathan," Kite said solemnly, wretched at the compounding of the man's grief.

Then Katherine was beside him, her plain face damp with tears. "I'm so sorry, Uncle William."

The paucity of words struck him: everyone was so sorry, as though they were apologising for their part in the sad little affair. "Thank you, m'dear," he said, touching her hand. "How is your father today?"

She shook her head. "My mother asked for you, but I did not like to distract you."

"I shall wait upon her later, Kate. It was good of you to come. Are you alone? If so I shall walk you home."

"No, no, that will not be necessary." She gestured unhappily to a figure whom Kite had not noticed before. Frith bowed.

"My condolences, Captain Kite, upon your grievous loss."

"Thank you, sir." Kite returned the bow. Frith had managed a different formula. It was more appropriate, but its uninterest was manifest.

"Your wife – is much afflicted, I don't doubt, Captain Kite."

"She is distraught, sir, as you may well imagine."

"Of course." Frith bowed again, then straightening up put on his hat and offered his arm to Katherine. Kite caught the glance that she threw at her honorary uncle and put his own hat upon his head. The priest was hovering for his fee. But as Kite walked towards that worthy he could not escape the slight hint of insolence in that small hesitation Frith had interjected to his reference to Puella. It was done by a man who knew of a secret power he had over his ignorant interlocutor.

Kite was seized with the conviction that Katherine, poor unhappy Katherine, had indeed got wind of something sinister. Returning home only to confirm what in his heart he already knew, that Puella had refused any food, he replaced his hat and made again for his door. He should, he knew, have invited the small funerary party back for some sustenance, but with the shadow of Puella's grief adding to the lugubrious morning he could not do it. Instead, he walked again to the Makepeaces' house where Bridget bobbed him her deferential curtsy and asked him to wait.

Mrs Makepeace came to him, red-eyed from weeping and watching at her husband's bedside.

"Oh, William, I am so glad to see you. He has not long now."

"Has the doctor . . .?"

Martha Makepeace shook her head. "He has gone." She paused, then added, "And he will not see a priest." The news did not surprise Kite, but he lowered his head in sympathy. He felt for Martha and her family, but his own situation continually overlaid theirs.

"I understand he was asking to see me, Martha," he said gently, and she nodded, recovering some of her old, familiar, brisk efficiency.

"Yes. Please forgive me. Come."

Kite followed her upstairs and into their bedroom. The curtains were drawn but Makepeace's pallid features were illuminated by a candle. His face was already cadaverous and immobile, the skin like wax, the lips all but gone and his mouth a dark hole through which he drew breath. His eyes seemed large, like a newborn child's, except that their rims were red and watery, and they fastened on Kite's figure as he loomed into the candlelight.

Makepeace lifted a hand and with a tiny gesture beckoned Kite, so that he bent to him.

"Makepeace, old friend . . ." he said, "it is Will Kite come to see you."

The dying man's lips moved and Kite bent to hear what he was trying to say, taking his hand and squeezing it gently. It felt like a scrap of discarded paper.

The words came out clearly, wheezed with long gaps between them, evidence of the effort that went into their enunciation. "You . . . must . . . forgive . . . me . . ."

Kite frowned and raised his head, to look Makepeace in the face. "There is nothing to forgive, old fellow."

But there was a blazing in Makepeace's eyes, a final desperate attempt to communicate, and then, quite loudly, just as Katherine came into the room, Makepeace said, "Forgive . . ."

"Oh, God." Martha was at the bedside on her knees as Kite straightened up and stepped back into the shadows. He caught Katherine's eyes and shook his head. She turned to the curtains, pulled them back and threw open the window. Then she went to the bedside and knelt beside her mother. Kite withdrew.

At the foot of the stairs Makepeace's manservant was waiting with Bridget.

"Your master is dead. You may send for me if there is anything Mistress Makepeace wishes me to attend to."

"There is no need to concern yourself, Captain." Frith's figure

emerged from the side parlour. "You have troubles enough of
your own, I imagine."

There was something unpleasantly insinuating about Frith's
presence, Kite thought, but he merely bowed and took his hat
and cane from Bridget.

"Thank you, Bridget," he said, noting the tears in her eyes.

Kite could not stay in his own house with Puella refusing to see
him, and although he remained there for the rest of that day, and
that night slept again in his study, he made for his company's
chambers off Water Street early the following morning, calling
for bread and coffee to be brought to him. A few moments later
Watkinson entered the office.

"Captain Jones is here, sir, and asking to see you."

"Christopher Jones? Good God, how did he get here?"

"I have not asked him, Captain Kite, but he is clearly travel-
stained."

"Ask him to come in."

A moment later Jones stood before him. He rocked a little,
like a drunken man, but Kite could see the mulatto ship-master
was exhausted. His blue coat was salt-stained and muddied, his
breeches filthy and his shoes caked in mud. The stock about his
neck was grubby and the deep rings beneath his eyes were purple
on his honey-coloured skin.

"Sit down, sit down, Jones." Kite rose and motioned to Jones
to pull up a chair into which the mulatto collapsed with a
terrible sigh.

"A glass, Watkinson, and hasten that bread, damn it. Captain
Jones is in extremis . . ."

Jones tossed off the glass of Jerez and rubbed a dirty fist across
his eyes. He tried to say something, but only a croak came from
his mouth.

"Take your time, Jones, take your time."

"I am sorry to hear of your loss, Captain Kite."

Kite nodded. "It is good of you to put the matter before your
own tribulations, Captain Jones."

"I am sorry for those too, sir. I had not meant – I mean, I know
the ship to have been of especial—"

"All our ships are special to us, Captain Jones. The loss of
one is of no more significance than the loss of another." Even
as he said the words, he knew them to be untruthful. The loss of

a ship with a valuable West India cargo was infinitely worse than one with two hundred tons of coal in her hold, but Kite could not add to Jones's obvious distress. He had been in command of the *African Princess*, the ship named after Puella, and Kite knew well that the wrecking of her had some mystical link in Jones's mind with the death of his own son and Puella's deliberate decline. His mixed blood placed him in part under the influence of such damning superstitions.

"How did it happen?"

"Bad weather, sir. Days of it. No glimpse of the sun, no sign of land till we struck. We were out in our reckoning, sir, way out, but if daylight . . . Well, sir, it wanted but two hours before dawn when— Had we had just a little luck, a moon, or bright starlight . . ."

Kite waited. To relive that terrible moment when normality turns in an instant to chaos was clearly an ordeal. He could imagine it well enough: an hour or so before the first flush of daylight in the east; the ship running fast before the wind; an overcast sky and the night black as the devil's riding boots; then the sudden shuddering lurch, the parting of stays, the crash of topmasts, yards, sails, all going by the board and the splitting of the hull on the unyielding rocks. Perhaps, too, the sudden high loom of a cliff and then the struggle to contain disaster as panic-stricken men came up from below, screaming about water pouring into the ship, only to find the ordered deck a ruination of broken spars and a weblike trap of rope and canvas. Within moments the sea would be breaking over the wreck and the first men would be swept to their deaths; then the impossibility of getting out a boat and the quick descent from discipline and order to the anarchy of every man clinging on for dear life. Even in a moderate breeze, the scene would have been hellish enough.

Jones finally finished his account. They had struck on Cape Clear Island and the ship had gone all to pieces before the next morning. He and eight men had survived. He had the ship's papers and her log, and had saved a quantity of gold bullion from her, but that was all. Her muscovado had washed like honey out of her split hull, the rum had run out of its stove casks with a stink that had brought a score of indigent Irish onto the scene, and while these hardy men had risked their limbs and even their lives to save some of the cane spirit for their own enjoyment, Jones and his men had clambered ashore by way of the fallen mainmast.

Jones stood and fished in his coat-tails, his fists dredging up the bright glint of gold coin. "I could not sleep well while I carried this, no, nor tarry on my passage. We were a week on the island before the weather allowed us to get to Baltimore and then it was a long march to Cork where we took ship. It was two days before we left."

"We heard that the wreck had been reported by a military officer conducting a survey on the coast, Captain," Kite said. "He found the name board and her port of registry washed ashore near Schull and had thought the crew all lost. We received advice from Dublin to that effect. But surely no ship came in last night?"

Jones shook his head. "No, I have come directly from Tenby."

"That is the devil of a journey!"

"Aye, sir, it is, but I did not feel that I could anywhere rest easy until I had got rid of . . ." Jones gestured at the pile of coin glinting on the desktop.

"And the log and papers?" Kite prompted.

"I have them outside, sir," Watkinson said, indicating the door to the counting house, "and there is bread and coffee arriving."

Jones had arrived in Liverpool in 1760 as mate of the *Spitfire*, which vessel Kite himself had commanded. They had brought in with them their prize, the French privateer *La Malouine*, later renamed *African Princess*, and in due course Jones had been promoted into her as master. He had married and in the intervening eleven years had bred a family of four boys and a single girl between his voyages to the West Indies.

For some of that time Kite too had continued voyaging, taking command of a succession of the ships owned jointly by Makepeace and Kite: the *Salamander*, the *Firefly* and the *Samphire*. Puella had from the first steadfastly refused to accompany him, preferring to stay ashore and bring up their child. But in due time the strain of living alone, a black mistress in a household of white servants, had begun to unnerve her. She had trouble with a manservant and threatened to beat him; he raised a mob which stoned the house and broke all the windows. Kite had to abandon his sea-going and take up a desk alongside Makepeace in the company chambers.

Captain Topsy-Turvy, as Kite was known in Liverpool for

upsetting the conventions of the day, became a diligent ship-owner, well known and well liked in commercial circles, but his wife became an unhappy and increasingly resentful recluse. She rarely rebuked him, devoting herself to her growing son, refusing to allow Kite to send him to school, but insisting upon the employment of a governess and then, a few months earlier, a tutor.

Kite had acquiesced to all her demands, content that with his presence quelling any popular reaction to Puella's colour she seemed to have made a satisfactory life for herself. Their own moments of intimacy had become few and far between, but even this he could bear if he occupied his mind with the business of ships and cargo. Of the two business partners he, rather than Makepeace, was the more dynamic, and he had thrown himself into the work of acting as ship's husband. In this role he left to Makepeace much of the arranging of outward cargoes. His own superior handwriting and the contacts he had made whilst working for the Antiguan merchant Joseph Mulgrave occupied him with the business of concluding deals on the homeward cargoes. By this means he kept himself appraised of developments in the West Indies and in the American colonies, writing to his erstwhile fellow clerk Wentworth at St John's in Antigua, and to Arthur Tyrell in Newport, Rhode Island.

Gradually, as fewer and fewer people saw Puella, and Kite's presence on the dockside became a matter of daily regularity, people ceased to concern themselves with the anomaly of a rich black women in their midst. Liverpool was already a cosmopolitan town and, now unseen, Puella began to slowly acquire a kind of mythical status. That Captain Topsy-Turvy married a black woman worth, it was said, five hundred pounds a year in her own right, was seen by many as a mark of his financial acuity. By others it seemed to bear out the notion that in trade lay a fortune for all manner of people; if a black slave could earn her manumission and gain such a fortune, what might not a decent white person achieve?

Kite was oblivious to this widespread gossip. Makepeace, on the other hand, had been largely responsible for fostering it. After Puella's disastrous attempt to beat her manservant, he realised that not only was Kite's presence at his wife's side necessary, but that something must be done to protect his own fortune from any tainting by oblique association with the black woman. He had initially hoped that Puella would sail with her husband but when this proved impossible the only thing to do was to encourage a belief in the lady's native grandeur. It was not difficult to put about Puella's nobility. Strikingly beautiful in her tall, upright ebony way, she did not disdain to enter Liverpool's social life in the early days of her marriage. This had coincided with a popular print showing a native king trading with "some Liverpool masters". The print had shown a beplumed black chieftain attired, enthroned and surrounded by an almost Gallic splendour, while some homespun captains stood respectfully at the foot of the monarch's dais. To the right of the king's pavilion, the masts and yards of the white men's slaving ships lay at their anchors in the waters of a distant but unmistakably African river; to the left, a landscape of wooden barracoons were depicted spilling thousands of black slaves across a plain, like a dark stream which flowed towards the waiting ships. In the foreground a spokesman for the Liverpool masters, his hat in his left hand, his right foot forward in a bow, offered his right hand in a gesture of amity to that of a half-naked but lovely young woman descending from the dais at her father's bidding. To offset the Liverpool masters, a group of splendid negro spearsmen, courtiers and royal mistresses appeared to applaud what had every appearance of a secular marriage. The meaning was clear enough, spelling out the commercial benefits to both the merchants of Liverpool and the nobility of "Guinea", while few remained insensible to the implication inherent in the imagery. The print, known popularly as *The Cornucopia of Africa*, seemed to find genuine proof in the union of Puella and Captain Topsy-Turvy, for although it had become known that Puella had been shipped as a slave aboard Captain Makepeace's own slaver, the *Enterprize*, the story of her false imprisonment and sale by a tyrannical usurper was confirmed by the common knowledge of her independent wealth. Makepeace had added a couple of hundred per annum to the real sum, and entirely suppressed the fact that her annuity was the gift of a wealthy West Indian merchant named Mulgrave, now long since dead. People forgave her her beating of a worthless Catholic Irish manservant, admired her elegance when she went abroad and, as time passed and she became increasingly reclusive, slowly allowed her to slip from the forefront of their minds.

*   *   *

When Jones had gone, Kite called Jasper Watkinson into his office. "As you know, Mr Watkinson, Captain Makepeace's death requires that we review matters relevant to our joint business. I have not been a party to the late Captain's testamentary provisions, but it will be necessary to make a settlement in favour of Mistress Makepeace. I shall also have to determine what interest young Masters Henry and Charles are to take in our affairs, or whether they are simply to receive the benefits of shares; neither has to my knowledge evinced the slightest desire to go to sea, nor any interest whatsoever in the affairs of the company. I also purpose to ensure that Mistress Katherine is well provided for."

"Captain Makepeace has already made known to me much of his personal financial stipulations, Captain Kite," Watkinson said with his customary deferential efficiency. "In my employment as chief clerk to Captain Makepeace, you will understand that, pending the reading of his will, I should not wish to breach any undertaking of confidentiality . . ."

"Yes, yes, I understand all that, Mr Watkinson, your personal attachment to Captain Makepeace is well known, but that is precisely why it is necessary to raise these matters with you. The circumscribed manner in which Captain Makepeace made some of his arrangements means that his death leaves me at a disadvantage. I shall entirely rely upon you as I usually do."

Kite smiled at Watkinson, though there was a worm of unease uncoiling itself in his guts. Watkinson was, Kite knew, ambitious; his wife was a woman of social pretension, admirably so, as far as Kite was concerned, for he saw no advantage in keeping a good man in the shade. But he sensed that Watkinson was seeking to throw smoke in his eyes and confuse him, for some reason best known to himself.

"There is absolutely nothing to concern you, Captain Kite, at least until the will is read."

Kite leaned forward on his elbows and put his fingertips together. "You know, Jasper," he said dropping his voice, "there is much work to be done. The company will require a new partner and the opportunities for your good self are, well, limitless if matters should fall out that way."

"I understand, Captain Kite," Watkinson said turning for the door. In the doorway he turned. "I am sure, Captain, I can rely upon your good offices in my behalf."

"I see no reason why not, Jasper. Do you?"

"No, sir."

And yet he did. All that morning Kite's thoughts drifted off the ledgers from which he was reckoning the loss occasioned by the wrecking of the *African Princess*. The ship had carried her own insurance and her loss would be borne by the company in its entirety, but his train of thought would not settle in the rut of even so uncomfortable a furrow as financial loss. He should be weeping for his dead son, but poor Puella's irrational behaviour had, over the years, eroded his capacity to brood. William was dead and no power on earth could bring him back; Puella was killing herself in the manner of her people and nothing he could do would prevent her. Makepeace was dead and something was in train that he sensed had some direct bearing on the conduct of the company that was now his sole responsibility, notwithstanding the benefits in law which accrued to Mrs Makepeace and her family.

It was dusk when he finally brought himself to reckon up the losses of the *African Princess* and her cargo. The cargo alone came to over two thousand pounds, and there were the wages of the crew to determine. He sat back, unable to work any longer, procrastinating as his wandering and distracted mind thought again of Puella. Out of spirits and fearful of returning home, he considered eating out. Perhaps he should be pleasant to Watkinson, but the chief clerk had already left, making his excuses and saying he had to call upon Mistress Makepeace and did Captain Kite mind him leaving to attend to his private business? Captain Kite did not mind. The *Samphire* was nowhere near completing her lading and no ships were expected now that the fate of the *African Princess* was known. They should have news of the *Salamander* within the fortnight, but no, Watkinson was free to go.

Kite considered matters for a moment, then he rose and went to the window. Despite the rain and wind, the panes were grimy, but he could see the River Mersey and the masts of several ships anchored in the stream beyond the dock. He thought of poor Jones and the wrecking of his ship on Cape Clear Island, of the dreadful quality of calamity and how Jones looked like a broken man. It had been Kite who had insisted his former mate should study navigation and make himself competent to become a master; he himself had therefore initiated the chain of events that had led to Jones losing his ship. But he did not believe there was a real link between the loss of the *African Princess* and the death of his son. They had not occurred on the same day, let alone at the same time. He rose, went out to where Watkinson's desk overlooked the counting house and the desks of the three junior clerks and, striking flint on steel, coaxed the lamp into life as the evening gloom settled on the dusty office. He sat at Watkinson's desk and drew the log of the *African Princess* towards him. He already guessed what he was going to find and when he did so he sat back.

Young William had contracted the rice-water fever within the hour of the *African Princess* striking the Irish coast. It was an uncanny coincidence.

But that was all it was; a coincidence, two disparate occurrences taking place at the same moment, a quite fortuitous matter. Why, hundreds, thousands of things would have occurred at that hour throughout the world. How many coaches had shed their wheels? How many horses cast shoes? How many women conceived? How many plates been dropped, barns caught fire? And if a man fell from his horse did it signify if his wife pricked her finger with a needle at the same moment?

Kite cursed. Men and women were not such logical creatures that they could entirely throw off the notion that there *might* be a connection. He did not believe it implicitly, as Puella would when she found out, but the coincidence was strange. He looked up. The junior clerks were looking at him, and he wondered if he had unwittingly exclaimed, then they bent again to their work and he rose and retired to his own inner office, to gaze again out of the grimy window.

Of course he would not tell Puella of the curious coincidence, just as he would not in fact tell her of the loss of the *African Princess*. If she was determined to die, it would be quite pointless. But, he recalled, he was responsible for her situation too. She was going to die and he was doing nothing about it beyond accepting the ancient horrors of the spirits. He suddenly thought what life would be like without her; even Puella reduced by heartache and misery was better than no Puella.

Beyond the glass window the river shone like a sword blade in the last of the daylight. The wind was still blowing, though with far less violence than it had been, and the late gale was now no more than a strong breeze. A flat was running upstream against the ebb tide. In an hour the flood would be making, and the sailing barge would carry it far upstream into the country beyond. He came to a sudden resolution: with William dead he would take Puella to sea again. They would shut up the Liverpool house and go back to Antigua, shipping out as passengers aboard the *Samphire*. He could not leave her to die because she believed in silly superstitions, in the predestination of random occurrences and the power of the spirits to divine, determine and destroy.

She was capable of bearing another child, and if she did not wish to share his bed again, she could be saved from her self-inflicted death, diverted and made to live again under the warm sun of the tropics. What a fool he had been to have so immersed himself in his business that he had almost lost her! He had no interest in other women and had only given himself to work for the benefit of young William, exactly as Puella had sacrificed her own happiness to the success of their son!

He reached for his coat and hurriedly pulled it on, then clapped his hat upon his head and hefted his cane.

"Good night, gentlemen," he called to the clerks as they watched him go.

"Good night, sir," they called after him, and then stared at one another.

"You should have told him, Mr Johnstone."

"You think he will not know soon enough?" Johnstone replied, closing his inkwell with a loud snap, adding, "if it is true."

"Of course it is true, and when he finds out, it will be too late. Watkinson will have sewn the matter up . . ."

"That's what you want, ain't it, Nathan, Watkinson to sew it all up so that you can be chief clerk . . ."

"Be quiet!" Johnstone said, rounding on his two juniors. "D'you think I care about being chief clerk any more with the cholera taking my wife? Captain Kite has just lost his son. How can I be telling him things that we only suspect to be true?"

"You should warn him though, Nathan, or we may all pay for it once that Master Harry arrives to console his bosom friends and accomplices."

Two

A Speculation

Kite arrived home too late. He was greeted by his house-keeper, Mrs O'Riordan, with the news that the mistress was dead.

"It is not possible!" Kite was incredulous. Even in decline, Puella could not die in so short a space of time.

"Her neck, sir . . ." Mrs O'Riordan was finding it difficult to retain her self-possession. "'Tis awful, sir . . . You see she asked that the chicken—"

"Neck? Chicken? What the devil are you talking about?" Kite looked from the woman's distraught face to the staircase. "Excuse me, Mrs O'Riordan."

He raced upstairs and flung open the bedroom door. The room was entirely in darkness and he bawled for lights, standing on the threshold, his heart thundering and his body trembling. At the noise of steps behind him he turned. Mrs O'Riordan, her body heaving with sobs and the effort of climbing the stairs at a run, held out the candlestick. Seizing it and holding it before him like a talisman, Kite entered the room.

The candlelight caught her eyes at once. Puella seemed to stare directly at him, a terrible accusatory glare that was at the same time piteous. Her head was flung back at an unnatural angle, hung over the edge of the bed so that her face was upside down. He moved towards her and, holding the candle above her, saw that she was quite naked. In the doorway Mrs O'Riordan gave a little shriek and he looked up at her.

"What happened, Mrs O'Riordan? Have you any idea?" He kept his voice low, under control, though a deep anger was rising in him.

Between sobs, the housekeeper explained. She had come, as the Captain had instructed, to offer food and drink at three in the afternoon. The Mistress had been sitting in her chair where, it seemed, she had been since poor Master William died. So she was all the more surprised when the Mistress asked for a live chicken to be bought and brought to her before it was killed in the house.

"It had to be live, sir, and it had to be killed in the house, sir, the Mistress was particular about that. And, begging your pardon, sir, but seeing the Mistress had her own ways like, I did as I was bid. I sent Maggie out to get a plump pullet . . ."

"What else did she say?" Kite asked, a cold sensation fastening about his chest like a rope lashing. "Did she ask for it to be cooked in a certain way?"

"N-no, sir, but to be truthful I didn't think much of anything else except that she'd be eating again, sir, and how pleased you would be at the news, though she did say as she was to be told when the chicken had been bought and she'd want to look at it to see if it was all right, sir, so I supposed that she would be telling me then how she'd want it to be cooked . . . She liked chicken, sir."

"Yes. She did." Kite leaned over her body and placed his hand beneath Puella's left breast. She was still warm but her heartbeat had long since ceased. "Go on," he commanded, his voice harsh with the effort of control.

"Maggie came back, sir, I took the pullet off of her and brought it up here to the Mistress . . ." Mrs O'Riordan paused and Kite looked at her.

"Was she still sitting in the chair?"

Mrs O'Riordan shook her head. "No, sir, she were lying on the bed. Like she is now."

"Naked, but not dead?"

Mrs O'Riordan saw the confusion she had caused. "No, no, sir, she wasn't dead but she was naked, sir, and that took me aback a little, though I have seen her that way before sir, as I think you know . . ."

"Go on, Mrs O'Riordan, please simply tell me what happened." He was breathing more easily now. The blind fury of anger had ebbed, and now, staring down at Puella, he was filled with regrets. If only he had come home an hour earlier, or fed her yesterday. He felt a wave of emotion surge through him, but he crushed it and listened patiently to his housekeeper.

"Well . . . Well, sir, she took the chicken and I supposed

she were going to feel it for plumpness, sir, but she kind of embraced it, sir."

"Embraced it?"

"I don't known how else to say it, sir, said like a prayer over it with her face all lit up, if you'll pardon me for saying so, sir, of a black person, sir, I don't rightly known how else to tell you, sir . . ."

"Casting a spell, perhaps."

"Oh, God, sir, that's terrible! That's wicked, sir, to be suggesting such a thing." Mrs O'Riordan crossed herself. "I know she was not quite a Christian, sir."

"Mrs O'Riordan, I respect your sensibilities, but you know there are women in Ireland as in England who make up potions for the shingles and the scrofula and they do so with incantations, do they not? So, was it like that?" He looked up at the woman standing, shaking on the threshold. "Well?"

Mrs O'Riordan nodded. "Aye, sir, I suppose that it was."

"And then?"

"She handed me back the pullet and said I was to break its neck quickly and to bring it back when she would tell me how to cook it. 'Twas no more than three-quarters of an hour ago, sir. I went directly downstairs, took the fowl and snapped its neck. I came back up the stairs and . . ."

"Please, Mrs O'Riordan, go on."

"She was like that, sir. Her neck all loose and – oh, God . . ." Mrs O'Riordan burst into sobs and fled.

Left alone Kite placed his hand beneath Puella's head so that he cupped her skull and gently lifted it. He was able to swivel it without resistance, for the vertebrae of the neck were detached from the remainder of the spinal column. As the chicken's neck had been broken, so had Puella's.

"I have never seen such a thing before, except in cases of extreme paroxysm among the insane," remarked Dr Bennett, taking snuff and dropping a considerable quantity down the front of his soiled waistcoat in doing so. Kite watched the doctor's huge nose wrinkle and sniff like that of a hound as it ingested the tobacco dust. An instant later Bennett's huge and ungainly body endured his own paroxysm. The pleasure thus engendered seemed to Kite to be of so suppressed a nature as to be merely an incomprehensible affectation, though he understood devotees claimed it to be beneficial.

"Of course rabies, in its final form," Bennett went on, "will bring on muscular spasms of such violence that small bones may break, but that the mere snuffing out of a chicken induces so dreadful a reaction in a human, even a black – begging your pardon, Kite – is much to be wondered at."

Kite grunted. The shock of Puella's death had passed, and he diverted his mind from dwelling on regrets. There were many hours yet until dawn and, given the unusual circumstances of Puella's death, he had felt it necessary to consult Bennett. The youthful experience of once, long ago, having thought himself under suspicion of murder had bred caution in him, but he was not surprised at Bennett's comments.

"You seem to reserve your own judgement, Kite. You know these people better than I; have you a theory?"

"Yes, and it may be more than a theory, for I believe there is a probability which I am unable to explain but which I have observed on more than one occasion, that the mind may be induced to release powerful agents. Such agents enable the physical being to do extraordinary things. I have heard of men leaping into trees to avoid lions, or of enduring terrible wounds in battle until some objective is achieved. The Africans of the Guinea coast place great confidence in the powers of the spirits they conceive to be all about us. They tap these in some way unknown to our more sophisticated and logical minds. It is perhaps a skill that we have lost through our greater leaning towards other things which, in the matter of our survival, we deem to be of a higher priority. They call these powers *obi*, or *obeah*. I do not understand the precise usage, but I know there are those who consider the magic not merely real but potent."

Bennett shrugged, his expression sceptical. "Then how do you explain the manner of her death? A kind of suicide?"

"Yes. She had nurtured a desire to die for several days following the death of our son. I had expected her to do this slowly, by starvation; she has acted in this way before when deeply troubled. I had in fact determined to stop her from this extremity, but thought that the matter was not one of urgency and it was perhaps better to allow her to grieve a little in her own way first." Kite pressed on, well aware that he was exculpating himself from a self-inflicted charge of neglect. "I myself have not felt much disposed to go on after William's death. But this afternoon I resolved to quit Liverpool for a while and to take Puella with me . . ."

"But fate intervened."

"No, Puella divined my intention. You must have noticed how married people oft times discover they have been thinking of the same thing when one opens a conversation and the other is already considering the same matter."

"You forget, I am not married, Kite. Who would marry a dropsical wretch like me?"

"You are not dropsical, Bennett, you merely eat and drink too much."

"It is the only pleasure available to an ugly man, but pray continue."

"She did not wish to continue her life and sought a means to end it. She disdained the knife, but needed only some means of tapping the *obi*, of reaching the agent necessary to induce, or release from her body, a last spasm, like your rabid or insane patient, so that she can twist and fling herself with such force that she breaks her own neck."

"But Mrs O'Riordan wringing the neck of a chicken—"

"Into which she had surrendered her own spirit, her own soul, Bennett, do you not see? If you can voluntarily pass into a trance, which is no more than a temporary and voluntary surrender of self, then you can do this with a finality, a last purpose to mobilise an effort of both physical and spiritual will which ends in voluntary death."

Bennett shook his head and gave out a great sigh. "Extraordinary," he breathed, "quite extraordinary."

They stood for a moment looking down at Puella and then the physician pulled the sheet over her. "She was very comely, Kite, that I must say. I have seldom seen so beautiful a form, black though it is . . ." He reached for more snuff, adding as he inhaled, "Love, I suppose, takes no notice of such things."

Kite stood a moment in silence. He had known Bennett for some years, knew him to be a man of integrity and intelligence, and a physician of no mean ability. "No," he said slowly, "but such things raise great barriers between persons, Bennett, even in death."

Bennett nodded and held out his hand. "You have so instructed me this evening, Kite, that I shall waive my fee."

"Will you join me for supper?"

"You don't wish to eat alone?"

"No, I do not." Kite knew that Bennett's presence would stave off the onset of a grief he felt he could not bear.

"And you will not serve me chicken?"

Kite was grateful for the black joke. "Mrs O'Riordan has a fine ham, Dr Bennett, and I can find a bottle or two, I dare say. To be candid, I should welcome your company."

"Very well. We should send Maggie out for the laying-out woman at once."

"Mrs O'Riordan has already called her, I expect she is warming her belly with a glass of porter in the kitchen below."

The two men descended the stairs and Kite made his wants known to Mrs O'Riordan, who had in part anticipated them. Over the cold ham, Bennett asked why Kite had called his wife by such an odd name.

"I never knew her native name. I could not bring myself to give her an English name, for though I purchased her from her enslaver, who happened to be Captain Makepeace, I never for an instant thought of her as my property. Calling her Nancy, or Molly, or some such seemed patronising in the extreme."

"Well, you had the wounds by then, I suppose," interjected Bennett, adding with his mouth half full of an enormous slice of ham, "the wounds of Cupid."

Kite nodded. "Yes. I was extraordinarily moved by her." He paused, lost for a moment in memories of Puella's love-making. "So," he resumed his explanation, "I simply called her by the Latin word for girl and to my mind the word came simply to signify Puella herself."

"Tell me, Kite, out of a clinical curiosity and availing myself of both my Hippocratic silence and the discretion of a friend, did you grow close to her? I mean by the question did you reach an intimacy comparable with your having married a woman of your own colour?"

"There are times," Kite said, "when I have observed considerable estrangement to exist between the partners in what I think you are alluding to in your inimitable way as a normal marriage. Certainly we had grown apart, as does any sea officer and his spouse, and this was made no easier for Puella by her being black and subject to some unkindnesses hereabouts. I was, of course, to blame for much of this and she never really understood how independent she in truth was."

30

"So she *did* have a competence of her own?"

"Such a sum as would keep you in snuff for about one thousand years, Dr Bennett," Kite said, smiling sadly.

"Oh. I had thought it mere jealous gossip."

Kite felt his spirits rally. Old Bennett was a shrewd mender of men and he warmed to his therapy. But they got no further, for at that moment the door to the dining room opened and a red-eyed Mrs O'Riordan stood bobbing her curtsy.

"What is it, Mrs O'Riordan? I thought you had retired long since."

"Oh, thank you, Captain, but I couldn't sleep and the laying-out woman has only just gone and now there's poor Mr Johnstone asking to see you, sir."

"Johnstone? What the devil does he want at this hour?"

"I'll be going, Kite." Bennett slipped a last slice of ham into his mouth and rose, revealing half a dozen new patches of grease on his coat.

Kite raised his hand without turning from the housekeeper. "No, no, Bennett, do you sit down, it is probably news of a ship, or some other matter." He raised his voice. "Come in, Mr Johnstone."

Johnstone shuffled in, revolving his hat in his hands. "Pardon me, sir, I did not know you had company, and Mistress O'Riordan has just told me that your wife – please accept my condolences . . ."

"Thank you, Nathan," Kite replied as Johnstone's eyes wandered to where Bennett, who had resolved to stay, was now hacking another slice off the savaged ham. Kite looked at the bereaved Johnstone and his pathetic, half-starved air. "You are hungry, sir. Pray take a seat, help yourself and then tell us your business. Mrs O'Riordan, another bottle and help yourself to a glass below stairs."

He smiled as the housekeeper bobbed a curtsy. She had already been helping herself, by the colour of her, but it was no matter.

Johnstone hesitated, made a half-heartedly self-deprecating gesture and then pulled out a spare chair as Mrs O'Riordan put a plate in front of him and fetched clean cutlery. Kite waited and watched; Johnstone literally drooled as he sliced the ham and placed it carefully upon the plate laid before him. For several minutes the two older men regarded the ravening of the younger. He did not look as though he had eaten for days and it occurred to Kite that he probably had had very little beyond some bread and tea. After a little, Johnstone recalled himself and, having drained a glass of wine, looked up at the others.

"I . . . I beg your pardon, gentlemen, I, er, I quite forgot myself."

"Please, take some more, but do tell us what brings you here."

Johnstone, who had already reached for the long-bladed carving knife and its accompanying fork, looked up as though paralysed. His eyes switched from Kite to Bennett and back again.

"Come, young fellow," put in Bennett, "what's the trouble? You have the look of a hare caught in a trap."

"Well, I . . . No, I cannot. The matter is confidential . . . between myself and Captain Kite."

"And you don't trust me not to blab your affairs all over Liverpool, eh? Is that it?" Bennett said with mock severity, laying his own knife and fork down with an air of genuine regret. "I am to be flung out of Eden, Captain Kite, by your damned clerk."

"I mean no offence, Dr Bennett," Johnstone responded with a swift anxiety.

"Ah, there's none taken," Bennett said rising with a low belch. "'Tis getting late and the ham will not sustain the two of us. Kite, I'm damned grateful to you for the fare and will leave you to your waterfront scuttlebutt or whatever evil nautical term you lay to your conversation." He held up his hands. "No, no, I'll see myself out, and I'll make sure Mrs O'Riordan leaves you in peace."

Kite sat again. "Good night, Bennett, and thank you for your company. I am obliged to you and greatly appreciate it."

"Good night, Kite. Think nothing of it. Good night, Johnstone."

"Good night, sir."

After Bennett had gone, Kite refilled Johnstone's glass. "Well, Nathan," he said, "the circumstances of this confidential visit must be extraordinary. Have you had news from Bidston of another ship in the offing, or news of a loss, or what?"

Johnstone swallowed the contents of his glass and stared at his employer. He was quite obviously mustering his thoughts and his courage, so Kite waited patiently. It was a night of revelations, he thought, but he had no desire to ascend those stairs again and see Puella, her eyes closed and her jaw bound up with a cloth.

"Captain Kite," Johnstone began, "I must ask you to believe that I have only two motives in coming here tonight. One is to protect my own interests. I mention this first if only to prove to you that I conceive my loyalty to you is not disinterested, and is thereby genuine. But added to that is a conviction that it would be wrong of me not to tell you that I fear something is afoot. Something, I fear, that is against your own interests."

He paused and Kite shifted uneasily. Was it not enough that a man should lose his son to cholera and his wife to the spirits of the *obeah* without a further visitation on top of the additional burden of the death of his partner and the wrecking of a ship? He thought of Watkinson's evasive and unsatisfactory conduct that afternoon, though it seemed like a lifetime ago. "Go on, Nathan," he said softly, sensing a further shadowy figure beyond the bounds of his present knowledge.

"I should perhaps have waited until something more concrete occurred, for I should not wish you to think of me as a conspirator or a spy of some sort . . ." Sweat stood out in beads over Johnstone's brow.

"How long have you worked for me, Nathan?" Kite cut in.

"Seven years, sir."

"And you have given me every proof of satisfaction. Now please, I beseech you, come to the matter directly."

"I believe you to have been cheated, sir. And I believe that further mischief is being hatched against you."

"By whom?" Kite asked. "To what purpose?"

Johnstone swallowed, held up his hand and shook his head. "Please, I beg you, sir, let me explain. 'Tis hard enough to comprehend, particularly as some parts of the matter are not clear, but I have fathomed out what I conceive to be a plan to dispossess you and over which the loss of the *African Princess* is but a fortuitous bonus to those who wish to encompass your ruin."

Kite could not imagine why anyone should wish to undertake so grievous a thing as encompass his ruin, but he suppressed his question and let Johnstone have his head. "Go on," he repeated.

"The *African Princess* was your own ship, sir, was she not, as the *Enterprize* was the personal property of Captain Makepeace? Your other ships were jointly owned in various proportions, some split with your own wife, some sixty-fourths being held by Mrs Makepeace, but the majority of the shares belonging to yourself and the late Captain. Is that not so?"

"Yes, that is so, though my wife and I owned the *Spitfire* entirely, while Makepeace and his wife wholly owned the *Salamander*."

"And in that way funds were laid aside to the principals in due proportion?"

"Yes, that too is so. And of course we shared the risks and any losses."

"Except where they were incurred by your own private property, so that you will personally bear the costs associated with the loss of the *African Princess*?"

Kite nodded. "But you are not suggesting that Captain Jones wrecked her deliberately, surely?"

Johnstone shook his head. "No, I am not. But did you know of the mortgages taken out on some of the bottoms?"

"Yes, we had remortgaged the *Samphire* to release some funds in order to speculate on a cargo for Spain . . . But you said bottoms; in the plural. To my knowledge we had only done it the once." Kite was frowning.

"And you were opposed to it, I believe? In the case of the *Samphire*, I mean. I speculate here, sir, but it does not seem likely that you would approve."

Kite nodded. "You are right. No, I did not like remortgaging a hull, just as I do not much like speculating in cargoes. I prefer that we offer a freight rate and let others pay. It is our business to offer tonnage and for others to buy and sell their commodities. I am a ship owner, not a speculator, a profiteer or a merchant. I do not have the aptitude or the interest for it."

"That is precisely my contention, sir. Nor did Captain Makepeace, but he became a victim and, well, I anticipate. The point is that most of your hulls are, in part or in full, remortgaged."

"I know nothing of this. It is inconceivable," Kite protested, then recalled Makepeace's last wish, his insistent desire for forgiveness, recollection of which had been driven out by the man's death and then the accumulation of his own miseries. He looked sharply at Johnstone. "So you are alleging that in proportion to the shares owned outside my own control, the vessels are not actually owned by Makepeace and Kite?"

"Yes, Captain, unfortunately that is just what I am alleging, and I am certain of it, for I have heard Watkinson discuss the matter with his principal."

The shadow moved out into the light. "Samuel Frith?"

"You knew!" Johnstone was astonished.

"I guessed. The man has made a proposition to Miss Makepeace."

"That is infamous!"

"Well," Kite said cautiously, unwilling at this stage to allow passionate emotion to obtrude, "it is perhaps not the most desirable state of affairs and Miss Makepeace certainly does not seek it, but as Frith is not married perhaps infamous is not quite the right word."

"But it is said, sir, that he has been Mrs Makepeace's lover!" Johnstone declared desperately.

"Is this more of your speculation?"

"It is common gossip, Captain Kite, that is all. But it may explain Miss Katherine's distaste for her own proposed union."

"Well, that is true, but what do you conceive Captain Makepeace has been doing with the funds Frith has been putting in his pocket? Has he been speculating in cargoes other than this shipment for Spain? I cannot recall evidence in any of our own ships apart from the *Samphire*, or those of others?"

"No, sir, that is where the remortgaging of the *Samphire* was clever. By making that known to you, and – though not without your own misgivings – your acquiescence in approving it being common knowledge, it signalled that Makepeace and Kite were not averse to the practice. Word of such matters spreads about the town while your personal suspicions would have been lulled for some time to come."

"Now that *is* speculation."

Johnstone nodded, then shrugged. "But if a man knows his wife has made a visit to the theatre in the company of a gentleman friend and does not object, he will not believe the rumours of adultery as quickly as will one who had never condoned such loose behaviour in the first place."

"That is somewhat sophisticated logic, Nathan."

"But you take my point?"

"Perhaps; but to what purpose? You have yet to tell me what is being done with the money raised by this remortgaging of ships."

"Master Harry spends, or should I say loses it, at the tables."

"You mean he *gambles* it?"

"Captain Makepeace was an indulgent father, or Master Harry a plausible liar. I gather Mistress Makepeace had frequent words with her husband, but then she had compromised herself and sought to secure her own future by marrying Miss Katherine to Frith."

Kite considered the matter for some moments and then shook his head, asking, "But why does Frith want ships? Tell me that. He is a wealthy man, for what possible reason does he want ships?"

35

"I am not absolutely certain, sir, but Watkinson is behind this matter, nursing his own ambition and guiding Frith. Frith I think has paid far less than the capital value of the ships. Makepeace was reluctant to dissemble directly, but content to leave the details to the chief clerk. Watkinson has undertaken much of the business to keep it from you, Frith has therefore not so much acquired ships as assets whose return far exceeds his own investment. I suppose Makepeace thought the sums advanced kept Master Harry out of trouble and might always be replaced, and that by securing Frith as his son-in-law the matter remained in the family and therefore in principle little had changed, since the ships would remain the property of the family!"

"Why could he not have acted openly?" Kite asked. "I could have disputed the matter and we might have divided the firm, but he could still have raised some capital in order to discharge Harry's debts."

"Because in the first place the matter of Master Harry's debts is serious; in the second place Watkinson did not want the size of the fleet diminished; and in the third place he wants you out of the way, pushed into the margins, sent back to sea as a mere master so that he can assume the powers of an active partner."

"Why does he so hate me?" But Kite already knew the answer and spared Johnstone the embarrassment of spelling it out. "Because I have lived with a blackamoor?"

"He would put it less charitably, Captain."

"Yes, I dare say he would," Kite admitted, considering all that had been said. "So now Makepeace is dead and Frith is already taking control both of the inconsolable widow and the wretched pawn of a daughter. But how would they rid themselves of me? Can you riddle me that riddle with your speculations, Nathan?"

"That is what I cannot reason out, Captain. Perhaps they will simply await your reaction. If you will forgive me for mentioning it in so indelicate a manner, the death of your wife will, in a sense, play into their hands, adding to your misfortune over the loss of the *African Princess* and making you vulnerable."

"Or perhaps very strong, Nathan," Kite said slowly. "You yourself are but recently acquainted with death. You have little to lose, I think, and risked my executing the messenger tonight, did you not?"

Johnstone flushed, then looked his employer in the eye. "I did say, sir, that I had every intention of protecting my own interests."

"Have you anything to keep you here, Nathan?"

"My late wife's mother, sir."

Kite leaned forward. "Would you be a conspirator, Nathan? As a partner, I mean?"

Johnstone frowned with uncertainty. "I should like first to know your mind, sir."

"Well, it is a little confused, but the *Spitfire* is expected soon and I have a mind not to tarry in Liverpool. Are you game for some more substantial speculation?"

"I have no money, Captain Kite. I, er, have never considered such a matter." He shrugged, clearly flustered.

"But you have an excellent brain, Nathan, and I might easily be persuaded to invest in it. Now tell me, what do you think their next move will be?"

"Well, sir, as I have said, and forgive my candour, but the deaths of both Captain Makepeace and your wife—"

"And the loss of the *African Princess* gives them an advantage, yes. I agree they will act soon while I am, so to speak, knocked down."

"Exactly, sir."

"Tomorrow?"

"I think it highly likely."

Kite thought a moment, then said, "We could, of course, transfer my own and Puella's shares in all our vessels clandestinely, as they have done, to Wentworth in Antigua. You could raise bills of sale and have the matter registered at the Custom House by tomorrow afternoon. I'd trust Wentworth with my life but—"

"You could be more subtle, sir, and avoid the risk of cutting off your nose to spite your face."

"Proceed . . ." And Kite listened while Johnstone explained his notion. Midnight struck as he concluded his dissertation and Kite smiled approvingly.

"You have given the matter some thought."

Johnstone shook his head. "No, sir, only a little in talking this evening."

"But tell me, how did you first become suspicious?"

"Well, it was not a matter of suddenly becoming suspicious, but Watkinson's manner towards me underwent a slow change. At first I was useful to him and I have to admit we were friendly, but then, when I married, I began to sense a distance growing between us. I thought at first it was that he wished to emphasise that he conceived his station to be above mine, but then I encountered him twice in deep conversation with Frith. Of course, I knew Frith to be a man

of substance, but also a man of low morals. Mrs Makepeace was
not the only woman his name was linked with. Moreover I heard
he had been to London in company with Master Harry and shortly
thereafter rumours circulated about Harry Makepeace's gambling
here in Liverpool. At about this time Watkinson sported a new suit
and cane, he appeared to be elevating himself in the world and his
manner towards myself and the junior clerks underwent a slow but
subtle change. I think he wished to conceal it, but he could not
avoid a certain supercilious manner affecting himself.

"I should not have taken much notice, I suppose, had I not
stumbled on him talking to Frith late one night. I had been down to
the dock with a jerque note for Captain Matthews of the *Firestorm*
and he had asked me to return some papers to the office. I did so
and found Frith, Makepeace and Watkinson enjoying a bottle of
wine in familiar ease. I'm afraid I listened. I heard sufficient. Your
wife was mentioned in no very flattering terms, I heard an opinion
voiced as to your judgement and your sense of trust. A little later
Harry's name was mentioned by Makepeace and – this caught my
attention particularly – both Frith *and* Watkinson spoke sharply
to the Captain, as though they both enjoyed the whip hand over
him. It was enough; I was about to leave when I heard Makepeace
shout them down in one of his bellows. 'Damn you both,' he
said, 'the *Samphire*'s worth more than that! I could mortgage her
for a thousand,' whereupon Frith said in his cold manner, 'Sit
down, Captain, you know perfectly well that to raise a mortgage
on the *Samphire* you will need Kite's approval.' There was
some movement in the inner office at this point and I fled."

"You were very wise to do so and I am grateful to you for your
confidence." Kite stood up. "I have a melancholy night ahead
of me, Nathan, one that you will have too recently experienced
yourself. We may both be dead of cholera ourselves within the
week, but we are not yet infected and may still confound our
enemies. Tomorrow you shall be at your desk promptly, but not
a word to a soul."

"You may rely upon me, Captain Kite."

"And my thanks to you for your speculation."

Three

A Great Sinner

Kite woke suddenly at dawn. He was cold and cramped but he rose and stretched stiffly, shivering miserably as he stared at Puella, where she had been laid out. From below he heard the first movements in the household, and as he touched the cold body with the tips of his fingers he felt a deep sense of guilt that his business with Johnstone overrode all other considerations. With an effort he went through to his study, rang the bell for coffee and hot water and wrote a letter to arrange for Puella's interment. She would be given Christian burial, of that he was sure, and would be laid to rest next to her beloved son. By the time Maggie appeared to answer his summons, his letter and instructions were ready. An hour later, improved in appearance if not in mood by a wash and shave, wearing clean linen and having broken his fast, he left the house. The straw strewn in the street to quieten the noise of passing wheels in acknowledgement of William's death had been dispersed by the gale, though wisps remained clinging to the cobbles where bird lime anchored it. He had ordered some more, and the windows of Puella's bedroom stood wide open, though he knew he clasped her *obi* himself and that she would not relinquish it to the Christian God.

He strode downhill, into the wind rising from the Mersey, towards the shipping office. Puella would truly understand the lifting of his spirits and he knew that in her death she had deliberately released him. Why, he wondered, had their love withered? Was that always what happened between men and women? Or had he really broken some ancient covenant, struck between God and mankind when the Ark grounded upon Ararat, that divided humanity into its disparate races?

If so, he thought, he had become a mighty sinner!

As he had hoped, he arrived before Watkinson, though

McClusky, the most junior clerk, had arrived to unlock the premises and Johnstone himself walked in some two minutes after Kite. McClusky evinced little surprise, for Captain Kite's habits were not regular and he was as likely to be late as early. He ran about tending inkwells and sharpening nibs with an impressive diligence. He would not yet know of his employer's bereavement, still less of the fact that before the day's end he would have elevated his station in life.

Kite caught Johnstone's eye, but the younger man looked swiftly away, a reaction that pleased him. A conspiratorial wink would have been scarcely appropriate, and a few moments later, as Peters, the other junior clerk, arrived, he saw Johnstone gather McClusky and Peters together, saw the involuntary twitches of their heads in his direction that betrayed the purpose of the impromptu conference: they were being told that Captain Kite was in mourning, though he wore no crepe about his sombre person.

It was exactly seven o'clock as Watkinson entered. He looked immediately at Kite; he, seeing that Peters was not then at his desk but came in a moment later, guessed that Watkinson had been informed of his bereavement. He affected to study some papers on his desk and then, just as Watkinson sat himself and gathered up some bills, rose and called to him.

"I do not know whether you have heard that Captain Makepeace died yesterday, Mr Watkinson."

"Yes, I had been informed, sir. I am most deeply affected and have sent my condolences to Mrs Makepeace."

"Very well. I understand the funerary arrangements are to be made by Master Harry when he arrives."

"I believe him to be already here, Captain Kite."

"If that is so, very well."

"And I understand, sir, that you yourself have suffered a grievous loss."

Kite fixed Watkinson with a stare.

"Please accept my sincere condolences."

"Thank you."

"She was a most gracious lady, if I may say so, sir."

"You may say so, sir, in my presence, though I hear that you say otherwise elsewhere." Kite smiled, watching Watkinson's discomfiture. He was thrown off balance and Kite struck. "Now that Captain Makepeace has passed the bar, Mr Watkinson, I

40

think it is time we dispensed with your services. You may leave at once."

Kite bent to his papers as Watkinson spluttered: "You cannot dismiss me! This is outrageous! I insist on knowing your reasons. I have done nothing to offend you . . . I may have made the odd joke at your expense—"

"Oh, Mr Watkinson, I do not care about the odd joke at my expense and my wife no longer cares about the odd joke at hers either, but I do object," Kite said, his voice rising as he looked up at the chief clerk, "to your selling our ships without reference to me."

"Good God, sir, I would never do such a thing! I have always obeyed the instructions of my employer. I did only what Captain Makepeace told me to do and acted scrupulously within the rights of Captain Makepeace as his agent for those numbers of sixty-fourths that the late captain or his wife owned."

"That may be true, Mr Watkinson, but the letter and spirit of my accommodation with Captain Makepeace was that I was to be informed of any such transaction affecting a vessel in our fleet."

"So I reminded Captain Makepeace, Captain Kite, and I am distressed to learn that he did not confide in you. I assumed he had done so. You agreed to the remortgaging of the *Samphire*."

"That is sophistry, Mr Watkinson, for you know I was opposed to it in principle." Kite sensed he was on slippery ground and losing his advantage. He had yet to draw Watkinson and the chief clerk was heady with indignation.

"That was a matter between you and Captain Makepeace," went on Watkinson, rallying, "to make me a scapegoat for your prejudice against a dead man—"

"I make you no scapegoat, Watkinson," Kite said vehemently. "Your prejudices are your own and as the sole surviving partner I have decided that I have no further need for your services."

"But you are not the sole surviving partner, Captain Kite. There is also Mr Frith . . ." Too late Watkinson realized he had stumbled into the trap. His triumphalism withered and he sought to regain his ascendancy. "I, er . . . I see that Captain Makepeace had not confided in you in that matter either."

"Tell me, Mr Watkinson," Kite said with steel in his tone, "that you knew nothing about Captain Makepeace's desire to conceal matters from me. Tell me you did nothing to encourage him to make a secret of it. Tell me you did not advise Mr Frith not to be open with me. Tell me you nurse no private ambitions of your own to secure your own place as a partner. Tell me you have not discussed all this with Mr Frith. Do please tell me all of these comforting things."

Watkinson spluttered again, sensing a further entrapment, yet eager to agree that all that Kite had suggested was true. "Absolutely, Captain Kite, absolutely . . ."

"Tell me all of this and I shall call you a liar, sir, to your face and, should you wish it, in front of witnesses, for there is one thing you do not know."

"I – do not know?"

Watkinson's face was losing its colour and went a deathly white as Kite smiled and said, "Yes, you are forgetting that I was at Captain Makepeace's deathbed."

Kite held himself from elaboration; the impact of the information stunned Watkinson. For a moment he stood swaying and then he turned and made for the door and the counting house beyond. Kite almost felt sorry for him as, at this moment and in evident anticipation of circumstances being quite otherwise, Frith arrived.

Kite noted Johnstone look up and rise at the unscheduled visitor, he saw Frith wave him aside, but then he saw a look of swiftly suppressed consternation upon Frith's face as he saw Watkinson's pallor. Kite moved swiftly round his desk and, even as Frith advanced on Watkinson to see what troubled him, leaned pleasantly from his inner office.

"My dear Mr Frith, you could not have arrived at a more opportune moment, do please come in. McClusky! Tea!" Kite ushered a reluctant Frith into his office and closed the door. "Wretched business, Frith, wretched. I dislike dismissing a man, but we cannot have untrustworthy clerks here. I daresay you wouldn't tolerate an untrustworthy clerk, would you? Fortunately for us Makepeace alerted me. Almost his dying breath, poor fellow. You'll have heard, yes? Of course you have, you are a close friend of the family, and, I understand, you have made an offer for Katherine's hand. Well, well. Do take a seat. Poor Makepeace was not terribly coherent and it is best that you tell me yourself what the two of you have been up to. I gather Master Harry . . . Are you quite well, Mr Frith?"

Frith eased himself into a chair. "It is not quite as black as Watkinson has no doubt painted it, Captain Kite."

Kite chuckled. "Watkinson certainly wrecked any feelings of reliance I, and indeed many others on 'Change, may have as to your financial probity, Mr Frith, but I sense, as a good judge of character, that I may assume that Watkinson sought to save his own skin at your expense."

"May I ask what defamatory notions he laid at my door?"

"Defamatory isn't the word, goodness me, no. Well, that you sought to dispossess me, the means I confess seemed over-complicated to a sea officer like myself, and that you sought to take over all Makepeace's business and that, forgive me, Frith, but you would surely wish me to be candid; in fact that you were nothing less than –" Kite dropped his voice – "Martha Makepeace's lover. There was more, of course, for they say the greater the scandal the greater the chance of its belief, but there was also mention, preposterous though it is, that young Henry Makepeace was to stand for Parliament and that you were busy putting him in your pocket even while you ruined him at the tables.

"All in all it's quite a tale, Mr Frith, don't you think?" Kite shook his head as though bemused. "As I was the only person in the way of your progress, it seems that you were to discomfit me. Truth to tell," he dissembled with increasing private amusement, "I can scarce believe it . . ."

"Neither can I," Frith rallied. It was clear that, in the short term at least, Frith was preparing to toss Watkinson to the wolves.

"Of course," Kite said, his tone of voice no longer flippant, "it is so preposterous that it may all be true." He rose and looked down at Frith as he writhed in his chair, alarm writ large across his face.

"Come, Captain, you cannot believe—"

"Oh, I am a simple soul, Mr Frith, a mere nigger-lover, of no consequence, don't you know." Kite smiled, then bent over Frith as his voice became hard. "Now, sir, I shall not ask you what your motives are, only what you will spend to buy me out, lock, stock and barrel. Come sir, make me an offer and then you may have your heart's desire." Kite straightened up, opened the door and called out, "Mr Watkinson! Come here, sir!"

Watkinson appeared in the doorway and Kite motioned him inside, shutting the door behind him. As he did so he caught Johnstone's eye and gave the most cursory of smiles. Then he turned to Watkinson and said, "Mr Watkinson, I have offered all my shares in the joint-owned bottoms to Mr Frith. If he buys me out, I shall have no objection to you continuing your employment here. If the offer is not satisfactory, however, I am afraid your continuing presence will be undesirable. Now I dare say you will wish to discuss these matters between yourselves and I suggest you occupy Captain Makepeace's office. I shall absent myself for one hour as I have some matters to attend to following the death of my wife."

Kite then ushered the two men out in silence and watched them cross the counting-house floor to disappear into Makepeace's former private chamber. He was careful not to draw the attention of the junior clerks to any communication between himself and Johnstone, but left the premises and walked purposefully uphill towards Makepeace's house. He felt a surge of hubris, confident of the success of the intrigue. "Oh," he muttered to himself, "I am indeed a mighty sinner!"

Crepe and straw decorated the façade of his dead partner's dwelling. Kite was shown into the drawing room where, a few moments later, Katherine came to him. She wore a mourning gown which did not suit her, emphasising her lack of looks. He rose and bent over her hand.

"My dear, I am sorry to trouble you on this of all mornings."

"It is good to see you, Uncle William."

"How is your mother?"

"She is asleep."

"Good. May I ask you a question of the most offensive nature, for which I ask your pardon?"

"If it is about Mr Frith . . ."

"It touches him directly. Was he ever in any way connected with your mother?"

Katherine nodded. "He has long been an intimate in this house. When my father was at sea he was frequently a caller and sometimes I suspected that he did not leave, or returned late."

"I understand. Now, listen carefully. I am in the process of detaching myself from the company. Frith and Watkinson have been intriguing to gain control without my knowledge, a fact that I have become aware of. There is also a matter closely concerning your brother Harry, who is, I gather, being put up for a seat in Parliament. Frith, it seems, wishes to increase his wealth, standing and influence at the same time; Watkinson is his creature and you are no longer central to their plan. Now, my dear, the sad truth is that your mother would make a better wife for Frith and, if you refuse him, he will almost certainly propose to her. You have nothing to fear and I shall see that you are provided for before I leave."

"You are leaving us?" Katherine's alarm was touching.

"Yes, I must, but it is time that you left this place and had an establishment of your own. I shall install you in my own house and you may have Mrs O'Riordan, Maggie and the three men as your household. I will leave you an annuity and you will still benefit from the profits of the company. There, what do you say?"

"It is most irregular . . . What will others say?"

"Your mother will say you are ungrateful, Mr Frith will come to terms with it, the population of this town will say Captain Topsy-Turvy is up to his mad tricks again and you, I will lay five hundred guineas on it, will have half a dozen suitors paying you court within a month of my departure."

"But I cannot accept."

"But me no buts, my dear Kate, I need you to do as I bid. I cannot abandon Mrs O'Riordan, I do not want to lose my property, but Puella's death has ended my life here. You will not, I know, abuse my trust and I am anxious to restore my spirits."

"You are going back to sea?"

"I am, the moment the *Spitfire* comes in." He smiled at her. "Come now, I have much to do, let me know your answer by this time tomorrow. Will you do that?"

She nodded. "Yes, yes, of course, and thank you for your kindness."

"Tush, Katherine, I am not being kind, I am merely being pragmatic."

At his own house he learned from Mrs O'Riordan that Puella's funeral could be held the following morning and that she had sent Bandy Ben to arrange for a coffin maker to call. The rickety old fellow returned and knuckled his forehead to Kite, who wished him a good morning. Ben was a misfit and although Mrs O'Riordan never owned to it, Puella had discovered he was some sort of a relative of hers. But he was a reliable message bearer, and while he hardly ever spoke, Kite had discovered that he had a quite uncanny facility with figures. Such attributes made him uncommonly handy to a shipowner whose communications with the docks were frequent and often entailed quantities more than mere facts. Bandy Ben could recite an inward ship's draught, the tonnage of her lading, the dues payable and the wage bill for her crew without recourse to endless chits of paper. But he could not otherwise communicate, and stood in sudden solemnity while Mrs O'Riordan spoke for him.

"There now, sir, Ben wishes you to know how sorry he is about the Mistress."

"I thank you, Ben. You are a good man. You will see that she is tended well by the coffin maker, I hope."

Ben nodded vigorously. "Five feet six an' seven-eighths of an inch, Cap'n," he said, repeating Puella's height.

"I put a dress upon her sir, this morning."

"Thank you, Mrs O'Riordan. Now forgive me, but there are matters of business coming to a head and I have to return to the counting house."

He left Mrs O'Riordan to her head-shaking and her muttering about business being too important these days, and asking whatever happened to a decent wake. If ever a body needed a wake it was that of the black Mistress, or she herself was not Siobhan O'Riordan from the Cove of Cork.

Neither Frith nor Watkinson remained at the counting house when Kite returned there. He had half anticipated their departure, but nevertheless felt a sense of disappointment. Johnstone followed him into his private office and closed the door behind them.

"Forgive the presumption, Captain Kite," he said, "but the birds have flown."

"That is not altogether a surprise, Nathan. Were they in good spirits when they left?"

"Watkinson made a show of it, certainly . . ."

"Oh?"

"He smiled at me."

"Putting a brave face on it, or crowing?"

"Impossible to say, but I suspect the former."

"I think you might be more optimistic; after all it is not Watkinson who has to put up the cash. By the by, do McClusky and Peters have any notion of what is afoot?" Kite asked, seating himself and drawing towards him the sheaf of papers pertaining to the recent refit of the *Samphire*.

Johnstone shook his head. "No, sir. But I should not linger here, for it might arouse suspicions."

He had hardly regained his desk when Frith, disdaining to knock, marched into the office followed by Watkinson. Kite looked up. Both men wore expressions of neither triumph nor defeat, rather of grim determination. Frith made his offer; it was based on the overall sum of all shares owned by Kite or his late wife.

"As I expected, at three pounds per share you undervalue the ships."

"You are holding a pistol to our heads, Captain. It is a fair offer under the circumstances."

"It is as fair an offer as you are prepared to make, but wait a moment. Mr Watkinson, please call Mr Johnstone here a moment."

Watkinson did as he was bid and Johnstone came in and shut the door behind him. "Gentlemen? What can I do for you?"

"Johnstone, I have a small commission for you. I should be obliged if you would seek a valuation on my shares in our ships. It is my intention to sell out. You may start with Mr Bibby and then seek out Mr Brocklebank. Do you understand, Johnstone?"

Johnstone made a fair stab at feigning his astonishment. "Yes, I understand, sir."

"Don't be a fool, man," cut in Frith, "Bibby will undervalue once he knows it is a buyer's market, so will Brocklebank and the rest. If I put ten shillings on my price, will you not accept?"

"I will accept nothing less than four pounds a share," Kite said coolly.

Frith sighed. "Very well then. I agree."

Kite saw the gleam of triumph in Watkinson's eyes as he turned to Frith and nodded. He had not been wrong; Mr Watkinson had this day hiked up his station in the world. But, thought Kite, with that went his expectations too. He rose and nodded to Frith. "Very well, Frith. I shall not trouble you further. Let us conclude the business. I shall ask, er, Johnstone there to draw up the bills of sale and he can deliver them to Watkinson. Mr Watkinson, your fortunes today have been somewhat mercurial. I wish you joy of your new opportunities. You may draw up a deed for my perusal to detach my name from this company. As soon as these matters are concluded, I shall leave in the *Spitfire*. Mr Johnstone, you may grub me up a cargo for the Antilles, if you please."

And as he walked from their presence he thought again of the magnitude of his sinfulness.

* * *

The day of Puella's funeral was worse than that on which her son's had been held. The little group of mourners, consisting of Kite, Mrs O'Riordan, Maggie and Bandy Ben, with Katherine Makepeace, Johnstone, McClusky and Dr Bennett, stood under a downpour which fell in torrents from a sky of lead. The vicar rushed the committal, took Kite's *pour-boire* with a shifty manner that was so full of eagerness to be away that it compelled Kite to go back to the graveside and stand and watch while the sexton and his mate filled it in. He was conscious of his preoccupation during the last few days, a guilt which only compounded the terrible certainty that he could have saved Puella from herself and that the fact that he had not done so only attested to the fact that he had been neglecting her for a longer time than the last few days of the cholera outbreak.

Beside him the sexton coughed, waking Kite from his reflections. He gave the two men a guinea and, after they had gone, said his private and heartfelt farewell.

He and Puella had grown as far apart as man and wife can grow under the harsh, ineluctable and imperative circumstances of life; but he recalled her not as she had become but as she had been when he first set eyes upon her on the deck of the slaver *Enterprize*. He knelt, touched his finger to his lips and placed them on the ground. "Fare thee well, my dearest and only love."

Then he went home to where Mrs O'Riordan served tea and oporto to the desolate and dripping group. He moved among them, thanking them for their time and trouble, urging them not to linger in their wet clothes, coming last to Dr Bennett, who was talking to Katherine Makepeace.

"I was saying to Miss Makepeace, Kite, that your poor wife was as much a victim to the cholera as your son. You should console yourself with that thought."

"It is kind of you to ease my conscience, Bennett, but I am not sure that you are right. But tell me, is the cholera still rampant?"

"No, it is on the wane; why, I cannot tell you, but this week the numbers have dropped and I understand that this diminution is widespread, thank goodness."

Kite noticed Katherine shiver. "Come, Kate, we must get you home before you succumb to some fever. If you'll excuse me, Bennett, I'll see Miss Makepeace home."

"There is no need. I shall attend to the matter myself." Bennett offered his arm to Katherine, who took it with a smile. He leaned towards Kite and said in a low voice, "Miss Makepeace has confided in me your intentions regarding her. I think it most kind of you and have counselled her accordingly. I hope you don't mind my interfering."

Kite smiled. "I could never mind you meddling, Bennett, you are too old a friend."

Bennett chuckled and led Katherine off, then the others made their farewells. Johnstone hung back until last.

"Are you all right, Captain?" he asked solicitously.

Kite nodded. "Yes, thank you."

"And you wish me to continue as we discussed?"

"Exactly as we discussed."

"Very well. Then until I hear from you, I wish you farewell."

In the following few days, Kite put his domestic affairs in order, arranging a tombstone for the grave of Puella and her son, instructing Mrs O'Riordan of the arrangements which would come into force after his own departure and making financial provision for the running costs of the house and an allowance for Katherine. Until these were concluded he kept his own company, sending Bandy Ben off with his letters and patiently awaiting news of the arrival of the *Spitfire*. It occurred to him that should she fail to berth his case would be altered, but his fortune was not entirely bound up in his ships and his bankers held sufficient in deposits, private and Government stocks, to enable him to purchase a new vessel. He wrote to London, where he held funds with Messrs Coutts, to arrange bills of exchange and letters of credit, satisfied that these arrangements, some of which had been suggested by the shrewd Johnstone, would allow him freedom to exploit his capital to further his ambition. He also wrote to his sister Helen, his sole surviving relative, who was now married to her naval husband. Henry Hope remained a lieutenant on half-pay and he knew their circumstances to be straitened. In his letter he informed her of the deaths of Puella and William, and of his plans for the future.

If Dame Fortune wills it, he concluded,

> I shall Reëstablish myself as an Independent Shipowner and therefore in a better Position than hitherto to offer Henry a Post as Commander of one of my Vessels, if he so Desires. While I Appreciate his Reasons for Declining this Offer in the Past, I should not like him to Think it Withdrawn in its Entirety and, while it is Temporarily beyond my Means

at Present, it will not be long before I am again able to Make him such an Offer should he by then find that his Advancement in the Naval Service is Further Delayed.

Kite did not think for a moment that Henry Hope would abandon his naval ambitions, but it would have been unthinkable to abandon his brother-in-law, particularly as he might have need of some reliable masters in the near future. He thought too of Christopher Jones, and wrote to him, explaining his decision to quit the firm of Makepeace and Kite and leave for the West Indies in the *Spitfire* as soon as she had discharged her inward cargo.

A week later Jones was on his doorstep demanding to see him to explain that he had called at the company's offices and had seen that Kite's name was no longer on the sign board.

"I have no desire to work for a locker-full of grasping clerks, Captain. Will you take me as your mate again?"

"You would relinquish your entitlement to command, Jones?"

Jones nodded. "For the time being. Don't think I have lost my nerve, though God knows the memory of the wreck dogs me like the pox itself, but another opportunity will come and you are not the man to deny it to me, I think, Captain Kite."

"Do not have too good an opinion of me, Jones. You would not find it echoed within the hallowed precincts of . . . what exactly do they call themselves now?"

"Makepeace and Watkinson, sir."

"So, Mr Frith enjoys living in the shadows, eh? No wonder I rumbled him so much. I had not considered that."

"I'm sorry?" Jones frowned.

"No matter, Jones, no matter."

"I was sorry to hear about Mrs Kite, Captain. She was a sweet lady and as comely as they can ever be . . ."

"She could not stand young Will's death, Jones." Kite sniffed. The candour of his old shipmate was touching and threatened to unman him. He stared at Jones, whose woolly hair showed flecks of grey, though his coffee-coloured complexion could never be mistaken for mere windburn. He held out his hand. "I am damned glad to see you, Jones, damned glad! You shall stay here until the old *Spitfire*'s numbers are made and then we shall have some work to do!"

"Just like the old days, Captain."

"Aye, just like the old days."

Part Two

Independence

Four

A Fall from Grace

In the month following the *Spitfire*'s arrival in the Old Dock and the discharge of her mixed cargo of sugar, indigo and rum, Kite and Jones laboured at her refit, an expense entirely charged to the account of Makepeace, Watkinson and Company, who still, as far as the outside world knew, were the agents for Captain Kite's vessel. The task was carried out with great thoroughness and without any hindrance. As Jones said with satisfaction as he, Kite and Johnstone conferred one morning in the cabin, it was precisely why the time had come to leave the employ of the company.

"Well," Jones had enlarged as Kite exchanged glances with Johnstone, "they might be able to determine betwixt a profit and a loss, but they have no one who knows the difference between a chess tree and a chestnut and that deficiency would soon render their other expertise null and void."

"You are only too correct, Mr Jones," Johnstone remarked as he put down a pot of small beer. "They will wake one day to the deficiency, but happily their self-conceit will obscure the facts for them for a week or two yet."

"Ahh," said Jones, "then you purposed all this?" He looked from one to another of them. Kite smiled, but Johnstone, now fully out of the shell of his former subservience, shrugged with mock modesty.

"Oh, we calculated that matters *might* fall out in this wise, yes . . ."

"You are too damned modest, Johnstone," Kite said smiling at the quondam clerk, "though I like you the more for it." He turned to Jones. "The fact is, Jones, that Johnstone here is the entire brains behind this enterprise, such intrigues being beyond the abilities of poor simple seamen."

"You do me too much honour, Captain Kite." Johnstone held out his pot as Bandy Ben, sent by Katherine Makepeace as manservant to Captain Kite, refilled it.

"Indeed I do, but it makes you an intelligent accomplice in my affairs, Johnstone." And in such a mood of convivial banter, the three men carried out the preparation of the *Spitfire* for her forthcoming voyage.

The *Spitfire* was a schooner, Spanish-built of mahogany in Havana eighteen years earlier. Limited in her capacity to carry much cargo, she was swift, armed and best suited as a small slaver or a privateer. As her ability to earn much by her lading was restricted, Makepeace and Kite had several times considered her sale, but although they had not taken part in slaving after his marriage to Puella, Kite had refused to sell her, arguing that another war with France or Spain would find her ample and rewarding employment. Her master, a young man named Moss, was eager to marry and had no objection to taking a voyage off, while the majority of her crew showed no reluctance to sign on again.

On a fine evening in the first week of June 1772, *Spitfire* warped out into the River Mersey and dropped downstream on the ebb tide, setting sail and standing to sea into the setting sun. Before dark she had crossed the bar and had laid a course north of the Great Orme, to double the Skerries and head for St George's Channel and the open ocean beyond. Thanks to the industry of Mr Christopher Jones and the hands, she was in first-class condition; thanks to the skill of Nathan Johnstone, she bore not only a quantity of blue and white chinaware for Jamaica, Antigua and Savannah, but the commercial mails for a number of mercantile houses whose principals were anxious about the increasingly fractious state of the New England colonies and eager to contact their agents and masters abroad. Captain Kite had made no secret of the fact that his ship was fitted out for any eventuality, that she was well armed and her magazines were full, for opinion in Liverpool was that the unstable condition of the Massachusetts was such that British goods could be at some risk, if the colonists lost their heads as they had already done in Boston. Kite's private agenda, concerted with Johnstone, had no warlike intent. He had simply equipped *Spitfire* to the best advantage, intending to sell her as a potential slaver in Cuba or Savannah and with the money purchase a ship better able to profit from the carriage of cargo, but there seemed no reason not to ride the wave of anxiety over the political troubles in New England, particularly as there were those who recalled Captain Kite's daring action in the last war when, greatly outnumbered, he had taken the French corsair *La Malouine*.

Kite himself had less faith in his martial abilities. His capture of the French corsair had been more a matter of luck than valour and owed more to the sudden appearance of Puella and the soot-blacked crew than to any spirit on the part of *Spitfire*'s commander. It had been these circumstances that had led to his renaming his prize the *African Princess*. But all that was in the past; the *African Princess* lay in pieces, strewn about the seabed off Cape Clear Island, and Puella lay in her cold, foreign northern grave on the hillside above the grey Mersey.

Kite felt a curious numbness over his loss. His slow estrangement from Puella made her death the more bearable, for the loss of young William had dissolved the one remaining bond that held them together. But he also knew that in the strange and self-inflicted manner of her death, she had bound her own spirit with that of her son while denying her body to Kite. On the one hand she took from him the sole means by which in time they might have come to a reconciliation, but on the other she set him free. He wondered to what extent she guessed he would return to sea, for he knew that one of the powers she possessed was a prescient sense that transcended mere female intuition. On those few occasions when they fought over their growing disassociation, she had once or twice flung at him the accusation that he would be happier at sea than in Liverpool, but when in desperation he had suggested that she accompany him again, she had always refused, arguing that she must remain in Liverpool and see their son brought up as a gentleman. Over the years he had made occasional voyages in command, partly to maintain his links with his trading associates like Wentworth in Antigua, and partly to run away from her unhappiness and the constant reproach of her presence. He felt his marriage had been the mistake many had prophesied it would be, and this had made him put a brave public face on it, extending its life against all probabilities. In her inimitable way, Puella had ended it by laying her ambiguous purpose on him like a paradoxical curse.

But while his crew hauled the *Spitfire*'s sheets aft and flattened her fore-and-aft sails as she stood west into the star-spangled night, he discarded his guilt. He was free of Liverpool and its festering cholera, he was free of all obligations beyond the bulwarks of the little schooner, and the pervading spirit of independence gave him an uplifting sense of hope, such as he had not experienced for years.

The schooner made a fast passage to the West Indies, during which she experienced fair winds and bright weather, reeling off the knots with an easy grace, her company settling into the pleasantly easy regimen of a ship's duty when the fates smile upon her passage. As they picked up the trades, Kite almost entirely threw off the megrims, troubled only by dreams which could be dispelled by a spell on deck and were easily diverted by his instruction of Johnstone in the vessel's navigation. It was soon clear to both Kite and Jones that, intelligent though he was, Nathan Johnstone did not possess those distinctive instincts of a natural seaman. He had no ability to act or to think swiftly, to react quickly enough to disarm even the most minor of problems, such as a kinked or fouled line which had been badly cleared for running. His mental skills, though gymnastic enough, were better employed in more orderly processes and he soon showed promise as a navigator, so that Kite recognised that he could easily outstrip Jones if it became a matter of necessity. As it was, he familiarised himself with the tabulated ephemeris and the manipulation of a quadrant, more to occupy his mind and to divert it from the incipient seasickness that dogged his first fortnight at sea than for any intellectual gain.

Jones, the mulatto mate, seemed not to resent his demotion. His respect for William Kite, both as a man and as his employer, combined with memories of his former status as mate under Kite's command to wind the clock back in his imagination. No man objects to reliving the happier periods of his youth, and the kindliness of the weather only added to the happiness of the illusion so that the pleasant voyage dimmed the horrors of wrecking the *African Princess* and drowning two-thirds of his crew.

The *Spitfire* warped into St John's a month later and that evening Kite and Johnstone sat at table with Wentworth and his plump wife, Kitty. She had once set her cap at Kite himself, but social convention and considerable wealth had buried the unpleasant little encounter, so that she acted as though it had never happened. Kite also sensed that Mrs Wentworth, who had certainly not forgotten her abject lust and his humiliating rebuff, derived some quiet satisfaction from the knowledge that he had not profited long from what she considered his unnatural marriage to his black mistress. Kite's misfortunes were not only a matter of mild pleasure to Kitty Wentworth; they also proved the rightness of her own opinion.

Wentworth had prospered mightily, having inherited a fortune from his late benefactor, Joseph Mulgrave. The house of Mulgrave, Wentworth and Co. traded on its own account and acted as agents for several plantations on the island of Antigua, and elsewhere in the Antilles. On the bare hillside, where Joseph Mulgrave's mansion had burnt down with a spectacular display of cunningly laid powder trains, fuses and slow-burning matches, he had built an extravagant villa fitted with every comfort. Looking at his complacent host, Kite found it was impossible to recall the fat and indigent clerk he had first known to inhabit Mulgrave's waterfront counting house. Now Wentworth looked older than his forty-odd years, corpulent and sweating, his face burnt brick-red by the sun, his nose red-veined with excess. He had had three children by Kitty, the oldest of whom, a boy, toiled as apprentice to his hard-working father; for Wentworth belied his appearance, being far from indolent and industrious in his pursuit of every possible avenue of commercial profit.

The Wentworths' table groaned under steaming platters of meats and bottles of wine for what was, in Wentworth's own words, "a private and intimate supper". He would, he assured Kite, be pleased to act as a proper host and dine Kite and his "associate", as Kite had introduced Johnstone, in a proper and fitting manner in due course. The evening's meal was, however, to run over old gossip and to dispose in part of the more congenial aspects of their business association, as well as to reveal to Wentworth the extent to which Kite had detached himself from his old involvement with the house of Makepeace.

As the cloth was removed and Kitty Wentworth rose to withdraw, she offered to show Johnstone the house and its immediate grounds which had been prettily lit by flaring torches. "I do not wish you to abandon my husband's table or his cigars or port, Mr Johnstone, but I am sure that he and dear William will talk so much of the good old days that it will bore you terribly . . ."

Johnstone looked, rather desperately Kite thought, from him to Wentworth, but the latter waved airily. "I think my wife is probably right, Mr Johnstone, as is usual. Do please feel free to take a turn with her if you are so inclined."

"Come, Mr Johnstone, it will be pleasant to hear of matters in England. I am so tired of the tedious doings of troublesome Yankees."

Johnstone bowed awkwardly to Wentworth and said, "If you will excuse me, sir, I have not had, hitherto, much occasion to smoke cigars and if my humble efforts at conversation will gratify your wife . . ."

"By all means, by all means." Wentworth waved them out, and as they left he slumped back into his creaking chair.

"The poor fellow has never, I think, been entertained in such style before," Kite said grinning and taking the offered cigar. "His fortunes have improved so rapidly of late that he can scarce believe it."

"You intend to make him a partner in this new shipping venture of yours?"

"Perhaps, if he wishes it. He has a shrewd mind and a better head for business than my own. Besides, I trust him."

"Well, he certainly seems to have declared his loyalty by making known to you this cabal against you. These rivalries," Wentworth expatiated between puffs of his cigar, "are bound to surface in any undertaking, and commerce is by its very nature conducive to the practice of trickery of one sort or another. By your account, though, you sound as if you might have succeeded in quietly ruining your own former associates."

"I doubt that it will come to that. But certainly, unless some unforeseen eventuality arises to support them—"

"Or they acquire a ship's husband or master mariner of sufficient acumen," Wentworth interjected with a knowing look. "There are a few such about in Liverpool, I dare say."

"Yes." Kite said, blowing smoke across the candleflames so that they guttered and turned the wraiths into strange forms. "But it was not my purpose to ruin them. I simply wished to extract myself once I realised the extent to which Makepeace had embroiled me. Johnstone saw a rather more tortuous advantage to be extracted and I had no objection."

"There could be one unforeseen event looming on the horizon to halt the decline in Makepeace and Watkinson."

"You are going to mention this trouble with the American colonists?" Kite said, smiling. " 'Tis true a few Liverpool ships have been taken up on charter as military transports, though most have come from London and a handful from Bristol, but I cannot see—"

"There is serious and seditious talk of rebellion, Kite. You heard no doubt of the massacre in Boston."

"Aye, but that was two years ago and it blew over. Besides, Boston, like many a sea port and like Liverpool itself on more than one occasion, has a rough populace given to excesses of one sort or another."

"You miss the point, Kite. You have been too long in England with all its comfortable certainties and ingrained misconceptions. I will do you the courtesy of not referring to them as prejudices, since I do not think that you native Englishmen can ever see your opinions in that light, but you and others like you would do well to listen to some of the grumbling coming from New England. I am not talking about any high-flown moral notions, but merely the pragmatic associations of men of business which will disintegrate if an open rupture is allowed to develop between New and Old England."

"Well, surely it is precisely because of those ties of commerce that there will be no rupture. I ask you, who will be the beneficiary?"

Wentworth shrugged. "Who knows? If it does come to open rebellion it will be easy for neither party."

Kite waved aside Wentworth's paranoia. "You are simply too fearful. Why, it would be like civil war . . . No, no, we have too much in common to throw away the advantages gained by the late war. Rest assured if there were any dissension, France and Spain would do their utmost to revenge themselves upon us for their recent humiliations."

"You prove my case, Kite. At the first spark of trouble they will fan the flames."

"Come, come, no one in New England could possibly want the French returning to Canada, for they would be into their own back yards inside a year."

"You don't believe there is a, what d'you sailors call it, a ground-swell of opinion, in favour of disassociation from the Parliament in London?"

"Perhaps by the very lowest who see in it some simple and superficial advantage to themselves. Only a fool would think the New Englanders capable of defending themselves without an army and a naval force."

"But supposing, Kite, there were men in New England who wished to be the new Whigs, the great landowners and nabobs of New England? Men who are excited by the thought of having their own parliament, their own rotten and pocket boroughs? Men who would apply the principles and practice of commerce to the principles and practice of government?"

"Are you telling me you consider such men exist?"

Wentworth burst out laughing. "Of course they exist!" He leaned forward and stubbed out his cigar, refilled his glass and shoved the decanter towards Kite. "Listen, Kite, you mentioned that damned massacre. Do you know what happened?"

Kite shrugged. "There was a riot, the military were called out, the Riot Act was read, the mob was intransigent, the soldiers fired to disperse the mob and some people were killed. A farce of a trial followed, men doing their duty were humiliated but the mob was unappeased. There, is that a fair and full summation, gleaned from English newspapers, which as any fool knows are bilious with prejudice?"

Wentworth nodded. "Well, that is a tolerably good recounting of the facts, but it misses the real significance of the event."

"Which is . . . ?"

"Enshrined in the fact that even you call it a massacre. You may, in your own mind, have put the word in quotation marks, considering it a mere matter of extreme exaggeration, but what would be your reaction if I said this incident was an unprovoked mowing down of innocent citizens by rolling volley fire of British lobster-backs?"

"I would say that it was an unpardonable exaggeration."

"You might be correct as a matter of veracity in its absolute sense, but you would not be believed in New England. In New England that is precisely how they regard the matter. Men and women living on remote farms and in small towns do not have the knowledge of the world that you have. They cannot conceive of any Bostonians, good people like themselves, as shouting incessant abuse at the military or pelting soldiers with stones. They cannot, I doubt, even imagine what a mob is, still less of what it is capable once it has coalesced into a monstrous hydra. All this, it has to be admitted, has been much helped by a mendacious engraving circulated throughout the province with every appearance of being a truthful and observed representation of what transpired. There was also some talk, I am informed, that the whole incident was cunningly fomented, since it started when a single off-duty soldier was seeking some work at a ropewalk and was taunted and provoked. Could this be established beyond doubt, you would find a conspiracy at the heart of it all, I don't doubt."

"And who are your informants, are they men of probity?"

Wentworth ticked them remorselessly off. "Oh, yes, Captain Hawkins of the *Dido*, Mr Wright, mate of the *Friendship*, Captains Douglas of the *Cleopatra*, Cracknell of the *Bostonian*, Greene of the *Emily and Jane*, Hubbard of the *New York*, and Maxwell of the *Lady o' the Lake* – all of whom except Hawkins and Maxwell are New Englanders or have been trading between here and the American coast for so long that they have forgotten they are British and have married and settled in the colonies. I rest my case."

"I see." Kite sat back and considered matters for a moment, then said, "Suppose I changed my mind and did not sell *Spitfire*, at least for a year or two, suppose I left Jones in her among the islands where he is happiest? I have sufficient capital to buy or charter a bottom."

"I'll come in with you if you sail as master. Young Johnstone can act as supercargo and learn the ropes." Wentworth put down his glass as if the gesture signified sudden resolution. "Yes, why not, what d'you say, eh? I'll go fifty-fifty with you on a bottom. You could pick up cargoes and trade up the coast and keep us wise to the gossip and the turn events are taking. The information alone will be helpful and you will see how best to exploit the situation if it changes." Wentworth paused, considering something. "I know of a ship, Spanish-built of good mahogany like *Spitfire*, but of four hundred or so tons burthen, the *Santa Margarita of the Angels* or some such Papist flummery. She's frigate-built and owned by a Spaniard in Maiquetia . . . Yes, she would do admirably."

"Maiquetia? That is on the Spanish Main, is it not?"

"Yes, but she is due here within a few weeks and I am certain we can acquire her. What do you say?" Wentworth was grinning like a schoolboy. "Come on, ain't you game?"

"I'm game, but let us take a look at her first."

"Done!" Wentworth rose. "Let us take a turn on the terrace and see what has become of Kitty and young Johnstone."

It was late when Kite and Johnstone walked back down the hill towards the harbour. They had eaten and drunk well and their bellies, unused to such rich fare, kept them quiet, or so Kite thought, as he struggled with a rumbling gut and thoughts of the projected new vessel. He did not want to break the news to Johnstone immediately, it being his habit to sleep on any decision. He knew the enthusiasm of the evening before could turn into regret when viewed in the colder light of dawn. It was some time, therefore, before he thought he ought to converse with his companion and broke the silence with a sigh.

"I hope this evening was not too intolerable for you. Old acquaintances can be somewhat self-absorbed, I am afraid."

"Not at all, sir."

"You ate well, anyway."

"Better than ever before in my life, sir."

"Good. And Mistress Robinson did not importune you, I hope?"

It had been intended as a joke, as a loose remark between men, to be taken as an irony, but Johnstone stopped abruptly. Kite, caught aback, had walked on a few steps before he realised what had happened and turned.

"What is the matter?" he asked.

"What did you mean by that question?" Johnstone asked, his voice tense.

"What did I mean by it? Why nothing; leastaways nothing of significance. If I meant anything, I meant that I thought you might have been less bored had you remained at table and that your manners did you credit . . ."

"She seduced me, sir," Johnstone said in a low voice through clenched teeth. "She made a fool of me . . . I . . . I thought you knew she had, that you guessed she might and that she had volunteered to take me into the garden out of lust."

Kite realised that, subconsciously, he had almost expected Kitty Wentworth to take the young man for her own pleasure. It occurred to him that perhaps Wentworth's children were not his own. His wife had been hot-blooded years earlier and although her figure had fattened, there was enough of the voluptuary in her to appeal to a young man in Johnstone's circumstances. The poor fellow had been deprived of his conjugal rights for several months now and his fall from grace was not surprising, except perhaps to himself.

"I did not think that, Nathan. But why confess the matter? Many men would have thought nothing of it."

"Because I am ashamed . . ."

"Did you not enjoy her? Did you fail to satisfy her?"

"That is the point, Captain Kite," Johnstone replied, his voice still low. "Of course it was pleasurable and she was hot for me. Or perhaps any man," he added revealingly.

"That we cannot tell, but why should you feel shame? Because your wife is not long dead?"

"Yes." It was too dark to see the expression upon Johnstone's face, but the enunciation of the word sounded as if he was being strangled.

"And you feel you have besmirched or betrayed her memory?"

"Yes," whispered Johnstone.

Kite stepped close to Johnstone and put his hand on the younger man's arm. "My dear fellow, you are no worse than the rest of us. I should be obliged if you would act discreetly while you are here, for if you have truly satisfied Mistress Wentworth she will most assuredly pursue you. Do not cause her to be bitter by taking another woman while we are here, simply do the gallant thing; we shall be here no more than a month."

"A month! I shall contrive to avoid the woman!"

"That would be ill-mannered of you . . ."

"But I have no desire to repeat my folly."

"Call it an indiscretion, Nathan. Consider it a privilege to have all your appetites satisfied in one evening, and a mark of good manners to have satisfied your hostess's wants too. Between us we have done well, for I have presented our host with something to divert *his* mind."

"That is most kind of you, sir," Johnstone said with a venomous sarcasm.

Kite laughed. "Oh come, Nathan, you should not have confided in me. I am not a priest."

"That you are not . . ."

"But I shall not make these facts public."

"I pray you will not, sir!"

"Come, Nathan, laugh at yourself. It will do you good, sir."

Five

The *Wentworth*

"Well, what did you think of her?"

"She will not be fast, but she'll be weatherly enough and would stand more and heavier guns than the six miserable four-pounders that she bears now," Kite said, sitting opposite Wentworth in the cool of the waterfront office into which he had once stumbled what seemed a lifetime ago.

"And she is well built?"

"No question of it. Truth to tell, I prefer mahogany to oak, as I think it less susceptible to rot and, in these latitudes, the damned ship-worm."

Wentworth nodded. "Very well, I shall make Diego Galvez an offer."

Kite looked out of the window. The *Santa Margarita de los Angeles* lay off in the bay. He would change her name, though to what he had not yet decided. He would have wider yards fitted in due course, for her rig was too narrow for his taste and he thought she would profit from wider courses and topsails.

"We could send *Spitfire* down to Maiquetia . . ." Wentworth was saying and Kite came to himself.

"There is no need. Galvez is on board, on his way to Havana with his wife and daughter. Ask him to dinner. He is, as you know, eager to sell and would release the ship once he has reached Cuba. I think he intends to settle there, for he is past his middle years."

"What is the daughter like?"

"Pleasant enough in her manner. She speaks excellent English, but she is not handsome. Why, do you indulge in indiscretions these days, Wentworth?"

Wentworth winked and touched the side of his nose with his right index finger.

64

"It is the heat, no doubt," Kite remarked drily.

Wentworth chuckled and Kite thought that he had never seen anything less like a libertine than the rotund figure before him – but then, he reflected, Mrs Wentworth seemed the very epitome of matronly virtue and he knew that poor Johnstone had enjoyed her embraces on several occasions now.

"By the way, Kite," Wentworth said, breaking into his reflections and tossing a newspaper across his desk, "I received this from Holmes of the *Morning Star* which arrived after you had gone aboard the *Santa Margarita* – you are not intending to trade under that name, are you?"

Kite picked up the paper. "No, but what do you think? You own half of her."

"Which of the two of us owns the angels?" Wentworth quipped. "Not I, I think."

"Then call her *Santa Margarita*."

"No, I do not like—"

"Call her *Wentworth* and be damned to it," said Kite, scanning the paper to see what it was he was supposed to be digesting. Then he saw the item and, as Wentworth smiled his approval at Kite's suggestion of the new name, he read the account of the burning of the *Gaspée*. Off the coast of Rhode Island, the British revenue schooner had been in chase of a local packet whose master was a suspected smuggler, and in chasing her into Providence she had run aground. That night boats from the sea port had approached the *Gaspée* and her commander, a Lieutenant Duddingston, had challenged them and forbidden them to come aboard. He was shot in the groin for his pains, whereupon over sixty masked men had boarded the vessel and she had been set on fire. A subsequent reward by the Colonial authorities of £500 had failed to tempt a single witness into giving information that would convict anyone involved in the deliberate act of piracy.

"If that is not an act of open rebellion, Kite, I don't know what is," Wentworth said.

"Yes, I confess that shocks me. You are right and the fact that no one will take the reward argues that it is men of influence who are behind all this trouble."

"They are indeed pirates; they should be hanged, all sixty of them. But in Rhode Island they are probably saying it indicates the unanimity of dissent, a general disaffection with Government and an indication of the loyalty of the populace to the ideals of liberty."

"And to hell with poor Duddingston."

"And to hell with poor Duddingston indeed, Kite. You will note that, unlike the so-called massacre at Boston, there is no mention of victims. Duddingston suffers as a proxy for the King and his ministers; not, of course, that they will care very much."

"No. But Lord Rockingham's government went a long way to redress the grievances of the colonists. If only he and not North were still in power."

"The impression here," Wentworth said, "is that North is the King's toady."

Kite smiled. "I think King's Friend is the correct designation of North's politics." He tossed aside the paper, a gesture eloquent with the dismissal of politicians in general and British ministers in particular. He stared once more at the ship beyond the window. "So, what do you say to *Wentworth*?"

"I think it makes her sound like an Indiaman and has an aristocratic ring to it, certainly. If you are to trade upon the Yankee coast it is as well that the King's late and conciliating minister should be so commemorated."

Kite frowned. "I don't follow."

"The Marquess of Rocking'm," Wentworth drawled the name as it was pronounced in London, "is Charles Watson Wentworth."

"Ahh. I had forgot. Then that is what she shall be," Kite said, standing, "and since I am intending to modify her sail plan I shall be satisfied with you having your name carved across her stern."

"Ah, you will trim her *kites*, then," Wentworth said with a chuckle.

"Very droll, Wentworth, very droll."

Captain Kite sailed from Antigua as soon as the sale had been completed and a cargo of sugar and rum had been loaded. He wished to be clear of the islands before the onset of the hurricane season and made first for Savannah with the last of *Spitfire*'s trans-shipped cargo of crockery. He had left Jones in command of the schooner and Wentworth had found employment for her trading between the islands. He had left Johnstone in Wentworth's counting house and Kitty Wentworth's bed. Johnstone was showing signs of tiring of his seemingly insatiable mistress, but he had not mentioned his liaison after that first, impetuous confession, nor had Kite raised the subject, for it was none of his business.

He was pleased to have established both Johnstone and Jones in posts from which they could profit. It had been essential to have them to help him refit *Spitfire* and leave Liverpool, but his desire for solitary independence had grown, prompted perhaps by the narrow society of St John's and the fact that much of the town was haunted by the ghost of Puella. He had never allowed himself to meander about the place; there had been no nostalgic wanderings off the track he had beaten for himself between the harbour, with its waterfront warehouses and counting houses, its sailmaker's loft and its chandlers' premises, the steps where the ships' boats picked up their officers, and Wentworth's villa. He went nowhere near the house which he and Puella had once rented and where their first son Charles had died, and he made a point of sleeping aboard either *Spitfire* or *Wentworth*, as the *Santa Margarita* was renamed with due ceremony.

It was never difficult to find a crew among the waterfront loiterers, and several of the ship's former seamen remained on her books. The matter of officers was more difficult, but Wentworth found a satisfactory first and second mate willing to serve and so Kite was able to sail in her as he had planned.

It was Kite's intention to trade on the American coast and to pick up a cargo of cotton from Savannah for Philadelphia or New York. He loaded a full cargo with an option to carry it to Liverpool, however, but before August was out he had discharged his entire lading of cotton bales at the Quaker city and then New York, somewhat relieved that he was not compelled to return to Liverpool so soon. In fact he picked up a part cargo of trans-shipped British and European manufactures, goods which ranged from fashionable gowns, millinery and a quantity of haberdashery, books, fine porcelain and glassware, cotton piece goods, silks and worsteds, to some fine guns and gentlemen's small swords. Although far from fully loaded, *Wentworth*'s part cargo when sold in Boston yielded the New York merchants a fine haul and Kite the high freight rate that Wentworth's agent had arranged.

"You see, Captain," this worthy had explained, "for some time now the Bostonians have not considered it fashionable to be seen purchasing goods from Britain. There is in fact what amounts to an embargo in that port. But of course, whether you are an ardent

Whig or a loyal Tory, you want the goods, so you quietly order them from New York and we ship them from here as though they are New York products."

"But that is ludicrous."

"It is also profitable, Captain, which as you know, overrides every other consideration in this life."

"But the *Wentworth* is a British ship; will that not raise a degree of this illogical prejudice?"

"No. The majority of the gentry purchasing your lading from the emporia of Boston will be Tory and therefore only careful not to excite attention in Boston itself. Most of the mob who are putty in the hands of the radical orators of New England will not know that the à la mode notions were carried in your vessel."

"But some of the mob will have discharged the cargo and will therefore know of its origins."

"Yes," said the agent with a trace of exasperation in his tone, "you are an Antiguan vessel and clearly have not come from England for most of your crew are negroes, mulattos or quadroons, with scarce a white face among them. As for yourself and your ensign, many British masters trade on this coast alongside their native Yankee cousins . . ."

And so for several months Captain Kite and the *Wentworth* were employed, mainly on the coast north of Cape Hatteras, until, with the onset of the worst of winter weather, Kite considered his plan of extending the *Wentworth*'s spars and sails. His experience of the ship convinced him that this was a proper course of action and he consulted his two mates, John Corrie and the forbiddingly named Zachariah Harper, a native-born Yankee.

"Well, gentlemen, what d'you think of my idea?" He looked first at Corrie, the senior of the two. He was a handsome man in his early thirties, but had lost most of his front teeth in a brawl and this detracted from his looks. He was married to a mulatto woman in St John's by whom he had had eight children and had proved himself a competent and steady man who knew his business both in working the ship and in the handling of her cargo. Corrie nodded his approval, his voice whistling through his broken teeth as he said. "It'll do no harm, Cap'n, none at all."

"Mr Harper?"

The second mate was a man with no claim to looks whatsoever. Indeed he was of such extraordinary ugliness that his face seemed to have no cohesion, being put together, as it were, from odds and ends of features. Neither eye matched its fellow, his nose was huge, his lips nonexistent and his chin jutted forward to a point upon which he grew a beard without a complementary moustache upon the upper lip. He had the large and pendulous ears of an old man and wore his hair excessively long. But he was powerfully built and Kite had more than once been glad to see him leading the hands aloft to tame a sail hurriedly clewed up in a squall. In short he was one of the finest practical seamen Kite had ever encountered and he waited to see what Harper would say.

"It is a good idea, sir," he said, "but we shall have to move the chess tree further forward and fit longer bumpkins over either bow to haul the tacks down, and that will necessarily govern the extent to which you can extend the yards."

"And the brace-leads will have to come aft," Corrie put in.

"That's less of a problem."

Kite nodded and then Harper asked, "Where will you have this work done, sir?"

"The only yard I have had personal experience of was at Newport, Rhode Island."

"Roberts's yard?" Harper asked. "I know it as a good place. I would not recommend New York, sir. There the prices are too high, they are so used to Government contracts."

"D'you have any objection to Roberts's yard, Mr Corrie?" Kite asked the mate.

"I have no opinion on the matter, Cap'n."

"Very well, Newport, Rhode Island it is. I shall write directly and see what we are able to arrange."

And as he sat at his desk after his mates had left the cabin, Kite felt a quickening of his pulse. Newport was the home of Sarah Tyrell.

Kite's knowledge of Roberts's yard in Newport, Rhode Island, had been a consequence of disaster. Several years earlier, while on his way back to Britain with the expectant Puella, the *Spitfire* had been severely damaged in a hurricane and he had put in to Newport, aided by Christopher Jones's local knowledge. Here the schooner had been repaired, her broken spars renewed and her hull thoroughly refitted. Here too he had bought Puella some warm furs for the transatlantic passage to an England lying under the frosts of winter. In so doing he had encountered Sarah Tyrell, the young wife of an older husband, Arthur

Tyrell, a merchant whose connections with Antigua were well established.

Mistress Tyrell had thought Kite louche in flaunting his black mistress, but had then made Puella's acquaintance and befriended the couple beleaguered by circumstances in Newport. Since then the house of Tyrell had been profitably associated with that of Wentworth in Antigua and Makepeace and Kite in Liverpool, and Kite had himself kept up a desultory correspondence with Tyrell, always asking that he be remembered to Mistress Tyrell and occasionally receiving reciprocal greetings, always couched in terms of absolute propriety.

There had been, however, an undercurrent to this exchange of pleasantries, for the physical attraction between Kite and Tyrell's wife had been mutual. It had amounted to no more than a brief exchange of veiled desire, a mere muttering of conventional pleasantries which had been charged with suppressed passion. In the ensuing years the possibility of their ever meeting again had grown increasingly improbable. But ever since he had read the account of the scandalous destruction of the schooner *Gaspée* off the Rhode Island coast, the possibility of again meeting Sarah Tyrell had quickened his heartbeat. Moreover, when the *Wentworth* sailed north from Antigua the thought of putting in to Newport had lain at the bottom of his consciousness. He had been half hoping, half fearing that, quite by chance, the ship would find herself loading a cargo for Rhode Island, but since this had not transpired he knew that fate was not going to oblige him. He could not wait to drift into what might add to his catalogue of great sins, for he knew he would not be surprised by the passion the sight of Sarah would arouse in him. He knew that he was being tempted, and that the notion of improving the *Wentworth*'s sailing qualities and the existence of Roberts's yard were perhaps in themselves fateful.

Well, it was no matter, he thought. He had no need to succumb to temptation like the unfortunate Johnstone. It would be pleasant to see both Sarah and her husband again, he told himself, and he ought as a matter of honour to tell Tyrell of the changed circumstances of the Liverpool firm that now styled itself Makepeace and Watkinson.

And so, after discharging his cargo in Baltimore, Kite succeeded in laying a few tiers of beer consigned to Rhode Island over shingle ballast and sailed for Newport.

*　　*　　*

When Captain Makepeace, master and commander of the slaving brig *Enterprize*, had thrust the nubile and beautiful young black slave at the canting young Kite, he had intended merely to draw the poison of virtuous complaint against the slave trade by the poultice of lust. He hoped thereby to drown Kite's disapproval, to reduce him to the lowest common denominator of his kind, to take from him the awkward intrusions of decency, humanity and compassion. Makepeace had been annoyed that Kite, whom he had picked up in the gutters of Liverpool, should turn out to be a dissident spirit. The captain had no need of an abolitionist among his officers and so sought to encompass the youthful idealist's fall from his self-appointed status of moralist. But Kite and what Makepeace conceived to be his black whore had fallen in love. At the voyage's end Kite had purchased his "Puella" and set up house first in St John's and much later in Liverpool. In fact, though they had then been mutually hostile, Makepeace had by his fatuous act touched off a train of events which in due course had led to reconciliation, friendship, the virtual abandonment of the slave trade by the old Guineaman and the establishment of the prosperous Liverpool house of Makepeace and Kite. That single act of silliness on the part of Captain Makepeace had shaped Kite's future, as well as that of his old commander, though Kite himself had been wholly passive at its inception. He had often thought of it as a turning point in his life and ever since he had seen such moments clearly. Whilst young William's death from cholera was not such a pivotal moment, the sacrificial and accusatory suicide of Puella most certainly was, for it had persuaded him to return to sea and try his fortune elsewhere than in disease-ridden Liverpool.

The laying of the *Wentworth* on a course to the north-eastwards was his decision alone, despite the consultation he had had with his officers. That was for form's sake, a matter by which he could ease his conscience, for his determination to take the *Wentworth* to Rhode Island grew in him by the hour. He was motivated not by the public consideration of refitting his ship, but by the private desire to see again a woman who had once stirred him. The refitting of the *Wentworth* was but a means to another end and, as he came below and turned into his swinging cot while the ship lifted to the Atlantic swells off Cape Charles, he knew that he had set a match to a powder train. How violent the explosion at its end, however, he had no means of guessing.

The following morning Kite was awakened not by Bandy Ben but by Harper. The second mate was dripping wet, his tarpaulins glossy in the feeble light which filled the cabin. Beyond the cabin bulkhead Kite could hear shouts and he felt his cot jar and sensed the heel of the ship as Harper shook him.

"White squall, sir! And worse to come!" Then he was gone and Kite was tumbling out of his cot and reaching for breeches and a greygoe to pull over his nightshirt as the deck slid away from beneath him. It was the first bad weather he had experienced since leaving the Mersey and it came as a nasty, humbling shock. Fighting to keep his balance he felt the *Wentworth* stagger under the onslaught of a sea which slammed against her weather bow and set every part of her fabric a-judder.

He reached the cabin door and wrenched it open, propelling himself through it half by his own volition while, it seemed, the ship herself gave him a hand as the next wave struck her and, just as he reached the foot of the companionway, he was suddenly soused by a chilling deluge of cold water. He cursed with the shock of it and fought his way up on deck. As his head came clear of the coaming he was aware of a number of sensations. The first was the residue of water pouring across the deck, the second was the shock of it as the wind whipped it up and flung it into his eyes where it stung them with its saltiness. As he dragged himself to his feet by the stanchion at the head of the companionway, he could hear the shriek of the wind and the cracking and booming noise of the blown-out main topsail. Below that the mainsail had been clewed up, but the loose folds filled and bellied with wind, a pale ghostly thing expanding and contracting like some huge, revolting grey bladder. This threatened to carry away at any moment while further forward the watch were hauling on the clew garnets of the forecourse. A group of men were at the foot of the larboard pin-rail abreast the mainmast, hoisting themselves into the weather shrouds.

Kite reached the helm where a large negro seaman named Jacob held the wheel, his huge legs braced wide on the planking.

"Bad night, Cap'n!" he called. "Ship's head nor'-nor'-west, sah!"

"Very well, Jacob. Can ye hold her yourself?"

"Aye, sah, Jacob'd hold the horse of the devil!" The big man grinned in the gloom and Kite was suddenly glad of the sight of his wide grin.

"Good man. Where's Mr Harper?"

"Second Mate go forrard, Massah Corrie gone aloft to take in de main tops'l!"

Kite looked up and could see that the figures he had seen going aloft were now negotiating the futtock shrouds. Hauling himself up to windward, he edged forward. Beyond the ship's rail he could see the sea had been knocked flat by the wind and for the first time the extreme angle at which the *Wentworth* lay heeled. He thought of her lack of cargo below and hence a lack of positive stability, he thought of the likelihood of the shingle ballast shifting to exacerbate the delicacy of their situation. Anxiously he stared aloft, aware that he was looking nearer the horizontal than the vertical. Even as his brain formed the thought, the inevitable happened. The faint yet threatening thrumming of parting stays suddenly reached its brief and terrifying crescendo in a series of cracks, each of which was followed by a thunderous sound, like the vigorous beating of a muffled drum as first the fore topmast went by the board, then the forecourse blew out and the falling wreckage took the main topmast with it while this in turn carried away the mizzen topgallantmast.

Kite heard the shrill screams of the falling men, heard the dreadful, dull thump as one hit the rail, his body smashed in an instant, and heard too the thin reedy scream of a man fallen unhurt into the wake astern of the ship. For an instant he stood stock-still, stunned by the overwhelming power of the gust of wind, uncertain whether or not some rope or stay in his immediate vicinity might not strike him as it parted, and then he was beside Jacob, bawling at him to let go the helm and get a chicken coop overboard for the wretch in the water to cling to.

The wreckage lying over the leeward side dragged the ship's head round to starboard and the stern rose as it passed through the wind. Against a sudden patch of lighter cloud he saw Jacob hurl the chicken coop overboard to the pitiful objection of its occupants while the *Wentworth* swung round to lie wallowing, her starboard side exposed to the wind as she dragged the wreckage of her upper spars slowly to the south and east.

"Mr Corrie! Mr Harper! Muster your watches!" Kite bellowed.

Someone called out, "The mate's overboard, sir!"

Kite swore. "Who else is missing? Mr Harper, are you there?"

"Aye, sir, all my men are accounted for."

Kite felt a surge of relief as the hands came aft and assembled just forward of the helm. Harper was too good a man to lose. He cleared his throat: "Boatswain, call the mate's watch."

"Aye, aye, sir!"

After a few moments they established that in addition to Corrie there were three men missing, all able seamen who had gone out along the foretopsail yard with Corrie to pass the gaskets and secure the blown-out sail. Kite digested the news, then he passed his orders.

"The mate's watch to get axes and knives and start clearing the wreckage. Jacob, aloft into the mizzen top and keep your eyes open. I'll not give up on those men!"

"Cap'n Kite! I've found Nicholls, sir," a man shouted and there was a general move to the ship's larboard side where Nicholls had fallen. He had struck the rail and then fallen outboard, not into the water, but between the deadeye-irons and the bulwarks, his legs trapped on the chainwale, his broken body trailing overboard in a bloody mess.

"Christ Almighty."

"Let him go, sir?" asked the boatswain.

Kite nodded and one of the men called out, "Shame!" while another muttered a prayer.

"Come, men," Kite pulled them together, "we've work to do . . ."

As if the squall had been fatally conjured for their own especial punishment, the wind dropped rapidly and by the time the sun rose it was almost a dead calm.

Then Jacob bawled, "Ah see him, sah! Ah see Massah Corrie," and Kite looked up to see Jacob up in the mizzen top and pointing out on the starboard quarter.

"No, sah!" Jacob called, his voice high-pitched with excitement, "I see two men! Two men!" Kite looked at the boat on the hatch and was about to pass orders to clear it away when first Harper and then Jacob, having slid agilely down a mizzen backstay, were over the taffrail and swimming powerfully for the bobbing heads.

"Get some lines ready, Boatswain," Kite called, but the matter was already in hand.

Within half an hour, the second mate and Jacob had dragged

the two survivors alongside the wallowing tangle of spars, sails and rigging onto which half a dozen seamen had scrambled to drag all four out of the water. About an hour later, as all hands with the exception of the rescued and rescuers toiled to cut the *Wentworth* free of her encumbering spars, the freshening wind backed steadily round and blew again with a steady force from the south-west, whence it had come the evening before.

By mid-afternoon the *Wentworth* had resumed her voyage. Sails had been set on her fore and main yards, her fore topmast stay and a temporarily rigged forestay running to her bowsprit which, with her undamaged spanker, made her manageable. Kite stood Corrie's watch for him, while he was left to sleep off the horrors of his ordeal. Harper seemed reluctant to leave the deck and Kite ordered him below. Still the second mate hesitated.

"For God's sake go below, Zachariah!" an exasperated Kite ordered, but Harper shook his head.

"I'm sorry sir, that I didn't get the sails off her quicker . . . I felt something was wrong an hour or so before there was any sign of trouble, but I couldn't determine what it was. I thought at first it were the compass, which seemed to me to be oscillating too much, but . . ."

"You did your best, Zachariah," Kite said quietly. "No man can do more and many would have been entirely overtaken by events. You should not reproach yourself."

"But—"

"Go below and get some sleep. At least Mrs Corrie is not a widow tonight. You may console yourself with that thought."

Harper sighed. "I cannot sleep, sir. Not yet."

"Then tell me . . . tell me where you come from," said Kite, attempting to divert the young man from the lugubrious train of obsessive thought he seemed determined to follow. "And tell me of the troubles that seem to be fomenting against England."

Harper shook his head. "Why, sir, I come from New York, but as to the troubles I know little of them, being at sea. It seems that there is a popular feeling against England which is due to taxes and no places for us in Parliament, but I have read that we have in our Assemblies more powers to govern our own lives than you have yourself, if you'll forgive me for saying so."

Kite nodded. "That is true," he replied, choosing not to muddy the waters of debate by a disquisition upon the purchase of politicians such as young Harry Makepeace would like to become. He wondered what had happened to Harry, and his sister Katherine, but then he dismissed the thought as Harper went on.

"My father says that in God's good time these North American Colonies must of necessity become a self-governing nation because they are capable of infinite expansion west of the mountains. He served in the French and Indian Wars and has spoken to men who have been over the mountains and others who have crossed the Ohio, and they say that there is land there that stretches over mountains and plains beyond the Mississippi and it is a crazy notion that all this land can be ruled by the Tory ministry in London. He says it is against all natural law and precedent and that time will effect a parturition."

"But land without population is not a nation and these lands belong to the Indians."

Harper gave one of his slow, engaging grins which seemed, in some curious way, to transform his face into that of a gentle ogre. "Cap'n, them Indians ain't God's creatures. As for population, well, I reckon we Yankees can fill a city or two like you English have filled London."

"I have never been to London," Kite confessed.

"Well, Cap'n, if you'd seen London you'd say that there were enough people to fill the valleys of Kentucky and maybe that'd be a good place to put them, seeing as how there's no room for them in that smoky city."

"That is a thought," Kite conceded wryly. "But what does your father say to rebellion?"

"Rebellion?" Harper seemed genuinely astonished at the idea. "Why, nothing, sir. Why should he?"

"Because I hear there are men in New England who would stir up rebellion and seize power in the people's name but for their own purposes."

Harper nodded. "Yes, that may be true sir, and they all do chiefly reside in Boston, but there are enough redcoats in Fort William and on the Common to keep a few hot-heads in order."

"So men of your father's opinion do not think matters will be forced, then? Only that they will evolve by a natural process?"

"I think so, sir. My father says that England has had her civil war and that she knows the danger of another and will avoid it."

"But all men may not think like your father."

"Well, they'll soon see sense if a redcoat points a bayonet at their bellies."

"What is the temper of Rhode Island?" Kite asked.

Harper shrugged. "I don't rightly know; there was some trouble there a while back when they burned that English schooner."

"The *Gaspée*, aye, I heard of that."

"But nothing came of it and it blew over."

"I think that is what worries me," Kite said.

"What, that it blew over?"

"Yes. When a schoolboy is not chastised for a misdeed, he commits another, usually worse, just to ascertain the boundaries of restraint. Weak parents indulge such behaviour and laugh it off. But consider, if the youth is motivated by malice, or any species of personal gain, he will play this advantage to the utmost. Cunning is learnt early, d'you know, it is not a sudden acquisition of the mature."

"I see what you mean," Harper said slowly, nodding his head as he digested the meaning of Kite's words. "Well, men's names are mentioned from time to time, even in New York we have heard that of Samuel Adams."

"And who is he?"

"He dwells in Boston, I believe, where he was found involved with some embezzlement. I don't rightly know what it was, but they say it made him a great champion of what they pleases to call liberty and freedom from the tyranny of England." Harper shook his head. "My father says that they who sow the wind usually reap the whirlwind with interest thrown in."

"Your father is a sensible man, Zachariah."

Harper yawned. "I think I shall go below now, Captain Kite. And thank you."

"Thank you, Zachariah."

Six

Sarah Tyrell

"They say lightning never strikes in the same place twice, Captain Kite," remarked Arthur Tyrell as he rose and took Kite's hand. The years since Kite had last seen him in 1759 had bowed him; he was shrunken with age and rheumatism, yet his eyes were as bright as Kite recalled and his mind undimmed by time. "Yet you have come again to Newport as a port of refuge, William."

"That is not quite correct," replied Kite, smiling. "I was bound here from Baltimore with the intention of having my ship put in the hands of Roberts' yard to effect some alterations in her sail plan."

"Well, from what I saw of her yesterday as she came in past Dumpling's Rock, she is much in need of that," Tyrell joked, "but Sarah will be disappointed if she thinks that you had any purpose other than to dine with us."

Kite felt himself colouring involuntarily. "That is most kind of her, Arthur."

"She is a constant woman, William . . ."

For one humiliating moment, as a sensation of weak-kneed guilt flooded him, he thought he was going to faint; that the old man before him had some strange yet potent powers of divination capable of seeing into the depths of his soul to expose the potentially adulterous phantasmagorias which had haunted the margins of his sleep for the last few nights.

"Pray do sit down and I shall ring for some wine."

Gratefully Kite sank into an adjacent chair, vaguely aware that he should have made some polite acknowledgement of Sarah's constancy. "How is your wife?" he asked as matter-of-factly as he could.

Tyrell smiled. "Did you know that when you sailed, she

followed you on her horse, riding to Castle Hill to watch your schooner until you had passed out of Buzzard's Bay?"

Kite coughed awkwardly. "No, I had no idea . . . It was a long time ago."

"You made a profound impression upon her, William, and it has long been my hope that you would return to Newport. I heard that a Captain Kite was trading on the coast in a vessel hitherto unknown to me and I assumed it was you."

Kite, uncertain of the purpose of Tyrell's revelations and embarrassed to pursue them, took advantage of the opening and explained to the old man of his separation from what was now Makepeace and Watkinson. Tyrell listened in silence, his elbows on his desk, his finger tips neatly touching, and when Kite had finished he nodded approvingly.

"By your account, you have acted wisely," he said, "but tell me, what of Puella? She was expecting, if I recall aright, and Sarah will want to know all the details, though you may tell her yourself for I will not countenance any refusal to make our house your own while you are here."

"You are too kind, Arthur, but to the matter of your question, Puella is dead, as is the son she bore. He fell a victim to the cholera so prevalent in Liverpool, and she . . ." He hesitated.

"She took to her bed and died," Tyrell said, "yes, you will recall I spent some time in the Antilles and have seen such things before." He paused then said, "So, you are a free man."

"I suppose I am."

"William –" Tyrell rose to his feet and turned to look out of his window which overlooked the harbour – "you may think me foolish, but as the years passed and you did not return to Rhode Island, I confess I was pleased, though I knew Sarah wished otherwise."

"Arthur, I—" Kite began, but without turning round Tyrell raised his hand and he fell silent.

"I married Sarah after her betrothed had been lost at sea. She appeared inconsolable and there was foolish talk of her having lost her mind. It was all poppycock, of course, she was simply very young and completely infatuated. The young man was not particularly admirable, and probably much improved by an early demise; but those were my own cynical observations. In due course and as I had anticipated she spoke less of him and enjoyed mild flirtations with a number of other men younger than myself. You were among them."

Tyrell turned and Kite said, "Arthur, there was never a moment's impropriety between us . . ."

Tyrell smiled, "Come, come, William. Except that my wife struck you with her riding crop."

"That was nothing, a misunderstanding."

"A mark of her occasional ungovernable passion, William, behaviour that, though thankfully rare, once caused her mother to consider her dangerous. Look, my boy, I shall be frank. I am an old man and Sarah is a headstrong young woman. She pined for you after you left our shores and for years I feared your return. But as before what the sea takes, it takes completely. Now, however, the case is altered; I am glad to see you, for we live in dangerous times and I fear for Sarah's safety. New England is becoming lawless. Have you heard what happened to the *Gaspée*?"

"Yes; the bare facts revealed by a New York newspaper."

" 'Twas a terrible affair. Terrible. D'you know what happened to poor Duddingston, the commander? He had to plead for his life, writhing in agony at the feet of the villains with two pistol balls in him. And do you know what they did with the wretched man? They let him have a boat in order that he might proceed ashore as if it was the greatest act of humanity they could do him! God rot them all!" Tyrell paused, to catch his breath, so angry had he made himself by his tirade. "Oh, there are those who will tell you that Duddingston was a foul-mouthed villain, that he stopped every vessel without pretext or justification, that he allowed his men ashore to cut firewood upon anyone's property and that he swore that if the whole of Rhode Island was aflame he would not lift a finger, or suffer his men to do likewise, to extinguish the conflagration. Most of this is true, so far as it goes, but it does not go far enough, for the truth must embrace both sides of the affair and the truth was Duddingston had been commissioned to extinguish smuggling! And if he was an insolent agent of the British Admiralty, as foul mouthed, arrogant and ill-mannered as Admiral Montagu at New York, then these qualities were matched by the insolence, arrogance and mendacity – which is but another form of bad usage of words – of those against whom he had to contend, which included every fisherman in the province! Duddingston could not obtain firewood by purchase, since none would trade with him, neither could he land and requisition it without some holy patriot claiming ownership of the land and denying access. I swear to you, Kite, there has been abroad such a manner of spinning the truth that one scarce knows right from wrong, or the law from the lawless!"

"Did anyone know who perpetrated the piracy?"

"Oh, yes," Tyrell said vehemently, resuming his seat. "A gentleman named Abraham Whipple led the rogues. Their only motive was to extirpate the predatory efficiency of the *Gaspée* before her commander put an end to their own illegal evasion of duties. He was supported by sixty-four worthy souls, chief among whom was John Rathburne, a sea officer like Whipple. As for Whipple himself, it was he who answered Duddingston's challenge when the commander ordered the boats not to come alongside the grounded schooner, and it was Whipple who abused Duddingston in as foul a language as ever Duddingston abused any other man. At this point a desperado named Bucklin shot Duddingston, who fell back upon his own deck, and having boarded the *Gaspée* the brave Whipple taunted Duddingston and sported with him in a tortuous manner."

"But why were these facts not laid before the justices?" Kite asked, adding, "For I understood a reward of five hundred pounds had been offered for evidence against the pirates."

"Oh, there was a far greater commotion raised than a mere reward. That only produced a poor black slave whom no one believed. Although he imparted the names of Whipple, Rathburne, Bucklin and half a dozen others whom he had seen embarking in boats at the landing place, all believed he acted out of motives of greed! Ha! What a pickled irony lies there, William, and how cogently such a motive can be argued and then digested! Lost among all the argy-bargy are the little facts of the affair; the robbing of Duddingston's silver spoons, the concerting of the raid by the beating of a tattoo, which is certain evidence of a conspiracy, the shouted order that all who would have revenge upon Duddingston should meet at the house of Mr Sabin.

"But all this, indeed everything that happened that night, was forgotten! When the news reached London, the Attorney-General, Mr Thurlow, obtained a royal Order in Council commanding the authorities of Rhode Island to deliver up the culprits for shipment to England and trial for piracy at the Old Bailey. But in the first place no one could be found that knew a thing untoward had happened in Providence that night and then Stephen Hopkins, our now mightily revered old Chief Justice of the Province, refused to obey the command, refusing to sanction warrants for the arrests."

"So the names *were* made known to him?"

"Oh, yes . . ." Tyrell fell quiet a moment and then looked up. "I am an old man, William, and had I not had Sarah to worry about I should perhaps have stood up and declaimed the names of Whipple and Rathburne from the rooftops myself. But I was not in Providence and knew them only by hearsay, though that hearsay had all the authority of heroic praise! Instead I heard of a black slave who was witness to the affair and I sent for him. I encouraged him to give evidence to the commissioners, thinking that I might strike a blow for justice and give the poor man a means of purchasing his manumission under the protection of the authorities." He gave a short, self-deprecatory laugh.

"I reckoned without Hopkins, who proved as great a coward as myself and considered London to be too far off to bother us. He proved the shrewder judge, for astonishingly the matter blew over, hush-a-byed by Lord Dartmouth, who was at the critical moment appointed Secretary for the Colonies. It was said that his lordship received a letter from a self-styled friend of Great Britain resident in North America. This patriotic correspondent assured Dartmouth that protracted pursuit of the incendiary pirates of Rhode Island would result in the entire continent catching fire. Beside that threat the burning of a revenue schooner was set aside as of no consequence."

"And Duddingston?"

"He died in my house, raving with the pain of a gangrenous wound in his groin wide enough to place your fist into. A month after his death a letter arrived in which their Lordships of the Admiralty appointed him to the rank of master and commander."

"That you gave so unpopular a man some shelter argues against you being a coward, Arthur."

"Oh, it was not me; it was Sarah. She had some mad notion—" Tyrell recalled himself. "I should not have said that. Please forget I mentioned it. No, no, it is not fair . . . Sarah was compassion itself." He looked up at Kite, shaking his head. "I should not have referred to Sarah like that."

Kite leaned forward and touched the old man's hand as it lay trembling on the desk in front of him. "'Tis no matter, Arthur, it was between ourselves; a confidence."

"Yes, well." Tyrell mastered himself. "Well," he said with a shuddering sigh that seemed to emphasise his physical frailty, "it brings me to the heart of this matter which is indeed between ourselves."

"Which is?" Kite frowned uncomfortably.

"William, I hardly know you, yet I liked you when I first met you and we have done business during the last thirteen years, and in that time I have learned that you are utterly trustworthy. You may think me foolish, but your arrival here today is mightily providential. I could almost believe that fate had stayed any inclination you might have had to revisit Sarah sooner, for I know you would not come to see me."

"Heavens, Arthur, I am here to see you now."

"Do not, I beg you, dissemble or misunderstand me. But now my mind is made up. She is yours, my boy, take her with you when you leave here, marry her when you can, for I shall not be much longer in this world. No, I am not given to moments of drama, William; but I recognise the fact and it is stupid to pretend otherwise. Lord Dartmouth may have prevented a conflagration sweeping the continent in seventy-two, but it will come this year, or next year. There will be some new outrage, engineered as the burning of the *Gaspée* was, by men whose own ambition is overweening. Already there is a new zeal abroad, and in every province there are now forming Corresponding Societies dedicated to uniting us in our resistance to acts of British tyranny such as were represented by Lieutenant Duddingston and his depredations hereabouts."

As Tyrell fell silent, Kite recalled his own analogy, expressed to Harper, of the bad boy pushing the boundaries of parental control until they burst.

"I am glad you have come, Kite," Tyrell said rousing himself. "And you *will* tarry at our house; I have much to discuss and arrange with you in the way of business." He rose, closed a ledger on his desk and carried it to a safe, the door of which stood open. He thrust the ledger inside and closed the steel door with a thud, turning the keys in the lock and then pocketing them. Turning, he confronted Kite, who rose to his feet. "Will you look after Sarah?"

"Of course, if both you and she wish it, I shall offer her my protection—"

"Then that is enough," cut in Tyrell with sudden resolution and, reaching for his tricorne, he added, "for the time being at least. Come, let us go home, I have need of my wife." And with this odd intimacy, he led the way out into the street.

Having divested himself of his hat in the hall of his house, Tyrell turned to Kite and gestured him to follow. "I do not wish to startle Sarah, William, so be a good fellow and wait for me to call you."

Kite nodded. He could hardly breathe and his heart was thumping in his breast. He felt ridiculous and eager, a paradox he could not reconcile as he stood behind Tyrell, who opened a door and went in search of his wife. Kite stared about him. He had a vague memory of the hall, of his arrival with Puella in her dress of brilliant red and yellow silk, and remembered the smell of rich food which is always a pleasure to a man inured to ship's fare. Now he heard Tyrell say, " . . . a surprise for you, my dear," and then he was being waved into the room.

She rose as he stood beside her husband and footed a bow. Her face was pale with astonishment and he thought for a moment she would faint. He stepped swiftly forward as she put out her hand and bent over it and as he straightened up she smiled, her eyes full of tears. "Is it really you, Captain Kite?"

"I should prefer it if you recognised me as William, Mistress Tyrell. It has been a long time and our former acquaintance was brief, but I recall we called each other by our Christian names."

"Yes, a long time." She retracted her hand with a gesture of awkwardness and dropped her eyes. "How is your . . . How is Puella?" she asked.

"Sadly she died. The air of Liverpool did not suit her and she died within a few days of our son, who was struck down by the cholera."

"I am so sorry. Was this long ago?"

Kite shook his head. "No, it occurred last spring, but it persuaded me to return to sea. I did not like an empty house. I resumed command of the *Spitfire* and having reached Antigua I purchased another ship. We arrived in her this morning, she is called the *Wentworth*."

"That is the ship with her topmasts missing?"

"The same."

"So you have come again to Newport for repairs?" She was laughing at the irony.

Kite half turned to her husband. "So everyone reminds me."

"My dear," Tyrell stepped forward smiling, "I have insisted that William stays with us while his vessel undergoes repairs. We have much to discuss and you will enjoy his company, I know. Now please do sit down and I shall order tea. William, do you write a note to the ship to have your effects sent up and I shall have it taken to the yard." Tyrell indicated an escritoire and a few moments later instructions were on their way to Corrie and Bandy Ben regarding Kite's location at the Tyrells' house and his need of a few necessities.

As soon as he had overseen this and the maid had brought in tea, Tyrell made his excuses.

"I shall take my tea in my study," he said to the maid, and then to Sarah and Kite, "I have some matters to attend to and I am sure you would like a some moments to yourselves."

For a moment the two sat in complete and baffled silence, then they both spoke at once and after a moment of foolish and constrained awkwardness Kite insisted that she continue.

"It is so good to see you, William," she said, her voice breathless. He thought he had never seen so handsome a woman. "I did not think we should ever meet again."

"I – er . . ." Kite hesitated, lowering his glance and stirring his tea with unnecessary vigour and concentration. He was at once confused and embarrassed, aware that after his earlier remarks Tyrell had left them alone to a purpose, yet unwilling to commit any breach of propriety that might be misconstrued. Simultaneously he was intensely moved by Sarah, eager not to let this opportunity slip past, impetuously anxious to say something which would adequately express his desire to establish that intimacy which had only previously existed in his own occasional, unfaithful fantasies. Distance and time gave no guarantee that Sarah felt any reciprocal emotion, only the strange illusion that it might be so, an illusion created entirely by Kite himself.

And yet he had left her that evening after they had all dined together long ago with pleasantries charged hot with innuendo. Moreover Tyrell had made no secret of Sarah's attraction to him, unless he had intended to exaggerate it in his anxiety for her future. For a moment the sudden intrusion of this thought had him stumbling tongue-tied, but he blundered on with an admission that not so much broke as smashed the ice between them.

"I had not intended . . . No, that is not correct. I had avoided coming here immediately I began trading on the American coast some months ago. At first I felt that it would prove awkward, that my association with your husband's business was not to be complicated by my own personal considerations and, since I was unable to pick up a cargo for Rhode Island, it seemed I was not destined to, but—"

"Then you were wrecked again, which must have struck you as uncommonly providential," she interrupted, her eyes uncommonly bright.

"You are laughing at my misfortune," Kite said smiling at her lightness of touch, "but that is not true either. In fact I *was* on my way here, quite deliberately intending to have some extensive work done to the ship. Then fate intervened and now has effectively extended our stay."

"Of that I am very glad. It has been so many years and much has changed." She paused, then added with an air of wishing the matter referred to, "I am sorry that you have lost Puella."

"Yes." Kite looked away. "I loved her, you know." An unaccustomed mist filled his eyes and it occurred to him that he had not wept over Puella until now, the moment when his feelings ran high for someone else.

"I know you did. But there was a strong attraction between us, was there not? All those many, many years ago."

Kite nodded, unable to speak. He sighed, cleared his throat and looked at her. "Yes, of course there was," he said thickly. "And it has not gone away. Time has enhanced your beauty, Sarah. It is a terrible thing to have been so moved by one woman and yet so sincerely love another."

"The distinction is usually between love and lust, is it not?" she said quietly. "I once thought I knew the first, only to discover that it faded and may have been no more than the latter."

"Your fiancé? Yes, your husband mentioned him . . . and what of Arthur?"

"Yes, it is love, of a sort. He has been very kind to me and I have not always been a comfort to him." She paused and smiled at him. "And what else did he tell you about me?"

"That you rode down to Castle Point and watched the *Spitfire* sail."

"He told you that?" She seemed astonished. "Yes, it is true. I watched the *Spitfire* until she was out of sight. And was that all, that and the intelligence that I had been betrothed?"

Kite shrugged. "He mentioned he thought that you regretted my departure."

"Did he tell you that I raged against my fate? Did he tell you that I was so furious that I nearly killed my horse and was gone into the back-country for three days? Or did he simply tell you that I was mad?"

"No, that he did not, nor do I think that you are. He did, however, express his concern for you in these troubled times and it is clear by his present absence that he wishes us to be friends."

"I hope that we are already friends, William."

"Of course."

"And I am delighted that you are here, truly I am."

"Sarah, I would not have you, or your husband, misunderstand. His anxieties are all about your future. As for myself, I am independent. Only the winds of heaven and commerce command me now that Puella is dead. I am at the service of you both."

"Most eloquently put, my dear William," said Tyrell, coming back into the room and closing the door behind him. "Unfortunately I am of the opinion that soon a stronger gale than that of commerce will be blowing; stronger and more irresistible than that of heaven's breath itself. I mean of course that of rebellion and war!"

"Come, Arthur, do not trouble yourself with these useless speculations, it will make you ill," Sarah said.

"Ah, my dear, circumstances will march past us if they have a mind to. God knows what the future holds, but I feel easier knowing that William is attached to you and is minded to trade on this coast. You are so minded, are you not, William?"

"Indeed, Arthur, I have no intention of returning to England while I may turn up a profit 'twixt North America and the Antilles."

"In that Arthur will be able to help you, I am sure, won't you, Arthur?"

"Of course, my dear. Now come, William, I will show you your room and your traps should be here within half an hour."

There followed six weeks of the most perfect harmony. Kite proceeded daily to Roberts' yard, discussed the work in hand with Corrie and Harper and then absented himself. Neither of the mates objected, being pleased to be left to get on without interference. From the yard it became habitual for Kite to walk to Tyrell's office, take tea or coffee with him, discuss cargoes and meet other ship-masters, agents and the like, and then return with Tyrell to his house for dinner.

In the afternoons when the weather served, he would go riding with Sarah. He was an indifferent horseman, but he improved rapidly once the livery stable provided him with a docile mare. They were too much noticed ever to indulge in the slightest intimacy, just as their behaviour behind the closed shutters of the house never infringed the generosity of Tyrell's hospitality. Neither of them wanted the pace of things forced, for they were long past the first, impetuous flush of youth. There was an unspoken, unacknowledged acceptance that things would not always be thus, that they would change and that the circumstances of that change would decide upon their mutual conduct. Paradoxically, yet perhaps not unsurprisingly, such restraint lent to their afternoons an unspoilt magic and a delight such as Kite had not thought himself fortunate enough to ever experience.

As was to be expected, there was some wagging of tongues. Kite was referred to as Mistress Tyrell's "English beau" and, unbeknownst to them, he excited some jealousy among a few men of Newport. But those rummaging for scandal of a more salacious nature could not persuade the Tyrells' servants to yield anything more than the honest truth. Sarah Tyrell slept in the same bed as her husband and the "English beau" slept by himself. After a few weeks this lack of adulterous news translated itself into a thoroughly satisfactory explanation. The English were mere milk-and-water shams, or worse, all public charm and private buggery. A red-blooded Yankee would have raised a cuckold's horns on old Arthur Tyrell's head long since! God knew, a few had tried! In this way the subject found a kind of equilibrium and then people forgot or ignored it, for there was a new subject to concern the gossips of Rhode Island. Rumoured news of a conciliating measure by Lord North's government had reached Newport; it was said that cheap tea was to be made available, and those who smuggled it to evade duty were concerned at a potential catastrophic loss of income.

None of these considerations impinged upon the happiness

of Sarah and her English beau as they headed north on their horses. Usually they took a quiet turn about the environs of Middletown, or up towards Portsmouth, but on one glorious day they rode hard, coming down to Howland's ferry and on impulse crossing the Pocasset River. On the other side Sarah whipped up her horse, Musketeer, with Kite in hot pursuit. She led him first uphill through trees which required careful negotiation so that she had soon lost the more cautious Kite, and he turned his mare back downhill to where, about a mile away, he could see the sparkle of sunlight upon water. As he came down onto the shore he saw on his left a few houses and, away to the south on his left hand, Sarah's Musketeer riderless at the water's edge. Fearing that something had occurred to her he dug his spurs into the uncomplaining flanks of his own mount and soon caught up with Musketeer. He reined in and turned about, calling Sarah's name, and then he saw her, coming down through the trees.

Catching Musketeer's reins up, he walked his mare towards her. "Are you all right?" he called and then he saw she was carrying her hat and limping, her hair dishevelled.

"No . . ."

"You fell?" he asked incredulously.

She nodded. "After pride," she said wincing, "which I have lost entirely."

Kite threw his leg over his horse and slipped down beside her and an instant later they were embracing in a welter of passion, all thought of injury forgotten.

Seven

The Tocsin

K ite cared not a fig for the debate on Lord North's Tea Act, which, it was maintained, threatened not only the smugglers of Rhode Island but also the china manufactories of Philadelphia and other native American industries. The measure that was presented by King George III's ministers as a conciliatory benefit to the American colonists was also intended to save the East India Company of London and to this cynical reason were soon attached numerous other attendant and incipient misfortunes which would, the propagandists insisted, bring ruin on America. It was argued that cheap tea would be followed by a flooding of every American market by cheap imports, Chinese porcelain being chief among them. This greatly alarmed the mercantile fraternity, and began to divide those hitherto firmly opposed to the lawless agitators of the radical party. This, aided by the alarm and despondency spread by the Corresponding Societies, steadily built up resentment against the eventual arrival of the cheap tea; resistance was increasingly referred to as patriotism.

While old Tyrell railed against these infamies and damned the King's ministers with incompetence, insensitivity and sheer stupidity, Kite turned a deaf ear. His relationship with Sarah had undergone a subtle shift since their intimacy in the woods on the shores of what Sarah had told him was known as Wanton's Pond.

" 'Tis appropriate, is it not?" she had remarked that afternoon as they drew apart and bent their thoughts to returning home. Kite had gallantly denied it, hopelessly in love with the dark-haired beauty. But their rides had become less frequent as work on the *Wentworth* neared completion, and even the most innocent of their intimacies more guarded as they reconciled themselves to parting. Neither wanted passion to ruin happiness, nor wished to compromise or dishonour Arthur Tyrell.

90

But the old man seemed as robust as ever, apparently fired up by political events and given a new lease of life. "If only," he would say, "the ministry would remove all the tax from tea, instead of merely reducing it, then every objection to its import would evaporate, such is the slavery of every American to the habit of drinking it! But they will not, and thereby they put a torch into the hands of these damned self-seeking and self-styled Patriots and Sons of Liberty!"

As the work on the *Wentworth* drew to its conclusion, duty drew Kite to Roberts' yard and entirely disrupted the cosy routine he, Arthur and Sarah had established. Late one morning in early June, as he sat in his cabin drawing up his accounts, writing to Wentworth and Johnstone in Antigua and making arrangements to pay the shipyard, he overheard two caulkers working on a stage under his quarter gallery. They were clearly unaware that Mistress Tyrell's English beau had taken to spending more than an hour on board, nor would he have listened had not a familiar name cropped up.

"What? Tea-tax Tyrell? They say that the old fool has a warehouse full of the stuff."

"Aye, he's Tory to the core an' no mistake."

"They should make an example of him and burn his damned tea!"

"Hush your mouth, Jethro, remember who the skipper of this barky is."

" 'Tis a shame and only adds reason to my arguments," the man named Jethro said, taking up his mallet and caulking iron again. The next moment the thud-thud of their labouring put paid to Kite's eavesdropping. Completing his work he gathered up his papers, placed them inside a leather wallet and rose from his desk. As he left the ship he avoided staring at the two men hanging under the starboard quarter and made his way towards Tyrell's offices on the waterfront to the south of the yard.

A small group of well-dressed men were assembled outside the adjacent newspaper office and one of them looked up as Kite approached them. He had clearly mentioned Kite's name because they all turned and stared at him, then as Kite made to pass them, they barred his passage.

"Well, well," one of them drawled, "if it ain't the English Cap'n."

Kite stopped and confronted them. "Gentlemen," he said coolly, "will you let me through?"

One of them whom Kite had seen frequently about the town stepped forward, ignoring his request. "I understand your ship is almost ready for sea, Cap'n Kite."

"She is, but you have the advantage of me, sir."

"I do, do I not, Cap'n? Well, well, that should not trouble you and nor will we if you sail soon."

"I shall sail when the work for which I am paying is complete, sir, and not a moment before."

"You are very bold, Cap'n."

"Aye, he is," added a colleague, arousing a chorus of assent among the group.

"If you will permit me to pass, gentlemen . . ."

"And if we will not, what then?"

Kite sighed. "Then I shall be obliged to walk another way."

The men deliberately stretched across the road. The little confrontation was arousing the curiosity of an increasing group of onlookers.

"Ain't you the nigger-lover? The man that Sarah Tyrell whipped when you first came to Newport, Cap'n?" one of them asked.

"She had some sense then," another added, and they laughed.

"And now you're cuckolding poor old Tyrell," the first man who had spoken went on. He was clearly their leader. He shook his head. "No principles, the English."

"That, sir, is a most offensive remark," Kite said colouring and aware that they had no intention of permitting him to escape without goading him to an extremity.

The leader leaned forward and thrust his face into Kite's. "And what are you going to do about it, Captain Kite? Call me out for satisfaction and meet me on the common tomorrow morning?"

"No, sir, because that is what you want."

"And you are afraid, you milksop."

Kite laughed. He had no idea afterwards why he did so, but the ridiculous provocation stung him not with the possibility of dishonour, but the folly of being led by such an obvious ploy. "Indeed, sir, I am afraid. Who would not be afraid of a combination of such bold fellows who would stop a single man and goad him with such puerile taunts? Heavens, gentlemen, only a fool would want to fight such gamecocks." And in the hiatus that followed, he pushed his way quickly through them and left them, walking quickly to Tyrell's office.

As he entered Tyrell's senior clerk looked up and Kite called him to the door. "Who are those men, Mr Borthwick?" he asked, pointing out the knot of troublemakers as they conferred. Borthwick removed his spectacles and peered up the street and then swiftly withdrew his head.

"Er, they are Captain Whipple's men, sir, officers and masters who associate with Captain Whipple."

"And the man in the bottle-green coat?" Kite pressed the nervous clerk, referring to the leader.

"That is Captain Rathburne, sir."

"So in short, Mr Borthwick, they are the men who burnt the *Gaspée*."

Borthwick drew in his breath sharply. "I could not possibly say, Captain Kite."

"Do you know why these men are assembled in Newport?"

"Good heavens no, sir!"

"Well, I shall have to be content. Thank you, Mr Borthwick."

"Thank you, Captain."

In Tyrell's office Kite told the old man of the conversation he had overheard between the caulkers and then outlined the intimidation he had suffered at the hands of Rathburne's gang. Tyrell listened in silence and then said ruminatively and half to himself, "I do not think the time can now be far off." Then he looked up at Kite and said, "I am sorry you have been thus treated, William, it is a crying shame."

"I had not meant to become embroiled in Colonial politics."

"I doubt you can avoid it," Tyrell said, then paused. "It is true I have some tea in the warehouse, but there is little of it left. The hypocrites have drunk most of it."

"Let me ship the balance; they will not be so particular in New York."

"No, my dear fellow. We shall fill you with ballast and perhaps some odds and ends of manufactures, piece goods, ship's stores and timber, but you must get the *Wentworth* down to Jamaica and load a full cargo of sugar and molasses. *That* I can sell, even to rogues, but hie you back soon, I pray you. Do not delay on any account. I shall have the bills and papers ready for you tomorrow."

"Very well."

"Go home now and make your peace with Sarah. Tomorrow, go aboard early and remain on board until you sail. We do not want another encounter with that fellow Rathburne."

Nor did it happen. Kite did not believe that his verbal riposte had warded off the provocative Rathburne, but he was offered no other insults and it might well have been that his keeping himself aboard the *Wentworth* as Tyrell had suggested was victory enough for Rathburne and his patriotic gang. His last afternoon with Sarah had been far from unpleasant, despite the fact that it was charged with their imminent separation. Both knew that, God willing, it was only for a few months and that their love could survive such an interval.

It was December before the *Wentworth* returned to Rhode Island, for she had sprung her new topmasts off the Florida Keys and Harper had discovered shakes hidden deep in the spars fitted at Roberts' yard that suggested someone in Newport had knowingly sold them defective timber, though it had passed the vigilant eyes of both the mates.

The thought occurred to Kite that his officers might have been bribed or even merely slack in their duty, but the consideration that the American-born Harper had been disloyal was too uncomfortable to contemplate, while Corrie seemed too straight a man to deliberately endanger his ship. Kite's own examination of the broken spars suggested that to all external appearances they had seemed perfect, but it was not impossible that, since there were two of them, a batch could not have been produced by some quirk of nature in the same stand of timber and their weakness had been known to the shipwrights and riggers of Roberts' yard. In the final analysis, however, Kite felt a lingering guilt himself. If he had been as assiduous as he expected others to be, the yard would not have dared to foist him off with damaged spars.

But although late, the *Wentworth* returned to Newport deep-laden and Kite entertained no apprehensions for the safety of Sarah or her husband during the ship's extended absence. During the voyage, he had encountered several Yankee masters newly arrived in Jamaica and from them had been reassured that matters in New England were much as he had left them. There were continuing fulminations against the proposed import of cheap Indian tea and a burgeoning fashion for publicly renouncing tea drinking, but no news of burnings or outright disorder.

Relieved, Kite and his acquaintances amiably discussed the political situation over a pipe, a cigar or a bowl of rum punch. In these discussions with Americans and a few British masters familiar with the Yankee trade, all of whom were sober seafaring men, Kite began to perceive the other side of the American coin. Setting aside all the machinating, exaggerating and mendacity of the extreme Patriot faction, there were bold principles of libertarian ambition emerging in America. Some were not entirely foreign to a man used to working in Liverpool, itself no stranger to radical politics. Most intelligent men of commerce on both sides of the Atlantic argued that they owed no feudal respect to those who birth alone had placed over them, and Kite could see that the increasingly popular independence of American minds grew out of the vastness and opportunity of the country in which these men lived. The similarities with the vigorous commercial expansion of Liverpool and Manchester were obvious, and the aspirations of men in these two centres of shipping and manufacturing were suffering in like fashion. It was clear that if established British institutions were incapable of accommodating Liverpool and Manchester, they were even less able to approve the expansion all native Americans felt to be their natural, God-given destiny. In fact the Crown was wholly opposed to American expansion, forbidding colonisation west of the Appalachians for fear of further disturbing the Indian tribes and drawing British troops, for which the Americans were unable to pay, into costly wars of frontier protection. While King George and his ministers considered the Colonies had sufficient local control over their affairs in their Houses of Burgesses, Assemblies and Councils, it was impossible for Great Britain to relinquish title to the country and hence the right to raise a paucity of revenue.

But taxation without representation in the Parliament in London was a rousing war cry, while any measure taken by London could, by its incompetent nature, be laid before a suspicious and malleable population as out-and-out tyranny. Kite rarely argued with men who pushed this point of view, unless it was to caution them against the consequences of rebellion, or to ask them whether if they detached themselves from Great Britain they could protect themselves against the hostile rapacity of France? But this was all too often blithely countered by a smooth assurance that if France turned upon an independent America, it would not be in Britain's interest to stand by in idleness.

"Our two countries will always trade. That's a matter of common sense. So you see, Cap'n," he was told more than once, "heads we win and tails you lose!"

When the now familiar landmarks of Rhode Island came into view on a cold, crisp December morning as the *Wentworth* beat up into Rhode Island Sound, Kite went below and donned his best blue broadcloth coat, fresh brushed by Bandy Ben, who had also polished his silver-buckled shoes and now offered them to his master as Kite kicked off the old pair he habitually wore on board.

"I think boots, this morning, Ben, for 'twill be frosty ashore. Do you pack those shoes in the portmanteau with my other clothes and have it all ready for transport ashore when we berth."

"As you say, Cap'n."

"What d'you think of Rhode Island, Ben?" Kite asked as he settled the heavy coat on his shoulders.

"Not as much as you, Cap'n, and it don't compare wi' Liverpool."

"You want to go home?"

"In due course, sir. Yes."

"You miss the place?"

"Truth to tell I miss Mrs O'Riordan's meat pies, Cap'n, an' the useful jobs I used to do for ye."

"I see." It was the longest conversation Kite had ever had with the man and he resolved not to keep poor Ben as a mere servant, but send him home at the first opportunity. Perhaps, he reflected as he picked his hat off the hook beside the door, he should have left him in Wentworth's counting house with Johnstone.

On deck Kite found Harper standing at the lee main shrouds, levelling a glass at the coast. "Well, Mr Harper, how do matters stand?" He looked aloft. "I see you have the signal flying for a pilot."

"Aye, sir. But the damned wind's drawing ahead all the time and Castle Hill is dead to windward."

"Very well." Kite digested the unwelcome news, then made up his mind. "Nevertheless, you can clear away both bower anchors and get cables bent on them."

"Aye, aye, sir." Harper called his watch aft and passed the order while Kite stared ahead, at the narrows between Rhode Island and the adjacent Connonicut Island with its lighthouse situated on its seaward point, Beaver Tail. He could see the masts and yards of shipping anchored in the far distance beyond the strait, lying as he well knew off the waterfront wharves of Newport, and his heart beat at the thought of seeing Sarah again.

"So near and yet so far," he murmured, for it was all too clear that he had donned his best coat somewhat prematurely. He looked aloft again. The yards were braced sharp up and were bearing on the catharpings, the weather tacks of the courses drawn down right forward and the weather leeches of the topsails stretched taut by the bowlines.

"Damnation," Kite swore, raising his own glass and sweeping the shoreline as if he might discover Sarah sitting Musketeer upon its green sward.

They beat fruitlessly all day, only working up closer to Beaver Tail and Castle Hill but unable to get a slant to pass through the narrows. Despite their signal no pilot boat ran out towards them.

"It's like the door being slammed in your face," Corrie remarked with a whistle through his broken teeth as he took over the watch at four o'clock in the afternoon. "They've given us up for today, I reckon."

"Yes," agreed Kite, but he still could not bring himself to admit defeat and go below and divest himself of the blue coat. All about him the hands glumly reconciled themselves to another night at sea, another night of beating back and forth, like a watchdog on a chain outside his master's door.

"Why, the damned wind even brings the smell of their confounded dinners down to us," he said pettishly, voicing his thoughts aloud.

"Aye, fate certainly enjoys rubbing our noses in our misfortunes," Corrie agreed.

Having spent so long refitting in Newport earlier that year, most of the men had, in the manner of sailors, made some friends or at the least established a presence in one of the several alehouses and taverns along the waterfront. Newport was famous for its distillation of rum and Liverpool men were famous for their ability to drink the stuff.

"And by the look of it, it's going to be a cold night to boot!" Kite added lugubriously as the red globe of the sun dropped quickly to the horizon through a sky untrammelled by a single wisp of cloud.

But as the sun set the strength of the wind died a little and, as darkness fell, the breeze backed sufficiently for them to lay the *Wentworth*'s bowsprit for the narrows. On the quarterdeck Kite saw the hands looking at him expectantly. He did not know that among them he had acquired a reputation, built on his past exploit of taking *La Malouine*, of being a lucky man. Only a lucky commander, they said, could have recovered men after they had gone overboard when a ship was knocked down by a white squall. So when he called out, "Keep her full an' bye! Call all hands! We'll stand inshore! Clew up t'gallants!" the watch on deck jumped to the fife and pin-rails with alacrity and even the watch below tumbled up with none of their usual grumbling.

"We'll not get through without beating, sir," said Corrie in a tactful reminder that they had no pilot, but Kite would brook no further delay.

"Then we shall have to tack in the narrows, Mr Corrie."

"And if the wind shifts again, sir?"

"Then we may have to anchor. Do you see to clearing the stoppers off the bowers."

"Very well, sir." Unable to raise any further objections to his commander's determination, Corrie went forward. A moment later Harper loomed up in the darkness, fastening the toggles of his greygoe.

"You're going in, sir?"

"Aye, I am; the wind's given us a slant. We may have to tack but do you go aloft and watch the land for me. I intend to stand close along the land under the Connonicut shore and then tack to gain ground to windward by poking our snout into Mackerel Cove."

Harper nodded. The inlet ran deep into Connonicut Island and would then give them clear water, past the Dumpling Rocks and Brenton's Point on the opposite Rhode Island shore.

"I'll watch out for you, sir."

With topgallants furled and courses clewed up, the *Wentworth* stood in for the harbour.

There are few things that compare with the taking of a calculated risk, Kite thought as he moved forward to take his station at the weather rail. Under shortened sail, the ship would handle quickly but not run away with him, while he could take tactical advantage of the entrance to Mackerel Cove and claw extra yards to windward before making a final leg into the anchorage beyond.

Kite put the *Wentworth* onto the starboard tack and stood across the entrance until, with the gleam of the lighthouse broad on the weather bow, he ordered the helm over and watched as the light traversed the bow. As Corrie yelled out the command to haul the main yards, he steadied the helm and laid the ship's head for the entrance. "Full and bye," he ordered and received the helmsman's repeated acknowledgement.

The breeze was holding steady and the *Wentworth* glided through the grey sea, the land lying dark on either bow. Slowly the loom of Connonicut Island grew closer and the orange fire in the lighthouse drew slowly abeam. The heel of the deck lessened as the ship came under the lee of the land and the hiss of the wash diminished to a chuckle as the *Wentworth* lost speed. Aloft the weather edges of the topsails lifted and fluttered.

Kite eased the helm a point, keeping the sails full, but giving ground to leeward. The long grey finger of Mackerel Cove opened up to larboard.

"She's luffin', sir!" the helmsman called.

"Keep her full and bye," Kite said, looking up to where the topsails shivered again.

"Wind's funnelling down the narrows," Corrie said, coming aft as the *Wentworth* paid further off to starboard and began to draw close to the Rhode Island shore.

"Aye, and I'll have to give her another point if we are to stay without coming aback," Kite muttered. "Do you stand by."

"Aye, aye, sir." Corrie went forward again and mustered the hands at their stations as Kite moved across the deck and stood beside the helmsman. "Free her off a point."

"Aye, aye, sir." It was Jacob, huge and reliable, who passed the spokes of the wheel from hand to hand, his black skin gleaming like ebony in the dim illumination of the binnacle light. Kite crossed the deck to the lee side. He could see the dark mass of Castle Hill climbing up against a background of stars as they gathered way, going faster now as they came clear of the lee of the opposite island.

"Deck there!" Harper's voice hailed from the foremast head. "Closing fast to leeward."

"Aye, aye," Kite called out, then asked, "Are you ready, Mr Corrie?"

"Ready, aye, ready, sir," Corrie responded and Kite held his hand for a moment longer then spun on his heel. "Down helm, Jacob!"

"Down hellum, sah!" and before the words were out of his mouth, Kite felt the cant of the deck ease, saw the bowsprit rake across the sky ahead and then Corrie was holloaing and the men were casting off and tailing on the forward braces.

The ship came up into the wind, faltered a moment, then paid off on the opposite tack as the main yards followed the foreyards round and Jacob was calling out, "Full an' bye, starboard tack, sir."

Kite breathed easier as the *Wentworth* sped back across the narrows, heading for the entrance to Mackerel Cove, where he again put her about. Once more on the larboard tack, the ship headed up for the lights of the town but as she drew closer to the open water they had to weather Brenton's Point and it looked as though their leeway was such as to cause them to tack again. There would be little room at this most narrow part of the strait, and on the opposite bank rocks extended to seaward.

Aloft Harper was calling out their distance and Kite asked for the bearing of the extremity of Brenton's Point.

"Steady, sir," Harper called out, his voice clear in the darkness as not a man moved from his station, instantly ready to tack. Kite kept his nerve and stood on. A steady bearing presaged collision, but then, as they again came out of the lee of Connonicut, a slight increase in wind strength and their own speed altered matters.

"She draws aft, sir!"

The collective sigh of relief was loud and then they were clear and Kite ordered the helm eased. They wore round Brenton's Point, passed two anchored brigs to the south of Goat's Island, then he brought *Wentworth*'s head into the wind about three cables from the shore and half that distance from an anchored schooner. With the sails aback he ordered the larboard bower let go. It went with a splash and the cable rumbled out after it, sending a slight tremor through the ship.

"Very well, Mr Corrie, make a fist of it. I don't want the Yankees waking up in the morning to see a British ship that looks as though her company can't make a decent harbour stow in the middle of the night."

"Aye, aye, sir."

Kite could hear the lightheartedness in Corrie's tone of voice. He turned. "That will do the helm, Jacob."

In the waist the men busied themselves with clewing up the topsails and lowering the yards. At the mizzen three seamen were brailing the spanker and Jacob slipped the white sennit lanyards over the wheel-spokes. Kite turned and strode aft to stare at the spangle of Newport's waterfront lights. He still wore his best blue broadcloth and it was surely not too late to call away a boat and have himself pulled ashore. A clock began to strike and he wondered what the time was; ten, he guessed, or perhaps eleven. He began to count, but the clanging passed ten, then eleven, then twelve and he realised it was no clock but the persistent ringing of the church bell.

"Nice of them to make us welcome," Corrie remarked as he came aft to report the anchor brought up.

"Probably the pilots complaining we're trying to cheat 'em," Kite joked flippantly, but the worm of unease was uncoiling in his gut. A similar thought must have crossed Corrie's mind for after a moment or two he said, "It sounds like an alarm . . ."

Kite listened a moment more and then agreed. "Aye, 'tis a tocsin, all right, but why?"

"There's a fire, sir, see, there, along to the left." Harper joined them.

"Give me a glass," said Kite sharply, holding out his hand.

"I have mine here, sir," Harper fished in his coat-tails and passed a small brass telescope to Kite, who raised it to his eye and wrestled a moment as he focused it.

"That's odd," said Corrie reflectively, "but that fire's only just catching and the bell's been ringing for some time."

"Aye, but that's just due to the distance we are offshore. The fire may have been burning for some time," offered Harper.

"I think Corrie's right," said Kite, closing the glass with a snap. "Get the boat swung out, Mr Corrie. You're to stay aboard. Mr Harper, you had better come with me. I think that is arson and I think I know whose warehouse is afire!"

Eight

The Tea Deum

B y the time the hands had got the boat swung off the booms
and over the side there was no doubt that the fire had gained
a firm hold of Tyrell's warehouse. As the boat pulled across the
harbour, the clang-clang of the tocsin growing louder, it was
equally clear to Kite that they were far too late, for the flames
were roaring skywards, dissolving into upwardly flung sparks and
completely consuming the tarred lap-straked building.

"There is nothing to be done, sir," Harper said as he sat beside
Kite, one huge hand on the tiller.

"It's Tyrell's place," Kite said. "I am going to remain ashore.
Do you go back to the ship and send the boat in for me at six
in the morning. Keep watch and watch with Corrie, there's
just the chance someone may have noticed our arrival and take
exception to it."

"Aye, aye, sir."

Kite stared into Harper's face, lit by the glare of the fire. If
he had entertained any doubts about the second mate's loyalty it
was likely the next few days would reveal his political persuasion.
Harper put the helm over and swung the boat under the overhang
of the wooden wharf and up to a ladder.

"Are you sure you'll be all right, Cap'n?" he asked.

"Of course." Kite reached for the ladder, suddenly angry to find
that he was still wearing his best clothes. As he hauled himself
up on the planking of the dock he paused. He was unarmed and
had not even brought a cane with him. As he looked along the
waterfront he thought he might need one, for he was staring at
a scene from Hell.

To the roar of the fire and the tolling of the church bell were
added the shouts and whoops of a milling crowd. There was
no sign of a single bucket of water, nor of distress, or even

102

a sense that the fire might be out of hand and a threat to the surrounding buildings. It was obvious to Kite that he was witnessing arson, and arson committed by the entire community upon a single individual. Aware of someone behind him, he spun round nervously, relieved to see Jacob behind him.

"Massa Harper said I was to stay with you, Cap'n Kite."

Kite nodded. "Very well, Jacob. I'm glad to see you." He paused, undecided as to what he should do. He must get to the Tyrells' house, and he said as much to Jacob, but then he was distracted by an intensifying of the noise of the crowd.

It was a mob now, forming what looked like a ring about the landward end of the warehouse and baying for something with a cacophonous pulse that he could not comprehend. Then he caught the cadence with its alliteration.

"Tea-tax Tyrell! Tea-tax Tyrell! Tea-tax Tyrell!"

Kite began to move forward, a knot of anger and fear bunching up under his heart. He began to shoulder his way into the crowd which kept up their chorus.

"Tea-tax Tyrell! Tea-tax Tyrell! Tea-tax Tyrell!"

Into the light flung across the adjacent street staggered a terrible figure which Kite recognised instantly, though he was stark naked and glossy with a covering of tar. Around him, dancing with excitement, came a dozen youths. Some had bowls under their left arms from which, as if in some obscene sowing rite, they gathered up handfuls of tea with their other hands and flung them over Tyrell. The others bore flaming brands with which they beat the ground behind the old man's heels, making him dance obscenely, to the vast amusement of the shouting crowd of men, women and children. This was Newport's version of tarring and feathering, a ritual adopted by the "Patriots" to intimidate their Tory enemies.

Tyrell tried to ward off the tea dust, blinded by it and the warm tar his thin body had been daubed with. Even where he struggled against the press of the mob, Kite could feel the heat of the fire, and if Tyrell uttered anything from his opened mouth Kite could not hear a thing. He was outraged and his fury increased his activity. He began to elbow people aside so that he attracted attention and men complained, and then he felt his elbow caught in a strong grip and he was being dragged backwards. He half-turned, aware that Jacob was pulling him back through the crowd.

"Unhand me, Jacob, damn you!"

But Jacob hauled him clear and as Kite, his face suffused

with anger, began to berate him, said, "Look Cap'n!" Such was the insistence in Jacob's eyes that Kite turned. Now he could hear Tyrell's screams cutting through the yelling of the mob which gradually ebbed as the enormity of their collective act struck them.

The flaring brands borne by the taunting youths had set fire to the tar which covered Tyrell's body and now he blazed and danced a grim dido of death. Even as he did so the burning walls of his warehouse collapsed inwards with a climactic roar and upwards spray of sparks; then the noise of the fire died down. Even the church bell had ceased tolling the tocsin, and the almost sudden lessening of noise emphasised the terrible death agonies of the tormented old man. Children turned away and buried their faces in their mothers' aprons while the women themselves began to sob and cry.

Someone shouted out, "Shame!"

Another called out, "Murderers!" and few voices joined in: "Incendiaries!" "Bastards!" "Patriot scum!"

As Tyrell's dying body arched with a last spasm of pain and terror, the air was filled with the stench of his burning flesh. Someone vomited and the crowd began to melt away.

"Take heart, citizens!" A man's voice bellowed. "Better one old man dies that a people is enslaved!" A thin cheer from the die-hard Patriots greeted this short speech. "Death to all tyrants!" the ringleader went on, rallying his supporters. "Liberty, and damnation to the British!"

"Come, sah," Jacob persisted, "I promised de second mate I'd look after you, Cap'n Kite. There ain't nothing we can do, sah. The old man is burnt blacker than any God-damned nigra."

Kite caught one last view of Tyrell. The old man had given up the ghost and his corpse lay shrivelled and burned. Then, as Jacob pulled him forcibly into an alley, Kite called, "Wait!"

Obedience was ingrained in Jacob and he paused as Kite turned to peer from the partial cover of the corner. There had been something familiar about the voice of the ringleader. The mob had become a crowd again and this had almost dispersed. Only a small group of men remained at the site of Tyrell's humiliation. One stepped forward and, undoing his breeches, relieved himself over the corpse, adding the stink to the smell of roasting flesh.

"Allan," one of them remonstrated.

The man named Allan looked over his shoulder. "I'm putting him out," he joked, "don't let anyone say I let him burn."

"You'd do better waving that thing at his widow!"

"Happen I will before morning."

"She'll be glad to be rid of him."

"Go give her the news, John."

The ringleader shook his head. "No, we'll make her sing the Tea Deum in the morning," he said. At that moment Kite saw his face.

"Let's get out of here, Jacob," said Kite, shaking himself clear of the black man's restraining grip and leading Jacob up the alley.

"Where are we going, sah?"

"To call on a lady."

The Tyrells' house was in darkness as they approached. Through the dark window-glass on the ground floor Kite could see the internal shutters had been closed, and he feared for Sarah's whereabouts. Where had she been when her husband had been caught by the Patriot mob? He banged on the door and stood impatiently for some moments on the threshold. A silence had fallen now on Newport and he felt this was preternatural. It was broken by distant drunken laughter. He swore and beat on the door again, leaning forward to catch any sound from within.

"Dere's someone in dere, Cap'n," Jacob whispered. "I see the shutters move."

Kite stepped back and moved to the window Jacob indicated. "It's Captain William Kite, just arrived from Jamaica," he called in a low voice. "Let me in!"

Then the shutter drew aside and Kite started as he stared into the face of the Tyrells' housekeeper, Bessie Ramsden, her head swathed in a nightcap. He saw her turn about and a few minutes later heard the noise of bolts being drawn.

"Oh, Cap'n, I'm so glad—"

"Where's your mistress?" Kite cut in.

"I don't know, she went out looking for the master."

"Damnation! I beg your pardon, but where is she likely to have gone? Where did Mr Tyrell say he was going?"

"He never came home tonight, sir."

"From the counting house?"

"Yes, sir."

"And is that where your mistress is likely to have gone to find him?"

"Yes, sir. We had word that the Patriots were on the rampage after what happened over in Boston last night."

"What was that?"

"Oh, they threw all the tea into Boston Harbour, sir, all dressed up as Mohicans."

"Yes, yes, but is there anywhere else Mistress Tyrell might have gone other than the counting house?"

"Only the warehouse, sir; the master took a small consignment of tea out of a snow last week."

"Dear God! Have you a pistol and a sword, Bessie? Be quick!"

"Here, come in, sir . . ."

In the hallway Kite saw the servants all armed with muskets. He turned and gestured to Jacob. "Here, Jacob, arm yourself. We are going out after Mistress Tyrell, that old man's wife." Kite turned to the housekeeper. "Bessie, I doubt you'll be bothered until the morning, but if I find the mistress, I'm taking her off to my ship until this trouble dies down." He forbore saying more and took what he recognised as Arthur Tyrell's small sword and a brace of pistols from a manservant.

"They're loaded, Captain Kite," the man said. "D'you want me to come with you?"

"No, do you stay here and mind these ladies. If anyone wants to know now or later where your mistress is, tell them she left to find her husband and you haven't seen her since. D'you understand me?"

"Aye."

"Good. Now come, Jacob. We've no time to lose."

Kite walked swiftly back into the silent town. Ironically a clock now struck midnight, the chimes ringing out mournfully over the rooftops. A few lights still glimmered between the interstices in the shutters and from one tavern the incongruous noise of riot sounded raucously into the night as a door opened and a Patriot reveller made for the latrine. They came to the waterfront and the smouldering remains of Tyrell's warehouse, which still glowed as the breeze gently fanned the embers. In the area where once the carts had loaded there was no trace of Tyrell's body and Kite heard Jacob muttering.

"The white man is powerful bad," he said and Kite was

compelled to agree with him. At the scene of Tyrell's dreadful death and humiliation Kite paused and Jacob could scarce contain his unease, hopping from one leg to another.

"Where the devil d'you think the monsters have taken him?" Kite asked no one and then he turned on his heel and made for the entrance to the counting house up a side street. The upper end window was that of Tyrell's private office and looked over the harbour. It was dark, but Kite thought he could see a dim flickering within. Was that the start of another fire, or did it indicate some activity inside? If so, was it more "patriotism" or did it reveal Sarah's whereabouts?

He crossed the street and tried the door. It was locked and he bent to the keyhole. Again there was a that faint glimmer, like a single candleflame somewhere in the interior. He turned his head and pressed his ear against the door. He was almost certain that he heard voices and, keeping his ear against the door, he tapped it deliberately with his knuckles. The whispering stopped. He tapped again, then heard a shuffling as of someone approaching the door cautiously.

He swallowed, then placing his mouth near the key hole called in a low voice, "It is William Kite, master of the *Wentworth*, newly arrived from Port Royal, Jamaica."

There was a short pause and then a man's voice, tremulous with fear responded. "That is impossible!"

"Borthwick? Is that you? Let me in, I am indeed William Kite."

"How can I be sure?"

Kite thought for a moment, then asked, "D'you remember me asking who a certain man was when a gang of Patriots tried to waylay me?"

"Aye, if you are Captain Kite you will known whose name I gave."

"You told me the name was Rathburne."

"And who is the mate of the *Wentworth*?"

"John Corrie."

To his relief, Kite heard a key grind in the lock and the next moment the door was cracked open. He stood to show himself.

"Who have you there?" Borthwick asked quickly, shoving the door closed again.

"This is Jacob, Borthwick, my quartermaster from the *Wentworth*."

Again the door opened and both men slipped inside. "Where is Mistress Tyrell?" Kite asked quickly and Borthwick jerked his head to an open door. It led, Kite knew, to a bay large enough for a single cart, from which valuables were brought into a strong room within the counting house through heavy double doors onto the street along the side of the building.

"Cap'n!" Jacob stood wrinkling his nose, the whites of his eyes alarmed in the semi-darkness. Kite could smell the burnt flesh and swallowed.

"Wait here, Jacob."

In the loading bay stood a small flat-dray and on it, lit by a single candle, lay the mortal remains of Arthur Tyrell. Kite shuddered and retched, then saw Sarah. She stood pressed into a corner, immobile and staring through wide eyes at what had once been her husband.

Borthwick shuffled in beside him. He pressed a handkerchief to his nose and mumbled, "I have been trying to persuade her that she cannot stay here all night, Captain Kite."

Kite nodded. "Thank you, Borthwick, thank you. Do you leave the keys with Jacob."

"I cannot, sir, I cannot."

"Very well, then, wait with Jacob." Borthwick turned and went out, leaving Kite with Sarah. There was no obvious sign that she recognised him, or even knew he was there, and he very slowly moved towards her, his hands outstretched.

"Sarah," he called in a low voice. "Sarah, 'tis me, William, William Kite . . . Sarah?" As he drew closer her eyes never left the charred corpse, nor did she appear to blink, though her cheeks were wet with tears. Yet she sensed him looming over her, for slowly she sank down onto her haunches, one arm coming up to shelter her head as though he was about to beat her with a stick. A faint whimper came from her, but it was clear she was insensible to his identity, though he murmured both their names. He crouched beside her, but still she remained withdrawn and his one attempt to touch her resulted in a swiftly indrawn breath, so that he moved back, perplexed.

He stood and, looking reluctantly at Tyrell's remains, had a thought. A whip stood alongside the dray, leant against the wall by the last driver. Moving slowly he took it up and then moved closer to Sarah. As soon as she was within arms' length he swung the whip and knocked over the candle. It guttered and went out, a moment later, as Sarah began to scream, he took her in his arms.

"Borthwick!" he called, aware that a flicker of flame ran along a wisp of straw on the board of the flat-dray. "Bring water, quick!"

"Oh, oh, oh . . ." Sarah was trembling in his arms as he gathered her up. Somewhere Borthwick stumbled and threw the remains of a jug of drinking water over the tiny fire and then in the next room the snap of flint of steel was soon conjured into a new light.

"Come, Sarah." With infinite patience, Kite led her out of the loading bay and into the main counting house.

"I should take her upstairs, sir, you can have some privacy there. I shall make some . . ." Borthwick had been about to say tea, but Jacob rose to the occasion.

"We'll make rum punch, sah. Do you light the cap'n up dem stairs, Massah Borthwick."

"Thank you, Jacob," Kite said as the clerk complied and he tenderly shepherded Sarah up the flight of stairs to Tyrell's private office. Here it seemed, she began to come to, blinking and looking about her, reaching out to touch familiar objects: Tyrell's inkwell, his tray of pens, the edge of a pile of papers. Slowly she made a circuit of his desk and then she looked up and seemed to see Kite for the first time, for she started, then stepped forward and, with her face a mask, raked her hand across his face.

"Sarah!" He staggered backwards, blood pouring from his cheek where her rings had cut him. It was a curious repeat of their first encounter when she had struck him with her riding crop. Into his outraged consciousness swam Tyrell's veiled allusions to his wife's high state of nerves, hints of instability, and now, he thought, of madness.

"Sarah!" He put his hand up to staunch the bleeding, and stared at her as she slowly realised what she had done.

"William? Is it you? It cannot be!" She began to shake, and tears suddenly poured from her eyes: not the suppressed weeping of her lonely vigil, but a full-blown and lachrymose collapse. Now she clung to him and slowly exhausted herself, voiding herself of the horrors of the night, as he leaned against Tyrell's desk and soothed her with soft, shushing noises, all the while stroking her lustrous dark hair.

At last, as though aware that the crisis had been passed, Jacob came up the stairs with steaming hot rum punch, leaving the jug with them as he retreated below again. "There was a boat, Captain," he said as his head reached the level of the upper floor. "I saw a boat tied up near where we landed. We can take that out to the ship when you are ready. There's no need to wait until the morning."

"Thank you, Jacob. Give us a few more minutes."

After a period during which Kite thought Sarah had fallen asleep, she stirred. "William?"

"Yes, my dear; it *is* me. We arrived this evening." He handed her a small tankard of the punch and she clasped it between both hands.

"Tonight of all nights," she said, sipping the hot liquid.

"Yes, tonight of all nights."

"The madness is an infection caught from Boston."

"So Mrs Ramsden explained." Kite took up his own punch and felt the warm glow expand in his guts.

"And Arthur would not lie low. Oh, God, do you know what they did to him, William?"

"Yes," he replied, "I do. I landed just as they finished . . ."

Kite wanted to make some excuse, to explain why he had not rescued Tyrell, but she went on.

"I saw it from this window. There had been muttering all day, after the news came from Boston. This evening a drummer went round the town, just like in Providence the night they burnt the government schooner. Arthur was restless and in the end he said he was going out. I begged him not to be foolhardy, but he insisted. 'All my life's work lies in that warehouse,' he said, and I argued that that was not only stupid, but untrue. His profits lay in the bank, in our house, in our property along the waterfront and our shares in ships at sea, but he would have none of it. 'It is a matter of principle,' he shouted. 'The law shall not give way to the mob!' and then he was putting on his cloak and hat and I said that I was going with him. He told me to stay, that you would look after me, that you had promised, but I said that whatever you had promised, you were not here . . ." She lifted the tankard again.

Kite said nothing; all that day he had been beating up and down outside the harbour in Rhode Island Sound, wondering why the confounded pilots were ignoring his signals. Now he knew why.

"After he left the house I followed him, catching him up before he reached Main Street. He was angry with me, then he took my hand and we came here. We were seen, of course. They were watching for us, I think. We heard them calling out.

"At first only a few of the waterfront loiterers followed us, but by the time we reached the door below there was a crowd assembling, and once we were inside and had found Borthwick Arthur made me promise to stay here. Before many more minutes had passed the crowd had become a mob. They were like animals, surrounding us and shouting their filthy abuse, people I have known all my life . . . Arthur was very brave; he opened the door and went out onto the step and asked them their business. They wanted him to open the warehouse and surrender the tea, so that they could brew it in the harbour as those others had done in Boston. I think that had he done so they would forgiven and forgotten his Toryism and have accepted he had changed his politics, but Arthur could not take the easy way out of this cruel dilemma and he refused to bow to coercion."

Kite remained silent, watching her and thinking how beautiful she was as she set down the empty tankard, her eyes blazing with indignation and her breast heaving with emotion. She drew herself up and her voice rose a little, cracking with the intensity of her feelings. "He had made me promise that whatever happened – *whatever happened* – I would stay here," she repeated, as though the knowledge exculpated and at the same time burdened her.

"He walked across the street with his keys to the warehouse, a great ring of them. I could see them gleaming in the lamps that people held up as they all fell silent. I wanted Arthur to throw open the doors of the warehouse and tell them to help themselves. The mob grew silent in anticipation, it seemed, of him doing this, but as they closed round him he drew back his arm and made to throw the keys over their heads into the harbour." She paused, shaking her head. "Then someone jumped up and caught them. John Rathburne, I think it was, and Arthur was pushed and shoved up against the door. The mob cheered and I lost sight of him, then I saw the door open and then close . . . It all grew silent again. I did not know what was happening until I smelt smoke. They set fire to the far end, the seawards end of the warehouse first. It was full of sugar. God knows what they did to him in there, but they stripped him . . ."

Sarah paused a moment, but she had control of herself now and went on calmly. "They stripped him and tarred him and in place of the chicken feathers they are so fond of they threw tea all over him and drove him back into the street and set fire to him."

"I saw the rest, Sarah . . ."

"But why, William? Why did they do that to an old man?"

"To unite them all, my dear. They are all complicit now, accessories after the fact, and though no one will ever be arraigned for murder, all their lives have been touched by the common crime."

"John Rathburne did it, he is their leader."

"I know, Sarah, and tomorrow we must take counsel, but tonight we must get you to a place of safety, the *Wentworth*. Come, I will send Borthwick home and he may let Bessie know you are safe with me. Let us get some sleep. Come."

He led her down the stairs and Borthwick put her cloak about her shoulders. Kite told the clerk his intentions. "If you can," he said, "return here for ten o'clock in the morning, but do not, I beg you, Borthwick, run any risks."

"I won't, Captain."

They stepped out into the now silent street. Smoke and heat still wafted across the street from the burnt-out warehouse and the dying embers glowed here and there, under the gentle impetus of the light breeze. Behind them Jacob emerged and Borthwick ground the keys in the lock.

"Good night, ma'am," he said, "good night, Captain."

"Ain't nothing good about it," mumbled Jacob, cocking the pistols. "Follow me, Cap'n," he said and led them obliquely across the street towards the wharves that jutted out from the waterfront.

A few minutes later Sarah sat in the stern of the stolen boat while Jacob and Kite each plied an oar. Answering the challenge from Zachariah Harper, they pulled alongside and with some difficulty in the dark Sarah was manhandled up the curving tumblehome of the *Wentworth*'s side. As they clambered aboard Jacob kicked the boat adrift.

"Nobody will know who took that boat," he said, handing the pistols to Kite.

"No, but they'll wake up to see an unexpected arrival lying at anchor in the harbour," Kite said.

Watching Kite escort Sarah to his cabin, Harper murmured, "Well, I'll be God-damned . . ."

"You'd better be for him, Mister Harper," Jacob said, "cos he's as angry as a five-legged hornet!"

Nine

Last Rites

K ite had left word that he was to be called at six o'clock and Bandy Ben found him wrapped in blankets on the deck of the cabin, his cot occupied by a remarkably beautiful woman.

"Cap'n, sir. Hot water."

Kite groaned; his body ached from lying on the deck. Then slowly the events of the previous day reinvaded his consciousness: the long hours of beating up and down off the Beaver's Tail, the tense passage of the narrows and then the terrible events beside the blazing warehouse culminating in Tyrell's scorched corpse and finally poor Sarah's ordeal.

At the thought of Sarah he threw off the blankets and rose to his feet. She lay in his cot like a beautiful but broken doll, fast asleep, her mouth slightly open, her hair tousled and her face and clothes fouled by sinister black smears. He caught the scent of her but it was impossible to avoid the smell of burnt flesh that hung about her dishevelled clothes and it occurred to him that she herself must have borne Tyrell's corpse into the loading bay.

He shook his head, turned to the hot water and shaved. When he had finished his ablutions he drew on his working clothes, the oldest of his coats that he wore at sea, and an old glazed hat which fitted tightly enough to withstand the odd gust of wind. Round his waist he buckled Tyrell's hanger and, bending a moment over his desk, scribbled a note for Sarah. Then he quietly left the cabin and encountering Ben told him to leave the lady until she woke and then to give her every attention.

"She is a person of importance, Ben; do you treat her kindly, for she has had a terrible experience." Ben grunted acknowledgement and Kite added, "While you wait for her to wake, be a good fellow and see what you can do to clean up my best coat and breeches."

113

On deck it was still dark. He found Corrie on watch and explained what had happened. The mate whistled through his teeth. "Zachariah said the fire looked bad, but I had no idea it was anything but misfortune . . ."

"Well, John, our consignee is dead, his warehouse is destroyed and his widow is asleep in my cot. I dare say we shall be able to sell our cargo to someone else and I shall attend to the matter later this morning. For now, however, I should be obliged if you will provide me with a boat as soon as possible. I have a mind to be ashore before the town is much astir. At ten o'clock send it back in for me. When Mistress Tyrell awakes, tell her I shall be back aboard at ten to take her ashore. I shall want Jacob turned out to accompany me."

"Zachariah wants to come with you, too."

"That's good of him, but do you not want him on board?"

"I can manage an anchor watch."

"I don't know how long we'll be, John."

"I'll manage."

"Very well."

Half an hour later, as the first glimmer of a wintry dawn threw the buildings of Newport into a sharpening silhouette, Kite stood again where he had witnessed the last moments of his friend. He walked into the charred timbers and heaps of ash that were all that remained of Tyrell's goods. Here and there embers glowed and the ash was still hot enough to warm his feet through the soles of his boots, but the sharp frost had cooled much of the previous night's conflagration. Smashed glass lay in piles, where bottles of wine and rum had exploded, while piles of barrel and cask hoops were all that remained of the large quantity of rum and beer Tyrell had had stored ready for shipping. Both were either distilled or brewed in the town and the incendiaries had damaged Newport's economy with a wantonness that shocked Kite. Of the offending tea there remained no trace.

Tyrell's warehouse was the last building on the waterside before it cut back in a dock, but on its far side rose the adjacent store owned by McFee, Browne and Kent. The nameboard announcing the owners was defaced by bubbled paintwork but, remarkably enough, it had not caught fire. A few buckets lay where they had been thrown at the end of the incident and the heavy frost that whitened the sloping roof showed where it had been thoroughly and constantly doused with water. There was no doubt that not only was the burning of Tyrell's warehouse arson, but it had been meticulously planned and carried out with great discipline.

A dog began to bark and somewhere a door slammed. Kite turned. A man was walking down the street that ran along the waterfront. He regarded the unfamiliar pile of ash and ruin that occupied the vacant lot and then noticed Kite and looked away. Standing still, Kite felt the heat burning through his boots and quit the site. It was too early to expect Borthwick to be at the counting house, but he checked, then walked off towards the Tyrells' house.

He found Mrs Ramsden a-bustle and obviously relieved when she opened the door to him. "Why, Captain Kite! Did you find the Mistress?"

"Yes, Bessie, she's safe aboard the *Wentworth*, but did you not hear from Borthwick last night?"

"We dursn't open the door to anyone if it wasn't you, sir. A man saying he was Borthwick came to the door, but I didn't reckon it was him, sir, and it was dreadfully late . . ."

"Very well, very well," soothed Kite, holding up his hand. "Pray do not distress yourself on that account, but I am afraid there have been terrible things happening in Newport."

He told her as sparingly as he could, but she was a curious and persistent woman, and despite the floods of tears and shrieks of dismay he could not, in the end, conceal the full horror of what had happened. By the time he had finished they had migrated to the kitchen and Mrs Ramsden felt the need for a tumbler of Tyrell's best rum.

"What are we to do, Captain? Oh," she went on without giving Kite the opportunity of replying, but dabbing her eyes with her apron and refilling her glass, "what a great mercy you came, sir! Had you not turned up, I don't know what would have happened to the Mistress, really I don't."

"No. The pity of it is, Bessie," said Kite, "that had I not met contrary winds yesterday I should have been in port twelve hours earlier and might have saved your Master."

"Oh yes, sir . . . To think of him being burned to death, oh, sir . . ." And she burst again into floods of tears. He waited until she had calmed down and then she repeated her first question. "What are we to do, sir?"

"I am not certain but I think we must see what transpires during the day. I hope the spirit of revolt will have had its fill of death and destruction, but it may not be so. There is, it seems, a very persistent faction in the town which is hell bent on mischief. Tell me, Bessie, what do you know of the man named Rathburne?"

"Oh, he is the worst of them, Captain, that I can assure you. John Peck Rathburne is one of Whipple's men – have you heard of Captain Abraham Whipple, sir?"

"I heard that he burned the *Gaspée*, yes, and I have marked him to be the ringleader of the active Patriots of Newport."

"Oh, he is, sir. The Master says— Oh, sir, forgive me . . ."

"That is all right, Bessie." Kite waited while she composed herself again.

"The Master," she went on, sniffling as she spoke, "used to say that he was the one man in Newport who was capable of real mischief. That was after the *Liberty* business."

"And what was that?"

"Oh, it was years ago, back in sixty-eight, I think, some business over a ship called the *Liberty* that belonged to Mr Hancock over in Boston. She had been taken by the Custom House officers for some problem over the duty that Mr Hancock should have paid or something. It was rather confusing, sir, seeing as how Mr Tyrell said, and I heard him say this, that the Crown officers were acting provocatively by strictly enforcing a regulation they had normally ignored. But Mr Hancock had annoyed them and I think they wanted matters done according to the regulation . . ." Mrs Ramsden had confused herself, but Kite could visualise the problem. It was probably waiving some procedure such as a strict entering of a ship for outwards clearance when the master cleared inwards at the Custom House. No doubt it had become a common practice to roll the two acts into one until, on this occasion, the Crown officers challenged the master of Mr Hancock's vessel, the *Liberty*, and accused him of not conforming to the letter of the regulation. Such things were done in Liverpool with a master who was a persistent problem to the authorities. But that, it seemed, was only half the story. "Go on," he said.

"Well, Captain, the Custom House officers used the *Liberty* like the *Gaspée* . . ."

"You mean they made her a revenue vessel?" Kite interrupted, incredulous at the inherent provocation of turning a seized vessel into a revenue cruiser.

"Yes, but all this was two or three years before the *Gaspée* business. Anyway, in the spring of the next year, sixty-nine that would be, the *Liberty* was lying here, off Newport. This raised a great commotion and they called a meeting and that John Rathburne was at the head of it, holloaing about Liberty being a matter for Americans and that it was all wrong for a ship with that name to be in King George's service and, oh, I don't known what all . . .

"Anyway, the upshot of it all was that they went out and burned her, said she wasn't British anyway. In fact I do believe that Mr Hancock himself came over from Boston and told them he didn't give a fiddle for the ship, what with him being the richest man in the whole of Massachusetts." Bessie Ramsden finished with a stout blowing of her nose which, Kite rightly concluded, signified she had overcome her moment of weakness. "So there you are, Captain, that's Captain John Peck Rathburne for you."

"A man with a fondness for burning things."

"Aye, quite." Mrs Ramsden pounded both hands upon her knees and rose to her feet. "And now, if you'll excuse me, sir . . . By the by," she asked, suddenly solicitous, "have you broken your fast? I'll wager not, and if you have it'll only have been that dreadful fare they serve on ships."

"Oh, 'tis not so bad when you've got used to it."

"Here, you sit down, sir, I've a fine ham, and we'll mash some tea and stir some porridge."

"And the condemned man ate a hearty breakfast," Kite murmured to himself as he relaxed, hoping that aboard the *Wentworth* they were looking after Sarah.

Kite reached Tyrell's counting house exactly as the church clock struck nine. Borthwick was already there but he shrugged his shoulders when Kite asked after his colleagues. "The word will have been passed to them to stay away, Captain."

"And you, do you wish to stay away, Borthwick?"

"I know the distinction between my duty and my inclination, Captain. Besides," Borthwick wrinkled his nose, "there is the matter of Mr Tyrell's remains."

"Yes, I have already considered that. I have been at the Tyrells' house this morning and before I left I sent word for a grave to be prepared for midday. Do you see that Mr Tyrell's attorney is summoned to the house with Tyrell's will and testamentary papers by two o'clock this afternoon. Now, before I leave you to go off to the ship again, I wish you to quietly see if there's a merchant who will take in three hundred and seventy tons of sugar and molasses, a small quantity of Spanish laces and similar wares."

"Very well, Captain, but they'll offer low prices."

"Then we'll sail for New York and sell it there."

Borthwick sighed and nodded. "This is a sad day, Captain Kite."

"Tell that to your fellow townsfolk, Mr Borthwick."

When he returned to the *Wentworth*, Kite found Sarah awake and dressed, sitting at his desk drinking chocolate. She rose angrily and accused him of abandoning her, but he swiftly responded.

"Would it have been proper to linger in the same accommodation as you, Sarah, beyond the time I had been called? Come, my dear, this will be a difficult day."

He watched her face soften. "I was frightened without you, William. When I woke I did not know where you were. Heavens, I scarcely knew where I was myself, until I remembered."

"Have you eaten?" he asked, swiftly changing the subject.

She nodded. "Yes, that odd little creature brought me hot burgoo and, as you see, I am completing my breakfast with this chocolate."

"That is Bandy Ben," Kite said, smiling for the first time, and she hesitantly smiled back. "You look better for your night's sleep. In fact," he said slowly, "you look uncommonly handsome."

She did not hear the compliment. "I cannot rid myself of the thought that with Arthur's death . . ." She hesitated, unable to bring herself to utter the words.

"Set those thoughts aside, Sarah, at least for the time being. Now, pray attend me and hear me out, for I have much to tell you."

It was odd, Kite thought afterwards, how events had conspired to throw them together, so that from the moment of his return to Rhode Island their fates had become inextricably entwined. There was never a formal proposal or any other of the regular conventions of courtship. She fell in with his plan not because he had assumed responsibility for her, but because it suited her and they were of one mind. For Sarah, outrage at the public murder of her husband, far more than the passion she felt for William Kite, made her aid and abet him. For Kite, friendship and respect for Arthur Tyrell obliged him to protect the dead man's helpless widow, while the commercial loss staring him in the face led him to acquire her help in solving their mutual problem. But both knew there was a distant objective behind this pragmatic union, and both knew that this governed the nature of their conduct upon that fateful day. It also enabled them to withstand the malicious intent of others who had already matured their own plan for the final disposal of the House of Tyrell.

Shortly before noon on the 19th of December 1773, the townsfolk of Newport were treated to a pitiful and dismal spectacle. A flat-dray, drawn by two nags and led by a huge black seaman wearing a cutlass, creaked its way up Main Street from the waterfront. Exposed on the dray lay what looked like a twisted and blacked log, such as one might pull out of a fire that had burnt out. It was scarcely recognisable as once having been a man. Behind the dray came a tall English sea captain in blue broadcloth, his cocked hat beneath his left arm, the glint of a silver-hilted sword at his waist and the scabbard-iron tap-tapping his gleaming hessian boots. He wore his hair unpomaded, his heavy clubbed queue bound at the nape of his neck by a black ribbon. He held his head up and his level grey eyes stared about him so that those who stood and watched dropped their gaze.

Upon his right arm walked Mistress Tyrell. Her voluptuous figure was set off in watered grey silk, over which she wore a black cloak whose hood was thrown defiantly back to reveal a cascade of hair tumbling about her shoulders. Like her escort, her head was also held high but she looked neither to right nor to left. Her eyes were fixed upon the disgusting sight of the black and shrivelled body of her husband which shuddered as the dray rumbled over the uneven surface of the street.

Behind Captain Kite walked Mr Borthwick in his common garb of black and grey, his arm supporting Bessie Ramsden, who was attired entirely in black. Four of the Tyrells' servants followed and the rear was brought up by a large and conspicuously ugly man, dressed in similar style to the captain, in a blue coat, apparel instantly recognisable to every person, man, woman or child in that seafaring place as the common clothes of a merchant sea officer. He carried in the crook of his arm a brightly polished blunderbuss, such as merchant vessels carry to deter thieves.

For the most part the people of Newport stood silently downcast, as though acknowledging their collective shame.

The men removed their hats, a number of the women sobbed silently and the smaller children peered from behind their parents' legs, scarce comprehending the grim sight. Only once, as the improvised cortege passed a tavern, was there heard an echo of the events of the previous night. A group of men, obviously appraised of the approach of the dolorous little procession, spilled out onto the street. Several had pots in their hands, others tobacco pipes and three wore their hats. Kite saw Rathburne standing slightly apart, hat on head and tapping his right boot with a cane. His face, a handsome one, Kite acknowledged, wore an offensive smirk and he stared at Kite quite unabashed. Kite felt Sarah's grip on his arm tighten. He held Rathburne's gaze until he could no longer do so without turning his head and he knew in that short period that he had made a mortal enemy. Sarah's grip eased as they passed clear of the group of men but behind them Kite heard the noise of exaggerated expectoration. Sarah grasped him again and he heard her indrawn breath.

"Steady, my love," he whispered and they slowly walked on.

In their rear a disrespectful murmur rose, then there was a laugh and as Kite guessed, having given offence as they intended, the gang withdrew inside the tavern.

There was only one person in the church other than the officiating incumbent, a man named Milton who, Kite was to learn later, was Tyrell's attorney. The funeral was short, swift and formal, spoken like the reading of the articles of agreement between a ship's master and his potential crew, Kite thought. Nor was the interment longer than was necessary, a circumstance hastened by a shower of snow driven in by a cold wind blowing from the north again. Afterwards, the little group of mourners slipped quietly away, traversing the back streets and heading out of the town towards the Tyrells' house. Here, irrespective of rank or station, Sarah had bid them assemble while some refreshments were served and Kite spoke.

"On behalf of Mistress Tyrell, I should like to thank you for your loyal support after the tragic events of the last few hours. It remains to be seen what the future holds for us, but I am certain that what provision can be made for you will be made."

"Thank you all," added Sarah, and she left the room, pausing only to address the attorney Milton. Kite saw the man nod, indicate his briefcase, pick it up and follow her. Kite joined them in the withdrawing room where he asked her, "Whom do you wish to attend, my dear?"

Sarah looked at Milton. "Mr Milton? What is your advice?"

"Besides yourself, ma'am, Captain William Alexander Kite, Mistress Elizabeth Jane Ramsden, Mr Solomon Lemuel Borthwick and Captain Thomas Edward Spenser Gray."

Kite called them in and they stood awkwardly about Sarah, who had sat on a single upright chair opposite Milton who was standing by a second. Kite recognised it as the one Tyrell himself favoured. "We seem to be one short," said Milton.

"Captain Gray is in the Antilles, Mr Milton, in the *Electra*," Borthwick offered.

"Then," said Milton drawing a sheaf of papers from his brief-case, "we shall have to proceed in his absence. If you would all be seated."

They did as the attorney bid them and an awkward silence fell. Borthwick coughed nervously, then Milton began to read. Kite looked from the window. It was the same one through which, less than twelve hours earlier, he had peered inwards at Bessie Ramsden in her night attire. He yawned, still tired after the exertions and turmoil of the night. The room was hot after the chill outside where the sky looked now like a sheet of lead. A soft and persistent fall of snow had begun to transform the landscape. Milton's voice droned over the testamentary clauses. The bulk of Tyrell's fortune had gone to his wife, as was to be expected, but there were special provisions for his housekeeper and chief clerk, who were both left two thousand pounds "for their loyalty and long and untiring service". Mrs Ramsden rocked as if about to faint, uttered a heartfelt, "God bless my soul!" and began to weep again.

Borthwick, by contrast, remained unmoved. He was charged with the conditional duty of advising Sarah "upon the disposal" of "the testator's commercial assets in their entirety, entirely freeing my wife from any encumbrance whatsoever". There was an exception to this, referring to the shares Tyrell had in various ships belonging to the ports of Newport, Providence and Bristol in the Colony of Rhode Island, which were to be made over to Captain Edward Spenser Gray, who was to enjoy or dispose of these as he saw fit on the sole condition that annually, or upon disposal, he paid five per centum of the profits raised thereby, net of all charges and taxes, to the trust mentioned in the next article.

Milton himself, in return for a legacy additional to his charges of one thousand five hundred pounds and an annuity of five per centum from an invested sum of five thousand pounds of which he and Sarah were the trustees, was "to advise my wife as to the best manner of drawing income from the residue of my estate". An additional provision was laid upon this trust, however, and at the mention of his name, Kite stirred from his brown study.

" . . . providing only," Milton read, "that this be in accordance with the wishes of Captain William Alexander Kite whom I charge with the duty, laid upon his honour as a gentleman, of ensuring as far as it lies within his power, of the future security, happiness and health of my wife . . ."

Milton looked up as the irrepressible Mrs Ramsden muttered in surprise and delight, expressing her pleasure and leaning forward and patting Sarah's knee before realising the unseemly nature of her presumption and flushing to the roots of her white hair. Sarah had gone deathly pale and had, Kite thought, been about to interrupt Milton and ask a question, but the attorney ploughed doggedly on.

"At the discretion of the said trustees of their heirs or successors, the funds shall be put at the disposal of any such children that my wife may have after my death."

Milton paused, then looked up. "Are there any questions?" he queried.

"When did Arthur sign that will, Mr Milton?" Sarah asked, her face pale, but her voice level and controlled.

"The day after Captain Kite sailed for Jamaica, ma'am."

"I see."

Milton folded the will and looked round. "I shall of course communicate with Captain Gray, Mrs Tyrell, as soon as that becomes possible."

"Yes, of course."

"May I ask something, ma'am?" They turned at the sound of Borthwick's voice.

"Of course, Mr Borthwick, what is it?"

"The question is to Mr Milton, ma'am, but closely concerns yourself."

"Well, sir," commanded Milton somewhat imperiously, "do go on."

"What is to happen about bringing the murderers of my late master to justice, sir?"

"It is a question that occurs to me too, sir," added Kite, lending weight to Borthwick's query.

"I think, sir, gentlemen, given the state of the country, we should find not a witness."

"But there were a hundred people . . ." Sarah breathed incredulously.

"You know it was Rathburne, do you not, sir?" Kite asked.

"I know only what I can get people to give as evidence in court, Captain Kite."

"I will give evidence in court," Kite said.

"I know, Captain, and perhaps, just perhaps, we might find another dozen brave souls to do the same, but you will find three times that number who will swear on oath that John Rathburne or any other person was at their house enjoying dinner or a game of faro."

"But what of the burning?"

"Oh, they will have seen a burning, they may have been among the numbers of men who turned out to fling buckets over the adjacent property to prevent the conflagration from spreading, but no one will admit to having seen Mr Tyrell, begging your pardon, ma'am, other than that he must have been within the warehouse when it caught fire and might himself have contributed to the ignition." Milton shook his head. "It will be the *Gaspée* affair all over again."

"So there is no redress?"

"You may try, Captain, but you will risk the most public and damaging humiliation." Milton looked pointedly at Borthwick and Ramsden. "If I might speak with you and Mrs Tyrell alone . . ."

"Of course, Mr Milton, I only wished to raise the matter out of respect for my late master." Borthwick rose, flustered and unhappy.

"That is quite understood, Mr Borthwick, and entirely to your credit. Your late master felt keenly that your loyalty was exemplary and he has provided for you most generously." It was a cruel and pointed dismissal, Kite thought, but if Borthwick felt it, he did not show it, as he led Bessie Ramsden from the room and closed the door behind them.

"I am sorry that Borthwick chose to raise the issue, ma'am," Milton said, turning to Sarah. "I was intending to touch upon the subject myself when we were alone. I have in fact some information that was laid before me this morning referring to this very fact." Milton shuffled the papers before him and lifted a single sheet of paper which had been folded as a sealed letter. "I shall not mince my words, for it pains me to be associated in any way with this sort of transaction, but this note," he held it up, "which is naturally unsigned, was delivered to me early this morning. It clearly states that any attempt to persuade the justices to pursue, and I quote, 'any line of enquiry which seeks to suggest the unfortunate death of the Tory merchant Arthur Tyrell was anything other than an accident, will not succeed'. As I said there is no signature, but there is a sub-scription which reads, 'By Order of the Committee of American Patriots of the State of Rhode Island', whoever, whatever and wherever that may be." He paused, then added, "By burying your husband, Mistress Tyrell, you have in part aided the Patriots' desire to have his death considered an accident. Now an inquest will be merely a formality, probably over within a few days and all but yourselves heartily glad of it." The attorney stopped again, allowing the import of his words to sink in.

Kite sighed. "It was my idea to have Tyrell buried immediately, the prospect of him lying—"

"No, it was not you, William. *I* wished it, you merely arranged it. That you anticipated my wishes is not important. This has been terrible, but I believe Arthur envisioned something like this occurring. Indeed," Sarah said, lowering her voice, "I might even consider that he precipitated it, for he was far from conciliatory to the radical faction."

Milton bowed his head in assent. "Sadly I think that is true, ma'am."

Sarah drew herself up. "Thank you, Mr Milton. There is much to be done. You will understand, I hope, that Arthur was aware that Captain Kite . . ." She held out her hand toward Kite and he crossed the room and took it, standing beside her as she confronted the attorney. "That Captain Kite and I are not . . ." She faltered, squeezing Kite's hand.

"Ma'am, I quite understand," Milton said hurriedly. "You and Captain Kite will forgive me if I say that few men could be immune from your attraction, Mrs Tyrell. May I congratulate you both."

"I'd be obliged if you will not fan whatever scandal is currently abroad, Mr Milton," Kite said. "This remains a matter of some delicacy, notwithstanding the provisions in the will which make it quite clear that nothing underhand was afoot behind Mr Tyrell's back."

"There is something more that I have to communicate with you, something of singular moment." Milton rummaged in his briefcase again and drew out a package wrapped in brown paper which he handed to Kite, who letting go of Sarah's hand took it, sat down again and reached into his pocket for his penknife. Cutting the sealed string, he noted the parcel was of a surprising weight and gave off a familiar chink. He began to unwrap it.

Inside the paper was a cloth which, once unfolded, revealed a small silver snuff box, two soft leather purses, one larger and heavier than the other, and a letter. Slitting the seal he unfolded and read Tyrell's neat and flowing hand out loud.

"'My dear Kite, you know the matter of which we spoke touching my wife, Sarah. I have given her into your charge because she' . . ."
He paused and looked from Sarah to Milton.

"Would you wish me to leave, ma'am?"

Sarah shook her head. "No, I am not ashamed of having a witness. Do go on, William."

"Very well. 'Because she has long regarded you with more than mere affection and, now that you too are alone in the world, I hope that you will find it in your heart to make her happy. Should either of you not consider this reasonable or practicable, should some rift come between you, I only ask that you do not part in anger. For this reason, beyond binding you to her insofar as your advice may help her, I have made no special provision in my will. You are not without means and I should not wish to sully a friendship and a business relationship with fiscal coercion which would, I know, be anathema to yourself. I therefore wish you to have my snuff box. It was a present from Mulgrave and is supposed to have been fashioned by a Spanish craftsman out of silver from the Inca mines. You are also to have my cane, my small sword and my brace of Cranston pistols. They are for duelling, but I have never had to use them. God grant that you do not, but the times are growing troubled and respect for order is being drowned by men who declare themselves Patriots. You are also to have the accompanying sum of money in the larger of the two purses, which, like the Cranstons, you may need for contingent expenses and are passed to you for that purpose. The smaller purse is to go to Sarah, should she need funds separate from your own. I wish you both God's blessings, and deem myself fortunate to have met you and to have fallen in with a man of . . . ' I am sorry, I cannot read any more. Anyway, he signs himself off in a flattering and, by me, undeserved manner."

The three sat in silence for a moment, then Kite said, tapping his hip, "I have already availed myself of his hanger."

It was a lame jest but served its purpose. Milton rose, "I will put matters in train directly, Mrs Tyrell."

"Thank you, Mr Milton. William, will you see Mr Milton out?"

When the attorney had gone Kite went back into the withdrawing room. "I am at a loss," he said. "Quite overwhelmed."

Sarah sat quite still, staring into the middle distance.

"Sarah," he said quietly. "Are you all right?"

She looked at him. "What does it mean, William, to feel all right? I hardly know." The she seemed to shake her head. "You will stay here tonight, will you not? I could not bear to be separated from you again."

He nodded. "Of course I will stay, Sarah. But excuse me a moment. Zachariah and Jacob are still in the kitchen and I must attend to a few matters relative to my cargo."

"Of course. Please, ask Bessie for some tea."

In the kitchen Kite found a merry scene round the fire. Although not yet three in the afternoon it was as cosy as Christmas Eve, with Jacob and Harper occupying the fireside settle and Mr Borthwick, clearly the worse for a swift imbibing of rum, leaning across the table over which Mrs Ramsden presided. Kite's entry produced a swift and guilty silence, but he was tolerant of their relaxation.

"I am sorry to disturb you, but Borthwick, can you tell me if any interest has been shown in our cargo?"

The clerk shook his head. "No, shur," he slurred, rousing himself. "I only had time to try two houses, but I don't think we will find anything diff'rent tomorrow."

"Sell direct to the distillery," Kite suggested, but Borthwick shook his head.

" 'Tis all shown up, shur," he went on. "The cargo's tainted goods . . . Shmells of the burning, shur. Take it to Boshton or New York."

Kite nodded. It was clear that he was going to make no progress tonight. He turned towards Harper and Jacob.

"Do you two get back to the ship. Tell Mr Corrie I'll be off in the morning."

"Aye, aye, sir." Harper rose, leant over and bussed Bessie Ramsden. "Thank you for the tea, Mrs Ramsden. You've a heart as big as my mother's, and no mistake." Jacob grinned widely and the two drew on their boots and coats. Then they left, a swirl of snow and cold air sweeping into the hot kitchen as they did so.

"Bessie, I don't think Mr Borthwick had better go home alone. Have we a bed we can put him in tonight?"

The housekeeper smiled. "Leave him to me, sir. Lord love you, sir, if the old master could see us now there'd have been some strong words said, and no mistake!"

Kite nodded. "Can you find something for us to eat? That ham was most tasty."

"You leave it to me, Captain Kite. You go and join Mistress Sarah and leave it to me . . ."

Kite rejoined Sarah in the withdrawing room, where he unbuckled Tyrell's hanger, laid it on a chair and made up the fire, waving aside Sarah's admonition that he should call one of the servant girls. "That isn't necessary, Sarah, I was making up fires before I even blacked boots."

"We are going to have to leave this place," she said, looking about her. "I do not want to stay here."

"No, I can understand that. I think the best course of action we can take is to try, once I have discharged this cargo, for a lading for Antigua. We will be close enough for the mail to allow us to settle your affairs here, while being away from all the fractious trouble that is brewing in this unhappy part of the world."

"Milton will sell the house; he may even buy it himself. He always admired it and told Arthur he liked it."

"There will be much of that sort of thing if people are terrorised for remaining loyal. Milton and his fence-sitting fraternity will pick all the cherries hanging in the garden."

"That is a quaint fancy," Sarah said.

"That is the first time I have seen you smile properly today, and I am very glad for it."

"And I am glad you are here, William. I keep trying to imagine what it would have been like without you."

And from the memories of the past hours they bent their thought to the future, making plans amid the strange circumstances of their present lives. They had adjourned to the chilly dining room to address the rump of Mrs Ramsden's ham when the pounding came on the door.

Kite opened it to find Jacob on the doorstep, his eyes wide with alarm.

"Sah, come quick! They am beating that damned drum again and Massah Harper says there will be more trouble!"

"Hold hard, Jacob!" Kite said, restraining the black man as he made to run off into the thick snow. "What is it to do with us?"

"We had just got to the wharf, sah, when we saw groups of men hanging about and smelled trouble. Mister Harper, he say, 'What's this? More trouble brewing?' and a man overheard him and told us, hadn't we heard, that damned English captain, he was going to get his come-uppance in real Rhode Island style. Mister Harper, he said that was one helluva good idea and nodded to me and I understood that I was to get back to you, sah."

"The ship," Sarah said, coming into the hall behind him. "They mean the ship, William. First the *Liberty*, then the *Gaspée*, now the *Wentworth*!"

Kite paused a moment, thinking fast. "Come in a moment, Jacob," he said, closing the door behind the negro, who stood dripping on the wooden floor. "Sarah, get me those pistols of Arthur's. Now, where did I put that sword?" He dashed into the withdrawing room, picked up the hanger and buckled it on. Emerging again into the hall he took his coat from the peg and drove his arms into it. "Where is the second mate now, Jacob? D'you know?"

"I reckon he'll be awaiting for us, sah."

But just then a knocking came again at the door and Jacob opened it to reveal the figure of Zachariah Harper. Even in the lamplight Kite could see the blacked eyes and the contusion about his face. Harper grinned. "There were three of 'em, sir. Only two ran away."

"There will be hell to pay if you've killed one of them," Kite said, then asked, "Any news?"

Harper nodded. "Yes, I'm afraid it looks as though they're assembling several boats. I think they're going to take the ship."

"God rot them!" Kite swore, jamming his hat upon his head as Sarah ran back down the stairs with the pistol barrels in her hands, offering him the butts.

"I've loaded them, William."

"Thank you." He took the pistols, checked the pans, closed the frizzens and stuck them in his waistband.

"Be careful, for God's sake," she said, but he bent and kissed her.

"I can't promise to be back, but lock and bar all the windows and doors. The password is 'Wentworth'." He turned to the two men. "Come, my lads!" he said, then opened the door and led them into the falling snow.

Sarah stood at the open door for a moment until they had disappeared into the swirling darkness. They she closed the door and locked it. Leaning her back against it for a few moments, she stilled her beating heart. The pace of events was overwhelming, but no one, neither Kite, nor herself, nor Bessie Ramsden, nor Borthwick, Milton, Jacob or the singularly ugly man named Zachariah, seemed to question what was already a fact: Captain Kite and the Widow Tyrell were already as one.

Ten

A Ship for Rhode Island

They stumbled through the thick snow almost blind, glad of its concealment, yet uncertain of their way, until Harper called for them to halt and they heard some drunken shouting which, in ten minutes, led them to the waterfront. Earlier, among the score or so of craft moored along the wharf, Harper had spotted a small rowing boat, too small for the gangs of Patriots that, if the noise was anything to judge by, were already pulling through the soft snowflakes towards the anchored ships.

"At least there will be no lack of warning," Kite said anxiously, as the other two scrambled down into the little boat.

"Aye, but John Corrie might think they're only revellers, sir," said Harper as he sorted the oars. "Christmas is not far off."

"Christmas?" queried Kite, pausing as he turned to step from the ladder into the wildly rocking boat. "I had forgotten about Christmas."

"We're ready, sir," Harper said. The second mate and Jacob had settled themselves on the two thwarts and each pulled a pair of oars.

"Very well, then let's cast off." Kite turned to get his bearings. The boat had no rudder and he would have to set their course from memory. "Give way together . . . Pull starboard . . . Now . . . pull evenly."

A moment later it was as if the world had disappeared. The boat surged along, floating on jet-black water in a tiny circumscribed area which was limited by the cold, pale and falling snow. As each white flake touched the surface of the sea, it vanished, but Kite took no interest in this. He was looking over his shoulder, trying to keep track of the wake and correct its deviation from what he tried to judge was a straight line in the direction to the ship. Somewhere ahead of him he could hear the noise of the Patriots and after a few moments he commanded: "Oars!"

Harper and Jacob raised the oar blades and held them horizontally as the boat carried her way through the water. Kite listened intently, trying to divine the direction of the *Wentworth* from any commotion, but the Patriots had fallen silent themselves.

"They'll have strung themselves out in a line abreast," Harper offered.

Kite nodded. "Just what I was thinking." They glided on in silence for a moment, his anxiety increasing with every passing second. Then, quite distinctly, they heard a shout which confirmed their supposition.

"Here she is!" the voice called, and there were several shouts as each boat identified its relationship with the locator of the *Wentworth*.

Kite was galvanised. "Give way! Pull starboard hard!"

Harper and Jacob laid back on their oars and the boat leapt through the water, the bow rising under the power of their strokes, with Kite in the sternsheets leaning forward as if he could impart impetus to their advance. Then he suddenly sensed something was wrong. A second later there seemed to be a huge black hole in the white curtain of snow as the hull of a vessel loomed out of the night. An instant later they struck her bow-on, the violence of the collision tumbling Jacob and Harper off their thwarts onto their backs. Kite was catapulted onto his knees in the sternsheets, striking his head on Harper's vacated thwart. The second mate lost his oars, and the boat's stem was sprung, so that as they ceased swearing and settled themselves again, Jacob exclaimed, "Boat's leaking, Cap'n!"

"God damn!" Kite said, but a voice above their heads interrupted.

"And what in tarnation may all you noisy buggers be up to running into this ship when any self-respecting Yankee would be tucked up in the lee of bum island?"

Kite settled his hat and looked up. A man's face stared down at them out of the darkness and a moment later another next to him held a light over the side. The assumption that they were part of the general uproar abroad on the waters of the harbour that night caused Kite to recollect himself. "We're looking for the English ship, the *Wentworth*."

"And what have the poor buggers over there done to upset your precious susceptibilities, then?"

"They're defying the Patriot Committee's regulations on the imports of tea."

"Are they indeed," the man drawled. "Well, well, and is that a lynching offence in Rhode Island? Well," he went on, not waiting for a reply, "she's not half a cable away on my larboard beam . . . I should hurry if I were you." The seaman nodded and they looked down to where a dark swirl of water, lit by the glimmer of the lantern, was just beginning to cover the bottom boards.

"Shove off, Jacob. Give way!"

They worked their way clumsily off the strange vessel's side. Jacob stowed one oar and he and Harper carried on with one oar each. Kite looked back and called out his thanks, recognising the schooner next to which he had anchored the *Wentworth* hours ago. As they rounded the bow with Harper holding water, they heard the noise of the attack. There were shouts and a pistol cracked in the darkness. Someone aboard the *Wentworth* was ringing the ship's bell rapidly as an alarm while above the uproar Kite clearly heard Corrie's voice calling all hands.

"Pull, damn you!" he shouted, but their progress was hampered by the rapid increase in the boat's weight as it filled and steadily lost buoyancy. Kite stared ahead, but could still see nothing beyond the white curtain and then, away to the left, he caught sight of a flash and a second gunshot sounded above the hubbub.

"She's filling fast, sir," Harper grunted between tugs at his oar.

"I know," Kite snapped and then he sensed the loom of the ship and hissed, "Hold water!" Over their heads raked the *Wentworth*'s bobstay, and as Harper and Jacob dug their oars into the sea Kite reached up and tried to stop them. The deceleration caused the water in the boat to rush forward and Jacob groaned as it rose round his legs.

"Up you go, Zachariah!" Kite commanded as he clung to the chain bobstay. Harper dropped his oar and Kite turned away as the second mate's feet momentarily kicked in his face and then disappeared into the darkness. "Now you, Jacob!"

Kite followed the quartermaster as the three men scrambled aboard over the bow and paused for a moment by the bitts to gather their wits. They could see the fight in the waist was already over. The Patriots had easily overwhelmed the

Wentworth's anchor watch. They, and the rest of the crew coming sleepily on deck at the summons for all hands, had been shepherded into a confused and disconsolate huddle by the mainmast. The Patriots not guarding the *Wentworth*'s crew were busy assembling lanterns and Kite could see Rathburne's face lit by one of these as he confronted John Corrie, his drawn sword scarcely an inch from the unfortunate mate's breast.

"Pipe down, the lot of you, and no harm will come to you," Rathburne was saying as Kite, drawing his own hanger, stormed aft and shoved his way through his cowed crew.

"Put up that weapon, Rathburne!" Kite brought his own sword blade up and his men surged forward. But his sudden emergence made no impression upon the imperturbable Rathburne, who merely held up his hand to stop any precipitate action by his own men. Calmly he turned his head to Kite and smiled. The next moment Kite felt the jar of sudden impact and the sword was struck from his hand and he, and not Corrie, was menaced by Rathburne's sword-tip.

Kite flushed with mortification as Rathburne rapped out his orders. "Get this mob into two boats and take them ashore. You may go with them, Captain Kite, and count yourself lucky that I am only seizing your ship."

"You have no right, damn you!"

"I have every right, Kite!" The rhyming remark produced a laugh from the Patriots, who immediately began to herd the *Wentworth*'s crew over the side. The lantern light jumped erratically from one face to another as Kite felt a rising tide of furious impotence.

"You cannot treat these men with such inhumanity, Rathburne – let them at least take their personal effects!"

"We will send what we do not require ashore in the morning," Rathburne said dismissively, sheathing his sword. Then he bent and quickly picked up Kite's sword, grasped the blade in both hands and snapped it smartly across his knee. Holding the two parts out to Kite he said, "You should not carry one of these unless you can use it, Captain Kite. It is a gentleman's weapon."

Kite kept a level head. "I shall ask you formally, Rathburne, by what right and for what purpose have you boarded my ship?"

"I am not answerable to you, Kite. I am requisitioning this ship for Rhode Island."

"What? Does Rhode Island have a navy?" Kite scoffed.

"It does now, Kite. Now get over the side while I still have my temper and thank God that you are a man of small significance."

Stung to the quick by Rathburne's cool arrogance, Kite said, "You are a murderer and a pirate—" But he bit his tongue as the tip of Rathburne's sword raked his cheek.

"There, sir, is a mark for you, where once Mistress Tyrell struck you to the amusement of the townsfolk. You may tup her, *Captain* Kite, as the pleasure takes you, for she is as mad a bitch as ever came on heat. But every time you shave, sir, you will recall how John Peck Rathburne fucked you! Now get over the side!"

It had stopped snowing when Kite woke and the humiliations of the night crowded into his recollection. A brilliant sunshine shone through the imperfectly pulled curtains and he sat up, his cheek drawn and scabbed from Rathburne's sword cut. Touching it he groaned with discomfort that was more moral than physical.

"You are awake." Sarah turned from the dressing table where she sat before the mirror in her satin robe, brushing her luxuriant dark hair.

"I am ruined," he said shortly, trying to recall the extent of their intimacy the previous night and then, seeing the blood-soaked shirt and neck linen thrown over the back of a chair, remembering his abject homecoming. He had been exhausted and, having had his wound cleaned up, for the intense cold had stopped the bleeding, he had been helped to bed and recalled only falling into the softness of Sarah's mattress before oblivion claimed him.

"Oh, God . . . They have the upper hand so completely . . . They have taken the ship, Sarah." He ran his fingers through his tangled hair. "What the devil are we to do? We are besieged here, damn them."

"John Rathburne sent three men here this morning about an hour ago. They have brought a portmanteau full of your effects. Your man Ben is below in the kitchen with that ugly fellow Zachariah, the negro and another man named John."

"Corrie?"

"Yes." She skilfully wound her hair into a tight knot and, lancing it to the top of her head, began to assume the cool and elegant poise that he so admired. "The rest of your men were put into a barn for the night."

"That is most kind of the Patriots," Kite said with a vicious and hopeless sarcasm. He threw off the bed sheets and rose, fumbling behind the sidescreen as he urinated into the chamber pot concealed behind it.

"I will send for hot water," Sarah said.

"We must go to Antigua," he said, emerging from the screen, "but first I would lodge a formal complaint with the Governor."

"That will do little good," Sarah replied. "Listen to me. I have been up most of the night and have considered our situation in the wake of what has happened and what I know of matters hereabouts. We have no place here, the Patriots will see to that. It would not matter that we declared ourselves the most ardent admirers of Sam Adams and John Hancock, that we hated King George and drank daily to his damnation, they would never believe us. What titles we have in law will be overturned the instant they begin the rebellion."

"They are intending to *rebel*?" Kite paused as he tucked his shirt-tails into his breeches. It was as though the actual import of what he had been involved in had only just fully occurred to him in the aftermath of the taking of the *Wentworth*.

"You think all this is some kind of childish prank?" Sarah asked in astonishment. "For years these people have committed acts of provocation to one purpose, to goad the authority of the Crown. Today, tomorrow, who knows when? Oh, William, you know perfectly well what this is."

He nodded reluctantly. "Yes. Yes, I do now. In the abstract, as touching the lives of others it was of no great personal moment but now . . . now it is very different."

"And do you wish the seizure of the *Wentworth* to be a *casus belli*? I do not want the murder of my husband to tear this otherwise pleasant place apart!"

"Have you no thoughts of vengeance?"

"On the few, yes. But not on the many. For those who like sheep baaed at Arthur's terrible end I have only contempt, William." Her eyes blazed as she regarded him, half turning on the stool before the dressing table. He was almost choked by the intensity of her passion and her beauty. Moved, he held out his hands.

She rose and came towards him. "We will take our revenge in due course, at a time of our own choosing, William."

He nodded and looked down at her. "I have not been very gallant, have I?"

She shook her head and took his hands. "No, sir, you have not," she said, her mood suddenly lighter. "You wallowed in my bed and this morning, you rose and took a piss in my jordan as though you had every right to be in my bedchamber." She was smiling. "In fact, Captain Kite, your behaviour has been monstrous and you should hang your head in shame."

But he could not match her flippancy. "Oh, Sarah, I have far more than you know to hang my head in shame over. I was disarmed by that man Rathburne on the quarterdeck of my own ship in the most humiliating manner."

"So, sir, your own loss of honour is greater than mine, is it?" she asked with mock severity.

"That is not what I mean."

She put her finger on his lips. "I know, my dear, but please right one wrong before you seek a more conspicuous and public satisfaction. You have only to ask . . ."

It took Kite a moment to comprehend her innuendo and then he threw off as much of his megrimmed mood as he could and dropped to his knees. He looked up at her. "It is too short a time for either prudence or convention, Mistress Tyrell, but what has convention to do with our present situation? You must therefore forgive me all my monstrous presumptions, I beg. Will you therefore consent to do me the honour of becoming my wife?"

She drew him up and they kissed. He felt the urgent pleasure of his arousal and pushed her backwards towards the invitingly rumpled bed, but she drew away smiling broadly, his blood smeared across her cheek. "Not now, William. You forget I have ordered you hot water."

"I am sorry, I had indeed forgot."

And as if she had been waiting outside – and perhaps she had, thought Kite – Bessie Ramsden knocked and brought in a large ewer of piping hot water. After she had gone and Kite bent over the steaming bowl, stripped to his waist and luxuriating in the perfume of Sarah's soap, he heard her say, "We may publish our banns in Boston, William, and marry there."

"After which we must go to Antigua." Kite said, picking up

a razor laid out for him, a distant look in his eyes. "That is our only chance."

"And shall we live in Antigua? I am not certain that I want to live in the Antilles. What shall you do? Go to sea and leave me alone in a strange place?"

He broke off shaving and looked at her, as though suddenly having to encompass her in his plans which were still full of revenge and the longing to obtain redress from Rathburne. "If you are right, my love, and rebellion breaks out in New England, much ill may befall us. You yourself said we have no place here, and we could return to Liverpool." He rinsed his razor and wiped his face, straightening up and turning towards her. "Sarah," he said, "it may be unwise to marry in Boston, or indeed anywhere . . ."

"But why?"

Kite reached for his shirt and wrinkled his nose at its soiled state. Sarah rose and, her face set, opened a drawer and drew out a clean shirt and stock. "Please, use these. But why should we not marry? I have just accepted your proposal," she concluded flatly.

"Because I would not make you so soon a widow twice."

She picked up his dirty linen and rounded on him angrily. "For God's sake, do not play games with my heart! Why should that be so?"

"Rathburne may kill me."

"Then he would have to kill both of us." Sarah said with finality.

"Come, Sarah, that is not logical."

"If I were to come to sea with you it would be perfectly logical."

"But you do not know what you ask."

"Puella accompanied you, did she not?"

"Yes, at the beginning."

"Well, we are at the beginning and I cannot play the role of passive wife any longer in these turbulent times. Think what being Arthur's spouse has meant to me, William, these last thirteen odd years. I am but four and thirty."

"Beg pardon, my love, but the sea life is nothing like anything you have experienced. Besides, having you with me will deprive me of my spirit, for I will be constantly anxious about your safety."

"Are the anxieties of being master of such a dimension? Why, I know of wives in Newport and Providence who accompany their husbands to sea. They are strong women, full of courage, but I do not think them my superiors in spirit."

"But you are a lady, Sarah, and besides . . ." Kite tailed off, taking up the clean crisp linen that had been Arthur Tyrell's.

"And besides," Sarah prompted, "you are concealing something from me."

"No, I have not yet revealed it to you."

"Then do not prevaricate. What is your purpose in returning to sea, if not to trade?" And then the thought occurred to her and she asked frowning, "You cannot mean you intend to seek a commission in the King's service?"

"Join the Royal Navy? No, no." Kite sat and pulled on his left boot. Then he pulled on the other while Sarah put her hands on her hips and shook her head.

"For God's sake, William, tell me what is on your mind and which, it seems, you are too terrified to admit for fear that I will faint, or something. I assure you that I shall not. I have learned to have a strong stomach, one that I venture to suggest may even tolerate the perils of the deep."

Kite stood and stamped his feet into his boots. "Very well, Sarah. But you must understand that if you wish to delay our marriage as a consequence . . ."

"Tell me, confound you!"

"I own another vessel, the schooner *Spitfire*. Do you recall her?"

"How could I forget," Sarah murmured.

"She is in the Antilles and, should matters go as we anticipate, there is every possibility of fitting her as a—"

"A privateer. Of course. I should have thought of it myself. They will issue letters of marque to put an end to Colonial trade and if you do not fit out your ships as privateers you will have lost all chances of profit, for you will not be trading with rebellious colonies tomorrow any more than rebellious colonies will trade with you today!"

Kite nodded. "I see you understand me perfectly. As for yourself . . ."

"But you do not understand *me*, William. I shall come with you in *Spitfire*. I can acquire such skills as may make me useful. I shall be an apt pupil, I promise."

Kite paused in the act of drawing on his coat. It no longer had any pretence at being smart, but it would have to do. "There is no doubt in your mind, is there?"

"None whatsoever. Our souls were linked long ago, William, when our fates were intertwined. This is but the outcome."

They embraced and Kite asked, "And shall our bodies find a compatibility of such a niceness, Sarah Tyrell?"

"Only while our minds remain in such perfect harmony," she breathed, adding, "but not yet, William, not just yet. I must shake the dust," she paused, "and the ashes of this place from my feet."

"To Boston, then. Milton may find us there with his papers and deeds. Shall you have him sell this place?"

"Yes. Or Rathburne's Patriots will burn it."

"I think not. Rathburne's ambitions may be such as to tempt him to sequester it. In the name of Patriotism, of course."

"Of course."

Part Three

Vengeance

Eleven

A Cargo of Flour

"My dear friends," Wentworth said, smiling broadly and bending over Sarah's bosom until his wife's disapproving eye burnt into his back, "I have excellent news for which I know you have been waiting these past weeks."

"When is she due?" Kite asked, leaping up at Wentworth's awaited arrival.

"Patience, patience." Wentworth settled himself in his chair and accepted the tea his wife passed him. "'Tis unpleasantly humid today, don't you think, Mrs Kite?"

"I think, sir, that were you sitting as close to my husband as you are to me you would judge it to be getting hotter by the moment."

"Oh, you do treat me so damnably bad, Mrs Kite," Wentworth said, pulling a face.

"But not as badly as I shall, sir," remarked Mrs Wentworth with as much forced humour as she could muster. "Nor as badly as Captain Kite," she added looking up at Kite.

"And do you sit down, Kite, please. Matters are very trying at present, with all the uncertainty in Boston; I pray you don't add to my troubles by standing up and waving your arms about in that remonstrating manner."

"I am not waving my arms about, Wentworth."

"No, but you look as though you might be in a moment or two."

"For God's sake, Wentworth, what is the news of the *Spitfire*? When is she due?"

"Sit down, and I shall tell you!" said Wentworth brightly.

"He is teasing you, Captain," Mrs Wentworth explained. "He is like a child when the fancy takes him. You have no recourse but to excuse him."

Wentworth turned to Sarah. "Do you think me like a child, Mrs Kite?"

"*Very* like a child, sir."

"There," sighed Wentworth, "then I shall sulk like a child."

"And Captain Kite will have to beat you like a child," Mrs Wentworth added, not without a hint of glee, as if in expectation. She nodded at Kite, who had sat down but remained poised expectantly on the edge of his chair. The banter was amusing to a degree, but the long weeks of waiting in Antigua had not been an unblemished pleasure and the constant presence of Captain and Mrs William Kite had strained relations with Mrs Wentworth. Her husband did not greatly care – whether he noticed anything amiss is to be doubted – but Sarah seemed to have swept down out of a New England winter with an overwhelmingly cool elegance that even the heat of Antigua could not melt. The round of social engagements with which Mrs Wentworth had at first encouraged them to occupy themselves had palled once it was obvious that the men of St John's, and in particular the officers of the garrison, were profoundly sensible of Mrs Kite's wonderfully voluptuous charms. Having been herself a garrison lady during her first marriage, Mrs Wentworth began to perceive that she was eclipsed by Sarah. This, and other petty differences, all of which demonstrated the plain fact that the two wives had absolutely nothing in common, produced a coolness between them.

Kite himself was sick of idleness. At their departure from Newport, he had not thought the months would have passed so slowly nor so little have been achieved. Having seen Sarah and those of her servants who wished it removed into Boston, he had paid off the *Wentworth*'s crew from his own private funds, obtaining a half-hearted promise from a few of them that if and when he returned there in the *Spitfire* they would rejoin him. He had told them he would be pleased if they did so but, so uncertain were the times, he urged them to look after their own interests first. He had other matters with which to preoccupy himself and Sarah; his return in *Spitfire* seemed to be too distant to worry about.

The settlement of Sarah's affairs, and the winding up of her interests in her late husband's business, proved a long-winded matter. Twice they had had to leave their lodgings in Boston and ride back to Newport to sign documents at Milton's chambers, a trip that was far from pleasant, given the inflamed mood of the countryside.

To their more personal satisfaction and dispensing with the prolonged tedium of formal mourning, they had published their banns in Boston and married quietly, sustained by their self-preoccupation as lovers through the tedium and imperfections of their long-enforced exile. Neither of them liked Boston, nor did they enter into society in any sense, though Sarah had several friends among the town's population with whom they occasionally dined. The newly-weds were in no position to reciprocate, nor did they feel moved to foster acquaintanceship amid the prevailing atmosphere of uncivilised disorder that dominated Boston. The majority of the citizenry inveighed by one means or another against British tyranny, with broadsheets, newspapers and street-corner gossip everywhere encouraging civil disobedience against the authority of the Crown. Evidence of this was produced at every turn, but centred chiefly upon the troops bivouacked on Boston Common. Such winter quarters contrasted badly with the cosy homes of the Bostonians, and while their officers managed to secure lodgings the common soldiers shivered in their tents, for it was as much a matter of principle for the Bostonians to refuse tea, as to refuse payment for billeting private infantrymen.

Kite had seen Samuel Adams once and had thought of seeking a confrontation with him over the *Wentworth*, but he had been prevented by Sarah, who counselled caution and inconspicuity until they again better controlled their own affairs. Nevertheless they once dined with Governor Hutchinson through the agency of a friend of the Tyrells', and Kite laid before him the circumstances of the illegal seizure of the *Wentworth*. Hutchinson promised "to see what could be done", but Kite soon realised that the man was losing his powers thanks to the damaging effect of revelations from his private correspondence, which had fallen into the wrong hands and had been maliciously circulated by the Patriot party during the previous year. Moreover, rumours were circulating that Hutchinson's civil authority would soon pass to General Thomas Gage, the military commander, and in May these predictions came to pass when it was known that Hutchinson was to sail for England.

To add to their personal uncertainty, it soon became clear that no one in Newport was going to bid for the Tyrells' house, as Kite had guessed. Though unwilling to do so, he and Sarah decided to offer it to Milton at a peppercorn rent, to prevent it falling into the hands of Rathburne or his ilk. With what Kite afterwards described as "a touching display of affected reluctance", the attorney finally agreed to taking a lease on the property in November and Mrs Ramsden had agreed to stay on in the house pending Milton's decision as to whether to remove himself into it or to acquire suitable tenants.

As for the Kites, having spent Christmas of 1773 trudging the streets of Boston seeking lodgings, they were in more comfortable circumstances a year later. Inviting some company to join them in a modest dinner party in their lodgings, they repaid some of the kindness and hospitality they had benefited from themselves. Kite had written to Wentworth, outlining his intentions, but he had replied that until a state of rebellion broke out, "a circumstance I very much doubt will occur, such a thing being so contrary to good sense and so damaging to trade", he could and would employ the *Spitfire* in a profitable manner. "She is not a vessel of any great capacity, but her speed makes her useful," he had added, concluding his reply with the remark that, "there is such a great deal of money to be made at the moment that I should be reluctant to relinquish the vessel and in view of your loss of the uninsured *Wentworth*, it would not be in your interest to curtail her useful voyages for three months at the earliest."

The remark had raised no apprehensions in Kite's mind at the time. He had become reconciled to frustration; inertia begets inertia and he had discovered great pleasure and diversion in Sarah's love-making. Nor did she seem unduly troubled; for her the long years of devoted but lacklustre marriage could at last be set aside and she found Kite a man of consistent and pleasing energy. Otherwise, to combat ennui and to wipe out the shame of his disarming by Rathburne, Kite had taken fencing lessons from a rather indigent army officer who, for a little private income to fund his habit at the gaming tables, gave private tuition. Most of his clientele were Tory gentlemen aware that a nodding acquaintance with self-defence might come in handy in the coming months. Under this tutelage Kite had rapidly improved his elementary technique, learned as a boy with a single-stick.

It had been late March before the transactions were concluded that terminated the business enterprise of Tyrell and Co. The residual property and assets had been transferred to Borthwick, Borthwick and Co., established by Tyrell's chief clerk and his brother, a sea captain from Providence. Kite, having managed to make himself useful to the extent of acting as agent for a number of Boston merchants who were anxious about the future, was at last ready to leave for Antigua and had secured a passage aboard the brig *Savage*. He had carried south to the West Indies a number of commissions undertaken on behalf of several parties, carrying letters of credit to Wentworth and others in Antigua, and securing measures to prevent losses if and when a run on the banking houses was precipitated by the breakdown of order which most now foresaw as inevitable.

Once at sea and caught up in the familiar routine of shipboard life, Kite wondered why he had delayed so long, swiftly forgetting the interminable wait for correspondence referring to all the complexities of Sarah's affairs. In the manner common to attorneys, Milton proved unused, even resistant, to haste. Nor did Sarah wish to leave until every possible knot had been tied and she could depart free of regrets or obligations. After a week enduring the agonies of seasickness, Sarah had found her sea-legs and began to take an interest in her new surroundings. Kite, having nothing to do, had taken the opportunity to school her in the business of the ship, the principles of navigation and of elementary sea lore.

Free of the frenetic atmosphere of Boston and her nausea, the *Savage*'s passage south had proved a congenial hiatus for her. At Antigua, however, further and seemingly interminable enforced idleness combined with anxiety and uncertainty to erode her belief in a future and in Kite's purposeful equanimity. Such had been the pressures of their existence in Boston that she had assumed that once they reached the Antilles a new existence would unfold. He assumed matters would move ahead swiftly, but he learned to his chagrin that *Spitfire* had only just departed and would be gone for many weeks. Having learned this he had at first made no further enquiries, reconciling himself to another wait and explaining matters to an increasingly impatient Sarah. Neither of them now enjoyed a rootless existence, and while their sojourn in Boston had been endured as a finite exile spiced with the novelty of their intimacy, they were irked by their life in Antigua as "guests" forced upon the Wentworths' hospitality.

To these irritating circumstances came the exacerbation of new uncertainty with the news from Massachusetts concerning the events of the 19th of April 1775. British troops sent out from Boston to seize illegal arms caches in Concord township had been opposed by militia drawn up on Lexington Green. The redcoats had dispersed the inexperienced "Minutemen" and marched on, but they had found little in the way of arms at their destination and having spoiled quantities of flour and other alleged "military stores" had began to march back to Boston. This proved to be a very different ordeal, and their return had been harried by highly effective sniper fire from every building on their long route, a profound humiliation for a detachment of British infantry.

For the Patriot party, the day marked not simply a victory over a British "army", but the long-awaited spark to the assiduously laid powder train of popular rebellion. For the men who had harried the British soldiers had not all been radical fanatics, but solid Americans for whom the British excursion into the countryside had been an outrage. In the ensuing weeks such men were coming in from far and wide to dig entrenchments cutting off Boston and transforming the town from the hot-bed of rebellion, to the beleaguered centre of royal authority in New England. Such news arriving in St John's only made William Kite grind his teeth in impotent frustration. He resumed his fencing, taking as a partner Nathan Johnstone who had been mysteriously absent on their first arrival.

Kite had had his first opportunity of speaking confidentially with his former clerk one afternoon as they had rested after a practice bout in a cleared area in the counting house where once as a young man he had lodged. Prompted, Johnstone revealed his own adventures. "I grew tired of Kitty," he said, "and somewhat ashamed of my conduct with respect to Mr Wentworth, who is a decent enough man when all is said and done."

"How did you detach yourself from Mistress Wentworth?"

"I spoke with her husband and suggested that I shipped with Captain Jones to better learn the ropes and see Havana, Guadeloupe, Basse-terre, Jamaica, St Kitt's and so forth." Johnstone smiled sheepishly at the recollection. "He jumped at the notion. I rather think he knew all the time what I was up to – the lady is insatiable, if you'll pardon me for saying so, but it is so undignified in one of her years – and perhaps he had sharpened his own appetites after a period of fasting . . ."

Kite laughed. "Yes, I recall she tried to seduce me once."

"Besides, I had become something of a laughing-stock among the garrison," Johnstone confessed.

"Ah, that I can imagine."

"Well, I removed myself into the schooner for some time, sailed with Jones and visited most of the islands while I have become a tolerable seaman as well. Then I acted as Wentworth's agent in St Maarten until –" Johnstone shrugged – "well, I returned here, delighted to find you back and, if I may say so, sir, so pleasantly circumstanced."

"I think you will find me a less tolerant husband than Wentworth."

"Captain Kite," Johnstone said hurriedly, "please believe I am not that devoid of honour that I would ever, in any circumstances . . . well . . . I mean to say, the matter is unthinkable."

Kite looked archly at the younger man, who had changed since they had last met. "Come, Nathan, let us lay on and see who first scores five."

" 'Twill be you, sir, you have the art to a nicety."

They came *en garde* again and the scrape and clatter of their buttoned foils filled the still warm air of the tropical afternoon.

Such diversions, though pleasant enough, were not satisfactory to the impatient Kite. The mock victories he achieved over Johnstone he wanted translated into real success; the defeats he suffered at Johnstone's hands became small, prickling reminders of Rathburne's unopposed run of luck. He wanted no proxy wins, he wanted blood and ruin to descend upon Rathburne and his vile gang of murderers and incendiaries and this perverse lust began increasingly to fill his being as the weeks dragged by during the long wait for news of the *Spitfire*'s return. It was for this reason that he grew so agitated when at long last that hot afternoon Wentworth walked up from the harbour and announced that he had at last received news of the *Spitfire*.

In that impatient moment he was far from considering Mrs Wentworth's suggestion that he beat his old friend as a joke. "By God, madam, that is a capital idea!" he cried. "Come now, Wentworth, cease your damned games."

Wentworth bent as though cowed. "Oh, oh, help, help," he pleaded in a squeaky voice, "please, Captain Kite, don't flog me!"

"Wentworth . . ." Kite cautioned, an edge to his voice and his face far from seeing the ridiculous and amusing side of Wentworth's conduct.

"She's just come into the harbour," Wentworth announced in a sudden rush, recovering his dignity.

"*What?*" roared Kite. "You have taken all this while to tell me she is already here?"

"Hold hard, Kite, I have asked Jones to come up to the house the moment he has completed his clearances, so you will have to wait an hour or so longer. Sit down, for pity's sake, and possess your benighted soul in patience." He turned to his wife. "Is there perhaps another cup of tea for a thirsty and abused messenger, my dear?"

Wentworth grinned at Kite, then leaned towards Sarah. "Do, I beg you, Mrs Kite, soothe the ingrate," he implored mockingly.

Wentworth's reference marked the strain in the relationship between the two men. Kite had known for some weeks that the delay in *Spitfire*'s arrival had been caused by Wentworth having sent Jones out on the last of several slaving voyages. He had promised Puella he would never again personally profit from such an enterprise and he was exceedingly angry that Wentworth had done so on his behalf. Untroubled by moral considerations of this delicate nature, and bowing only to the imperatives of the market-place, Wentworth had waved aside his objection, justifying his act on the grounds that Kite had "distracted himself on the American coast with no very clear indication of his intentions relative to the *Spitfire*". This, he had claimed, left him free to employ the vessel in the manner he deemed most profitable to the *Spitfire*'s owner. Since the voyage had proved highly profitable, he was unable to comprehend how Kite felt he had the slightest grounds for complaint. He had no idea that Kite would suddenly want his vessel back "on a whim". Kite did not argue; it was enough that she was safe and would be at his disposal. Indeed his principal preoccupation was what he would do with Captain Jones, now that the man had regained his self-confidence along with the habit of command.

In the event, this problem never arose. Jones had made sufficient money to take a small house into which he installed a handsome quadroon with whom he declared he wished to "relax, at least until the coming hurricane season was past, and perhaps for longer".

"'Tis the languor of his tropical blood," Wentworth had explained with a singular lack of insight and a good deal of prejudice. Kite was not disposed to argue the point. Instead in a burst of released energy he hastily removed every trace of the *Spitfire*'s slaving voyage, constantly aware that in the mahogany-built *Wentworth*, Rathburne and the Rhode Islanders had, as they might themselves say, "gotten themselves a tarnation fine little man-o'-war at a real Yankee bargain price". Refitting and rearming *Spitfire*, he made of her not merely a private ship of war, but a privateer bent on a most private mission.

He received assistance from an unexpected source, Nathan Johnstone, who volunteered to join the ship.

"A privateering voyage," Kite explained, "is in the nature of a speculation. I cannot afford to pay you."

Johnstone waved these considerations aside. "I shall, if you will permit me, venture a little capital and ask that you take me as a gentleman volunteer. I have no desire to remain longer among the islands and to serve with you for a few months will take me north to –" he shrugged – "who knows what?"

"Very well," Kite agreed. "I shall make you gunner. You may take charge of the arms chest, the powder and the shot, along with the guns."

Johnstone nodded with satisfaction. "That seems a very sufficient inventory for a clerk," he said, smiling, as the two men shook hands.

"Now I suppose I must show you the principle of a magazine."

"It might be of use, certainly."

In the last few days of refitting the schooner, Kite felt a mild sensation of panic as the news arrived from Massachusetts. The investment of Boston by rebellious Americans was, it was claimed, of such a provocative and forward nature that General Gage must soon evacuate the town or utterly defeat the rebels. British fortunes in New England now hung, like the Damoclean sword, by a single thread. It was enough. Shipping a quantity of powder and shot and placing it in Johnstone's prepared lazaretto, Kite loaded *Spitfire* with rum and a consignment of imported flour, and on Wednesday the 17th of May 1775 the schooner sailed from St John's, heading for New England.

"I cannot pretend that I am not glad to see them go, my dear," Kitty Wentworth said pointedly, slipping her arm inside that of her portly husband and falling into step with him as he took a turn on their terrazzo as the sun set. "We can enjoy our own and the island's society again now." She paused, threw him a quizzical look and observed, "Your friend Kite is much changed, and not for the better, I am afraid."

Wentworth stopped and turned to his wife. "I fear the same must be said of *his* friend Johnstone. Come, my dear, tell me if you love your husband. Do you?"

"Of course I do," she replied coyly.

"Come then . . ." He took her hand and led her hurriedly into the house, shutting the chamber of their bedroom door and swinging round on her. "Come, madam, I have an urgent need of you!" he said, taking off his coat and kicking off his shoes.

"My dear, you are all haste, surely a little tenderness . . ."

"Devil take it, you have been hot for him for weeks! Ever since you quenched Johnstone." Wentworth advanced on his wife who backed towards the bed, half alarmed and half acquiescent. "Now let me show you what manner of man I can be when my wife is aroused . . ."

"Oh, sir!" she exclaimed, laughing, seeing his engorged state spring from the confinement of his breeches as she fell back upon the bed and lifted her skirts. "It has been some time!"

"Aye, madam, and we shall be glad of their visit if only for this moment . . . of – rapture at – their – departure . . ."

Kite and his wife found Boston a very different place from what it had been but three months earlier. It was now a town under formal siege, with rebel positions straddling the narrow isthmus of the Neck and cutting off communications with the rest of New England. The harbour, overlooked by Dorchester Heights in the south and Bunker and Breed's Hill in the north, was full of shipping. A handful of Royal Naval cruisers, a number of military transports and numerous merchant vessels, both American and British owned, all lay at anchor below the commanding heights.

If Boston had seemed to be full of soldiers before, it was now stuffed to overflowing, British troop reinforcements having arrived during Kite's absence. The contrast was marked by more than a mere increase in numbers, for where before the troops had tended to distance themselves from the hostile townsfolk, now this augmentation seemed to empower the troops, so that they were less self-effacing and conducted themselves with a certain swagger. Kite marvelled at this, particularly among the young subalterns, seeing that since the colonists had so effectively chivvied the British infantry back into Boston after their sally towards Lexington and Concord in April, and had since then prevented them from repeating the exercise. The besieging of Boston by a hay-seed army of militia seemed to him to be a humiliation to which the gay young officers seemed indifferent. Moreover, he soon realised that Boston was short of every necessity and was filled with more than the hungry mouths of several thousand extra soldiers. In fact Boston's political colour had been changed dramatically, for men and women too terrified of the Patriot party to remain in the surrounding countryside had come to seek refuge under the bayonets of the King's soldiers and this wretched population now optimistically awaited the exertions of General Gage and his army to restore them to their homes.

Making his way to the Commander-in-Chief's headquarters after attending to the usual inward formalities at the Custom House, Kite reflected upon the increasingly desperate situation. At the Custom House the Collector's clerk had brought the newly arrived ship-master up to date with the situation and then assured him of a profitable sale of his cargo, particularly if he permitted his own brother to act as agent in order to avoid the painful consequences of government requisition.

"I do assure you, Captain Kite, that between ourselves there is an eager market with payment in ready money for flour, but you must not delay. Once your inwards clearance is processed you may well have to surrender the lot for a pittance."

"Tell me," Kite countered, "have letters of marque and reprisal been issued against the rebels?"

The clerk looked astonished. "No, sir." He dropped his voice to a confidential tone. "There is a marked reluctance on the part of General Gage to admit that a state of open rebellion exists, let alone war!"

"Good God, sir! You mean to tell me that these hostile preparations don't signify?"

"No, sir, they don't. Only two days ago, on the twelfth, the General issued a proclamation offering a free pardon to every person in the province with the exception of John Hancock and Samuel Adams."

"Which fell on deaf ears, no doubt," Kite commented drily.

"Indeed it did, Captain. But if you wish to dispose of your cargo . . ."

"Yes, yes." Kite frowned, thinking for a moment and then asked for directions to General Gage's headquarters. With an assurance to the Custom House clerk that he would let him know directly about the disposal of his cargo he hurried out into the street.

There was an appearance of military activity outside Province House, Gage's headquarters. The open doorway was guarded by two sentries, both wearing the tall caps of men from a grenadier company, while two orderlies held the nervous heads of five officers' chargers. Just as he approached, one of these men grabbed the reins of a sixth horse as it galloped up and its rider slid to the ground and threw them to the orderly. The young scarlet-clad officer fumbled in his saddlebags as the brilliant June sunshine twinkled off the silver crescent of the gorget at his throat. Having drawn out of his saddlebag the bundle of papers he had brought to headquarters, the young man strode up the steps two at a time. Kite made to follow but one of the sentinels barred his way with his musket.

"I have dispatches for General Gage," he lied, adding with more truth, "I am Captain Kite, master of the schooner *Spitfire*."

The soldier looked at him and the briefcase that contained his inwards clearance papers. "Where are these despatches from then, Captain?" he asked with a truculent and suspicious air as his fellow sentry came over, but a voice behind them interrupted.

"Good God! Is that you, Uncle William?"

Both sentries snapped to attention as the officer who had preceded Kite into the dark interior of the requisitioned house retraced his steps. Kite looked from the unco-operative visage of his interlocutor into the good-looking and sunburnt face of Harry Makepeace.

"Good God, Harry! What the devil are you doing here? I thought you had taken a seat in Parliament."

"Long story, but come in, come in." Makepeace waved the sentries away and led Kite through the hallway and into a withdrawing room given over to acting as the ante-room to the adjutant-general's office. "I heard the names 'Kite' and '*Spitfire*' and well, here you are . . . Do you have despatches for the General?"

Kite shook his head. "No, not exactly, but I'd like to see a senior military officer, if you can arrange it. I dare say your own mission warrants a quick entry . . ."

Makepeace laughed. "These?" He held up the papers from his saddlebag. "These, dear uncle, are the daily returns from my regiment. They represent the extent to which military duty is entrusted to a mere captain of infantry in Boston these days," he said ironically.

"I did not know you possessed any great military knowledge capable of more fitting employment, Harry," Kite responded with equal irony and a smile.

Makepeace assumed a serious face and like the Custom House clerk an hour earlier dropped his voice. "Even a young fool just out from England with reinforcements for his regiment and a purchased captaincy knows it is utter folly to allow those damned rebels to dig themselves in and surround Boston. Why, they'll be up on Dorchester Heights and Bunker Hill before Gage—"

"Captain Makepeace!"

"Sir?" Makepeace turned. An officer had opened the door of an inner room. He wore the lace of a major and his outstretched right hand was ink-stained.

"I am waiting for your battalion's daily muster *again!*"

"Major Hayward," Makepeace said with plausible aplomb and turning to indicate Kite, "this is Captain Kite of the schooner *Spitfire*; he has urgent business with the adjutant-general . . ."

"Not as urgent as yours will be if you don't hand over your papers."

"Come, Hayward," said Makepeace, winking at Kite as he handed the papers over, "there is no need to be unpleasant just because you owe me twenty guineas."

"I shall whip your arse at the cart's tail if you are insolent, Makepeace. This is an army headquarters, not a gaming house."

"More's the pity, but what about Captain Kite here?"

"*What* about Captain Kite?" asked Hayward, looking down and studying the muster lists Makepeace had given him.

"I want a letter of marque and reprisal for my schooner, sir, from the Commander-in-Chief in his capacity as Governor of Massachusetts," put in Kite boldly.

"You have twenty-six men sick in the 59th, Makepeace." Hayward looked up at him, ignoring Kite's interjection.

"Some sort of flux, sir. Nothing serious, the surgeon says."

"Fat lot he'll know about it," Hayward said, looking at Kite for the first time and frowning. "What did you say?"

Kite repeated his request adding, "I've a cargo of excellent flour that I shall be pleased to trade for such a commission."

Hayward started, grasping the import of Kite's words. "You want a commission for your schooner to act as a privateer in exchange for your cargo, is that correct?"

"You have it, sir. She was very successful as a private man-o'-war during the last war."

"I can vouch for that," put in Makepeace helpfully.

"I wouldn't, if you wish to render Captain . . ."

"Kite, Major Hayward."

"If you wish to render Captain Kite any kind of service." Hayward sniffed and looked at Kite. "I can simply requisition your cargo, Captain. It would be a lot easier."

"I can be of considerable use to the government, Major Hayward, and I would not advise you to requisition my cargo."

"Why not, pray?"

"I could weigh anchor and go and sell it, along with the gunpowder and shot I have laid by, to the rebels."

"That would be a treasonable act."

"But your taking my cargo without recompense would be another action to discredit His Majesty's name in Massachusetts and I have already lost a ship and my wife has lost an entire business, all of which was taken by the rebels without any compensation from either themselves or His Majesty's Government."

Hayward turned away. "I cannot enter into any discussions about your personal misfortunes," he said over his shoulder as he retired to the inner room.

"Major Hayward," Kite called after him, "you may have a hundred tons of flour for a letter of marque and fifty guineas to clear the pestilence of debt from your shoulders."

Hayward spun in the doorway, his face colouring. "You would try to bribe me, sir?"

"'Tis the way business may be done, sir," Makepeace interjected quickly. "Captain Kite is a man of capital good sense, Major, and means you no affront. Allow me to wipe out your debt, sir, for a letter of marque."

Hayward hesitated. "I shall see what can be done."

"Today, sir," pressed Kite.

"Before I see you at the tables . . ." Makepeace added.

Hayward looked from one to another of them and then, drawing himself up said coolly, "Damn the pair of you. You may discharge your cargo, Captain, and Makepeace, you can pass word to the QMG."

"My pleasure, Major Hayward," grinned Makepeace, saluting the closing door. "Well, Uncle," he said as they strode out into the sunshine and he shook his head at the orderly, "let us take a glass of wine before I return to my battalion. I am intrigued, you said 'my wife' – was that all a fabrication?"

"No, Harry, I remarried. A lady from Newport, Rhode Island, named Sarah Tyrell."

"I was sorry to learn about Puella. And young William." Makepeace paused and eyed his adopted uncle. "I gather it was your bereavement that decided you to quit Liverpool and dissolve your business association with us."

"Yes. That and the fact that Frith was not a man I had any sympathy with."

Makepeace turned and ducked into a tavern, where he called for a bottle and sat himself down.

"I am sorry to hear that. I have always found him congenial enough."

"I am sure you have, Harry, and I am sure he went to some trouble to be so to you. I found him otherwise."

Makepeace poured the wine and left Kite to pay for it. He took the opportunity to drop twenty guineas onto the table.

"I thought the sum was fifty," Makepeace said, picking up the gold coins.

"I do not have that sum with me, and in any case I only mentioned fifty to Hayward. You expressed satisfaction with the repayment of his debt."

"You have lost none of your shrewdness, Uncle." Makepeace's tone was dry.

"Thank you," Kite replied. "I was sorry to hear you are still gambling."

"Oh, don't be censorious. To be truthful there is so little else to do. We sit here day after day waiting for God knows what. The enemy seem to possess at least as much military competence as we do, which isn't saying much. There was some muttering about the seizure of the southern heights at headquarters yesterday." Makepeace sat back and stretched out his legs. "Alongside such incompetence, a night's gambling seems a small enough sin."

"What are my chances of getting Hayward to comply with my request?"

"If I remember, a letter of marque is a complicated document, ain't it?"

Kite nodded. "But it legitimises my actions and I have my own accounts to settle. If the rebels won't do business our way, I shall do it theirs."

"Gage has done everything possible to appease them; I cannot see him making an exception for one merchant master."

"Then my money is wasted."

"I fear it may well be. What will you do?"

"Keep my own counsel."

"You don't change, Uncle William."

"A man only has his character, Harry. It may prove his best friend or his worst."

"Ah, now you sermonise."

"What's the news of your mother and Katherine?" Kite asked, changing the subject.

"They are well, despite your abandonment," Makepeace responded without malice, "though you were kind to sister Kate, I own. She prospers and is engaged to Dr Bennett . . ."

"Ah, that is good news and it does not entirely surprise me. And your mother?"

"She has married Frith. I thought you knew, from your earlier remark."

"No, but I suspected it. And Charles?"

"Ah, my sober and upstanding brother. He has come down from Cambridge with an eye on chambers in Lincoln's Inn and a seat in the House." Makepeace paused. "Truth to tell, Uncle, he would make a better fist of it than myself."

"And what of you? Will you follow a military career?"

Makepeace shook his head and refilled his glass. "Frith thought military experience would stand me in good stead at the hustings so, here I am, eager to serve my King and Country."

"That is very good of you, Harry. I hope his Majesty appreciates your devotion."

Makepeace grinned. "*I* hope that General Gage gives me something useful to do, otherwise my invaluable military experience will consist entirely of gambling, wenching and drinking. Which of the three would you recommend?"

"Ah, there you have me, Harry. I have only ever gambled in business, when I came out evens over all, I suppose. As to wenching, I did little of it, taking up with Puella and remaining faithful to her until her death. Now I have Sarah."

"Whom I must meet. Where is she now?"

"Calling upon friends."

"And of course you don't drink."

"Not to the excess that qualifies me for an opinion, no."

Makepeace drained his glass and stood. "You are dull, Uncle William, but rich and therefore admirable in your own way."

"I am not rich, Harry, I have lost a great deal in America." Kite stood and faced the young officer, holding out his hand.

"I shall remember that when I lead my soldiers to attack the confounded rebels," he said as they shook hands. "Which I suppose we must do eventually."

"I am content to seek my own revenge, Harry."

"I am sure you are, Uncle Will, but do not let that famous character of yours mislead you. Remember your stout masts break in a storm while the gull wafts away to leeward."

"Most poetic, Harry," Kite said smiling and putting on his hat as Makepeace led the way out into the hot sunshine.

"Most philosophic, Uncle Will," Makepeace corrected. The two men were about to part when Makepeace hesitated. "There is something . . ."

Kite noticed a troubled look cross the young man's face. "Yes? What concerns you?"

Makepeace looked straight at Kite. "I had every reason to dislike you, Uncle William. Frith was strong in his language when referring to you, but Kate said his opinion was prejudiced, so I am entrusting you . . ." He drew a signet ring from his right hand and handed it to Kite. "Give this to my brother, will you? There's a good fellow."

And then he was gone. Kite stood a moment watching him return for his horse. He felt a chill despite the heat of the sun and shuddered. Then he admonished himself for falling foul of the spirits Puella would have said hung about the young man's departing figure.

Looking down at the ring he slipped it into his waistcoat pocket. "Bloody fool," he muttered of himself and, turning, went in search of his wife.

Chapter Twelve

Boston

During the next two days Kite waited in vain for his letter of marque. Despite Hayward's remark that he might discharge his cargo he waited upon events, in case he might yet require its value as a bargaining counter. He called daily at Gage's headquarters at Province House but never succeeded in seeing Hayward again, despite sending in messages. Nor did he catch Harry Makepeace bringing in the muster lists of the 59th Foot and he gradually gave up any hopes of legitimising his meditated vengeance. On the morning of the 16th of June, having spent the night on board *Spitfire*, he had himself pulled ashore and landed on the Long Wharf at the foot of King Street. Instead of making for Province House as had become usual, he turned right and headed for the lodgings in Hanover Street where he had installed Sarah so that she might enjoy a little society while he fretted about the vessel.

Breaking his fast with her he announced his mind was made up. "I am growing weary with waiting, my dear. I do not wish to languish twice in this godforsaken place and am considering acting entirely on my own account." He looked across the table at her, anxious to know what she would say.

"*Entirely* upon your own account?"

He nodded. "It seems I must. The rebels have made of this a civil war and I am not minded to let them cruise in the *Wentworth* without doing something about it. Today I am intending to sell the cargo to the highest bidder, for it is clear that the military have forgot all about me."

"Well, I have some news for you, William, which I think you will account good."

"Oh? Please, do tell me."

"Yesterday evening, after you had left me to return to the

Spitfire, I received this letter. You have the knack of inspiring loyalty, Captain Kite."

"I do?" Smiling at her, Kite took the paper Sarah held out to him and read it.

Dear Madam,

Having seen Notice of the Arrival of the Spitfire, Schooner, under Your Husband's Command and having made it My Business to Acquaint Myself of Your Lodgings, I should be Obliged if you would Make Known to Captain Kite that I and Six or Seven other Stout Fellows are Desirous of Joining Him should He find Employment for us. I shall say no more save that a Matter Touching Your Recent Misfortunes is Known to Me and that, Notwithstanding any future Acquaintanceship or Employments, I am Most Desirous to Make Known certain Facts to Captain Kite or to Yourself. Please send Word at Your Earliest Convenience to, Your Humble Servant, ma'am,

Zachariah Harper.

At the Sign of the Bear, Fish Street, Boston

Nine of the Clock Post Meridian, this 15th of June 1775

"Well, well. Zachariah Harper. I had almost forgotten him. He speaks of six or seven stout fellows. I shall send word for him shortly, but I must first settle things with you."

"I know what you are going to say, William, but I am not going to be left here in Boston. You have just called it a godforsaken place and I do not think it will improve; rather otherwise, I guess, so I wish to make it quite clear that nothing is going to persuade me otherwise than to keep my word and accompany you wherever you go. My happiness is not to be found anywhere other than by your side."

"I am overwhelmed."

"I have not been idle these past two days. I have not told you before because I knew we should dispute the matter, but now it is too late for disagreement. You have no option but to fall in with my wishes."

"I have no wish to quarrel, Sarah."

"That is as well." She smiled at him and he was moved by the radiance of her expression. "I have almost completed my trousseau and will be ready to join you this evening."

"Your *trousseau?*" Kite was utterly puzzled. He had long expected that Sarah would not sit supinely ashore and, truth to tell, he had no great desire to leave her behind. The strategy had not worked with Puella and was even less likely to do so with the headstrong Sarah. Besides, he would rather she threw her lot in with him entirely, for he had ceased to think of life as a preparation for tomorrow, but a matter for today.

Sarah shrugged. "Perhaps I should say my traps, or my dunnage. I forget the nautical noun. In any event I have acquired some boots and breeches and will look as pretty as these British subalterns I see mincing about the streets . . . By the by, have you noticed there is a lot of activity in the streets today?"

"You mean military activity?"

"Yes."

"I cannot say that I noticed, but perhaps you are right."

"Well, you will fill your head with freight rates and stowage factors, so I suppose I cannot expect you to be observant as well."

"I have been filling my head with other matters, but I suppose today I must think of obtaining ballast." Kite drew the napkin off his lap, wiped his mouth, rose and leaned over his wife. "Do you see if you can buy a dozen bottles of oporto, a decent cheese or two, a dozen laying hens and do the duty of a wife at least for today before you pull on breeches."

"Very well," Sarah said, rising in a susurration of silk, "though they will cost a great deal."

"No matter."

"Very well. I shall be ready to leave before sunset."

"I shall try and come for you myself, otherwise the boat will wait by Woodman's wharf."

"You may send Zachariah. I should like to see his misshaped countenance again."

"Then I must go and seek him out."

Zachariah Harper was not at the Sign of the Bear, so Kite took himself to the Custom House and found the clerk who had performed his inwards clearance.

"I think you are too late, Captain," the man responded when Kite raised the issue of discharging his cargo.

"What d'you mean?"

"Would you care to borrow the long glass, sir." The clerk indicated a large telescope resting on a rack secured to the wall.

Kite picked it up, went to one of the several windows that overlooked the harbour and levelled it on his schooner. A lighter lay alongside and, conspicuous in the sunshine, the scarlet uniform of a British officer told its own story.

"They have requisitioned it, by God!" he exclaimed, lowering the glass and turning to the clerk, who nodded.

"I did emphasise the necessity of acting in haste, Captain," he observed dolefully.

Kite closed the glass with a snap and returned it to its resting place. "A plague on both your houses," he said, half to himself.

"I beg your pardon, Captain?"

"No good will come of any of this, you know."

"Any of what, exactly, Captain?"

"Civil war," he said.

"D'you think it will come to that?" the clerk asked, his face no longer wearing the bland expression of bureaucratic time-serving, but the concern of a Crown official in a position of obvious and potentially unpopular faction if the rebels took Boston.

"It's my experience that it already has," Kite said, picking up his hat.

He was about to leave when the clerk asked, "Would you care for your outward clearance now, Captain? It might help you later."

The appeal for help, laying Kite under at least a technical obligation to aid the clerk if and when events warranted it, was transparent. But the offer also played into Kite's hands. "Very well," he said, waiting impatiently while the clerk made it out.

He walked from the Custom House in a fury at losing his cargo, but his boat was nowhere to be seen and he recalled he had sent it back to the *Spitfire*, intending to remain ashore until after noon. Now, unless he hired a boat, he was marooned while the military authorities seized the cargo of flour for their own purposes. He calmed himself. The troops had been pushed to the limit of their endurance in Boston and he should not so far forget his own humble origins to begrudge them their daily bread. Besides, it would be utterly futile to protest against the removal of his cargo and while he wondered, for a self-deluding instant, if Hayward had actually organised the drawing up of a letter of marque, he doubted it. In short, he wished for no further delay. Calming himself he decided to accept the fact that he could not easily reach his ship. There were no obvious boats plying for hire and he recalled the authorities had been busy requisitioning them too, so he abandoned any notion of rushing out to the *Spitfire* and involving himself in a tedious row he could never win. Having met Hayward and his military methods, he believed that like the situation he had found himself in at Liverpool, it was sometimes better to cut and run, keeping a distant but more important objective in mind. Suddenly resolved, he headed at a brisk walk for the Sign of the Bear.

Harper was not at his lodgings but, just as he wheeled away to seek a cargo of shingle for ballast, another familiar face hove in sight.

"Jacob!"

The big negro turned and recognised his old commander. "Cap'n Kite! Why, sah, 'tis wonderful to see you." His grin was heartening. "Massah Harper has all the men mustered and we was thinking of taking a boat out to your little schooner. Why sah, she look damn fast!"

"Well, Jacob, she schoons with the best of them, that's a certainty." Kite smiled and nodded his pleasure at seeing Jacob. "It is good to see you. Tell me, where is Mr Harper now?"

"He sent me back here to the tavern, to pick up his portmanteau. He's with the other men at Hutchinson's Wharf."

"Has he had any success at finding a boat, Jacob?" Kite asked.

"Seems to be some difficulty, sah, but if you stand fast but a moment, Cap'n, I'll be right back . . ."

The sun was hot on Kite's back as he waited for Jacob to return. Sarah was right, there *was* an increase in military activity this morning. Some of the boats from the men-of-war anchored off the town, the *Glasgow*, *Somerset* and *Lively*, were assembling in the dock south of the North Battery, as though some movement were being meditated. Kite stared south across the sparkling waters of the harbour to where Dorchester Heights rose. Was Gage intending to occupy the elevated position? Was that why all the boats were being requisitioned? It made sense, of course, for if the rebels raised batteries upon the eminences, they would command the anchorage and thus reinforce the besieging works about the town. Boston and its harbour would become untenable and what that meant to the position of the Crown authorities was unthinkable. It was surely something to be avoided at all costs, even by the appeasing Gage.

"Captain Kite!"

Kite turned to see Harper approaching, his hand held out and his ugly face cracked by a smile of genuine pleasure.

"Zachariah!" They shook hands and Kite said, "I thought you were at Hutchinson's Wharf – I have just met Jacob."

"Ah, well there are no boats to be had, so I thought that I would come back here and save Jacob the labour of carting my gear."

"I have my own boat coming alongside in an hour or so," Kite explained, "so we can take her, but tell me how you are."

They exchanged pleasantries and Kite learned that although most of the *Wentworth*'s crew had dispersed, the passage of time had brought half a dozen back to Boston, all of whom were willing to ship out again with Captain Kite.

"Why me, Zachariah?"

"They trust you, sir, and the experience of being kicked out of the *Wentworth* has turned them against the rebels. Besides, most have no life ashore here, being from the Antilles or Liverpool, and seek only employment afloat."

"Come," said Kite, "let us walk a little and I will explain our situation." The two men walked along the quays, heading north along Fish Street, in the direction of Ship Street and the North Battery. Kite explained his failure to obtain a letter of marque but his intention to attempt the recapture of the *Wentworth*, the presence of Sarah and Johnstone as gunner, and his need of men willing to risk their lives in their commander's interests. "I make no bones about it, Zachariah, I want only willing volunteers. I have yet to put this proposition to the men on board, but I would be obliged if you would tell me whether you think your men will serve under such terms."

"If you take the *Wentworth*, sir," Harper asked, "she will be restored to you. What then is the inducement for the men?"

"Good pay for four months and a bonus if I take the *Wentworth*."

"We could be adjudged pirates . . ."

"I think not, unless by the rebels in some court of their own creation. I am willing to risk that."

"You have every confidence in your enterprise."

Kite stopped and confronted him. "I may fail, Zachariah, but I shall not give up because the British Governor of this province has not the wit to protect the rule of law." He paused, then asked, "Well, what about you yourself?"

"Me?" Harper looked surprised. "Oh, I'm your man, sir. Don't fret, I'm certain the rest will be too, but I'll sound them out."

"And try and be discreet. I doubt we can keep the matter secret in this place. It would be better if we wait until we are all on board."

"Aye, aye. I shall see to it."

"Very well," said Kite, satisfied. "Now, do you bring your men to Woodman's Wharf while I shall try and find a cargo of ballast and I will meet you and your volunteers there in, say –" he looked at his watch – "an hour."

Kite had no luck in securing any ballast. The siege had halted all outward trade and although some of the ships lying in the harbour had secured ballast, many still required it before they would be able to sail to seek a homeward cargo elsewhere along the coast. The chances of this were diminishing daily, for the news arriving in Boston by every hour indicated that, far from the rebellion being confined to New England, there were signs of colonial truculence everywhere. In short the normal flow of American exports was falling off. This further frustration only served to worsen Kite's temper when he returned to the rendezvous where he found Harper and his men waiting.

Explaining the situation to Harper, he expressed his annoyance. "It puts paid to a swift departure," he said.

"We can get our own, sir."

"I had thought of that, but any landing hereabouts will attract the attention of the rebels."

"Then we can land on one of the islands in the outer harbour."

Kite looked at the ugly face of the American. He was grinning and Kite laughed and slapped him on the shoulder. "Damn me, Zachariah, why in God's name did I not think of so simple a solution?"

Harper shrugged. "Don't ask me, Cap'n."

"By Heaven, you've quite restored my spirits!"

"Where there's a will, there's a way, they say."

"And they are damn well right!" Kite cheered up, particularly as at that moment he saw the *Spitfire*'s longboat picking her way through the anchorage, her oar blades flashing in the brilliant sunlight.

During that afternoon Kite and the schooner's company took little notice of events elsewhere. The sudden withdrawal of lighters, which brought an abrupt halt to the discharge of the cargo of flour, served as a welcome relief by withdrawing the gang of wharf-labour, rather than alerting them to impending military events of any great significance to themselves. The rumours that Dorchester Heights were shortly to be occupied by the British seemed so sensible, and the operation so overdue, that it was dismissed as a matter for the authorities to be getting on with. Kite and his men had other fish to fry.

To his satisfaction, Kite discovered that no one had any misgivings about serving aboard the *Spitfire* and that all were willing to enter into formal articles, to be signed the next forenoon, binding themselves to a four months' term of service during which the recovery of the *Wentworth* was to constitute their chief objective. At the termination of that period, they would either be re-engaged or discharged with their pay in Boston, New York, or St John's, Antigua.

On the passage from Antigua to Boston, Kite had shared the watches with the *Spitfire*'s mate, her former slaving mate, Hamish Lamont, with Johnstone standing a watch alongside Kite to gain experience. Now he appointed Harper as his second mate and Jacob as an additional quartermaster, drawing up a watch bill with the customary stations for sail-handling and action. He would rather have had Harper as his mate, but Lamont was a quiet, competent enough officer whose only fault so far had been to allow a young subaltern sent out by the Quartermaster General's office to persuade him to open the schooner's hatches in order that the army might seize the cargo of flour. Lamont was apologetic, but Kite waved the incident aside and as the lighters were withdrawn the matter blew over.

Once Kite had consulted Lamont over the watch bill, the two men set to drawing up the orders for the regulation of the *Spitfire*. At sunset Harper was sent ashore to pick up Sarah as arranged. When she arrived, Kite left her in the cabin to settle herself and took a turn on deck. The evening was warm and in the waist some of the men had gathered to smoke and sing songs. Over the almost windless waters of the harbour the stillness of the night settled, and the anchor lights of the men-of-war, the merchant vessels and the military transports joined the lamps and lanterns in the houses and taverns along the waterfront, their reflections long tongues that flickered on the black water.

Kite sent for Harper and when the second mate joined him he asked, "In your letter to my wife you mentioned, if I recollect the phrase aright, that you knew something about a matter touching my misfortunes. I presume that you referred to the loss of the *Wentworth*. Was I correct?"

"Indeed, sir, you were. I happened to ship in a snow owned in Boston but trading with Rhode Island. I found myself among men of the radical persuasion and dissembled to the extent of not disagreeing with their sentiments. Fortunately none of them knew me and we encountered none that did so, since we generally called not at Newport but at Providence. Anyway there is great agitation in Rhode Island and the representatives which they have sent to what they term their Congress have been charged to form a rebel naval force. The names of Whipple and Rathburne are much talked of as being men fit to lead such a squadron either in the name of Rhode Island or of the United Colonies. Whipple commanded a privateer called the *Gamecock* in the last war and is thought to be a capable man. Of course I listened when they mentioned Rathburne, and upon enquiry as to whether this navy would have any ships, they said that it already had, Captain Rathburne being in command of a fine frigate-built ship, the *Rattlesnake*. Admitting that I did not know of her, and enquiring what was her armament and so forth, I was told that she had only lately been acquired, that she had been a British vessel named the *Wentworth*. Now she is armed with eighteen guns and fitted to cruise against British trade anywhere between Halifax and New York. I dropped the matter after that, and kept my own counsel."

"That was wise of you."

"I had little option, Cap'n. They made other remarks regarding their collective smartness in outwitting the dumb fools aboard the ship . . . You can guess I had no choice but to pipe down."

"Of course."

"I shouldn't be sorry to wipe the smiles from their faces, though," Zachariah said. He stifled a yawn. "If you'll forgive me, Cap'n, I must get my head down. I've the anchor watch at midnight."

168

"Not at all, Zachariah. And thank you for the intelligence. It's a long stretch of coast, but who knows what tomorrow will bring."

Thirteen

Bunker Hill

K ite woke in the night and lay in the darkness listening to the faint noises of his schooner. The vessel lay almost motionless in the still, calm water, with only a faint creaking coming from the rudder stock as it moved slightly, constrained by the sennit-work beckets looped over the tiller on the deck above. Beside him the faint sound of Sarah's breathing came to him, and as though aware of him being awake, she turned uneasily. He felt supremely happy, as if neither the night nor the future held any fears for him, though both were pregnant with possibilities.

He pondered this, for such a grim hour was usually filled with unbidden horrors and apprehensions. Yet the feeling of well-being persisted and he realised that for months that had run into years he had never felt any sense of tranquillity. Even though the prolonged period of sadness following the death of Puella had ended with his marriage to Sarah, the seemingly interminable difficulties of settling their affairs and the unsatisfactory sojourn in Antigua had given him no fulfilment. Indeed the difficulties seemed to him to be fate's recompense for the joy of his love for Sarah. For although this had always seemed like an oasis in a desert of desolation, like an oasis it could only be left for further travail through the wilderness. Now, however, all seemed different. He felt a sense of purpose that had begun to form as he had undertaken the simple task of assembling his crew and drafting his standing orders to them. This and the satisfaction of reassuming full command of the *Spitfire*, free of the constraints of consignees' demands, had been crowned by Sarah joining him, throwing in her lot with an abandon that stirred him. He turned towards her.

It was already growing light and he could see the detail of her beautiful face on the pillow beside him. A wisp of hair drifted over a cheek and he looked down over her body as it lay under the light coverlet.

"You are awake." Her voice startled him and he looked at her face again, bent and kissed her. She drew back the sheet. "Come," she said, and he moved over her tenderly as the dawn flushed the eastern sky.

Afterwards they fell asleep and it was late when Bandy Ben woke them with news that the whole place was in uproar.

"Why is that?" Kite asked, reaching for his breeches.

"Because the rebels are here," Ben said with a confusing lack of accuracy.

"You had better go up on deck, my dear," Sarah urged, thinking like Kite that the Americans had attacked Boston itself.

On deck in the brilliant sunshine of mid-morning, Kite found the entire crew lining the rail. He joined Harper and Lamont, who had their telescopes trained on Boston.

"What the devil's going on?" Kite asked. "Are the rebels in Boston itself?" he asked, his tone full of incredulity.

"No, sir," said Harper turning and handing over his glass, "take a look above the North Battery."

From the position of the anchored schooner, the North Battery formed the visible extremity of Boston. Beyond, on the far side of the entrance to the Charles River, was a low hill, marking the end of the Charlestown peninsula. The hill rose to a greater height known as Bunker Hill which, from Kite's vantage point, lay directly above the nearer North Battery. On both hills could be seen swarms of men, the brown scars of earthworks under construction and the occasional brief flash of a swung pick or shovel catching the sunshine.

"Well, I'm damned."

It was quite clear what had happened; either as a matter of coincidence or of pre-emptive initiative, the rebel commanders had decided to occupy Bunker Hill on one side of Boston before the British claimed Dorchester Heights on the other.

From beyond Boston, unseen in the Charles River, came the boom of gunfire and Kite noticed a small brown shower of earth fly up, as one of the warships pitched roundshot into the rising entrenchments.

"This will set the cat among the pigeons," Harper remarked. "General Gage will have to do something now," he added, to which Kite could only agree.

"There's a flood-tide running," Lamont said, "and high water is about two o'clock this afternoon; surely they'll not try pulling barges and flat-boats across the Charles River with the ebb under them."

"It will take time to muster the troops, though," said Kite, recalling his own brief military experience in the taking of Guadeloupe years earlier, "and they'll need artillery to dislodge the rebels."

They could hear the distant rattle of drums beating and, perhaps more imagined than perceived, though it seemed real enough in their recollection afterwards, a buzz rising from Boston itself. Like a disturbed hive, the town would be swarming with troops and citizens. Some would be eager for the moment of decision that seemed now to force itself upon the reluctant Gage, some fearful of the outcome. Kite could guess that many of the military would be all agog to drive the insolent rebels from their position on Bunker Hill, while a few more perceptive souls might regard the task with some concern.

"May I see?"

Kite turned at the sound of Sarah's voice. She wore her grey silk day-dress and her hair was loosely caught up at the nape of her neck, so that the light breeze caught it, while the sun shot lights through it. He thought her very lovely as she steadied the glass against a stay and levelled it on the distant hill. For a moment they remained contemplating the rebel activity, aware that the crew were equally fascinated by the turn of events, then Sarah asked, "Should we not do something?"

"Do?" Kite said, frowning. "What can we do?"

"Well, we cannot just sit here like the audience at a play, surely?" Sarah lowered the telescope.

Kite was nonplussed. "Is it our business to do anything?" he asked, looking at his two officers, as though seeking some reassurance from them as men in the face of this odd, female notion. Both men shrugged and shook their heads, then Johnstone asked, "What do you mean, Mistress Kite? Have you an idea in what way we might prove useful?"

"General Gage will send his army across the river to attack the enemy, surely," Sarah said. "And if so, may we not assist?"

"They will go over in flat-boats, harbour lighters such as the one which took part of our cargo yesterday, and the boats of the men-o'-war—" Kite began, but Sarah interrupted him.

"Well, we have a longboat they can use."

"Yes, but they will not require our help," Kite assured her.

"And we have some guns," she persisted.

"Sarah," Kite responded, a hint of exasperation in his tone, "the *Somerset* has a broadside of over thirty pieces."

"And you don't have a letter of marque," Sarah riposted quickly.

Kite saw her logic. "You think that by helping Gage we will ingratiate ourselves to the extent of the General issuing us with a letter of marque?" He laughed at her. "I am sorry to disappoint you, Sarah, but I think this will occupy the General's mind with rather more important matters than a letter of marque for a would-be privateersman."

"Maybe your wife has a point, Captain," said Lamont, "not so much in respect of the letter of marque, but we may be able to assist a little and the benefit to the men of firing the guns would prove useful."

"That is a point, sir," Harper put in.

Kite vacillated. It was true that they might be able to do something, but they might equally get in the way and incur the displeasure of the authorities. Then the second mate added, "It would not take long to weigh and work our way across the harbour."

Kite felt himself being boxed into a corner. On the one hand he was reluctant to get involved. He had a lingering feeling that to do so would compromise the clear and happy intent with which he had woken in the early hours of that same morning. On the other hand he was aware that to act in a manner offensive to the rebels was long overdue, both personally and nationally. At the same time his rejection of an entreaty from Sarah, coming so soon after their love-making, seemed an unkind and dismal response and Sarah, as if divining his train of thought, came to his rescue.

"There will be wounded if there is fighting," she reasoned.

"Aye, we could do something there," Lamont said.

At this point Johnstone rejoined them. He had been studying the fortifications on the hills from the forecastle and Sarah turned to him as to an ally, asking him for his opinion.

"Well, I'm no strategist, but I suppose that it is better to be involved than to sit here and watch."

"Very well, then," Kite said, "man the windlass and the halliards."

An hour later they anchored again some three cables east of Moulton's Hill. To the south-west of them, lying in the narrow strait between Boston and Charlestown where the Charles River debouched into the outer harbour, the *Falcon, Lively, Somerset* and *Glasgow* lay, their guns firing at the rebel positions ashore. Both Bunker Hill and the lower eminence in its front, known as Breed's Hill, now bore well-defined entrenchments and they could see the white and grey of the rebels' shirts as they continued to ply pick and shovel to the grassland. Over on the Boston side a battery at Copp's Hill was opening fire on the rebel positions while on the placid waters of the harbour, which sparkled under the hot noon-day sun, a flotilla of some thirty or so boats began to slowly cross the Charles River, heading for Moulton's Point.

The brilliance of the day added a fairground aspect to the occasion. The sun danced not only upon the water, but upon the oar blades of the boats, and twinkled on the bayonets of the soldiers crammed into them. Up on the hills, whose altitude though not great was now more obvious to the observers aboard the *Spitfire*, they could see the rebels not as remote dots, reflecting points of light, but men preparing for battle. Yet despite this, there seemed no great drama in the moment, for it was too pretty to be the prelude to slaughter. Even the gouts of earth and stones sent up by the guns of the warships and Copp's Hill seemed mere theatrical tricks.

Staring through his telescope, Kite raked the shore of the Charlestown peninsula and noticed the works which extended off the flank of Breed's Hill, a stone wall that ran to the foreshore and was surmounted by a rail fence. He pointed it out to Lamont and Harper.

"They are manning it," he said without removing the glass from his eye, "and I think it might be in range of our long chase guns. We have our colours hoisted and at least as legitimate a reason for engaging the rebels as they have of threatening us; shall we try a shot or two?"

"I have no objection, Captain Kite," said Lamont.

"Nor I, sir," added Harper, grinning. "We shall have to close the range, though. If we get the anchor a-trip and let the tide carry her upstream a little?"

"Very well," said Kite closing his glass with a snap. "Lying to the flood like this, we shall need to clap a spring on our cable and manhandle the starboard bow chaser into a midships port, but let us see what we can do."

The casual consent of the commander set the Spitfires into action. Since the order had been given to shift their anchorage they had been in excited anticipation that they would be up to some form of mischief before the day was out. Now they turned-to with a will. Harper led a few men forward to haul short the anchor cable and let the schooner drift closer in, while a second party of seamen eagerly slipped the breechings of the starboard six-pounder bow chaser and dragged it aft. A third group ran the smaller four-pounder out of its port and a fourth hauled a rope from the starboard quarter, outside the schooner, and made it fast to the anchor cable as Harper veered this and brought *Spitfire* up to her anchor again. This, the spring, was then adjusted so that by sharing the schooner's weight between cable and spring the *Spitfire* was slewed across the tideway allowing her six-pounder to be brought to bear. By manning the helm, she was held more or less steady while the six-pounder was laid on the rail fence and the line of militia behind it.

By this time a column of redcoats could be seen advancing from Moulton's Point, parallel to the shore towards the rail fence. It was clear to Kite that the British intended to attack along the low ground and envelop the higher position on Breed's Hill and that his gunfire might indeed prove of some use to the advancing infantry. To what extent this was true he was never to know, for the six-pounders moving forward with General William Howe's light infantry companies had been supplied with roundshot for twelve-pounders. Moreover when they loaded grape to clear the enemy, the boggy ground prevented them from getting close enough to be effective.

On board the schooner Harper insisted on laying the *Spitfire*'s six-pounder, and he judged the matter to a nicety, his first shot ploughing up the ground in front of the rail fence with a fine feather of earth and pebbles. Kite saw the fall of shot quite clearly, as he did the second where it struck a perceptible shower of stones up and threw a few men back out of the rebel line. He was equally ignorant of his target, who were Colonel John Stark's New Hampshire infantry, but his shot, though it wounded a few men, actually fell on a second rail fence thrown out in front of his main position by Stark to encumber the British approach. Thus his action only stiffened the resolve of Stark's soldiers so that, as the British advanced on them and Kite was compelled to hold his fire, they were as steady as regular troops.

Kite and his company watched in dismay as the rebel volley fire, controlled by Stark and other officers who were familiar with British musketry drill from their own experiences in the Indian Wars, stopped the advancing column. Despite pressing forward again, the British were met by a second volley, and then as they tried to clear the farmers' boys from their positions with a rapid bayonet charge, by a third.

For a few moments the disciplined order of the column dissolved. As the smoke from the volleys of the rebels rose in clouds, the British infantry milled about in front of the rail fence, firing piecemeal in a furious, frustrated response. To Kite, watching intently through the glass, memories of just such a moment on Guadeloupe flooded back. His heartbeat quickened and a lump rose unbidden in his throat, for then the men with whom he had impetuously charged had carried the field, but he was now watching brave men on the edge of defeat. Even as the realisation came to him the British infantry began falling back, then he could see beyond them another column, which had struck across higher ground towards the American positions, also in retreat.

"Open fire again!" he yelled, lowering the glass, but the tide was turning and it was some moments before the spring had been adjusted and his gun's crew could again lay their weapon upon the rail fence. By then General Howe's men had reformed and were advancing again, the greater portion of the British heading not for the rail fence but the redoubt which crowned Breed's Hill. The light infantry, however, persisted in their attack upon Stark's position and were received and driven off in the same manner.

Watching the British infantry on the higher ground Lamont exclaimed, "They are wearing their knapsacks!" They all stared as the distant waves of redcoats toiled up the hill. "Why in God's name would they want to do that in this heat?" he asked, looking round, but he received only shrugs in response, for it was clear that the rebel position was not going to fall to the British regulars as easily as they had anticipated. As the second attack crumbled and the red-coated infantry fell back again, more boats were seen crabbing across the Charles River from Boston, bearing reinforcements to join a large body of soldiers from the earlier attacks who now massed on Moulton's Point, where they were dumping their knapsacks. Amid these men, the observers aboard *Spitfire* could quite clearly see wounded soldiers being borne down the hill, while lying in front of the rebel entrenchments small, individual red dots told their own story.

"It is not going well," Sarah said, her voice half questioning, as if seeking assurance that, on the contrary, it was all some dreadful ruse which would produce victory in a few moments.

"No, my dear," said Kite, his own tone harsh, "it is not going well. In fact it is damnable."

"There are dead and wounded on the hillside."

"Yes, there are."

"If we sent away our boat, William," she said in a low voice, as though her earlier suggestion had been responsible for all this death and destruction, "we might be able to offer them some help."

"Yes," said Kite hurriedly. "It is infinitely preferable to pitching shot . . . Get me the apothecary's chest." He turned to Lamont. "Bring the longboat alongside, Mr Lamont, and have her manned."

He was halfway to Moulton's Point, urging his boat's crew to pull as hard as they were able, when Howe launched the third attack, straight up the hill in the hot afternoon sunshine. He watched the red lines waver as the rebels held their fire and knew in a moment of insight that they were picking off the British officers. Their gorgets would sparkle bravely in the sunshine as the sun westered, inviting targets to young men used to bowling over rabbits and coneys at fifty or sixty yards. As the longboat pulled into the landing area the noise increased and they could smell powder, mixed with the rank stink of sweat and smoke, for beyond the milling troops Charlestown was ablaze. The foreshore was a litter of boats and bodies. Many regimental drummers were acting as stretcher-bearers and the wounded lay in writhing rows, the crimson of their coats and the white breeches disfigured with bloody stains and gouting wounds. Blood ran over the ground and was soon soaked up by the thirsty earth.

Kite bent to his task. The son of an apothecary, he had a rudimentary knowledge of medical matters and had once acted as a surgeon aboard ship. No one challenged him as he sent the longboat back to the *Spitfire* for fresh water and some linen for bandages. It was clear that the military authorities had made little effort to provide a field dressing station at such short notice, and he was filled with a sense of rage at this neglect. It was all of a piece, he thought as he bent with needle and thread and closed a flap of flesh over a sword wound, with the inefficiency and the misplaced preoccupations of men like Major Hayward.

For the most part the men lying in the sun were officers, and many of them had been hit by musket balls. Aimed low, these had driven deep into their soft bellies or their thighs, causing fearfully painful wounds; many were mortal but few were quick in their fatal effect. Kite did what he could to ease these men's suffering with a little water when the longboat returned, but the majority were almost bled white by the time they had been brought to the foot of the hill for treatment. He bumped into a regimental surgeon who filled the air with a thick torrent of profane oaths, aimed at the bumbling incompetence of which he himself was a part. The man was drunk, but he drove his probe remorselessly into an officer's lower abdomen until the wretch was dead. Next to the surgeon Kite had more success. He dug out a ball which had flattened itself against the femur of another officer and was delighted when no gush of blood followed the extraction.

"You are lucky," he said to the young man, holding up the offending lead projectile. The youth was already pale and rolled his eyeballs as he passed out. "Poor devil," muttered Kite as he turned to the next man.

"Help me hold him," the drunken surgeon muttered as he readied his saw and laid it across the wounded man's left leg. The knee was shattered and, as Kite bore down upon the man's shoulders, he recognised the face staring up at him.

"Harry!"

"Oh God!" It was as far as Harry Makepeace got before his teeth were bared in a grimace of extreme pain. A moment later he had passed out and Kite turned to look at the surgeon. It was already too late. The cauterisation of the arteries was imperfectly done, the fumbling was fatal and blood ran from Harry Makepeace as from an insurance company's fire-hose.

"Damnation!" The drunken surgeon swore and moved on to the next casualty, leaving Kite beside the dying son of his old friend. It was soon over and after the death of Makepeace it seemed to Kite that the afternoon dissolved into one interminable series of bloody wounds, each of which confronted him with a mounting sense of abject failure. He had no obligation to be kneeling on the foreshore tending the remnants of Gage's assault force, yet he could not tear himself away. He felt himself bound to grovel amid the dust and the blood and the vomit, surrounded by the groans and cries of anguish and pain, and to do whatever seemed possible. It was little enough, for he had little equipment, nothing in the way of those unguents with which his father had insisted a wound might be kept clear of infection, only a handful of torn sheets for bandages and pledgets, and only water from the harbour to clean open wounds. As for drinking water, there was insufficient of this to ease more than a few men, and most died with a raging thirst to add to their last agony.

Kite was dimly aware that Sarah and Harper had joined him and were moving among the wounded with water and a kind word here and there. Sarah collected messages, last-minute wishes to be communicated to wives and sweethearts, fathers and brothers. A few other kind souls from Boston had arrived to help, so they were less conspicuous among the military scarlet as the afternoon drew to its close. News came down the hill that Howe had finally forced the rebels from their positions and chased them back up Bunker Hill and beyond. This raised pathetic little cheers from the wounded and dying men.

As the sun set, Kite, Sarah and Harper were relieved of their self-imposed duties as the dead, dying and wounded were taken back across the river to Boston. Kite gathered the others on the beach and waited for the return of the longboat from Boston, whither she had taken a number of the wounded. They stood in complete silence, unable to meet each others' eyes in the deepening twilight. At last Harper announced the approach of the boat and they were just waiting for it to close the beach when a young and dishevelled officer ran up to them and bowed to Sarah.

"Madam," he said breathlessly, "I bring you Lord Rawdon's compliments and thanks for attending him. He asks who was his ministering angel?"

Sarah looked at Kite and stretched out her hand. Her fine eyes were filled with tears and he could see her swallow. He took her hand and squeezed it, nodding his approval. She said with a cool dignity, "I am Mistress Kite, sir, from the schooner *Spitfire* of which my husband here is the commander."

The young officer turned to Kite and made a short bow, taking in the sodden state of his garments which reeked of gore. "His Lordship is obliged to you, madam, and to you, sir, and," he added, seeing Harper standing there, "to you too."

"It has been a bloody day, sir," Kite said without expression. The young officer nodded. "Indeed it has, sir, but at least it is ours."

"At a cost," Kite responded quickly, "and one which I doubt you can sustain. Pray give our compliments to Lord Rawdon and wish him a speedy recovery and a better victory than this over the rebels."

"I shall drink to that, sir." The young officer made a final bow and turned on his heel just as the forefoot of the longboat drove onto the beach beside them with a crunch.

"You were too hard on him, William," Sarah murmured.

But Kite shook his head. "Such a victory is a greater evil than defeat," he said.

"Then why wish him another?"

"Because if the British troops fail to smash these rebels quickly, there will be an infinity of scenes such as the one which we have just witnessed." He paused and added, "This is a war, Sarah, not a shooting party."

After they had regained the *Spitfire*'s deck and Sarah had gone below, Kite lingered for a moment or two. Two men had not returned in the boat from Boston and he wondered why Johnstone and one of the seamen had gone missing. It was no great matter, he thought, staring at the hills which he could now barely make out in the darkness. He felt the weight of the day cling to him like the stench of powder, blood and dust that clung to his coat. The spirits of the dead and the damned seemed thick in the heavy night air and then he felt a faint but purifying zephyr gently fan his face.

A faint trace of the dawn's optimism inexplicably slowly stole over him. He felt the dreadful affair of Bunker Hill slough off him and knew that Puella's shade and the spirits of the *obi* kept him close company.

Puella's generous spirit had led him to make love to Sarah that morning and suddenly he felt fate's benediction with relief. Others had been destined to die on Bunker Hill that day; for William Kite there was still a tomorrow.

Fourteen

A Moth Drawn to a Candle

The discovery that Johnstone and one seaman had landed in Boston from the longboat the previous evening to assist with the wounded had caused little concern on Kite's return to the *Spitfire*. Although the boat was sent back in for them, neither had materialised by midnight and such was the confusion in the town that Jacob, who had been acting as the boat's coxswain, had decided to return to the schooner without them. Long before Kite received the news of Johnstone's absence Sarah had removed her fouled clothing and fallen into the sleep of exhaustion. He too was dropping with fatigue and was more concerned with divesting himself of his own filthy clothing. Hearing Jacob's report of the state of Boston, he thought that Johnstone had most probably become so involved with the removal of the wounded that at the late hour at which he was free to return to the ship he had been too tired, and had found lodgings ashore.

The following morning he ordered the schooner prepared for sea, passing word that the longboat should be sent ashore again during the forenoon to pick up the two missing men. Meanwhile the empty water casks were hove up on deck and Lamont supervised their stumming, prior to sending them ashore for refilling, the rigging was rattled down and overhauled, and the final preparations made for their cruise. The morning, being almost windless, persuaded Kite to hoist *Spitfire*'s sails and check them over, allowing them to dry out after the night's dew and for some new cringles to be worked into the bolt-ropes of the foresail and fore topmast staysail, the neglect of which might cost him his prize if he ever got sight of her.

Attending to such details absorbed him, temporarily driving out of his mind the concerns he had for locating Rathburne, and entirely wiping from his mind the two absent men. The events of the previous day had, however, cleared from his mind any lingering doubts about his intentions. The British "victory" at Bunker Hill had not merely been Pyrrhic, it was an illusion. Kite knew that the stand the Americans had made had come as a profound shock to the British officers, for he had overheard enough comment while tending the wounded. That it had been brushed aside in that laconic off-handedness that characterised the casual attitude of the young blades did not fool him: he was himself Briton enough to recognise the underlying worry.

An eighteen-year-old ensign who while having a bullet wound in his upper arm dressed drawled that "brother Jonathan is a tough nut to crack, by Jupiter" had proved himself courageous enough. But his shuddering frame could not hide the impact of the enemy's action, which had struck deeper than his flesh wound. Such bravado, Kite knew, was a requisite quality among these stupidly brave young men, for no one could doubt that they had driven Jonathan from his entrenchments by raw courage and sheer persistence. Admirable though these qualities were, they were limited and could not win a long war. It was this consideration which had stirred Kite from sleep and occupied his thoughts that morning. The rebels had had it all their own way and he felt that he *must* strike at Rathburne. To translate that resolve into action meant locating Rathburne with all the advantages of surprise on his side, for he was in no doubt at all of how tough a nut Jonathan was to crack.

It was while Kite scoured his schooner for defects that the lighter approached with a hail of "*Spitfire* ahoy!"

"What d'you want?" Lamont queried.

"The rest of your requisitioned cargo, if you please," a man dressed in the blue uniform of the Customs Service responded with mock civility. As the lightermen shipped their sweeps, the barge bumped alongside and the lines were thrown, the Customs officer stood and looked up at the schooner with her sails hanging loose in the hot summer air.

"You shifted your anchorage, Captain. Not thinking of leaving, I hope?"

"I most certainly am. I've my outward clearance, mister," Kite declared, "but that was not my intention by moving our anchorage. That was to do what we could to help the army."

"I'm sure it was," the Customs officer replied with flat ambiguity.

"Had I wished to leave, I should have already done so," Kite answered with some asperity.

"I don't doubt it, Captain," the other rejoined, his voice suspicious as he made for the rope ladder thrown over the *Spitfire*'s side. On deck he held out his hand and added, "Come, sir, things have been all topsy-turvy of late. We abandoned your discharge the day before yesterday for military reasons and now have a greater reason for wanting your lading ashore."

"Things went ill, then," Kite asked, pretending ignorance. The Customs officer shrugged his shoulders and looked away. "We were close inshore, we saw a great deal," he added.

"Well, 'tis true that the cost of yesterday's victory was somewhat excessive, but the chief worry is the fact that Boston is isolated. Without supply from the sea our position here will deteriorate."

"Then you are welcome to my cargo, but you would be well advised not to antagonise too many shipmasters. We are a tediously fractious breed."

"So I observe, Captain."

"Almost as intransigent as Custom House men," Kite said with a grin, seeing the signs of anxiety on the native-born colonial's face. The officer relaxed and wiped his hand across his sweating face. "Come below for some refreshment. My wife has some lemonade aboard."

Sat in the cabin with a glass of the cool drink in the easing presence of Sarah, the Customs officer unbent to the extent of revealing that rumours of evacuation were beginning to circulate among the tense and overcrowded drawing rooms of Boston. "Things could go very ill for us," he said, referring to the loyal portion of the population. In response, Kite briefly outlined the mauling he and Sarah had endured at the hands of the party calling themselves Patriots. Leaving the Customs officer to fulminate on the perfidy of such men, Kite offered him some rum, which he drank with as much eagerness as he had the lemonade, so that he manifested no surprise when Kite asked if he had heard of John Rathburne.

"Oh, indeed I have, Captain, indeed I have. He is one of those men most implicated in defying the levies and duties placed upon trade, not to mention a man tainted by criminal acts. You'll have heard of the *Gaspée* affair?" Kite nodded. "A noose is too good for that fellow," the Customs officer went on. "Truth to tell," he said, leaning forward with an air of confidentiality, "the man is a pirate and deserves to hang in chains betwixt high and low water. My God, Captain, along with Whipple and a handful of others, mostly from Rhode Island I might add with due respect to y'r wife, such a fate would be too good for the dogs – begging your pardon, ma'am."

"Please don't worry, sir. I am entirely of your opinion."

"Are you aware that he is at large in an eighteen-gun ship named the *Rattlesnake*?"

The Customs officer nodded. "Indeed. I heard he was at Salem or Marblehead."

"But," said Kite, rising, pulling a chart out of a folio and spreading it on the cabin table, "that is not far away!"

"Not at all, Captain; why, the man is as bold a devil as any. For all I know he was in that redoubt yesterday. Yes indeed, I should not be at all surprised if he was."

"Well, well." Kite tapped the chart thoughtfully then, suggesting his visitor relax until the cargo was discharged, excused himself. "I must go on deck for a moment. Sarah, my dear, do please entertain our guest for a while."

Running up on deck he began to pace the starboard side of the after deck, ignoring the fine cloud of white dust that settled over everything. Such was his preoccupation that he failed to notice Lamont trying to attract his attention. After about twenty minutes he suddenly stopped and spun on his heel.

"Mr Lamont?" he called and the mate emerged from under a whitening fold of the mainsail that hung almost to the deck from the dipped gaff above them.

"Captain?"

"What news of Johnstone?"

"None, sir, I'm afraid."

"Damn! And how long until that confounded flour's out of the ship?"

"Another hour, two at the most."

"Very well."

But the lightermen stopped for dinner and the two hours dragged on into the afternoon so that by the time the lighter bore all the *Spitfire*'s cargo the Customs officer was dead drunk and Kite sent the barge ashore without him, ordering two men to pitch the inebriated official into Johnstone's cot.

"By God, sir," Harper remarked with a broad grin, "these recruiting methods are worthy of the Royal Navy."

"Believe me, Zachariah," Kite responded, warming to the second mate's drollery, "I have no intention of shipping that wastrel in place of Nathan Johnstone. Now," Kite went on lowering his voice, "do you know any reason why he should still be ashore?"

Harper dropped his eyes to the planking on the deck. He was a poor dissembler and his awkwardness was almost palpable.

"Zachariah?" Kite prompted.

"Well, sir, he was ashore with Carse, sir . . ."

"And? Is this significant?"

"Well, sir . . ."

"Come on, Zachariah, spill the beans, damn it."

"Carse is a Bostonian, sir, and, er, he has an uncommonly pretty sister."

Kite was aware of Jacob grinning as he coiled a rope within earshot. "Well, Jacob, is this true? What do you know about it?"

Jacob hung the rope over a belaying pin and confronted Kite. "Well, sah, all I can say is that Massa Johnstone is drawn to de wimmin like a moth to a candle."

"D'you know where this Carse lives, Jacob?"

"I do, sir," Harper admitted. "His parents run a boarding house. I stayed there between voyages."

"Very well, then. Let us have the longboat manned. Zachariah, do you come with me. Hamish," he turned to the mate, "secure the deck in my absence and get her ready for sea. We'll pick up ballast from one of the islands tomorrow."

"Aye, aye, sir."

Kite went below to consult Sarah and a few moments later he scrambled over the side.

Even almost a day after the affair on the slopes of Bunker Hill the streets of Boston fairly seethed. There was an air of nervous expectation about the place after the long months of complacent inactivity. The few troops on the streets had a slightly battered and hangdog look, and yet there was a typically British disregard for disaster in the attempt by all parties to continue with everyday affairs as though nothing of note had occurred.

Carse's boarding house stood up an alley off Ship Street and an enquiry from Kite soon revealed that Johnstone was indeed in the place. It was clear from the attitude of the serving-girl that his presence was a matter of some amusement as she rolled her eyes at Harper with a giggle.

"Damned wenches," muttered the big American.

The two men were shown into a tawdry parlour whose whitewashed walls were ochre with tobacco smoke. Harper sat down and stretched his long legs out in front of him while Kite stared out of a grimy window. A few moments later Johnstone came in. He was in his shirt-sleeves.

"Ah, Captain Kite."

Kite turned from the window and regarded him. "Mr Johnstone," he began formally, "for your absence from the schooner yesterday, I put your motive down to humanity."

"Indeed it was, sir."

"But it seems that this is no longer the case."

"Carse and I were very tired, sir," Johnstone began.

"But I am told that you are probably late abed for purposes other than sleep."

Johnstone grinned and looked from Kite to Harper and back again, seeking a measure of understanding from two fellow males. "Well, sir, I have formed a sincere attachment—"

Kite broke in. "You know, Nathan, when you first agreed to sail with me you were a grieving widower, as was I."

"And you have married again, Captain Kite," Johnstone interrupted sharply, "pray do not forget that."

"I do not even consider it, Nathan, but do not forget that you are engaged to be gunner aboard the *Spitfire*."

"Well, sir, I wish now to break that engagement and establish another." Hostility and determination were clear in Johnstone's tone.

Kite frowned. "You wish to stay in Boston?" he asked incredulously.

Johnstone nodded. "I do, sir. I intend to marry, sir."

"And what of the rumoured evacuation? What will become of you then?"

He shrugged, a trifle smugly, Kite thought. There was no point in pressing the matter, though. "Very well. I presume you wish to gather your personal effects. Will you come off with us now?"

"I will come out in an hour, Captain."

"As you please. And you may keep your prospective brother-in-law with you."

"That will not greatly trouble him, Captain Kite."

"It will not greatly trouble me either."

Kite and Harper returned to the ship in silence and it was only when they regained the schooner's deck and Kite noticed with satisfaction that Lamont had had the crew refurl the sails that Harper caught his sleeve. He turned.

"Beg pardon, sir, but I couldn't say anything in the boat." Harper spoke in a low voice.

"Well?"

"It's Carse, sir . . ."

"Go on."

"I think he's attached to the Patriot party, sir. I surmise that Johnstone may be falling for the other side."

"Johnstone's to become a rebel?" Kite asked with astonishment.

"The movement is widespread, Captain Kite. If their rebellion succeeds it will mean new opportunities and Nathan's an ambitious man."

"He's certainly a changed man," Kite said grimly, adding, "damn him." Then reflecting upon what Harper had said he asked, "And what happens if their rebellion doesn't succeed, eh? Tell me that?"

"It may well do so, sir. This is a big country and the British army cannot hold it all." That was true enough, Kite thought ruefully, thinking of the clumsy attempt to hold Boston, let alone the whole of Massachusetts. "There is land west of the mountains, sir. The rebels will retreat there like the Israelites into a land of milk and honey."

"Indians and swamps, more like," said Kite with a sudden bitterness. Then he looked sharply at Harper. "And what about you, Zachariah? You are a born American; if the Patriots win, what will you do?"

"I don't know what I shall do if they win, Captain, but for the time being you may rely upon my loyalty. I will fight with you as long as you will have me."

Kite looked hard at the big man. It was a curious world, he thought, damnably curious when a man who owed him much deserted him, and a man who owed him nothing protested a touching loyalty.

"You have my hand and my word on it, sir," Harper said, holding out his paw.

Kite took it and instantly regretted it, for he felt the pressure in the big man's grip. "I shall take your hand and your word, Zachariah. All that I ask is that if your loyalty wavers you will leave me and not deceive me."

"There would never be any question of that, sir."

"Then I am content," he said as Harper released him. "I do not wish to know when Johnstone comes off to recover his gear. He will get a surprise to find a King's officer lying in his cot. Pray put both of them over the side with the ship's garbage," he said over his shoulder as he made for the companionway and the society of his wife in the cabin below.

He was dozing in a chair when the knock came at the cabin door. Sarah laid aside her needlework and went to see who it was.

"It's Mr Johnstone," Sarah announced as Kite stirred and rubbed his face.

"What?"

"It's Mr Johnstone, my dear."

"I don't want to see him."

"I think you do, Captain Kite," said Johnstone gently, forcing his way into the cabin with an apology to Sarah. Kite was awake now and rose quickly to his feet, alarmed at Johnstone's insolence in view of his changed political sympathies.

"Damn you, Nathan! I know you have turned your coat by your intended union with Miss Carse, but you will gain nothing from me."

Johnstone held up his hand in a pacifying gesture. "Captain Kite! Please! Pray give me a moment of explanation, I beg you!"

"Sir, the so-called Patriot party have given me much cause for deep and lasting grief, so you cannot suppose that I wish to debate New England politics."

"I know that, Captain Kite! That is precisely why – Mistress Kite, can you not intercede? I know you of all people have no reason to sympathise, but pray give me a moment."

"William, perhaps," Sarah began, her lovely face marred by anxiety, "you might heed Nathan for a moment."

"Please, Captain!"

"Oh damn it. Very well."

"Thank you. I make no bones about this matter –" he looked from one to the other of them – "and I know that I owe you, Captain Kite, a great debt for your kindness. That is why I come with a proposition."

"A proposition!" Kite expostulated.

"William!" Sarah bade him to instant silence and he clamped his mouth firmly shut.

"I confess that I behaved badly in remaining ashore, but Miss Carse is a most agreeable girl, not at all the type of daughter one would suspect of a common tavern-keeper. It is true that her father and three brothers are radicals. I have had long discussions with them – that and not dissolution was the reason for my sleeplessness – and I am convinced that despite all the horrors and excesses of the mob that presently calls itself a party of patriots, there is much to be said for the libertarian instincts of these Americans. Furthermore, Captain, I believe that were you not so circumstanced, and were you not laid under so deep a grievance, both you and Mrs Kite must agree that much justice lies in the claims of the radicals. I cannot, nor would I wish to, plead their cause with you now, but I will say that there is a movement particularly advocated by the Rhode Islanders to form a naval force on behalf of the United Colonies. You cannot pretend to avoid what this implies and I wish you and your enterprise well, for in the personal you deserve your vengeance. To this end I will tell you that I know that Captain John Rathburne's ship *Rattlesnake* presently lies in Marblehead harbour."

"I already know that, if that is your proposition."

Johnstone shook his head. "No, it is not, and it eases my conscience somewhat that you already have intelligence of Rathburne's whereabouts. No, my proposition runs as follows: if this rebellion succeeds it is my intention to found or ally myself with shipowning interests in New England. Sooner or later Great Britain and America must re-establish relations, and while this might be politically strained, commercial pressures will prevail and a trade between, say, Boston and Liverpool will be revived and will flourish again. Such a trade will profit those ready to exploit it and I would have it that both the names of Johnstone and Kite were reunited under such happier circumstances. You must see, Captain Kite, that I am a rootless man unless I seize those opportunities that providence offers me. There is nothing to draw me back to Liverpool, though I own a personal attachment to your own person. Therefore, as long as you have your property in Liverpool I shall know where to find you."

"And if your rebellion fails, what then?"

"Judging by yesterday's events, I do not think it will, Captain Kite, but if it does, the revival of trade will be necessary and those who first re-establish it will first profit from it."

Kite looked at his former clerk. "You astonish me with your audacity, Nathan," he said quietly, turning to his wife. "Have you an opinion, my dear?" he asked. "You are, after all, an American."

"It is a bold notion, William, and since Nathan's fortunes lie beyond the compass of our own plans, not without merit whichever way matters come to pass."

Kite nodded. "I do not like the manner of its inception, for it goes against the grain."

"Commerce, William," Johnstone said boldly, sensing the softening in Kite's mood, "is of primary importance in this world, that you and I both know, as does Mistress Kite. Let us part as the friends we have hitherto been." He held out his hand.

Kite looked wary, then took the outstretched hand. "You and I shall both pursue our private goals and subject ourselves to the caprice of fate, Nathan, but whichever way the cards fall, and always supposing we shall both survive, let us hope that we may again shake hands in amity. Very well, I agree."

When Johnstone had gone Kite poured two glasses of wine and, handing one to Sarah, asked, "Do you despise me, Sarah?"

She took the glass and sipped at the wine, staring at her husband over its rim. "No," she said when she had swallowed and lowered the glass, "for such rifts will occur throughout the Thirteen Colonies if this civil war becomes general. Besides, you two will not act in concert until after this present matter is resolved, and in the aftermath men of goodwill must come together. But that will not be for a long time."

"Aye," Kite nodded, "and there is many a slip betwixt the cup and the lip."

"And we have a private matter to attend to."

"Whatever justice Nathan conceives to lie with the Patriots cannot lie with John Rathburne. He has passed beyond the law."

Fifteen

Beacon Island

The *Spitfire* sailed from Boston harbour the following morning under the influence of a light breeze and her headsails, slipping easily between Governor's Island and Castle William, above which flew the bold colours of the British Union flag. Passing through King Road and doubling Spectacle Island, Kite brought her up to her anchor close to Long Island. Having before sunset established the fact that he might ballast the ship from stones and shingle on the shore, he made arrangements for the hire of three local boats and some labour the following morning.

For almost a week the crew and a few local farmhands and fishermen not otherwise employed toiled at the tiresome business of loading stones and shingle into baskets, placing these in the longboat and the local craft, pulling them out to the anchored schooner and transferring the contents into the hold. Here the ballast was shovelled out into the wings and forward and aft throughout the length of the hull, to stiffen the schooner and render her stable. Long acquaintance with the *Spitfire* had determined the draft and trim at which she sailed best on all points, though this was inevitably something of a matter of compromise, and Kite made frequent observations at bow and stern. Despite a gnawing anxiety to get away and nail Rathburne in Marblehead before he escaped – and he could not rule out the strong possibility that Carse would reveal his intentions – he was nevertheless determined not to act precipitately. That *Spitfire* should be as carefully prepared as his forethought and endeavour could make her remained his paramount consideration; he had been too long at sea not to know that one should leave as little to chance as possible.

"Providence," he explained to Sarah over dinner one day, "is a false goddess unless a proper and deferential sacrifice is first

191

made to her. She lends her support only to those who prepare themselves."

Such a sententious proposition would have seemed a pomposity had not they witnessed the fighting on Bunker Hill a week or so earlier. As it was, the terrible effects of military bungling lent a creeping purpose to their activities, and while the crew grumbled about the fossicking of their commander they admired his taking of pains, particularly as he was not averse to joining in with them as they worked. For Kite, such physical involvement was in part a panacea to his impatience, and in part a need to hasten things as much as he could, for he was aware of a smouldering agitation in Sarah, whose docile acceptance of the circumscribed life of a ship-master's wife was, he knew, a temporary expedient. While the Spitfires and their hired help scrabbled and dug up the foreshore of Long Island, she went for walks across the island, wrapped in her own solitude.

In due course, however, the task was completed and Captain Kite pronounced himself satisfied with his vessel. The final layer of ballast was left in its wicker baskets on top of the dusty deposit in the hold. Next morning, the decks having been washed off, the hatch battened and the longboat hoisted inboard and placed on her chocks, the men went cheerfully forward to man the bars of the windlass. As they did so to the rousing chorus of a shanty, Sarah appeared on deck. She wore breeches, boots and a man's shirt and bore in her arms a cascade of brilliant red, white and blue silk. Calling Jacob to help her she bent the large pendant to the mainmast head flag halliards and had him run it aloft. As the breeze lifted it, it streamed out revealing its motto, red letters on a white, red-edged ground: *Spit-Fire and Seek Revenge*. On reading it, or having it read to them, the men raised three cheers and in no time at all Harper was calling out that the anchor was a-trip and the main and foresail halliards were manned. Ten minutes later *Spitfire* was heading for the north point of Long Island and the open sea of Broad Sound beyond.

There was no sign of the yards of the *Rattlesnake* in either Marblehead or Salem, though Kite stood as close inshore as he dared. He then stretched out towards Cape Cod, thinking Rathburne would cruise there on the chance of taking British merchant ships making for Boston. But here too he was disappointed and he set course for Halifax, an alternative cruising ground for a man intent on damaging British trade. Kite spoke with every ship he could bring-to in the hope of receiving news of his enemy, but the trail had turned cold.

"Or you have been deceived," Sarah said as they ate one evening with the coast of Nova Scotia grey on the northern horizon. "Put back for Boston," she added sharply, "that is where the focus of rebellion lies."

"I should like to think your tone was bred of certainty," he said smiling. "But I suppose he may well have gone to cruise in the Irish Sea."

" 'Tis too far from the seat of events, William. Think, we speak of a man who seeks every possible advantage from rebellion. Would you go far from Boston if you were such a man?"

"You are persuasive."

"Say rather that I am intuitive." Sarah paused and then added, "And we have wasted three weeks on this fruitless quest."

Kite considered the matter for a moment and then nodded his head and rose from the table. "You are right, my dear. I shall go on deck directly and put the vessel about."

"Well, Zachariah, what d'you make of her?" Kite's voice was tense with expectation and he went so far as to remove his eye from the spyglass and turn and contemplate his second mate impatiently, as though he could worm from Harper the answer he wanted by fixing him with a glare. The big American was not to be hurried.

"Look at those yards, man; they are the *Wentworth*'s, or I'm a Dutchman!" Kite said.

"They are certainly longer than one would expect on such a vessel," offered Lamont helpfully.

The *Spitfire* was close-hauled under fore and aft canvas, her square topsails furled and her sheets hauled aft as she thrashed to windward in a stiff breeze under a grey sky. It neither felt nor looked like a July day, for the overcast was mirrored in the sea and the wind drove the spume off the wavecaps in wicked little gusts that sent it over the weather bow with an intermittently vicious hiss and patter.

"Well, sir?" Kite asked, again staring through his glass as the schooner bucked under them. Harper lowered his own glass and confronted Kite. "I'm not certain, sir, I cannot be sure."

"Oh damn you, why 'tis as plain as that damned great nose on your face!"

"Well, we shall know in an hour or two, when we come up with her."

"If this wind remains as strong as it is, or strengthens further, she will have made Salem or Marblehead long before we come up with her," Kite said disconsolately.

"Then we will blockade her, or cut her out," Lamont said cheerfully.

Kite shut his glass with a snap and took himself below, while Harper and Lamont exchanged glasses, the mate raising his eyebrows. "Is he often like this?" he asked, and Harper shook his head.

"No, but then I have never seen him in such circumstances before. I am reasonably certain that ship is, or was, the *Wentworth*, but to raise his expectations would be foolish. We have to recall that if it is the *Wentworth*, the vessel was once his own property. It cannot be easy to see your own property so flagrantly used by another man."

Lamont grunted. "Like finding your wife abed with a neighbour."

A strengthening wind and nightfall failed to resolve the question for them, and Kite hove-to rather than drive to windward in the darkness. They reduced sail, hauled the headsail sheets to windward and lashed the tiller so that the *Spitfire* bobbed easily into the seas, her decks now dry. A tolerable if not a comfortable night now lay in prospect for them all. In the cabin, Kite pored over his charts. The strange sail had been on their lee bow and was clearly not intending to double Cape Cod, which suggested she was bound for Boston, Salem or Marblehead. Heaving-to was not likely to lose them their quarry, if quarry she was, for she must tuck in somewhere or stand across their bow during the night and, if she did that, she must surely be seen, for she would have to pass close while the wind lay in the west-south-west.

Writing up the *Spitfire*'s log he was convinced the ship they had seen earlier was indeed the former *Wentworth* and, bracing himself against one of the schooner's more violent curtsies to the oncoming seas, he recorded as much in the wide right-hand column of the log-book under the heading *Observations*. By the time he had sufficiently composed himself for bed, Sarah was already asleep. Staring down at her for a moment before he doused the lantern, he marvelled at her ability to stay cool. That she had a temper he had ample evidence of, but it seemed to have lain dormant for many weeks under a paradoxically seething calm.

He blew out the lantern, bent and kissed her, murmuring her name into the darkness.

He was on deck again at dawn, but now the wind had dropped and the sky had cleared so that the visibility extended for miles and he could see the blue line of the shore from Cape Ann in the north to Cape Cod in the south, with the faint outline of New Hampshire beyond the former. Only half a dozen sails were in sight, but none of them even remotely resembled the old *Wentworth*. He swore under his breath, walked forward and hoisted himself into the foremast rigging. He climbed with slow deliberation until he could throw one leg over the topsail yard and then he scanned the horizon again, but it brought him no satisfaction.

"Well," he muttered, "we shall have to start again."

Regaining the deck he found the watch had been roused and were anticipating him passing orders. "Very well, Mr Harper, let fly those heads'l sheets and let us lay a course for Salem. Full and bye on the larboard tack. Then you may set those topsails and the flying jib." The tempting smell of coffee rose from the cabin skylight and he was about to disappear below when he added, "And keep a sharp lookout."

"Aye, aye, sir."

By noon they could see there was nothing of comparable size to the *Wentworth* lying in either Salem or Marblehead, so the helm went over again and they stood south on the starboard tack, heading for the cluster of islands known as the Brewsters that lay off Boston and between which the two safely navigable ship channels wound. Kite was bitterly disappointed, the more so since he remained convinced that it had been the *Rattlesnake*, the former *Wentworth*, that he had seen the previous afternoon. In this despondent mood he went below in search of a light meal. Within an hour, however, his mood had changed and he was roused from the doze into which he had fallen by a hammering at the cabin door and the intrusion of Harper's ugly but happy face.

"It's her, sir. I've no doubt of it!"

Kite was on deck in an instant. The afternoon was now bright and sunny, the wind a steady breeze which offered the *Spitfire* her best chances, while in the lee of the distant land the sea was negligible. He recorded these details automatically; his attention was entirely engrossed by the ship to windward of them, some three miles away.

"She suddenly emerged from Nahant Bay," Harper explained, "and she carries no colours . . ."

"Meaning she wishes to conceal her intentions." Kite completed the sentence. But as if prompted by the schooner to leeward, a British ensign rose to her spanker gaff, matching the one at *Spitfire*'s own main peak. Kite registered a bearing along with the fact that they were sailing faster than the *Rattlesnake*. He was reluctant to give up the leeward position from which Rathburne might escape, but wished to be certain of his quarry before bringing his enemy to action. On his present course Rathburne looked as if he was going to make for the north ship channel, and pass inside the North Brewster Island before hauling round and beating up into Boston harbour. Perhaps the rebels had taken up more positions in their absence, or perhaps Rathburne was intending to raid shipping in the outer roads; either way he could afford to give a little ground.

"Let us also play the innocent, Mr Harper," Kite ordered. "Do you put her on the other tack and let us cross his stern. When you have done that pass word that the men are to muster at their general quarters. Have Mr Lamont report to me, but do everything without ostentation."

"Aye, aye, sir."

As the *Spitfire* came up into the wind and the watch hauled the topsail braces and shifted the headsail sheets, Kite kept his glass trained on the *Rattlesnake*. He could see the small form of two figures on her quarterdeck and fancied he recognised Rathburne, but he knew it for a foolish assumption and concentrated on the hull of the ship. It was the work of a moment to recognise the stern decorations of his own vessel, for all the emblazonment in new gilt letters of the name *Rattlesnake* upon her transom timbers. Jumping in the lens of his glass he could see a man staring back at them through a long glass. It was impossible to identify the person at such a range and, even if it was Rathburne, the sight of the *Spitfire* would mean nothing to him, unless Carse had betrayed them. Mercifully, however, whoever it was could not possibly read their name, while schooners such as the *Spitfire*, despite her Spanish origins, were sufficiently common in New England waters as to excite no suspicions. Kite explained all this to Sarah, who had come on deck and, as was her custom when her husband was handling his ship, stood quietly beside the main windward rigging.

"Captain Kite?"

Lamont, rubbing the sleep from his eyes, reported himself as required and Kite said, "That is my ship, Mr Lamont, and I intend to retake her. At the moment I am playing the innocent and attempting to pick my own ground. Have the men go to quarters quietly and prepare the guns. Double shot them but do not run them out through the ports until I pass the word."

"I understand, sir."

As if it was the most natural thing in the world Kite ordered the schooner round onto the starboard tack again and stood after the *Rattlesnake* a cable or two to windward of her track. "If he is making inwards to Boston, as I think he surely must be," he said to Sarah, "I shall try and cut him off and catch him inside the passage, where his draught and the trickiness of the navigation will hamper him."

"You think he intends to raid shipping in the roads?"

"Yes, that would seem to be very possible."

"Might he not decide that we are a suitable prize?"

Kite shrugged. "Possibly, but we are only a small schooner and he may be after larger craft." He stared ahead and out over the starboard bow. "If you'll excuse me, my dear, I must slip below for a moment."

Having steadied on her new course, he went below to consult the chart. Picking it off his table he rolled it up and took it on deck where he gave it to Sarah to hold. Then he turned to Harper and relieved him of the conn.

"I'll take the ship," he said formally.

"Very well, sir. Full and bye, starboard tack, course sou'-by-west and we're overhauling our friend."

"Very well. Now Zachariah, I'm intending to slip between Deer Island and Niches Mate, and to avoid the reef off Deer Island we must wait until Castle William lies clear between the two. It will require a tack or two, but we will arrive in the roads before our friend, as you call him, and may well pin him against the islands when we offer battle."

Harper nodded; the bigger and deeper *Rattlesnake* would almost certainly run down inside the Brewsters and join the south ship channel, entering Boston harbour by way of Nantasket Road. The action of both vessels would be seen as perfectly usual and Rathburne would not compromise his approach for fear of losing the initiative he so clearly thought he possessed.

For the next half an hour the two ships parted company, the *Rattlesnake* continuing south, leaving Kite to concentrate upon making the lead of Castle William in the distance lie between the southern point of Deer Island and the northern point of Niches Mate. He then tacked in along the lead, the *Spitfire*'s square topsails clewed up and the schooner handling under fore and aft canvas like a yacht of the Cumberland Fleet. An hour later, inside Long Island a mile from the anchorage where they had loaded their ballast three weeks earlier, they hove to and awaited the *Rattlesnake* driving up from Nantasket Road.

But after the passing of yet another hour she was nowhere to be seen, and it was Harper who, clambering aloft, reported her yards with the sails clewed up, bearing roughly south-east.

"If you ask me he's anchored, sir," Harper said as he regained the deck and reported to Kite. Kite asked Sarah for the chart and unrolled it. Harper leaned over his shoulder and laid a finger on the paper. "About here, I'd say, Captain. Near Great Brewster Island."

Kite looked up then sang out, "Helm hard over! Let fly the heads'l sheets and let fall those topsails! Brace the yards round for the starboard tack!"

The *Spitfire* gathered way and Kite steadied her for the run down Nantasket Road, stamping up and down the deck with impatience as the schooner raced to the south-east, the wind broad on the beam and the white wake flying out astern of her. It was an exhilarating half an hour as the shores of Long Island to starboard and first Gallops and then George's Islands sped past to larboard. Soon they could see from the deck the upper yards of the *Rattlesnake* over the islands and, as they cleared the southern extremity of George's Island, Rathburne's intentions became clear.

The *Rattlesnake* had been brought to her anchor close to the south of the Great Brewster Island and her boats were plying between off-lying Beacon Island, one of the so-called Little Brewsters, and the anchored ship. Beyond the anchored *Rattlesnake* lay a schooner.

"Well, I'll be damned, they are going to damage the lighthouse!" Kite announced, closing his glass. "Well, let us see if we can frustrate their plans!" He raised his voice. "Run out the guns!"

In fact, unbeknown to Kite, the schooner had been on the scene for some two hours and the work of destruction was far advanced by the time *Spitfire* arrived to contest the matter. Nevertheless, clewing up the square topsails, they approached the anchored rebel vessels with Sarah's pendant streaming from the main truck. Running past the *Rattlesnake*, they fired a broadside into her, taking her completely by surprise but apparently effecting little damage. Continuing past the *Rattlesnake*, Kite ran very close to the rebel schooner and fired into her also, shooting away her main gaff, wounding both her masts, beating in a portion of her bulwarks and lodging a few shot in her hull. Gybing, Kite stood back towards Beacon Island and threw shot into the cluster of boats, then put up his helm and ran past the eastern flank of the island, firing at the parties of men ashore. He was now compelled to break off the action and work round the island, to beat up from the south before engaging the *Rattlesnake* again.

There was little doubt that the *Spitfire*'s gunnery had damaged the rebel schooner, whose name Sarah said was the *Concordia*, but Kite was conscious of having thrown away the chance of overwhelming the *Rattlesnake* by surprise. However, he knew that had he concentrated upon her, the *Concordia* would have undoubtedly engaged the single schooner and overwhelmed them, so he was not too dispirited as he passed south of the island. He did not need a glass to see the rebel party on the island as they bore off stores and equipment from the lighthouse, nor to guess why shortly afterwards a curl of smoke became a raging fire where the rebels burnt the wooden parts of the pharos.

"Sarah, my dear," he said turning to his wife, "do you bring up the small arms with Ben, my pistols and the like."

She smiled and, her eyes wild, ran below.

As the *Rattlesnake*'s anchorage opened up again, Kite ordered Jacob to put the *Spitfire*'s helm over, then told Lamont to double-shot the guns of both batteries and to withdraw the breech quoins.

"I shall pass close across her stern," he announced. "You may fire at will, but make certain every shot tells. Any man not at a gun may take up a pistol or musket here, aft of the mainmast. You may knock heads, not hats, off."

Heading north, Kite ordered the main and foresails triced up, slowing the rate of advance, though he kept the headsails drawing. "I'm intending to tack on his quarter, Jacob, where he has no gun to bear upon us, and then run back across his stern and fire the larboard guns. D'you follow me?"

"I follow you, Cap'n Kite!" The tall negro bared his teeth in a wild grin and Kite caught the infection of excitement in that wild, fearless moment. As they closed the enemy, he saw the schooner was making sail, having cut her cable, and escaping to the north-east; then they were swiftly approaching the *Rattlesnake* and her stern began to loom over them. Forward the first gun fired, then the second, and the boom of the discharges rolled along the *Spitfire*'s side in a series of concussions that echoed between the two hulls. A musket shot struck the rail beside Kite and he saw the pale blur of a face behind the open sash of one of the stern windows. Sarah, her hair blowing in the breeze, her arm outstretched and steady, levelled a pistol and as a musket barrel emerged she fired so that the barrel was hastily withdrawn. Beside her Bandy Ben passed her another loaded pistol and she pinked a figure that leaned over the taffrail.

As the *Spitfire* drew off on the quarter an after gun was fired, but the shot flew wide and then Kite ordered Jacob to put the schooner's head through the wind, exposing her stern to the enemy who fired a number of muskets and a swivel gun into her cabin windows. One pane of glass shattered noisily.

The second pass across the *Rattlesnake*'s stern was at a greater distance than the first and the enemy had mustered more men with small arms in the cabin and at the rail. Aboard *Spitfire* a man at a midships gun was hit, another had his hat knocked off and several holes appeared in the schooner's sails, but she drew clear little the worse for her audacity. What damage she had inflicted on the *Rattlesnake* Kite was uncertain, for the smoke from the schooner's guns drifted slowly to leeward and blocked their view, but it was clear that the rebel ship had sent most of her crew ashore and was actually as vulnerable at that moment as she would ever be.

"I shall run directly alongside," Kite called out, motioning Jacob to put the helm over again and warning the men at the sheets to tend them as the schooner gybed. But he got no further, for there was a shout from forward and out of the smoke blowing to leeward came the bows of two boats which thumped alongside and then men were swarming over the side yelling like banshees.

"We've run into their bloody boats!" Lamont yelled, as he grabbed a boarding pike from the rack. Kite suddenly realised that he bore no arms, but then Bandy Ben yelled, "Captain!"

and threw him his sword. He was aware of Sarah beside him, a pistol in one hand, a sword in the other, and he lunged forward as the guns' crews rose from their pieces and thrust rammers and sponges at their assailants.

"Jacob," he roared, "ease the sheets and get her before the wind!" Then he plunged into the fray, slashing and thrusting as the Spitfires prevented the boarders from forcing their way further aft. To his left he caught sight of Harper hacking right and left with a tomahawk, and beyond him the masts and hull of the *Rattlesnake* as they glided past. By an irony, the presence of the rebels on the deck of the *Spitfire* prevented the rebel gunners left aboard from firing into the schooner as she swept by Kite felt a man cannon into him as Sarah withdrew her sword and an American voice yelled that the boats had gone and that they were being carried away. In a moment the fight ended with the attackers diving over the side and swimming back to their ship or to the two boats bobbing in the wake of the *Spitfire*.

As they drew clear, Kite took stock. One man lay dead, a pair of his own crew sat between the guns nursing broken heads, while another had a cut arm. At the foot of the foremast, Harper had pinned a single rebel, a youth of about sixteen whose feet barely touched the deck.

"Who is your commander?" Harper demanded.

Half choking the young man gasped out the name "Rathburne" and Harper let him go. Slumping onto the deck, the boy strove to regain his breath before getting unsteadily to his feet. "You can swim back to your ship, or stay a prisoner," Harper said as the boy stared astern at the growing distance between the *Spitfire* and the *Rattlesnake*.

"I surrender, sir," the youth gasped and Harper conducted his prisoner aft to where order was re-establishing itself as *Spitfire* stood out to sea.

Kite crossed the deck to the dead man. It was the rebel who had fallen heavily against him and whom Sarah had thrust through the shoulder. He had a head wound from which the blood still oozed, and a pistol ball had smashed in one eye to penetrate the brain. He nodded to two seamen.

"Throw him overboard," he said, then turned to the mate. "Secure the guns, Hamish." He smiled at Sarah, who appeared undaunted by her encounter with the enemy. "You have despatched one of them," he said, "though they drove us off, I fear," he added ruefully as Sarah, Lamont and Harper gathered round the pitiful boy who represented their sole trophy.

"Brother Jonathan is a tough nut to crack, Captain," said Harper, and Kite looked at him sharply, momentarily forgetful of where he had heard the phrase before and disproportionately fascinated by the long shadows cast by the setting sun.

"What's your name, son?" the second mate asked his prisoner.

"Joe Paston, sir."

Harper looked at Kite. "His commander's name is Rathburne, sir."

"I see," said Kite, recalling himself at this news. "We had better lock him up in the gunner's cabin."

"I'll see to it," Harper said, pushing the lad towards the companionway.

"Wait," said Kite. Turning his full attention to Paston, he asked, "Where was your Captain during the fight, Joe?"

"He was ashore, sir, a-burning the lighthouse."

"He wasn't in the boats, then?"

"No, sir."

Turning aft, Kite pulled his glass from his pocket and levelled it astern. Against a flaming sunset he could see the hummocks of the islands and the tall stone lighthouse tower from which a column of smoke still rose into the air. To the north, in silhouette against the brilliant sky, the sails of the *Rattlesnake* showed her heading north, towards Marblehead.

"Brother Jonathan is a damned tough nut to crack," he muttered and then he felt Sarah by his side.

"I failed to retake my ship," he said, taking her hand and turning towards her.

"You are not a natural killer, William, but you shall succeed at the next encounter."

"I wish you were not so certain," he said miserably, bowing under the weight of obligation.

Sixteen

The Gun

Having withdrawn offshore, Kite hove the *Spitfire* to again and the schooner lay that night upon a placid sea. He went forward to tend the men wounded in the action and found them merrily bragging over their scratches and bruises. The mood among the hands was one of elation, because they did not share their commander's sense of failure. For most of them it was their first taste of action and while firing the guns and enduring an enemy's return of fire blooded them, the short but physical encounter with the American boarders was a more satisfactory affair. In this their little victory was incontrovertible, and their pathetic prisoner evidence of their triumph.

Kite came aft again. Lamont and his watch had the deck and Kite paused beside the binnacle. He stared round the horizon. The night was moonless and the almost cloudless sky was dotted with stars; Arcturus blazed above them while the steady light of Saturn lay close to their southern meridian. Lamont coughed and Kite looked up as the mate approached until the dim gleam from the binnacle lamp showed the features of his face.

"What d'you propose doing now, sir?" Lamont asked.

Kite shrugged and shot a glance at the man at the tiller. Whatever he said would be carried below and it would be churlish to withdraw and whisper in secret.

"Well, Hamish," he said with a confidence he was far from feeling, "we roughed them up a little, but we have lost the initiative and they will know our identity now. If they rumble that we are neither a naval schooner nor a revenue cruiser, which is not very difficult, they will make enquiries. One way or another, bearing in mind the situation regarding Carse and Johnstone, our friend Captain Rathburne will soon know that the *Spitfire* is involved in some personal crusade. With half the enemy ashore burning the lighthouse, we didn't effect much . . ."

"Oh, come on, sir, that's a gloomy view, we did a wee bit more than rough up that schooner!" Lamont protested. "We knocked the tar out of his deck seams."

The helmsman grunted his agreement. "I see I am out-voted," Kite said wryly.

"I've been thinking," Lamont went on, "if we had a few more men and one heavy long gun . . ." The mate left his sentence unfinished and watched his commander's face. But Kite was unpersuaded. Where could they come by either a long gun or more men willing to join in a forlorn and private revenge?

"Well, if you can think of where we can come by a gun, I'll consider the matter," he said. He could smell something like a stew filtering up from the cabin below and he felt suddenly famished. He smiled at Lamont. "For tonight I shall wish you a good night. Keep a good lookout and call me if you are at all concerned."

"Aye, aye, sir."

In the cabin Ben served supper, and after he had cleared away and Kite had written up the log, Sarah came and stood beside her husband. Pushing her hands through his hair she ruffled it playfully.

"You are too serious a man, William."

He looked up at her and put his arm about her. "Who would not be, with a wife as lovely as you?"

She pulled a face at him then she bent and kissed him. He rose and they embraced, then Kite tore off his coat and blew out the candles. The cabin was not in total darkness, for not only did the starlight throw up a pale reflection from the dark water but the easy motion of the schooner, in troubling the surface of the sea, stirred up a phosphorescence that illuminated it with a numinous light. Lit by this cold glow, they both unrobed and stood naked before each other before coming together in a sudden and overpowering passion. Afterwards they lay together on the deck in a tangle of limbs and a disarray of clothes and blankets.

"You must have made love to Puella in this place," Sarah whispered.

"I did," Kite replied, "but you should not—"

She placed a finger on his lips. "I am not jealous . . . She was a sweet person whom I wronged, and sometimes I fancy she still sits in the shadows, keeping me company when you are on deck."

"I have never thought of her as a ghost," Kite said.

"If she is, she is a friendly one," Sarah said contentedly, "and she believed in the spirits."

"Yes, she did, and I am certain that her spirits linger here."

"And she bore you a child."

"Sarah, it is not important."

"But I am with child, William, and I think Puella's shade is not displeased."

He was incredulous, then delighted, and in the quiet of the night he reckoned the matter out. Sarah must have conceived the night before Bunker Hill, the night he had felt so optimistic about the future.

At ten o'clock the next morning the senior of the two lighthouse keepers on Beacon Island off Nantasket Point took the spyglass from his junior colleague and levelled it at the schooner just then dropping her sails and hoisting out her boat after having come to an anchor.

"No colours," the junior keeper observed nervously to his principal.

"Another damned rebel, then," the other replied.

"I thought perhaps she looked a little like that man-o'-war schooner that intervened yesterday," the junior offered, reigniting a stale argument.

"That weren't no government schooner, Jim," the senior keeper said firmly, "she was more like a privateer with some private pendant flying, I noticed . . . Hullo, there's a boat pulling ashore."

The two men watched the boat's oars catch the sunlight as her crew plied them, propelling the schooner's longboat in towards the landing place. In the stern sat a man in a cocked hat; beside him was what appeared to be a woman.

"Well, I have no idea what this is all about, Jim, but get them scatter guns. After yesterday, I don't trust no one." The principal keeper remained on the wrecked parapet of the tower as his colleague scrambled below. The previous day had been a terrible shock and he feared worse was to come. He stared again through the glass. Was the "woman" a ruse? A seaman dressed in a gown? The fact that the lighthouse had escaped total destruction the previous day had been entirely due to the timely arrival of a strange and unidentified schooner, but the rig was common, and in the outrage of the rebels' looting of the lighthouse neither of the keepers had taken in any details of the intervention on their behalf taking place a mile away. As it was the rebels had burnt the wooden parts of the lighthouse, removed all the lamp-oil and the gunpowder for the fog signal gun, stolen the hay and a thousand bushels of barley from the island's barn and terrorised the little community. They had departed swearing to come back and complete the job after they had dealt with the intruding schooner. When they had made off, they had taken the two pulling boats which belonged to the island, leaving the keepers and their families isolated and fearful. Was the arrival of this schooner the promised threat of further destruction, or the return of the friendly vessel?

There seemed to be a great deal of activity in the waist of the schooner, which suggested some intention which could only be hostile. The older keeper watched the boat approach the landing then turned for the ladder leading below. The rebels had burned the wooden staircase and he swore volubly. He was no longer a young man and the staircase had been bad enough, but negotiating the temporary ladder his colleague had rigged up made his rheumaticky limbs creak with effort.

At the open door at the base of the tower the junior keeper handed him a blunderbuss.

"Thank you, Jim," the principal keeper said as they waited for the party to come up from the landing place. They could already see the boat pulling back to the schooner having landed its passengers. The principal keeper felt his stomach twisting with apprehension: there was something unnaturally threatening about all this and he was too old for more excitement. A moment or two later the two keepers were approached by a middle-aged man in a dark blue coat, white breeches and boots. He appeared to point something out to his companion, though what this was neither keeper could decide, but the stranger wore no sword and appeared relaxed and smiling, while at his side, her hand resting upon his arm, walked a woman in a bottle-green riding habit. Beneath the hem of her skirt polished boots gleamed intermittently in the sunshine and as they came closer the two keepers could see that, far from being a seaman in disguise, her feathered tricorne shadowed an uncommonly beautiful face.

"Good morning," the blue-clad gentleman said, doffing his hat and smiling. The two keepers kept silent, their blunderbusses held across their chests. "You suffered no casualties in yesterday's attack, I hope?" he enquired.

"Would it have mattered to you, if we had?" the principal keeper asked truculently.

"I am Captain William Kite," the gentleman said, ignoring the affront and replacing his hat. "I am commander and owner of the privateer-schooner *Spitfire* . . ."

"We don't wish to treat with any damned rebels, Captain, nor do we want any trouble. We are here for the benefit of mariners."

"My dear sir, we are not rebels," Kite expostulated. "I was hoping that our intervention yesterday afternoon prevented the rebels inflicting much damage upon your station." He looked up at the smoke-marred tower. "But I see that has not proved to be the case."

The two keepers exchanged glances, seemingly mollified. "They did enough," the older man said, "and threatened to do more. If you were willing, would you take word of the attack into Boston? The rebels stole all our stores, oil and powder, not to mention our boats. Perhaps General Gage will send us a garrison."

"Yes, I will do that if you wish to draft a despatch, but I have first to ask a favour of you."

"Oh, what is that?" The principal keeper narrowed his eyes suspiciously.

"I wish to take on board your signal gun. I see the rebels did not take that. It is a twelve-pounder, I believe."

"It is an eighteen-pounder," the younger of the two keepers said, but the older held up his hand.

"I can't let you do that. 'Tis a signal gun to be fired in case of fog."

"I have a need of it," said Kite, "and you said the rebels stole your powder. Besides, you could pretend that the rebels took the gun as well."

"They did try and spike it, 'tis true," said the junior keeper.

"Hold your tongue!" his senior snapped and then, screwing up his face and looking from Kite to his wife, he asked, "Why would you be wanting an eighteen-pounder?"

207

"Because I have a particular desire to engage that ship that landed her crew here yesterday."

"The *Rattlesnake*?"

"The *Rattlesnake*," Kite agreed, "formerly the *Wentworth*, a vessel not long since owned by myself and seized as an act of piracy by a Captain Rathburne."

"John Peck Rathburne, eh? God, I know that bastard – begging your ladyship's pardon."

Sarah graciously excused the principal keeper with an inclination of her head. "Do you know him?" she asked sweetly.

The principal keeper nodded. "Aye, I am originally from Rhode Island. I should have recognised him! I recall him now," he turned to his colleague, "he was that bugger in the brown coat, d'you recall? He led the incendiaries . . ."

"He is very good at burning things down," Sarah said, her voice suddenly harsh.

"Ah, well, I wish I'd a-known . . . Not that we could have done much, just the two of us with our wives and a few children, but still."

"Could you not say that he made off with your eighteen-pounder?" Kite repeated.

"He stole off everything else!" the younger keeper exclaimed. "He'd have taken the gun if he could have! But for your arrival he might have done just that!"

"Without powder, you can't use the thing to defend yourself or warn any ships of fog, can you?" Kite persisted.

"No," the principal keeper said ruminatively, "but what will you do for shot? We have none here."

"We shall manage," Kite said, "and I can offer you gentlemen a little money by way of smoothing matters with your superiors, whilst adding my evidence that we saw the rebels bearing your gun away . . . You may write all this in your despatch which I will send into Boston at the first opportunity."

"I am not much of a hand at the writing."

"I can write," said his younger companion.

"Aye, but you'd not know what to say."

"Perhaps," put in Sarah, smiling benignly, "while my husband and his men shift the gun, you and I can sit down and compose your despatch."

The principal keeper rubbed the side of his nose with a grubby finger. "How much would you be thinking of, Captain?"

"Would fifty pounds between you be a sufficient—"

"Sixty," interrupted the junior keeper.

"I told you to hold your tongue."

"Don't squabble, gentlemen," said Kite gently. "To be truthful fifty is as much as I can reasonably afford and sixty is out of the question, but shall we say, for the ease of division, fifty-four gold sovereigns? Twenty-seven pounds each must surely exceed your individual annual emoluments."

"Fifty-four pounds is fine, sir," said the principal keeper hurriedly, watching as Kite, fishing in his coat-tails, drew out a purse.

"Shall we withdraw into the pharos," he asked amiably, "and conclude our business in private?"

The eighteen-pounder weighed two tons, and although it proved possible to move it some way towards the landing on its carriage it was clear that the path was too uneven to facilitate the matter properly. This eventuality had been foreseen, however, and Harper and most of the *Spitfire's* crew arrived ashore with spare spars, some timbers and a quantity of cordage and blocks, permitting the rigging of two pairs of sheer legs. By erecting one pair of sheers directly over the gun, it was lifted off its carriage and then lowered onto short billets of wood, made largely from dunnage and toms brought ashore from the schooner. By securing lines to the trunnions a combination of men and a pair of small horses hired for the day from the farm on the island worked the gun further towards the landing, the sheers being moved to assist over the roughest of the ground.

By sunset, aided now by the downward slope of the land towards the beach, the gun reached the high-water mark. Kite was unwilling to lose an instant, and so he sent off to the schooner for a pot-mess, fed the men round an open fire on the beach and then urged them on to complete their task. Under the stars the men of the *Spitfire* toiled on into the night.

While Kite, Harper and the greater part of the *Spitfire's* company concentrated on dragging the gun down from its position near the lighthouse to the place selected for its embarkation, a smaller party of seamen under Lamont worked on board the schooner. Their task had been to construct a raft from materials on board and some taken off the island. A number of water casks were emptied and placed inside a rough framework of lashed spars, held together within this structure by a net to which they were individually lashed. The whole structure was then covered with a storm trysail of heavy-grade canvas, folded in half for additional strength and stretched by means of a rope lacing. This extemporised raft was then dragged ashore and anchored in water reckoned deep enough to float it even when loaded. At about nine o'clock that evening the relocated sheer legs lowered the heavy gun onto the contrivance. It bore the two tons of dead weight well and by ten o'clock, the men having wearily pulled the two boats towing their cumbersome burden back out to the anchored *Spitfire*, the gun lay alongside the schooner. The foresail throat halliard had been overhauled and shifted from the fore gaff jaws to the end of the fore boom and this was topped up with the sheet, unshackled from the deck, left on it as a purchase. By this means the eighteen-pounder was finally deposited upon the *Spitfire*'s deck, inducing a slight list. By midnight the carriage had followed and the hands were piped below, orders being passed to turn out again at daylight.

The following morning, having obtained additional stout timbers from the roof of a partly burned outhouse adjacent to the lighthouse keepers' dwellings, Harper and Kite began to fashion an extempore barbette just forward of the main hatchway where the longboat usually nestled on her chocks. They had compensated for the additional weight of the eighteen-pounder by striking four of the small broadside guns down into the hold, simultaneously clearing the larger weapon's field of fire. Before securing the hatch, the deck was shored up from below to take the weight of the heavier gun. Having completed bolting the necessary beams to the deck, a traversing slide was built on the barbette. This was liberally slushed with tallow and linseed oil and topped by the gun's carriage, shorn of its wheels. Finally, twenty-six hours after Kite had opened negotiations with the keepers to acquire the gun, all forty hundredweight of the large iron weapon was laid on the carriage, the cap squares were closed and pinned, and the men raised a ragged but spontaneous cheer. Before sending them to dinner Kite ordered a practise firing. A charge of powder was brought up on deck, wadded home and, with the gun pointed away from the island, fire was applied to the touch-hole.

As the charge in the chamber exploded, the gun carriage recoiled satisfactorily along the slide, though the whole ship shook with the reverberations of the thunderous discharge. But the gratifying concussion brought smiles to the faces of the men and two of them executed an excited little caper, to the delight of their watch-mates and the general merriment of all hands.

"Belay that bloody dido," Lamont said with a laugh. "Larbowlines away for dinner," he ordered and with the larboard watch sent below for their midday meal, the starbowlines manned the windlass and the halliards. Half an hour later the two keepers on the parapet of the wrecked lighthouse stood and watched the schooner as she disappeared behind George Island and headed towards Nantasket Road, heading for Boston.

"These are strange times," the principal keeper remarked philosophically, his fingers jingling the gold in his pocket.

"Aye, they are," concurred his colleague with a laugh.

"She was a handsome woman, that Mistress Kite . . ." the older man said wistfully.

The younger man nodded enthusiastically. "Aye, she was that. And she knew all the right words to say to explain matters."

"Aye, and she had to help you with spelling some of them words, too."

The older man smiled at the recollection. Then he stirred and said, "We had better put that money safe away; I don't want them dirty bastard rebels getting their greedy paws on it if they come back."

"No," the younger man said, grinning, "not like they took the fog-signal gun."

The two men laughed and congratulated themselves. "Not a word now, Jim lad, not even to your sainted mother."

Kite hardly dared to suppose that his luck had changed when he met a naval cutter in the King Road. If he could pass to her commander the task of informing General Gage of the attack on the lighthouse, he could the sooner be about his own affairs. He gave the schooner's waist a quick glance: the eighteen-pounder lay concealed under a tarpaulin and looked like a pile of deck cargo. They had also taken Sarah's pendant down while the displaced longboat was under tow astern, making the *Spitfire* look even more like a merchantman than she really was.

To attract the attention of the outward-bound cutter, Kite had a bow chaser fired to leeward and then hove to and hauled the longboat alongside, ordering half a dozen seamen into it and leaping in to take the tiller himself. He felt his spirits lift as he clasped the despatch largely dictated by Sarah and painfully written out by the junior keeper of the Brewster lighthouse and the boat danced across the wavelets towards the cutter which was in turn heaving-to. Scrambling up the little vessel's side Kite raised his hat and introduced himself.

"Captain Kite of the schooner *Spitfire* of Liverpool."

"John Gilbert, lieutenant-in-command of His Britannic Majesty's cutter *Viper*, at your service." The two men shook hands.

"I am on passage, Lieutenant Gilbert, but have been in contact with the lighthouse on the Brewster. They were making signals of distress having been attacked yesterday by rebels. We did what we could, but the lighthouse has been damaged and its stores completely looted. The keepers are anxious for the continuing existence of the pharos, not to mention their own safety, for I understand the rebels threatened to return. I have here their report of the incident."

Gilbert took the offered packet and nodded. "We were on our way out there, Captain Kite, having heard some rumours from the village of Hull on Nantasket that smoke had been seen rising from Beacon Island."

"Forgive the presumption, sir," Kite said, "but the faster a garrison is placed on the island, the better. I believe the keeper's report to be comprehensive, having urged him to write it to secure the prompt response of the authorities, and it may well be advantageous to convey it directly to Boston rather than waste time merely confirming the details. General Gage or the admiral will need to put troops or marines ashore as soon as possible in order to deter a further rebel descent on the island."

Gilbert considered a moment and then nodded. "Very well, Captain. My thanks to you. I will see what I can do. Tell me, where are you bound?"

"To Halifax, sir. I cleared outwards from Boston a couple of days ago, having discharged a cargo of flour from Antigua."

"Very well. And thank you, Captain."

The two men took their leave. As he put back to the *Spitfire*, Kite had the satisfaction of seeing the cutter swing round and her sails trimmed for a return passage to Boston. He wanted to escape all entrapment and involvement, and the encounter had been fortunate. Besides, a report brought by a naval officer would have more impact than one brought by a mere merchant master, so the meeting with the *Viper* was to the advantage of all parties anxious to defend the rule of law.

Both Lamont and Harper wore anxious expressions as they met him at the rail. He scrambled back over the *Spitfire*'s side and the longboat was passed astern again on its painter.

"Well, gentlemen, that was the cutter *Viper* and Lieutenant John Gilbert proved most obliging. I think the coast is now clear for us to proceed, so let us work out clear of the islands and thereafter lay a course for Cape Cod."

"You are going in chase of the *Rattlesnake*, then, sir?" Harper said.

"Why, Zachariah, what else should you suppose I would do?"

"Nothing, sir, but . . ."

"But we need to be certain, Captain Kite," interjected Lamont, "so that we can better prepare ourselves."

"Indeed, I agree. We shall dine together once we have sufficient offing, in order to do just that. But for now let us work out clear of the Brewsters."

"Aye, aye, sir."

And hauling round herself, *Spitfire* headed again for the passage between the islands and the open sea beyond.

Chapter Seventeen

Nantucket Sound

That evening the light in the cabin burned late. Hitherto the cabin had been Kite's private quarters, but that night, leaving the deck to Jacob, Kite entertained his two officers in formal state. This was not entirely a disinterested matter, for he had formed a liking for both men and they, it seemed, rubbed along together very well.

"We all need a good night's sleep, gentlemen," Kite said, as Ben cleared the dishes and Sarah made to withdraw at least from the table. "Stay with us, my dear," he said, restraining her, "for this whole affair touches you as much as the rest of us and we should welcome your opinion, should we not, gentlemen?"

Lamont and Harper both concurred; Mistress Kite was a woman whose society it was difficult to avoid enjoying and besides, Captain Kite's hospitality, rare though it was, proved lavish enough when he dispensed it.

"I think ye've earned a place at our council, Mistress Kite, and a welcome one, if I may say so," Lamont said, "if your conduct in the late scrap with the rebels was anything to go by."

"Hear, hear," said Harper as Ben completed his task, drawing the cloth and setting a decanter of Madeira on the table. Kite drew the stopper and passed it first to Lamont.

"Now," he said, clearing his throat, "I am certain that our friend Rathburne has retired to Rhode Island to refit. I am equally certain that he will be back to raid the Brewsters again and, one way or another, that he knows who and what we are. He is not a man, I conceive, to let matters drop. On the contrary he is likely to come looking for us so, if we are to regain any initiative, we must fight on our own terms and for this the eighteen-pounder gives us our best chance." Kite paused and looked round the table. "Zachariah, you are looking troubled; what is the matter?"

"Sir, I heard you talking to Hamish here, and saying that we could make up langridge and may even find some rocks in the ballast to charge the big gun up with, but if we could threaten him by implying we have a heavy calibre weapon capable of battering him from a distance . . ."

"I have thought of that." Kite leaned forward eagerly. "The bore of the eighteen-pounder is a little larger than the sheaves in a number of the heavy blocks on board. We have several spare blocks in store, and by fitting rope grommets we can match the bore. A few pairs of these with bolts such as we keep for the channels between each of the sheaves will make good bar shot and my plan of attack is this . . ."

Carefully, and in some detail, Kite explained his intentions, concluding: "So it does not greatly matter in what circumstances we encounter the *Rattlesnake*, only that when we do so, the gun crew acts with absolute coolness. I am therefore going to order you, Hamish, to handle the eighteen-pounder. Pick your men carefully and impress upon them the absolute necessity of following the plan." He paused and stared at Lamont, letting his import sink in.

The mate nodded. "I understand, Captain."

"Good. Now, Zachariah, I am depending upon you to take the forward guns and the headsail sheets, while I shall handle the after guns and the ship herself. Both of us will be prepared either to lead the boarders or, if matters go against us, to defend the ship. To that end I shall require you to see that all the men not selected by Hamish for the eighteen-pounder have weapons prepared and to hand. We will issue small arms tomorrow morning and, depending upon how long we have to wait for Rathburne, draw charges and renew them every morning or after any rain or excessive spraying. Is that understood?"

Lamont and Harper both nodded.

"Good. Now, since it may be some days before we find our quarry, we will divide the ship's company into three watches. I will prepare watch bills tomorrow forenoon and we will commence the three-watch system at noon."

"You mean to keep a watch, then, Captain?" Lamont asked.

"Yes. When we meet Rathburne, we will require all our men to exert themselves to the utmost and by this means we can all benefit from the rest." Kite paused again, judging the impact of his words. "Finally," he said at last, "while I do not intend that we commit ourselves to a useless fate and I am confident that this will not become necessary, if events do go against us I shall not willingly submit. This man has done me and mine," he paused and looked at Sarah, whose expression was one of rapt attention, "a deal of harm. I am not out for revenge, but for the only form of justice that men of Rathburne's stamp comprehend." He stared round from face to face. "Now, any questions?"

Lamont shook his head.

"Beg pardon, sir, and you, Mistress Kite, but what of your wife, sir?"

"I shall fight," said Sarah simply, speaking for the first time since the council of war had started.

"But is that wise?" Harper asked, colouring so that Kite wondered if he knew, or guessed at, Sarah's condition.

"No, it is not wise, Zachariah," Sarah said coolly. "It would be wise to retire quietly to England with my husband," she reached out and placed one hand over Kite's as he leaned forward clasping his glass, "but then I am an American and I am not much given to wisdom, Zachariah, much like yourself." She smiled with such charm that the three men all laughed.

"Well," said Kite, raising his glass, "here's to our next encounter with the *Rattlesnake*."

After the two mates had gone, Harper to his cot and Lamont to take over the watch on deck, Kite turned to Sarah. "Zachariah has a point, Sarah. Does he know of your condition?"

"Certainly not!" she exclaimed with a laugh, tossing her hair in a charmingly youthful motion. "As for Zachariah being right about my lack of wisdom, you know my sentiments. My child will not wish to be born an orphan and I would rather die at your side than survive to be at Rathburne's mercy, whatever happens to you."

Kite laughed. "You might lack wisdom, my love, but you certainly do not lack honesty!"

"Come," she said rising and matching the gentle roll of the *Spitfire*. "If you are keeping the morning watch, we should get some sleep."

They cruised for a day or two in Rhode Island Sound without success. Outside his own watch, Lamont and a pair of seamen he had selected for the big gun's crew carefully prepared the extemporised ammunition for the eighteen-pounder, while Harper, in his watch below, prepared the small arms, made up cartridges, checked the knapping of flints and the edge on cutlasses, tomahawks and boarding pikes.

After a while Kite set the *Spitfire*'s bowsprit east from Block Island, cruising the shores of Buzzard's Bay and Martha's Vineyard, nosing into New Bedford and scouring every inlet along Nantucket Sound. They sighted fishing boats and the occasional coasting vessel, as well as two Royal Naval frigates and a sloop of war, but *Rattlesnake* had vanished, or so it seemed. Kite held to his theory in the face of an increasing if gentle and well-meant disagreement with Lamont.

"You have put too much trust in your judgement of the man, Captain Kite," Lamont argued. "It is all right for you, with a single objective, but Rathburne, for all his hot-blooded temper, is only a part of the rebel movement. He may well be subject to orders."

In the end Kite had to admit that the mate's opinion that Rathburne had retreated, not to Rhode Island, but to the coast of New Hampshire, or perhaps that of Maine, was probably correct.

"If they are meditating another descent on the lighthouse," Lamont continued to argue with increasing conviction, "they will waste little time and could have dropped into Plymouth or Portland before returning to raid the Brewsters again."

Kite capitulated with a good grace and once again they doubled Cape Cod, this time heading to the northwards, standing inshore towards the Brewster Islands. But here they saw the red dots of British uniforms ashore, and signs of men working on scaffold boards around the lantern of the lighthouse tower. Beyond the hummocks of the islands they could see too the masts and spars of two vessels lying at their anchors. One appeared to be a man-o'-war cutter and Kite thought her the *Viper*.

"Well, the lighthouse seems secure enough from further attack," Kite said gloomily, tucking his glass away and giving orders to put the *Spitfire* about yet again. He leant his weight to the tiller as the sheets were trimmed and the men milled expectantly in the waist. They were enjoying the relaxed regimen of the three-watch system, but the delay in bringing their enemy to book was beginning to grate. It was almost noon and most of the ship's company were on deck, either idling in the sunshine or waiting to relinquish or relieve the forenoon watch. He turned and regarded Sarah, Lamont and Harper, bracing themselves as the schooner swooped over the waves and ploughed through intermittent patches of brilliant sunshine.

Kite frowned uncertainly. He remained convinced Rathburne must return to Rhode Island sooner or later and decided that he might more certainly be induced to do so if word reached him that Rhode Island itself had been attacked. And suppose that he had never left Newport at all? Suppose all this time Rathburne, aware that the British were repairing and fortifying Beacon Island, had betaken himself quietly home? What a fool he had been to think that by simply trailing his coat up and down outside the entrance Rathburne would fall for his foolish enticement! Damn the man! If the *Rattlesnake* was in Newport Road, then it was time he was made to feel the weight of his enemy's wrath. Moreover, he thought with sudden resolution, it was the one way he could recoup almost all the initiative he had lost by his earlier encounter off the lighthouse.

"I intend to go back to Rhode Island," he said suddenly. "We will enter the harbour and attack any shipping we find there." As Lamont opened his mouth to venture an opinion, Kite added "But me no buts, Hamish. I am resolved."

"I was not going to argue, Captain Kite, only to suggest we could the more quickly attack shipping in Salem or Marblehead."

"Damn Salem and Marblehead," Kite said with a sudden ferocity, "I have no quarrel with either place."

"No, nor I," put in Sarah, stepping forward and uncharacteristically thrusting her opinion into their debate, "but I have a strong reason for returning to Newport!"

"I have no argument with your proposition, ma'am, nor that of your husband. Besides," Lamont added wryly, "perhaps Master Rathburne has been there all the time."

"Exactly what troubles me!" concurred Kite.

"What about you, Zachariah?" Sarah asked, staring at the big American.

"Where you go, ma'am, Zachariah Harper will follow. But he will the most willingly follow you back to Newport."

Sarah smiled. "I am obliged to you, sir," she said, bobbing him a flattering curtsy on the canting deck, and Kite and Lamont grinned as Harper's ugly face flushed brick-red.

*   *   *

On their return they beat through Nantucket Sound under a grey sky that fitted the grimmer mood aboard the schooner. Word had been passed among the crew that they had abandoned their hunt for the *Rattlesnake* off shore, and that Captain Kite was determined to attack any vessels lying at anchor off Newport. The plan found no dissenting voice on board, for all were by now spoiling for a fight, emboldened by their action with the rebels on the 21st of July and intent on inflicting greater damage on the enemy. Whispers of acquiring a prize or two began to circulate, following rumours of Captain Kite's need of more money to sustain his vendetta against John Rathburne. There were more rumours, said to be facts though the source was never revealed, that the *Rattlesnake* was known to be lying at anchor there.

Passing between Nantucket Island and Martha's Vineyard on the afternoon of Monday the 31st of July 1775, *Spitfire* lay down under reefed canvas as a summer squall passed over her, her decks darkening under the onslaught of driving rain as she ran her lee scuppers under. Astern the longboat tore along in her wake as the white water rushed out from her stern with a wildly seething hiss that Sarah, sitting reading in the cabin, exclaimed was like the noise of a snake.

The realisation that she had spoken out loud made her start. She was alone, Kite having run on deck as Harper raised the first alarm of the approaching squall.

"What foolishness," she murmured, staring about her, but her heartbeat had increased and the hairs on the nape of her neck were standing up in a strange sensation, like the excitement before love. "Was I so lost in my book," she asked herself, "and so roused from my abstraction?"

The strange, almost concupiscent feeling did not diminish as the moments passed, but her heartbeat remained strong and her breathing light and hurried so that she placed an involuntary hand on her breast and rose, braced against the extreme heel of the deck, her other hand steadying herself on the deck beam overhead.

"Puella . . . ?" she whispered, dropping her book and staring into the dark recesses of the cabin. "Puella? Are you there?"

And it seemed to Sarah that in the hiss of the sea, the shriek of the wind in the rigging above and the creaking of the labouring hull as it accelerated through the sea, that Puella answered her in a voice that was audible, yet could not be heard.

"Puella," Sarah whispered, no longer frightened, but highly excited, "shall things be well with us?"

And again the word came without sound, but full of conviction and certainty, so that Sarah sank back into the lashed chair. Gradually her pulse subsided and she was flooded with a great joy, like the afterglow of love. Her hand strayed downwards from her breast to her belly, as if seeking the life growing within her, and at this sensual moment the wind dropped. The heel of the schooner's deck eased suddenly, and a patch of sunlight fell about them, illuminating the wake that rushed like a millstream out from below the windows of the cabin.

Five minutes later Kite, his cloak and hat running with water, came through the cabin door, his face split with a grin. "My God, Sarah, but did you feel the old girl *go*? Why, damn me, I think she is spoiling for a fight!"

He helped himself to a drink from the decanter nestling in its fiddles against the cabin bulkhead and turned to her, glass in hand. She shook her head. Seeing one hand upon her belly and recalling her condition with sudden contrition, Kite crossed the deck and dropped to his knee beside her.

"Sarah, forgive me, but are you well?"

She looked at his face and smiled, placing her right hand reassuringly upon his arm, whilst leaving the other on her quickening womb. "I have never been better in my life, my darling," she said.

Kite shook his head. "You must not fight, my dearest," he said, "you must not exert yourself."

"Shhh." She placed an admonitory finger on his lips. "I have put two fine flints in your Cranston pistols and shall do as I promised, William. Not even you are going to come between me and the man who murdered Arthur."

"Sarah . . ."

"But me no buts, as you are fond of saying to others. I do not love you any the less, but Arthur has no other champion but me."

"That is not true," Kite began, but Sarah overrode him.

"You are my new and happy life, William, but my old one is not quite over. Providence is never quite as tidy and accommodating as we should like her to be."

"I am anxious for the child, Sarah."

"Rest easy on that score, my dearest William."

220

"But you cannot be certain, and it would be foolish to take risks . . ."

"Shush! I *am* certain. Don't ask me why, but I am."

And although he pressed her no further, he involuntarily stared about the cabin, as though searching for something.

By passing south of Martha's Vineyard, it was Kite's intention to deceive any watchers on the shore and to look as though he intended to make a passage to New York. But after dark, when the wind had dropped to a light westerly breeze, he headed the *Spitfire* north towards Rhode Island. His plan was to pass the Narrows at dawn and descend upon the unsuspecting ships anchored off Newport in the first hour of daylight. He had therefore arranged to be called an hour before his watch commenced at four in the morning.

Harper called him at three and he eased himself from his bed-place trying not to wake Sarah.

" 'Tis six bells, sir," Harper said in a low voice, "and the wind has fallen light."

"We are not yet close up to the Beaver's Tail, then?" Kite queried.

"No, sir."

"Damn! Very well. I'll be up directly." Kite reached for his breeches and boots. The first flush of dawn showed the panes of the stern windows as pale rectangles, giving him just sufficient light to find his clothes. He must shave and dress carefully, for he would be in action later and knew that he must compose his mind in order to concentrate on taking *Spitfire* into Newport Road. At least the delay gave him a little more time.

He was tying his stock when the door burst open. "What the devil—?" he began as behind him Sarah stirred and Harper's figure loomed in the doorway.

"Sir! It's the *Rattlesnake*!"

"*What?*"

"She's coming down the coast from the east—"

"From the *east*?" Kite grabbed his coat and hat. "Come!" He paused only to call Sarah: "It's Rathburne, Sarah! Wake up!"

But she was already awake and he caught sight of her legs as she swayed to her feet. An instant later he was pounding up the companionway behind Harper.

221

Eighteen

Point Peril

They were closer in than Kite had supposed when Harper had warned him the wind was light. The lighthouse on Beaver Tail was broad on the larboard bow, with Brenton's Key almost ahead. Price's Neck and Coggeshall's Ledge stretched away to the east, grey against the dawn sky. And there too was a ship, running down from the east, no more than five miles away.

"The wind's changed," Kite said, fishing for his glass.

"It was in the east at midnight, sir. Hamish said it went right round at about six bells in the first watch. I've called all hands," Harper went on, and Kite was aware then of men milling in the waist. "I'm certain it's the *Rattlesnake*, sir," he added as Kite levelled his glass.

Kite needed only a moment to recognise those extended yards. He shut his glass with a decisive snap. "So am I."

He strode forward to stand on a gun truck, one hand holding the main shrouds. "My lads!" he called as the men's faces turned towards him like the features of ghosts in the dawn. "My lads, that ship is the *Rattlesnake*. You all know she is the vessel we have been searching for. I do not know why we have not encountered her before, but now that she has so obligingly appeared I urge you all to do your duty. Follow the orders that I or Mr Lamont or Mr Harper will give you and we shall prevail. Remember, we have justice on our side. Good fortune guard you all! Now take up your battle stations!"

"Three cheers for Cap'n Kite!" someone yelled, and as the cheers died away the *Spitfire*'s company broke away for their quarters.

Lamont and Harper came aft and there was a brief moment of conference. "Well, do you recall the plan?" Kite asked anxiously. Both men nodded. "Good luck then." They shook hands and as

Kite turned to Jacob on the helm and passed orders so that the schooner swung round towards her foe, Sarah appeared. She wore breeches and an old coat of Kite's, cinched in to her waist with a seaman's belt from which the butts of her two pistols protruded. On her head she wore the tricorne with its ostrich feather. He could not suppress a smile.

"You are a veritable pirate, my love," he remarked.

"You forgot your sword," she said, producing the weapon from behind her back.

"The devil I did! I'm mightily obliged to you, Mistress Kite. Will you give me a kiss for luck?" Their lips touched and then he said quietly. "Do take care, Sarah. Would that I could, but I cannot watch over you."

"I would not have Captain Kite become Nanny Kite. You have your task to do and I shall do mine. All will be well."

Kite brought the *Spitfire* hard on the wind, which was growing with the daylight. As soon as he had steadied the schooner on her course, he ordered Harper's men to let fall the square topsail to close the distance as rapidly as possible. As the men on deck toiled at the halliards, Sarah ran up her red and white battle flag with its legend, *Spit-Fire and Seek Revenge.*

In the waist Lamont had cleared away the eighteen-pounder and its prepared ammunition was being brought up from below.

"Where is our prisoner?" Kite asked Jacob, into whose charge Joe Paston had been given.

"He's below, sah."

"Bring him up on deck, Jacob," he ordered, taking the helm and leaning against the heavy tiller. He had forgotten what hard work steering was, particularly with the *Spitfire* going to windward hand over fist like this. He stared ahead. The *Rattlesnake* was slightly inshore of them, on their lee bow, and Kite guessed what Rathburne would do as they came up and he recognised their hostile intention. The thought quickened his heartbeat, but brought a vicious little smile to his face as a cold resolve fastened itself around his innermost being. He had dodged this arrogant Rathburne's parries for so long, made a clumsy riposte off Beacon Island some eleven days earlier, and now he was intent upon a fatal reprise.

Returning his attention to his own deck he called out, "Mr Lamont! Are you ready?"

"Ready, sir!" came the mate's response.

"Mr Harper?"

"Ready, aye ready, sir!"

"Very well. Mr Harper! The moment I luff, I want the square topsail off her!"

"Aye, aye, sir!"

"Mr Lamont! You may first train to larboard. You other gun captains, the larboard battery will be the first to engage."

A chorus of acknowledgement greeted his instructions and at this moment Jacob reappeared with an ashen-faced Paston. "Master Joe," Kite addressed the boy, "how are you this morning?" Paston mumbled something and Kite went on, "Do you keep my wife company. She will look after you. We are about to engage Captain Rathburne, as you can see." He looked at his wife. "Keep an eye on the boy, my dear. He'll make an admirable shield. Oh, and Joe, don't try any tricks, or someone might have to shoot you dead."

Paston shuffled miserably across the deck towards Sarah. He was shivering with cold and fear and looked quite incapable of any form of trick.

Grinning, Kite looked ahead again. The *Rattlesnake*'s ensign was hidden from him by her forward sails, but if he was in any doubt as to whether the approaching ship knew of their own identity this was now removed as a great pendant rose to her main truck and suddenly fluttered out to leeward. Kite raised his glass and had no trouble in reading the inscription: *Don't Tread on Me*, which wound alongside the undulating image of a rattlesnake. He glanced up: above his head Sarah's pendant matched the rebel banner and he felt a surge of ridiculous elation thrill him. Behind him he could hear the snap of the British red ensign as it flew from the main peak.

"That is *my* ship," he growled, unconscious that he spoke at all as the two vessels closed the distance between them and he studied the *Rattlesnake* through his spyglass. And equally unconscious, he raised his voice so that the sound of it quelled any chattering between the men as they crouched or squatted at their stations, or soothed the nerves of those for whom these last minutes before action were filled with the awful anticipation of death.

"Steady, boys, steady . . . She's coming down like a lamb to the slaughter just fine and dandy-oh . . . Steady, Jacob, keep her full and bye, full and bye . . . That's fine . . . Soon now he'll bear up and try . . . Soon now . . . Soon . . . Now wait for it . . . Come on, Captain Rathburne . . . Come on, now . . .

"*There she goes!*"

The *Rattlesnake* suddenly altered course as Rathburne bore up, hauling his yards, crossing the *Spitfire*'s bow and exposing his starboard broadside. Kite lowered his glass as the points of yellow light rippled along the *Rattlesnake*'s side to be extinguished an instant later by grey smoke which drifted off towards them in a lazy cloud. Then the balls whistled past, two passing through the square foretopsail, several plunging into the sea alongside, the rest whistling away God knew where as the deep and shocking rumble of their discharge reached the approaching *Spitfire*.

"Hold your fire, my lads, not yet," he called, "not yet. Mr Lamont, shift your gun to starboard, shift to starboard! Keep it laid upon the target!"

Lamont waved acknowledgement and his crew shoved the heavy gun so that it traversed across onto the starboard bow. Aboard *Rattlesnake*, Rathburne had backed his main yards, stalling his ship almost dead in the advancing track of the schooner and prepared to rake the approaching *Spitfire*. This would be the moment of their greatest trial.

"Steady, my boys . . . Stand this and you will stand anything . . ."

The distance between the two vessels was closing fast. Just as the second broadside twinkled along the *Rattlesnake*'s side, Kite called out, "Starboard guns, hold your fire until we come under his stern! Marksmen, make ready! Mr Lamont, when you are ready!"

And then the thunderous impact of the *Rattlesnake*'s shot was among them. A ball struck an after gun, tumbling it off its truck with an echoing clang followed by the rending of the carriage as it split apart. A man jumped clear, but fell over and struck his head on an eyebolt while a shower of wooden splinters exploded into the air and caught another member of the gun's crew. A second ball flew through the topsail and a hole appeared in the foresail, while a third and fourth struck the hull forward, one passing through the bulwark and carrying off the leg of a man waiting innocently to clew up the square topsail.

"Larboard a half-point," he said to Jacob and raising his voice, roared, "Clew up that topsail!"

They were rushing down towards the *Rattlesnake* and her higher freeboard began to loom over the starboard rail as the *Spitfire* struck back. The obstruction of the larger ship's hull killed the breeze as the schooner passed into the wind-shadow, but

Jacob coolly ran the *Spitfire* close under the *Rattlesnake*'s stern. Choosing his moment, Lamont jumped back from the breech of the elevated eighteen-pounder. The big gun belched fire and thunder, the smoke of its discharge streaming back over Kite, Jacob, Sarah, Paston and the men at the after guns. All about him, Kite could hear the crackle of musketry, hear the shouts and the cries, but he ignored them, intent upon the task in hand, standing rigid beside Jacob and as they came out into the wind again under the *Rattlesnake*'s larboard quarter. "Hold her steady, Jacob . . . Now! Down helm! Headsail sheets, there Zachariah!"

The *Spitfire* swung round onto a course approximately parallel to that of her enemy, but as the starboard guns opened fire and the air was again filled with the ear-splitting concussion of the broadside, Kite noticed Rathburne was hauling his main yards round to catch the wind. As *Spitfire* drew steadily ahead, *Rattlesnake* also began to gather way and move forward, but Lamont had the eighteen-pounder fire again, then again, and Kite was aware of only an intermittent response from the larboard guns in the *Rattlesnake*'s broadside.

As the two vessels moved ahead, the smaller schooner was now on the larger ship's windward bow. Kite realised that for a moment or two he had a decided advantage, for only the forward guns of the rebel ship bore, while the traversing eighteen-pounder could sweep the waist and quarterdeck of the *Rattlesnake*. But Rathburne was equal to the occasion and in the face of this withering fire, tacked his ship through the wind in an attempt to rake the *Spitfire*'s stern, extend the range and re-engage with his starboard broadside. "Down helm! Lee-oh!" Kite roared as the more responsive fore-and-aft-rigged schooner conformed, to take station again on the *Rattlesnake*'s windward bow and resume her destructive cannonade.

Suddenly the full force of a double-shotted broadside swept them and Kite felt the enemy balls strike the *Spitfire*'s hull, sending up showers of splinters all along the bulwarks and dismounting a second gun forward. A man screamed with pain and another fell stone dead beside the mainmast, while one of Lamont's gun crew slumped slowly to the deck, leaning on his rammer.

"Keep up the fire, my lads!" Kite shouted, looking about him for Sarah. For a moment his heart skipped a beat as he saw her stand up, her shirt soaked in blood. Then she caught his eye and smiled bravely and gestured at the still body lying at her feet: the blood was another's and Sarah had been comforting the dying man. "Is that Paston? Where's Paston?" he called, casting about him and fearing the dead man was in fact the American prisoner, but the boy was crouching between the guns, released from duty as Sarah's shield by her sudden concern for the dying seaman.

The two vessels were now close hauled, standing to the east-north-east and exchanging fire. It was clear that Lamont's fire was having its effect on the larger ship, for while he could no longer throw anything remotely heavy at the enemy, the loose canvas bags of langridge were having a devastating impact on both the *Rattlesnake*'s personnel and its rigging, slowly but surely robbing Rathburne of his ability to manoeuvre his ship. Lamont's ammunition consisted of canvas bags into which all manner of odds and ends of metal junk, nails, broken bolts, shackle pins, broken glass bottles, stones and musket balls had been sewn. To these horrific missiles he added short lengths of chain, old off-cuts from the schooner's bobstay and her yard slings and other rubbish which habitually littered the carpenter's shop on any vessel. At a short range, thrown on a high trajectory, the latter sliced through rigging and sails, while on a lower path the former swept the enemy deck or flew in through the open gun ports. It occurred to Kite in a prescient moment that Rathburne's ship's company was under-strength, that the imperfect response from the *Rattlesnake*'s larboard guns was evidence that they were not fully manned, even by men crossing the deck from the starboard battery. Perhaps he had landed men somewhere, and this had had something to do with his apparent disappearance and his present attempt to reach Rhode Island.

Kite looked about him. His own vessel was in a state, but she remained manageable and, though riddled with holes, her sails still drew. As the two vessels continued to exchange fire, he grew increasingly alarmed at their position, for beyond *Rattlesnake* the higher land was falling away to a river valley. He looked astern; already Seakonnet Point was behind them while up ahead the land curved round across their bow towards Point Peril and the Old Cock and Hen Rock. They were working their way into the bay into which the Coakset River debouched into the sea and this neglect of navigation by Rathburne, a man familiar with the locality, convinced Kite that his enemy was in trouble.

"His fire's faltering, William," Sarah called, and Kite, sensing the same thing, was truly puzzled. Amidships, Lamont continued to pour his fire at the enemy, while the larboard broadside guns which remained in action still threw their shot at *Rattlesnake* with unabated fury.

"What's that you're saying?" Sarah suddenly asked Paston, calling out, "William!" to attract her husband's attention and pointing to the boy, who was watching the *Rattlesnake* with a grin. He suddenly looked up at Sarah, realised he had been speaking his thoughts out loud amid the prevailing thunder of the guns, and shook his head. "What did you say, Joe?" she said, one hand going to a pistol butt in her belt.

"Come here, boy!" Kite ordered and as the trembling youth came close, he hauled him up onto the rail. "What is it, eh?"

"Nothing, sir."

"Tell me, damn you!" Kite shook the lad. "Tell me!"

He could feel Paston shuddering with terror and then, as the guns barked and shot flew past him, endangering him from his friends' fire, the lad stuttered, "The lobster pots . . . the Two Miles Rock . . ."

For a moment Kite failed to understand, but then he saw the flags on the light spar buoys marking the lobster pots around the rock lying in the middle of the bay. Did Rathburne intend to run his ship aground? Or had Kite's manoeuvring unwittingly driven him into a position from which he could not escape?

Just then one of Lamont's seamen ran up to him. "Sir, the mate says he has only three rounds left, sir!"

"What?"

"The mate . . ."

"Yes, yes!" Kite waved him aside and raised his voice, aware now that he was hoarse with shouting. "Cease fire! Cease fire! Jacob, down helm, put her about! Mr Harper! Headsail sheets! We're going about!"

As the schooner turned and her big main and foresails shook with a rattle of blocks as she passed through the eye of the wind, Kite watched the islet that formed Point Peril track across the *Spitfire*'s bow, then he spun round and stared astern. A few shots followed them, as the schooner's vulnerable stern was exposed, but the risk betrayed the truth: Rathburne had shot his bolt and even as Kite realised that the storm of raking shot was not going to follow them he saw the *Rattlesnake*'s foremast shudder and then crash forward in a tangle of falling spars and torn sails.

"She has struck the Two Miles Rock," he said flatly. Then, turning forward, he called out, "Secure the guns and ease yourselves, men. You have done well. Mr Lamont and Mr Harper, do you lay aft, if you please!"

"William, look!"

He spun round and stared to where Sarah was pointing. Extending his glass and raising it to his right eye he could see, just beyond the *Rattlesnake*, under her stern, a pair of boats in the water, men lying on their oars. Had they come from the shore, or had Rathburne's slackening fire meant he had diverted his men to lower the boats from the waist? Then he saw the wooden davits that Rathburne had erected under the mizzenmast since he had stolen the ship: their falls trailed in the water. Rathburne was abandoning his ship. Kite was furious. "I knew it had been too damned easy," he said, turning with a sudden cold anger at what he knew Rathburne was about to do. The telescope closed with a metallic snap.

"What is it?" Sarah asked, seeing the terrible expression upon her husband's face.

"That *bastard*," Kite bellowed, though it came as a cracked roar from his strained throat, "is going to burn *my* ship!" He strode forward. "Get back to your guns and load 'em! Boarders are to be ready! Second Mate! Headsail sheets! You men amidships, veer that fores'l sheet! Jacob, up helm! Lamont, load that gun of yours with all the shit your can lay your hands on!"

"Up hellum," intoned Jacob.

Kite turned aft, kicked Paston and called to Sarah, "Come you two, help me veer this mainsheet." Then, raising his voice again, he shouted, "Stand by to gybe! Overhaul those sheets now . . ." Bending, Kite, Paston and Sarah tended the big mainsail as the *Spitfire* cocked her stern up into the easterly wind. "Watch there! Watch there!" Kite called out and then to Paston and Sarah he warned, "Be careful when she gybes . . . Now! Heave in!"

Frantically they hauled the sheet so that when the wind caught the other side of the huge mainsail above them and carried the heavy boom across the deck with a murderous swing they checked it with the sheet before it had gained an excess of momentum. The moment of dangerous flurry over, the sheets were trimmed, and with her men once more at their battle stations the *Spitfire* stood back into the bay towards her enemy.

Kite was frigid with anger. The concentration of nerve and

judgement necessary to the handling of the *Spitfire* in the action had not yet drained him of his reserves of energy, while the realisation that he might yet lose his rightful property induced a terrible, cold rage. It was directed against Rathburne not solely as a man, but against him as an agent of that capricious providence of which Sarah had so recently remarked. To receive another blow to his fortunes argued that fate had, after all, a grudge against him, and this he could not yet fully contemplate, though the notion lurked on the edge of his sensibility. For the moment, however, he was a thing of sinew and bone, of blood and a raging desire to level with the pirate who, under some illusory banner of assumed rectitude, had merely exercised the ancient tyranny of might.

"Train to larboard, Mr Lamont, I'm coming alongside his starboard gangway! D'you have some lines ready fore and aft! Gun captains, remove your quoins and double-shot your pieces! Boarders make ready! We'll storm her after the first discharge!"

Kite stared ahead as they approached the *Rattlesnake*. She drew more than the schooner and, though he had given the matter little thought, he guessed they might lie alongside her without themselves touching the reef. He could clearly see figures running about her waist, and men staring in their direction, then a gun was fired, followed by a second. He was vaguely aware of the tearing sound of the passing shot, felt a dull thump somewhere and heard someone scream in agony, a noise that subsided into a whimper. One could ignore that, he thought callously, it simply spoke of a soul in agony. He moved closer to Jacob.

"Set up the main and fore topping lifts, and stand by all halliards," he called. He watched with mounting impatience as the seamen threw the coils off the pins and singled up the turns ready to drop the heavy gaffs and the two headsails. He must keep way on the schooner enough to carry him directly alongside. More guns were fired from the *Rattlesnake*, but this was no concerted broadside, thank God!

Kite chose his moment. "Lower all! Handsomely with that foresail now!" Dropping his voice and sensing Sarah by his side, he muttered, "It would never do to smother Lamont with falling canvas at the crucial moment." Then he turned, and his eyes falling on Paston beside his wife, he motioned to him. "Come here, boy!" he ordered and as the trembling youth came close he thrust him forward. "Get up onto that rail and let those rebel dogs see you."

"William . . . !" Behind him Sarah protested, but he was not listening. With her sails lowered, the *Spitfire* was losing way, but her jib boom was only seventy yards from the *Rattlesnake*'s side. "Put the helm over, Jacob!" he sang out as the thunder of six or seven of the *Rattlesnake*'s guns fired, but now the balls passed over their heads and, with the *Spitfire*'s sails doused, it no longer mattered if they cut away a rope or two.

Forward, the jib boom fouled in the wreckage of the *Rattlesnake*'s foremast where it hung over the side in the water. Her swing was arrested, but several of the gun captains had anticipated this and were busy spiking their guns round as Lamont, traversing his with far greater ease, set his linstock to the eighteen-pounder's touch-hole. The gun fired with a tremendous roar, confined as the noise was by the proximity of the *Rattlesnake*'s side, and then Kite drew his sword and called the boarders away.

He scrambled up the old *Wentworth*'s remembered tumblehome and over the bulwark onto her deck.

The scene that met his eyes could scarcely be believed and, as the wave of boarders followed, it seemed they paused in shock. Their shot had dismounted no guns, nor had it much damaged the sturdy fabric of the *Rattlesnake*'s upperworks, but the stones and nails, the old bolts, copper rovings and odds and ends of metal and glass had driven in through the open gun ports and swept over the rail to wound and maim. Men lay twisted in the agonies of painful death, lacerated and bloody from a score of flesh wounds. Many still groaned as their life drained from them and a few, the least wounded, dragged themselves painfully about, withdrawing from the enemy just then heaving themselves over the rail with a muttering of oaths and slithering in the slimy mess that ran across the once clean decks of the West Indiaman. Somewhere someone was sick and behind Kite, Sarah stood on the rail astounded at the horror before her.

In that instant of stunned hiatus Kite smelt the smoke, and a moment later, as though playing some hellish trick, like a madly sinister and deadly jack-in-the-box, a score or so of men poured up from below, armed to the teeth. "The incendiaries!" He lunged forward to strike at the nearest man. "You bastards!" he said, almost losing his footing in the gore. Then, recovering his blade, he parried the man's sword thrust, and riposted swiftly, running the fellow through.

A few feet away a man stood his ground at the foot of the mainmast and beside the binnacle. "Captain Kite!"

Kite recognised the figure in his brown coat. "Rathburne, you dog, surrender and give up my property!"

"You shall never have her, Kite! She is bilged and burning!" But as Kite sought to get over a pile of three tortured bodies, he felt a hand grab his ankle and, looking down, slashed at the mortally wounded rebel who sought to encumber him. Breaking clear he looked up in time to see Rathburne spin round, drop his sword and clasp his upper left arm.

"Remember Arthur Tyrell!" Sarah shrieked from the rail, from where, without advancing a foot, she had shot at Rathburne. Then Kite closed the distance between them and had Rathburne up against the mast. "I should kill you, you dog, and would do so if it would not lower me to the level of a pirate like yourself . . ."

But Rathburne spat in his face and as Kite jerked back and wiped his eye, Harper was beside him, his face pale under its covering of powder smoke. "Get back to the schooner, sir! They've fired her with trains to the magazine! Look, see where they run!"

Kite was aware of the rebel seamen rushing aft to clamber over the taffrail and down into their waiting boats. Two men turned at the stern and shouted for their commander: "Cap'n Rathburne!" But then they saw Kite, his sword drawn and its point against the familiar figure backed up against the mainmast. Behind the vicious-looking Englishman were more men, including a large, ugly-featured fellow brandishing a tomahawk who stood above Rathburne and the English commander. Both rebels turned and threw themselves over the side.

"You will burn in hell yet, Rathburne, like you burned Tyrell . . ." Kite said, his sword point an inch from Rathburne's face.

"Damn you, Kite, damn you!" Rathburne, his face contorted by the pain of his broken arm, glared defiance at his persecutor.

"Come, Zachariah," Kite said, getting an arm about Rathburne, "help me get this bastard aboard." As they rose unsteadily, with Rathburne between them, he called breathlessly to the immobile Sarah, who seemed rooted to the spot by the terrible scene before her. "Sarah! Go back aboard. Tell Lamont to hoist the sails!"

The fire had already taken hold of the *Rattlesnake* and was burning fiercely below as they struggled across the deck towards the *Spitfire*, shouting at the boarding party to retire and fall back. Reaching the rail they lowered Rathburne down to where a few seamen helped them, then Harper was running forward along the *Spitfire*'s deck, shouting orders and hacking at the ropes securing the two vessels.

Dumping Rathburne beside the binnacle to which Jacob swiftly cast a line connecting it to the wretched man, Kite leaned on the tiller. "Bear off forrard!" he yelled, but Harper was already hacking at the tangled jib boom and, his leg against the *Rattlesnake*'s forward channels, was thrusting with all his might as more men joined him, taking alarm from the column of smoke and flames roaring up out of the *Rattlesnake*'s hold.

But the wind pinned them against the larger ship's hull, and although Lamont had some men toiling at the halliards they could not shove the schooner's head clear. For a moment Kite thought the game was up. Any second he expected the whole world to be rent asunder in an immense and terrible explosion as the *Rattlesnake*'s magazine blew the ship apart, but the minutes passed. Very slowly, they began to drop astern, grating all along the *Rattlesnake*'s side, with Harper and his men managing to shove them clear of the worst of the obstructing channels so that little real damage was done to the *Spitfire*. Then her stern was clear of the stern of the *Rattlesnake* and Kite could see the rebel boats pulling ashore where a small crowd had gathered. Finally drawing away, the *Spitfire* blew round broadside to the wind, her jib boom pointing ashore as her sails filled and she began to gather way.

"Sah," warned Jacob, "it will get too damn shallow inshore, sah. Don't press revenge too hard, sah!"

"What?" Kite was vaguely aware of the increased rhythm of the oarsmen ahead of them as the fugitive enemy tried to escape.

"Jacob's right, William," said Sarah beside him, and he looked round into his wife's eyes. He would never forget her appearance, for she looked like a corpse, her beauty oddly stark, drained of colour yet not of form. She would look like that when she died, he thought, shocked at the awesome revelation. "Don't pursue vengeance any more. We have done enough slaughter for one day and have Rathburne a prisoner."

Suddenly Kite relinquished the tiller. "Jacob," he said unsteadily, "take the helm and put her about."

"Helm's a-lee, stand by to tack ship!"

Slowly the schooner began to turn up into the wind. It seemed to Kite that they must at any moment run ashore, but then the long strand of Hen's Neck beach with its grass-covered dunes was swinging past the bow, followed by the burning *Rattlesnake* and then the hummock of Point Peril and the Old Cock and Hen Reef beyond. A few minutes later, her sails trimmed, the schooner *Spitfire* stood out to sea, the embroidered pendant still streaming from her mainmast head.

Kite looked at his old ship. The mainmast rose like a flaming tree and deep red flames flared within the roiling column of smoke that poured up out of her burning hold. "She has not exploded," he remarked to no one in particular.

"She was bilged," a voice said, and Kite looked down to where Rathburne had propped himself against the binnacle and stared astern. "The water," Rathburne gasped with an effort, "must have flooded the magazine." The sweat stood out on Rathburne's forehead as, gritting his teeth, he concluded his explanation: "Before the fire reached it." The two men looked at each other. "You . . . you are a lucky man, Captain Kite."

"No, sir," Sarah breathed venomously, "you are a lucky man, Captain Rathburne, for you deserve to be as dead as my late husband!"

Rathburne merely looked at her with contempt and then, with an effort replied, "Perhaps, Mistress Tyrell, if you had been a good shot, I would be."

Sarah drew in her breath smartly, but Kite put up his hand between them and then beckoned Paston over and ordered him to make his commander comfortable on deck by bringing some blankets and a pillow up from below.

"What, have they got you too, Joe?" remarked Rathburne with a brave smile at the frightened lad. "Well, well. I thought I had broken my promise to your mother."

And Kite, staring at the two of them, wondered why he felt so little except an immense and wearying sense of loss.

Nineteen

Rathburne

K ite straightened up. "There," he said, holding the pistol ball up in the forceps, "that is what did the damage."

On the cabin table Rathburne relaxed and Jacob let go of him with a sigh of relief. It had been a long probing and the American was soaked in sweat, but he lay quiet at last, the extraction complete. He opened his eyes and looked at the lead ball.

"Give it back to your wife," he whispered.

Sarah lent over and wiped his face, ignoring the remark.

"Now, Rathburne, I have to suture you," Kite said. "You have lost a deal of blood, but the wound is clean. Infection and dirt are close companions, so I think you have little to fear."

"I fear nothing, Kite . . ." the wounded man hissed, trying to sit up, but Jacob seized his shoulders and forced him back on the table.

"We know you for a brave fellow," said Kite abstractedly, holding a needle up to the light coming in through the stern windows and drawing thread through it.

"So very brave," added Sarah, "especially with flint and tinder . . ."

"Damn you . . ." But Rathburne carried his diatribe no further as Kite bent over him again.

The American commander remained silent for the next quarter of an hour as Kite, having cleaned and closed the wound, bandaged his arm, then stretched and splinted it. When he had finished, they laid him on the cabin deck, where a seaman's palliasse had been laid as a temporary bed.

"Well," said Kite washing his hands in the basin Ben brought in for him, "that is the last of the wounded. How many of them were there?"

"Two rebels, Captain Kite, four slightly wounded of our own,

235

three severely wounded and one mortally," Ben answered without hesitation.

"Mortally? Ah, yes, Dodd, the stomach wound . . ."

"And six dead, sir," Ben added, completing his computation.

"Thank you, Ben."

"I will wash down the cabin," Ben said, indicating the blood-soaked table top, the stained deck beneath it and the bucket full of bloody rags.

"Let us have five minutes' peace, Ben." The rickety-legged man nodded and, picking up the bucket, left the cabin.

"He is a treasure," Sarah remarked as Kite turned and drew the decanter from its fiddles, pouring three pegs of rum and handing one each to Sarah and Jacob. "And thank you both for your assistance."

Sarah had sunk into a chair and the tall negro stood and leaned against the forward bulkhead. Both drooped with fatigue as Kite too eased himself into a chair. "Come, Jacob, sit down." Kite indicated a vacant chair, but Jacob shook his head and merely buckled his legs, his back sliding down the bulkhead so that he sat upon the floor. Before any of them had finished their rum, they were asleep, unaware of Ben slopping out the cabin round them.

On deck Hamish Lamont and his watch slumped at their stations as, battle scarred and exhausted, the ill-tended *Spitfire* sailed into the night, her head to the south.

Kite woke to find himself in his bed with Sarah alongside him. He could not recall how he had got there, nor what the strange noise was that had woken him. Raising his head he peered about him in the darkness. He could see nothing, but then thought that perhaps he should have been on deck, on watch. Had they been below to call him? Had he drifted off to sleep again? He threw his legs from the cot and then, as he stood unsteadily on shaking legs and felt the strain of yesterday's exertions, the events of the preceding hours came back to him in a rush. In the next instant he almost stumbled over Rathburne's groaning form as the wounded American turned uneasily in fevered sleep. So that was the source of the strange noise!

Kite stooped and placed his hand on Rathburne's forehead. It was hot, but that was to be expected, and he eased the blankets into which the unconscious man had twisted himself. Then he rose, dressed quietly and went on deck.

Harper had the watch and straightened up from the binnacle as Kite appeared. "Good morning, sir," he said formally, testing Kite's mood.

Kite grunted acknowledgement and Harper, after a moment's hesitation, slumped back over the binnacle.

"What o'clock is it?"

"Six bells has just been struck, sir, about ten minutes ago."

Ten past three in the morning, Kite thought as he fell to pacing the deck. And what was he going to do with the day that would shortly dawn? For weeks, no months, he had set his mind to the problem of recovering the *Wentworth*, and now that objective had been wrenched from him he was at a loss. Instead he had Rathburne lying below, a liability and a burden to him. Why in God's name had Sarah not shot him through the heart and put paid to the wretch?

Kite seethed with fury at the notion of having to tend him. Yesterday, as he had looked after the wounded, he had not thought much of the matter. Rathburne was just one of those who required attention after the fight, and as such he had had his just share of Kite's imperfect skills as a surgeon. Now, however, his mind was on a different tack and, as the first faint trace of daylight began to edge the horizon under a sheet of grey overcast, he realised something else. The utter loss of the *Wentworth* meant a severe reduction in his fortunes, for while he had a chance of recovering the ship he had not let his mind dwell on the outcome of her irretrievable loss.

He was not a poor man, it was true, but there had been considerable outlay in fitting the *Spitfire* and since then the costs of her running and manning had made severe inroads into his capital. Moreover, he now had Sarah to support and, God willing, her unborn child. He felt the prickle of sweat break out along his spine. The coast under his lee, perhaps by now all of it, was hostile while Sarah herself was no longer in the first flush of her youth. How was the child after the horrors of yesterday? He recalled the way she had looked, drained of all colour, like a bloodless corpse. What physiological changes wrought that effect and did not have an impact upon the foetus in her womb? Great God! But why was the world so full of unanswerable questions?

He paced the deck in an agony of indecision and loneliness, his tousled hair, half escaped from its ribboned queue, swept by an impatient hand as he flew up and down the deck muttering to himself. After half an hour of this wild abstraction he went below again, leaving Harper and his watch to heave a collective sigh of relief.

Two days later, still trailing her longboat astern, but with no ensign at her peak, the schooner *Spitfire* stood in towards Newport Road between the Beaver Tail and Brenton's Key. From her mainmast head flew a large white flag, fashioned from one of the few bed-sheets on board. Standing well up amongst the anchored shipping the schooner was hove to and her boat hauled alongside. A crowd of observers had congregated along the waterfront once the word went round, and the crews captive aboard the ships watched as the *Spitfire*'s boat was manned. Word went round that a body was being lowered into it and that this was followed by the figure of a blue-coated gentleman and a woman in a green riding habit wearing a feathered tricorne. The boat shoved off and headed for the shore; in its bow a boat-hook was raised and from this a smaller white flag, made from a table napkin as it happened, hung limply as a sign of truce.

As the boat approached the wharves and headed for a slipway, a group of the more curious of the male onlookers moved towards its intended landing place, their voices querulous as to the purpose of this strange event. Fifty yards off the landing the strange oarsmen rested and the blue-coated gentleman stood up in the boat's sternsheets. Without removing his hat or giving any sign of courteous salutation, as the rebel newspaper the following day reported sniffily, the sea captain called out:

"I am Captain William Kite of the British privateer *Spitfire* of Liverpool. I have here Captain John Peck Rathburne, a native of Rhode Island . . ."

At this intelligence, the newspaper afterwards stated,

> a murmur of incredulity and anxiety ran through the assembled populace whose strong feelings were mitigated when they learned from the British commander that Captain Rathburne was not dead, but merely wounded in the arm, a wound which, we are pleased to be able to assure our readers, will soon mend and enable Captain Rathburne to further the noble cause to which he has espoused and for which he almost gave his life.
>
> "Captain Rathburne's ship, a frigate of this Free

Province of Rhode Island, the *Rattlesnake*, having run
aground after an action with a ship of the Royal Navy,
had been burned and Captain Rathburne wounded in
the action. Captain Kite, we are assured, was employed
to provide safe passage for Captain Rathburne. Having
landed its precious burden, the British boat withdrew.
Captain Kite is rumoured to have had some interest in the
Rattlesnake which, readers will recall, was most gallantly
carried off this port some months ago by a boarding party
under Captain Rathburne.

"Reports have also been passed to the Editor that with
him in the boat, Captain Kite had a lady not unknown
in Newport which delicacy forbids us to dishonour, but
who, having been but recently widowed, has cast aside
her proper weeds to become the whore of a British
seaman. To such low ends must all who cling to the
Tory cause reduce themselves . . .

And thereafter the Editor relieved himself of a good deal of
bile at the expense of truth, all of which was of inestimable value
to the cause of "Continental Union".

Pulling back to the *Spitfire*, Kite managed a grim chuckle.
"I wonder what they will make of that?" he asked Sarah,
adding, "Not to mention your presence. Do you think you were
recognised?"

"Oh yes," Sarah replied. "I was pointed out by several of the
ladies on the wharf."

"An' not a few gennelmen noticed you, ma'am," remarked the
seaman pulling at stroke oar.

"I am notorious, then," Sarah said with a smile.

"Undoubtedly." Kite smiled back.

In the two days since the action, they had done much to restore the
damage to the *Spitfire*'s upperworks, but she was leaking badly
and the men had to spend an hour at the pumps every watch,
for which labour Kite maintained the three-watch system and
made for Halifax. Here he spent the remaining days of August
1775, emptying the schooner of her ballast, hauling her down
and effecting permanent repairs to her two shot holes and the
split strakes that admitted water in a dozen places. The stoutly
built schooner had stood up well to the early gunnery of the
Rattlesnakes, for this had proved the most deadly.

During his brief period on board, Rathburne had recovered sufficiently to give them an account of his side of the affair. This had not been a matter of weakness, for he was fiercely anxious to know why so inferior a vessel as the *Spitfire* had taken his "frigate".

Having given them an account of the first attack on what he called "the Boston lighthouse" which had been led by himself and Major Joseph Vose and during which the only thing they had not carried off had been the fog-signal gun, Rathburne had made a second descent on the night of the 30th and 31st of July. In the interim the *Rattlesnake* had been in Plymouth Harbour, sailing at dawn on the 30th with a number of whaleboats in tow and having embarked a detachment of three hundred New Hampshire troops under Major Benjamin Tupper.

The troops had overwhelmed the garrison of thirty British marines under two officers with the loss of only two men, and then captured a dozen carpenters and bricklayers working on repairs to the lighthouse and its outbuildings. All, including the two keepers, their wives and families, were withdrawn by Tupper, and Rathburne had returned to Plymouth, where he had completed negotiation for the purchase of a British vessel from her captors. Like the *Wentworth*, she had been illegally seized, and a party of influential Rhode Islanders, desirous of forming their own coast guard, had offered a sum of money to acquire her. Rathburne had accordingly placed half of the *Rattlesnake*'s company aboard, to refit her and bring her round to Newport, which accounted for the parlous state of his own ship when she had engaged the *Spitfire*.

"She was not your ship, Rathburne," Kite had said gently, as he sat at the side of his enemy, "she was mine."

"You lost her and I acquired her by force of arms." Rathburne's eyes glittered with passion as well as fever.

"Is force to justify everything in your new country, Captain?" Sarah asked, her hostility to the man who murdered her first husband unmitigated by the catharsis of action.

"Why did you not shoot me through the heart, madam?" Rathburne turned his eyes on her.

"Because I wished to see you suffer."

Rathburne looked at Kite. "Your wife is mad, Captain Kite. I wish you joy of her."

"I am not mad, Captain."

"Hush, Sarah, he is still fevered—" Kite began when Rathburne interrupted.

"Feverish but sane . . ." he said, breaking off to chuckle mirthlessly. For a moment the trio remained awkwardly silent, then Rathburne turned to look at Kite with a sudden intensity. "That midships gun of yours, where did you get it? Was it from the lighthouse?"

Kite inclined his head and Rathburne murmured, "Of course," and turned away, closing his eyes.

"It was my wife's idea," Kite said quietly, taking Sarah's hand.

"She *is* mad," Rathburne added in a low voice and without opening his eyes, "Quite, quite mad."

The decision to land Rathburne conspicuously was Kite's. He had no wish to take the man prisoner and, despite his assurances to his patient, had no idea whether he would yet survive. But on the morning of his departure from the *Spitfire* Rathburne was fully lucid, though still weak.

As the longboat approached the landing place, Kite bent over him and spoke to him for the last time.

"It would seem that the entire populace has turned out to welcome you, so I shall wish you a full recovery and have done with you."

"No, Kite, you shall hear more of me. You too are mad, like your wife and all your foolish countrymen." Rathburne's tone was low and intense in its vehemence, but Kite had grown weary of the American's bombast and straightened up as the boat glided towards the waiting crowd.

The *Spitfire* sailed from Halifax at the end of the first week in September. The eighteen-pounder had been struck down into the hold along with all but four of the smaller carriage guns, and on top of them Kite had loaded a full cargo of timber. Her stability thus secured, the men made their final preparations for sea. Kite offered any that wished to take it their discharge. Four seamen availed themselves of the opportunity of remaining in North America; the rest, having been paid and permitted leave to enjoy a short debauch ashore, rejoined for the transatlantic passage.

Battened down, her longboat once again nestled in its amidships chocks, her sails and rigging repaired, the schooner had stood bravely out to sea at first light on Saturday the 2nd of September, to run east towards England before the equinoctial gales.

Twenty

The Return of Odysseus

Katherine Makepeace looked up at her husband. He stood by the unshuttered window against which the wind dashed the rain.

"Bennett, my dear, do close the shutters and come and sit by the fire . . ." Dr Bennett grunted but continued to stare out into the dark street. "Are you waiting for a summons?" Katherine asked, fearful that some inconsiderate and ailing soul would deprive her of her husband's society on this foul night.

"No," Bennett replied.

"Don't tell me that Milton wishes to pay a call?"

"No."

"Then why do you stare out of the window?"

"To be truthful, my dear, I do not know, beyond the fact that I am entertaining an apprehension."

"Ah . . ." Katherine nodded. Her first guess was correct and her husband was dissembling. She had come to learn that her husband's "apprehensions" were apt to precede some cataclysmic event occurring to one of his patients. She bent again to her needlework, a little irritated but resigned.

Then Dr Bennett suddenly closed the shutters, crossed the room and rang the bell. He remained standing until Mrs O'Riordan entered the room.

"Siobhan, my dear, do please warm the bed in the back bedroom."

"Captain Kite's old room, Doctor?" Mrs O'Riordan's face bore an expression of astonishment.

"If you please."

"Are we expecting company, Bennett?"

"No, we are not *expecting* company, Kate, my dearest, but I apprehend it may arrive." The doctor bent, threw out his

242

coat-tails and sat down while the two women exchanged glances. Having rolled her eyes to heaven, Mrs O'Riordan bobbed her habitual curtsy and swept from the room; Katherine looked at her husband, but the doctor had closed his eyes and clasped his hands contentedly across his portly belly. She resumed her sewing with a sigh.

The two sat in silence until Bennett broke it with a gentle but persistent snoring. Katherine looked up again at her husband; he had been called out at five o'clock that morning and had a right to doze in the warm room, she concluded charitably. He was a good man as well as a good physician, attentive without being demanding, and she had long since despaired of having children. It was a shame, though no child of hers would carry on the Makepeace name and, with Harry dead, all hinged now on Charlie. Nevertheless, she would have liked children and flattered herself that she would have made a competent mother. Her train of thought strayed now to Harry, her poor wastrel brother, who had thrown up his chances of a political career, annoyed his stepfather, upset his mother and bought himself a commission.

"I shall make a name for myself in North America," he had declared with a laugh to his sister on the eve of his departure when he had appeared resplendent in his scarlet coat and his powdered wig. His battalion had been embarked in one of Makepeace and Frith's vessels, for war transportation was proving lucrative to the shipowners of Liverpool, despite the downturn in general trade with America. Poor Harry had made no impression upon America; on the contrary, the continent had made a fatal impact upon him. Bunker Hill! How could so beautiful a creature as Harry Makepeace die on the slopes of so prosaic a place? His mother had wept for a week, inconsolable over the loss of her favourite child. They had had a letter of condolence from Captain Kite, one of several he had written since he had left England, saying that he had met Harry in Boston before the battle and had learned afterwards that Harry had been "among the fallen".

Here her reverie was abruptly ended as her husband jerked awake with a start. "Here they are!" he exclaimed.

"My dear," she said gently, "you are confused by a dream. There is no one."

"I heard the bell!"

"No, Bennett, you heard nothing."

"There it is," the doctor said, his face beaming as, from the hall, the sound of the front door bell jangled.

"Good Lord," exclaimed his wife, growing pale.

"Well, well," muttered her husband, getting to his feet and walking to the door. "I shall have to see who it is at this hour."

As Bennett left the room, Katherine laid aside her work and rose to her feet. From the hallway she heard her husband's voice raised in surprised welcome.

"Good God, William, is that you? Well, well, and you have a lady with you . . . Ah, there you are, Siobhan, look who the gale has blown to our door . . ."

"Why," Katherine heard Mrs O'Riordan say as she primped her own hair, her heart beating, "Captain Kite, sir, what a pleasure!"

"Kate!" Bennett called and she joined the merry confusion in the hall. "Lo, Odysseus has returned," he said with a delighted laugh, "and brought Penelope with him!"

Katherine looked at the strange woman who was slipping off her cloak, catching a glimpse of dark hair and a face of astonishing beauty which smiled magnetically as it caught her eye. Kite bowed over her hand then Bennett ushered them into the drawing room, where Kite introduced his companion.

"My wife, Sarah . . ."

Dr Bennett bowed and Katherine nodded, welcoming her new guest while Bennett drew up chairs and invited Kite's wife to seat herself. Katherine studied her with interest, noting enviously that though her own senior by several years, the new Mistress Kite was indeed a woman of outstanding beauty, with fine dark hair, a fair unblemished complexion, clear eyes, even teeth and a sensuous mouth. Her riding habit, though worn and stained, seemed a little small and though graceful in her movements, Katherine formed the suspicion that she was pregnant.

"Well, well," Bennett said from a side table where he poured oporto into glasses, "a warm welcome to you both. When did you berth?"

"We arrived this morning, before the wind got up," Kite said, "and were fortunate to berth directly on the tide." He took the offered glass and expressed his thanks. "There were the customary delays, but I was determined that Sarah should not spend another night on board." He reached out and took his wife's hand. "She is expecting . . ."

"I knew it," Katherine said, smiling and clapping her hands with pleasure.

"You see, my dear," Bennett said, "I told you I had one of my apprehensions."

They explained the uncanny presentiment of arrival that Bennett had experienced and Sarah said, "You are very kind. I hope we shall not put you to too much trouble."

"Who else should you go to, my dear lady?" Bennett replied enthusiastically. "The house is yours and I am entirely at your service professionally and as a private person."

"Thank you, Dr Bennett."

"Dear lady, please call me Joshua." He leaned forward conspiratorially. "It would give me exquisite pleasure, for my wife denies me the intimacy and insists on calling me 'Bennett'." He pulled a face and sipped his wine, "'Tis such a damnably *dull* name, don't you think?"

"Oh, I don't know; I have heard it used as a Christian name in America."

"Ah, but not by Christians, surely. By Red Indians, I suppose?" Bennett's eyebrows rose quizzically over the rim of his nearly empty glass.

Sarah laughed. "Of course by Christians." She turned towards Kite. "Shall we call our son Bennett, William?"

"If it please you, my dear Sarah, though I fear William Bennett Kite is something of a mouthful."

"William Arthur Bennett Kite," Sarah corrected, adding wistfully, "I should like Arthur to be thus memorialised."

"As you wish," Kite said, smiling indulgently.

Katherine asked: "Who is Arthur?"

"My first husband. He was killed by the rebels."

"Oh, I am so sorry," said Katherine awkwardly, quickly adding, "so was my brother Harry . . ."

"Lord, Katherine, I had forgot," began Kite as Katherine shook her head.

"Do not worry, William, the time for grief is past and you were kind enough to write at the time. Besides, this is a cheerful occasion and not one on which we should dwell on death. Pray tell me what you would like to eat." Katherine turned to Sarah. "I know little of ship's fare beyond the fact that it is distasteful. What would you like?"

Sarah shook her head. "You are very kind, Katherine, but I am not hungry. We had a fresh pie brought aboard from the shore and did not intend to put you to any trouble."

"It would prove no trouble at all."

"Well, I shall have another drink," put in Bennett, "and I doubt not that you will join me, Kite, eh?"

"Obliged, Bennett."

"You'll be glad to be home then, William?" Katherine said. She added pointedly, "And we must find alternative lodgings, Bennett."

"Eh, what's that?" Bennett said, looking round from the side table. "Oh, yes, my goodness me, we must, we must."

Kite held up his hand and shook his head. "No, no, it is not our purpose to evict you, though I should like us to remain here until after Sarah's confinement."

"As I said, dear lady, this is the very place for you in your condition." Bennett handed Kite his refilled glass. "There is ample room for us all and we had anticipated your arrival, for the bed is airing as we speak."

"Your forethought does you credit, Bennett," Kite said. "But in all seriousness, we shall need some time, for I have my fortune to repair and I do not think this war will benefit us here, in Liverpool."

"War? What war?" Bennett looked up, halted in the very act of resuming the comfort of his chair, his face transformed by incredulity.

"Why, this war in America . . . The war in which Harry was killed," Kite said with an air of bafflement.

"But though Harry was killed, Bunker Hill was a victory for the King's arms and surely it has put paid to all notions of outright rebellion?" Bennett was frowning.

Kite and Sarah exchanged glances and Kite shook his head. "My dear Bennett, Bunker Hill was only the beginning, and Harry lost his life not as some unfortunate but necessary consequence of the military art. There was little artful in the attack on Bunker Hill and Harry, in common with some ninety-six other infantry officers, lost his life largely through incompetence."

"Oh!" exclaimed Katherine, her hands to her mouth. "That is too cruel!"

"Not necessarily his own, Katherine," Kite temporised, "but that of General Gage and General Howe."

"But how d'you know all this?" Bennett asked, throwing an anxious look at his wife.

"We were there, Bennett, among the wounded when the first two attacks failed. It was no brilliant military exploit but a hard-fought battle in which the rebel yokels stood their ground and repulsed our infantry like heroes."

"Damn it, Kite, that is treasonable!"

"Oh, Bennett, pray do not take up the stupid opinion that likens admiration for an enemy to some form of treachery. It was widespread among the officers in Boston before the battle and they thought if they took brooms to the summit of Bunker Hill they could sweep the farm boys out of their entrenchments. Now I understand that the defeated hay-seeds have fortified Dorchester Heights and the talk is increasingly of our evacuating Boston."

"*Evacuating* Boston? Good God, is this true?"

"It is all too true, Joshua," said Sarah, "and on another occasion, I shall tell you how my first husband lost his life and how my present husband fought the rebels at sea."

"Good God, Kite, you have resumed privateering, have you? I had not heard that letters of marque and reprisal had been issued."

"Nor had I," remarked Kite drolly, "but the whole matter has gone beyond such touching niceties, Bennett. Believe me, we are at war and will have a hard time of it before it is over."

Bennett blew out his cheeks and nodded. "Aye, I can see that, and if we become preoccupied with our misguided transatlantic cousins, I would lay money on the French trying their luck against us."

"I should not wonder if the Americans will not seek an alliance with them," Sarah said, "though they may make strange bed-fellows, to be sure."

Katherine looked at her sharply, astonished at her presumption.

"No, nor I," agreed Kite, seemingly unruffled at his wife expressing her political opinion so frankly. "And if so, we shall have to consider our personal position most carefully, though we have left Nathan Johnstone behind; you will remember him as my clerk—"

"Oh yes," said Bennett, "I recall him; a widower."

"Now remarried, I shouldn't wonder, to a rebel lass and intending to settle in Massachusetts."

"Good Lord, what will become of him after the rebellion?"

Katherine asked, emboldened by Sarah's candour. "Will he not hang for a traitor?"

"If we win," said Kite, "do you suppose the King's ministers will order every rebel hanged? There are thousands of them. Besides, it presupposes our troops will prove victorious."

"And you do not think they will be, do you, Kite?" Bennett asked, his voice sober with concern.

Kite shook his head. "No, not in the end. They will have their Bunker Hills and declare them victories, but in the end I think the task too vast. The country is enormous."

"Well, what do these rebels want?"

"Independence – a new country . . ."

"A new England? I thought they had that."

"No, something entirely different," put in Sarah, "a country where any man may rise and not concern himself as to how he does it."

"A republic, then?"

"Yes."

"And a man like Nathan Johnstone can change his nationality in this rebellion, and emerge as an . . ."

"American," offered Sarah coldly.

"Well, well," said Bennett, digesting the news. "Well, well."

They sat in silence for a moment, the gulf of different experiences lying between them, then Kite recalled something.

"Kate, my dear, it is remiss of me," he said, reaching into an inner pocket of his coat. "I seem to be forgetting everything important this night." He held out a small paper package sealed with wax. "It is Harry's ring. I think Charles is to have it, but I do not intend to wait upon Frith, so perhaps you would deal with it."

Her hand shook as she took the little packet and broke the seal. "How did you come by it?" she asked.

"I was with him when he died. It was quite circumstantial."

Kate looked up from the ring which lay in its crumpled square of paper. "You never said so in your letter."

"No. There is always much one does not say in such letters."

After they had retired for the night, Kite was unable to sleep. Beside him Sarah's even breathing told where she had sunk into the unbelievable luxury of a feather mattress. He recalled another homecoming, when he had taken the expectant Puella north to his native Lakes and how he had come down the following morning and been filled with such optimism that it seemed the whole world must be imbued with the same sensation of hope. But so much had happened since that bright moment of expectation. Puella and her son were dead, killed by the cholera for which this place was notorious, he had all but abandoned Liverpool and as the world moved on the fortunes of men rose and fell. He thought of Johnstone in Boston hitching his fate to the apparently rising star of Yankee republicanism, of Wentworth and his unfaithful wife in St John's and of the late Captain Makepeace's widow now in her marriage bed with Frith, her former lover. He thought too of John Peck Rathburne in Newport, and the Rhode Islander's defiant declarations; would they ever meet again? He sought an answer in the darkness, but there was no sense of Puella's presence. Perhaps she slept at last, and then he recalled the odd little yarn of Bennett's "apprehension" of their arrival tonight.

Well, well, how strange. Puella had killed herself in this very room and yet he felt no terror at the thought, only a profound sadness for her unhappiness and a vast gratitude at her act of manumission to himself. That her *obi* approved of his new wife he was in no doubt, but he was not a man of sufficient self-conceit that he could content himself with such a thought, even as Sarah lay breathing evenly beside him. No, William Kite, the self-declared privateersman, had murdered a hundred men on the deck of a ship he conceived to be his own property wrongfully taken from him. What had happened to the apothecary's son who had once splinted the wings of birds and bound up the wounds of pet dogs?

The terrible image of the carnage upon *Rattlesnake*'s deck filled his mind's eye; the writhing bodies, torn to pieces by the ragged, homespun and extemporised weapons of death, the stink of blood and shit, mixed with the smoke coiling out of the ship's hold. He shook off the haunting thought and Rathburne returned unbidden in its place, Rathburne defiant even in his pain, telling him his wife was mad.

No, Sarah was not mad; they were all mad! Poxed with insanity in all their vain endeavours! And he, William Kite, was adding to the world's overflowing portion of folly, for he had fathered another human life even now quickening in his wife's belly.

What would become of his third child? Would he or she survive? Would cholera revisit his family and take the infant? Was that how nature revenged itself upon the ludicrous creatures that called themselves humans? The sensation of panic rose in him and he was aware that Puella's spirit had gone now, leaving him alone and frightened in the darkness. How quickly a man's mood swung!

He eased himself from the bed and went to the window. Peering through the curtains he watched the grey daylight grow over the rooftops of Liverpool and felt his own apprehensions recede. He must not linger here in Liverpool to expose either Sarah or her child to the dread rice-water disease, despite Bennett's offer of himself as man-midwife. He must take all possible care of them both, for fate had given him a new lease on a life he had once thought finished and such opportunities came to few souls.

Having resolved the matter, he returned to the bed, careful not to disturb the sleeping Sarah. He lay quietly for a while and then, as the sun rose, he slipped into a dreamless sleep.